PRAISE FOR *MEDUSA*

"*Medusa* by Nataly Gruender is a deeply poetic retelling that brings you so close to the character of legend you feel yourself intwined with her. I felt her pain, I railed against the injustices committed against her, and I wept in pride when she turned a power that she feared into something she could claim for her own. It was beautiful and thought provoking. Gruender's lyrical and metaphoric lines made the seamless connection between a woman of legend to a woman of now. I'll be thinking about the evocative words for a long time after reading."

—Hannah Nicole Maehrer, #1 *New York Times* bestselling author of *Assistant to the Villain*

"*Medusa* by Nataly Gruender is an imaginative and thought-provoking retelling of the myth of Medusa. Gruender is not afraid to tackle the more challenging aspects of Greek mythology, resulting in a novel that is completely relevant to modern readers."

—Laura Shepperson, author of *Phaedra*

"This vivid debut flips the script by transforming Medusa's curse into a source of power so she can meet fate on her own terms. A perfect read for mythology fans."

—A. D. Rhine, author of *Horses of Fire* and *Daughters of Bronze*

"Nataly Gruender's subject in *Medusa* is not just the gorgon herself, but the social milieu of the gods, the relationship between mortal and immortal, and that eternal hobgoblin of the Greeks: fate. You might think you already know Medusa's story, and how it ends, but en route to its destination, *Medusa* tackles timely subject matter: sisterhood, men in positions of power abusing their privilege, and what it means to be beautiful or ugly in the gaze of others. Gruender accomplishes all of this with gripping sentences that will stop you in your tracks, or turn you to stone."

—Phong Nguyen, author of *Bronze Drum*

"In *Medusa*, Nataly Gruender offers an evocative and sympathetic voice to one of history's most maligned and misunderstood mythic figures, the feared Gorgon, Medusa. Often dismissed as a vindictive and vengeful monster, in Gruender's hands, Medusa's story is fully told, one of a beautiful mortal woman that became a monstrous immortal legend; born of and victimized by gods, stigmatized by mortals and destined to fulfill a prophecy that is both her curse and her gift; a power that will sustain her rise in the wake of those who seek her fall. With profound dignity, grace and wit, Gruender's *Medusa* is a delightful addition to the pantheon mythic Greek retellings."

—Aimee Gibbs, author of *The Carnivale of Curiosities*

"Gruender's ingenious debut...brings a truly new spin to Medusa's story, casting her as a tragic but resilient character who seeks to live on her own terms. This holds its own."

—*Publishers Weekly*

SELKIE

SELKIE

NATALY GRUENDER

GCP

GRAND
CENTRAL

NEW YORK   BOSTON

Grand Central Publishing
Hachette Book Group
1290 Avenue of the Americas, New York, NY 10104
grandcentralpublishing.com
@grandcentralpub

First Edition: August 2025

Grand Central Publishing is a division of Hachette Book Group, Inc. The Grand Central Publishing name and logo is a registered trademark of Hachette Book Group, Inc.

The publisher is not responsible for websites (or their content) that are not owned by the publisher.

The Hachette Speakers Bureau provides a wide range of authors for speaking events. To find out more, go to hachettespeakersbureau.com or email HachetteSpeakers@hbgusa.com.

Grand Central Publishing books may be purchased in bulk for business, educational, or promotional use. For information, please contact your local bookseller or the Hachette Book Group Special Markets Department at special.markets@hbgusa.com.

Library of Congress Cataloging-in-Publication Data

Names: Gruender, Nataly, author.
Title: Selkie / Nataly Gruender.
Description: First edition. | New York, NY : Grand Central Publishing, 2025.
Identifiers: LCCN 2025006964 | ISBN 9781538765371 (hardcover) | ISBN 9781538765395 (ebook)
Subjects: LCSH: Selkies—Fiction. | LCGFT: Mythological fiction. | Novels.
Classification: LCC PS3607.R716 S45 2025 | DDC 813/.6—dc23/eng/20250311
LC record available at https://lccn.loc.gov/2025006964

ISBNs: 9781538765371 (hardcover), 9781538765395 (ebook)

Printed in the United States of America

LSC-C

Printing 1, 2025

For my mom, who told me stories

And for my dad, who listened to mine

SELKIE

Prologue

EVEN WHEN THE MOON was full, the water was an inky black expanse. Quinn could strain her eyes and see only a few meters ahead of her at best. At this depth, she depended more on the feel of the currents against her sensitive whiskers and the knowledge that her friends swam close by. The five young seals swam in close formation, every so often twisting to brush against whoever was closest and get some reassurance that they weren't alone in the dark.

Quinn and four of the herd's younger selkies were heading toward the shore. They were giddy with nerves, each of them daring to pull ahead of the group for a few moments before falling back.

They were not supposed to be out. They were not supposed to go to shore. They had been raised on stories of the greed and harm that humans had inflicted on selkies. It seemed like every member of their herd had had someone taken from them because of human selfishness. With these stories, they had been given a healthy fear of the shore close to human towns.

Quinn's mother was no different. As long as she was in the

water, her mother told her, she could easily evade human capture. But the shore was human territory.

"Then why can we change?" Quinn had asked. "Why are we able to remove our pelts?"

Her mother had nosed along Quinn's forehead, her whiskers twitching and tickling Quinn's nose. They were curled up together with the rest of the herd. Long, sleeping bodies stretched out around them, crowded together on the narrow strip of beach of an island that was free of humans. The seals closest to them grunted and shifted as Quinn whined, and her mother quickly shushed her.

Quietly, her mother told her, "There are many versions of this tale. Some say that one of our ancestors was a normal seal who observed the humans from the water and grew jealous. The longer they watched the humans, the more they wished to come ashore and join them. But our bodies are slow on land and lack the grace of human limbs. So our ancestor wished to shed their fur, wished for their limbs to grow long, and wished to find balance on their feet. One night under a full moon their wish came true. They walked on land with two feet, their seal skin trailing behind them like a heavy cloak.

"Our ancestor approached the humans they had envied for so long. The seal's human form was beautiful to the people of the town, and they were coveted by many to remain on land and become someone's spouse. The seal trusted one of these humans with their pelt and married them. But as long as the human hid the pelt from the seal, our ancestor could not return home, and as months and years passed, the seal began to long for the ocean. The human limbs and life they had envied became confining. They wished to swim with the herd again. To be surrounded by the great expanse of the sea.

"The seal pleaded with the human they had married, but the human would not return their pelt. Ever since the seal had arrived, the town had experienced uncommonly favorable weather and luck with their fishing trade. What had previously been a poor, struggling community now thrived, and they attributed their good fortune to the seal's presence. The humans were not willing to let the seal leave for fear that without them, their blessings would wash away with the tide.

"Betrayed by their partner and desperate to return to the ocean, the seal waited for night and searched the home they shared. They discovered their pelt buried at the bottom of a chest in the attic. Once the fur was in their hands, the call of the sea was unbearable, and they ran from the house and leaped into the water.

"Our ancestor stayed at sea for seven years. One day, when the herd was passing by the shore of the town where the seal had first shed their pelt and walked on human legs, their curiosity compelled them to swim up to the beach and see the town they had left behind. When their round head broke the surface, a nearby boat of fishermen spotted them. Ever since the seal's escape, rumors had spread of the good luck that selkies could bring.

"The fishermen thought to improve their fortunes after many years of poor catching seasons and set out to capture the seal with their great nets. Of course, they could not know that this was the same seal that had spurred these stories all those years ago. The seal, easily recognizing human selfishness and greed, swam away as fast as their fins could take them. They dove deep into the water and went back to their herd, warning them of the dangers of humans.

"But our ancestor's wish could not be so easily undone. That seal's children, and all the children born after, inherited the ability to shed their skin and take a human form. And with this came the curiosity that led our ancestor to shore in the first place. Every generation warns the next of the dangers of humans, but each is spurred by the need to see it for themselves, to take off their pelt and walk on land and see what life is like out of the water."

Her mother gave Quinn a hard look. "But know this, Quinn, many have given in to that curiosity and were never seen again. Humans bring nothing but suffering to our kind. I hope you never give in to the desire that our ancestor plagued us with."

The shame of sneaking away from her mother and the rest of the herd made Quinn's heart stutter in her chest. Her mother had told Quinn the story of their ancestor years ago and made sure she never forgot it, but Quinn was older now. She wasn't the young, reckless pup that could be tossed and rolled in every current like a loose piece of seaweed. Quinn had been on many migrations with the herd, had explored the depths of the ocean along the coast that they inhabited, and could hold her own against creatures twice or three times her size.

Not every selkie who dared venture onto land and remove their pelt disappeared. Many made it back to whisper stories to their friends and the younger seals when the adults were out hunting. Quinn didn't want to live on stories. She wanted to experience it for herself. Her mother's begrudging lessons on how to remove her pelt itched at the back of her mind, urging her to test it out on land where she could use her legs the way they were meant to be used.

This feeling was shared among the other seals Quinn's age. Four of the most daring had agreed to join Quinn and seek out the humans' shore the next time they came to stay on the island.

Like their ancestor before them, the five seals slipped away from the herd under the cover of night, carefully avoiding the night watch. Quinn was leading the way. Still, her mother's stories echoed in her mind.

It was not a very long swim to the humans' beach. As the seals rose with the climbing ocean floor, the water lightened from black to a reluctant indigo, the full moon's weak light finally able to disperse the shadows at a shallower depth.

The seals twisted themselves even tighter as they swam closer to the beach. One popped her head above the water and ducked back down. She snorted bubbles, signaling that the shore was free from humans.

They dallied in the shallow water for a few moments, building their courage back up after the dark journey and waiting for someone else to be the first to shed their pelt.

Quinn rolled and twisted among her friends, but her heart wouldn't settle in her chest. She slapped her flippers against her sides and broke away from the group. The others tightened up behind her and floated in the gentle tide, watching.

Quinn let her fins touch down on the seafloor first. It was pebbly and shifted under her weight as she scooted up the shore until her head broke the surface.

The beach was flooded with moonlight, casting long shadows off large rocks and illuminating the cliff face that curbed the far end of the beach. A pier sprouted out of the water thirty meters away, its boats abandoned and bobbing in the tide. Quinn could see a narrow trail leading up from the pier and over the cliff. But as her friend had seen, the shore was empty. Quinn used a weak wave to propel her farther out of the water before she began to drag herself up with her flippers. When she made it to the edge of the surf, Quinn stopped and cast another look toward the cliffs, searching for any sign of movement. She found none.

Before her guilt could make her turn back, Quinn began to shed her pelt. She peeled her hands out first, the flippers stretching and splitting open like clams to reveal long, thin fingers and their useless, dull claws. She used her hands to pry her head free next, pushing the pelt off her mouth and nose, up over her eyes and off her ears, and gasping at the sudden dulling of her senses. The smell of the ocean was muted by her human nose. These eyes could barely see past the cliffs.

She kept going. Her fur slid off her shoulders, and the bare skin pebbled against the chill. With her upper body free, she crawled farther up the shore and flipped onto her back to wiggle her stomach and hips out. The rocky beach was slick and uncomfortable against her back without a layer of blubber to cushion her. The knobs of her spine and sharp shoulder blades protested the unforgiving beach.

She was panting, her lungs nearly half their normal size and struggling to fill. It was much harder to remove her pelt on land than it had been in the water. Using her hands to push and shove at the pelt, she revealed the long stretch of her thigh, her round knees, her calves. With a few sharp breaths, Quinn hauled herself up into a seated position. The pelt protected her backside from the rocks. Only her feet were still trapped inside.

A splash called her attention to the water, and she saw her four friends had all crept up the shore to watch her transformation. She grinned at them even as she heaved for breath. In a final burst of energy, Quinn kicked her feet free of the pelt.

She stared at the delicate bend of her ankle, her toes. She bent one leg and straightened it out again just to see the movement of the muscle and bone.

Still in the water but getting closer and closer every moment, one of her friends barked.

"Come try it yourself," she told him. Her voice was a surprise, so unlike the language the seals used both in and out of the water. She put a hand to her throat. The column of her neck was so exposed in this form, with only a thin stretch of skin protecting the veins and bones.

Her friend barked again but dragged himself up the shore anyway. Not to be outdone, Quinn shifted her weight and got her feet under her. She knew from the stories that humans walked on two feet. She had seen them do it once, far in the distance, and she figured the movement would come to her once her body had all the right pieces.

By the time she had wobbled to her feet, the other three seals had made their way onto the beach. She grinned at them again, even as her legs trembled. Her friend who had barked at her had already freed himself from his chest up and matched her smile. He had wide, dark eyes, a sharp nose and chin, a full mouth with shining white teeth that flashed in the moonlight. His dark hair was wet and hung in a long, thick tumble over his shoulders.

Quinn looked down at her feet and saw her pelt of fur, molded against the rocks of the shore like a dead thing. She didn't like how it looked when it was separated from her. Carefully, she bent at the waist and lifted the pelt with both hands. The weight of it was a comfort; a physical reminder of who she was even as her body found this new shape.

The others had also begun to find their feet. Like their seal bodies, they were all slightly different. The male seal who had come out of the ocean after her was broad-shouldered and taller than everyone else, while the other male was much shorter and thinner. The two female seals varied in height, but Quinn was the tallest of the three of them. She was thicker around the waist and seemed to have sturdier legs. The other two were struggling to stay standing.

Clutching her pelt like a lifeline, Quinn lifted one foot and took a step. The movement was jerky and uncoordinated, but she kept her balance and stayed upright. The others were watching her again. She took another step, and another. They came quicker and easier the more she moved, even as the unsteady beach shifted and slid under her feet, and Quinn felt her blood rushing through her long limbs, urging her to do more.

She gave in and broke into a run. Her wet hair stuck to her shoulders and back, but the pelt fluttered at her side. Every step made her feel stronger. She laughed, a delighted sound that made her smile even wider.

One of her friends called out behind her, and she stumbled to a halt. They were following her, though none of them were quite as fast as she was. The taller male caught her first, though he nearly knocked her off her feet as he figured out how to stop by running into her. They spun around, limbs and pelts flying, and she laughed some more.

The others joined in and soon all five of them were dashing across the beach. Occasionally one of them would stumble and trip, and they would laugh and marvel at how easily human skin bruised or tore. They grew bold. They pushed themselves faster. The tall male, tired of carrying his pelt, spread it over a large rock at the edge of the beach far away from the pier. Quinn followed him and did the same. She ran her hands over it once it was spread out, sinking her fingers into the thick, damp fur. One of her friends called out to her, and she turned away.

Quinn and the other seals danced and ran up and down the beach. With the wind biting at their skin and their voices carried off into the night, their parents' warnings faded away. What could hurt them now that they'd conquered their human bodies?

They kept up with the movement for as long as they could, until their legs screamed at them and their forearms and elbows smarted from too many falls on the rocky beach. The smaller male retrieved his pelt first, unerringly finding it amongst the others on the rock. The two females went after him, clutching each other's shoulders and giggling. The tall male and Quinn trailed behind. Quinn could tell her body ached to curl back into its pelt and be supported by the water. She had accomplished her goal and lived the story she had been hearing about since she was young.

Her friends returned to the water with their pelts and tugged them over their skin. They reversed the process of taking them off, putting their feet in first and shuffling the fur over their limbs. They went to their knees and then their bellies in the surf. Human hair and faces disappeared beneath the pelt. One of the seals blinked huge, black eyes at Quinn and huffed.

"I'm coming," she said. She turned to the rocks where they had all laid out their pelts, her hand outstretched.

The rocks were bare. Quinn frowned and circled the rock, trailing her hand across the surface. Had one of the others taken her pelt? But they would have known it wasn't theirs right away. Had they hidden it?

She darted a look at the shore and felt her heart kick up. The others had already disappeared into the waves.

Legs suddenly unsteady beneath her, Quinn searched the other rocks. Had it blown away in a gust of wind? But her searching yielded nothing.

The white light of the moon was harsh and cold. Quinn's pulse was rattling in her ears, and she let out a despondent noise.

"Are you looking for this?"

Quinn froze. The voice was male and young, but it wasn't the voice of her two friends. She looked over her shoulder.

A man stood among the boulders. He was human, wearing bulky clothes to ward off the night's chill. In his hands he held Quinn's pelt.

Another noise escaped Quinn's throat, this one more of a growl. It was wrong for him to be holding it. Quinn felt like he had his hands on her, all over her.

"Give me that," she demanded.

The man held it closer to his chest.

"Are you a selkie?" he asked her. "You must be. My grandfather told me stories of your kind."

His voice was shaking slightly, though Quinn couldn't tell

if it was from fear or something else. He had a gleam to his eye that Quinn didn't like. She braced her weakening limbs as best she could.

"Give it back," she yelled, and lunged for her pelt.

The man avoided her easily. Her strength nearly gone, she caught herself on a rock as he stepped out of reach.

"You can't go back to the water without it," he said, not really speaking to her. He took another step away, and Quinn gritted her teeth. She reached out a desperate hand. The man took another few steps.

"The stories were true," the man said, his pale eyes wide. "So that means you can get me what I want. Luck and fortune—a family." He dragged his gaze along Quinn's body, and it sent a chill like nothing she'd ever felt before down her spine. "You're very beautiful."

She bared her teeth at him.

"If you want it," he told her, "come with me. Follow me." He turned and made for the path that led over the cliff.

Quinn could feel the distance between her and her pelt stretch, and it was like the man was ripping her heart in two. She sobbed. Behind her, a short bark and a splash made her look back. Four dark heads hovered at the surface. She wanted nothing more than to join them.

But the man was right. Without her pelt, she could not go back to the sea. This human body could not carry her through the currents or withstand the pressure of the depths.

She had no choice. Blinking through salty tears, Quinn searched for the man. He was at the top of the cliff, waiting for her. With a cry, Quinn shoved herself away from the rock and steered her feet toward the path.

The sky had been clear when the seals had first broken the surface and come ashore. Quinn hadn't noticed when the clouds had rolled in, but they were spitting at her now, the raindrops growing fat and stinging the farther she made it up the path. The wind pushed and tore at her hair. The man had her pelt tucked tight to his body so that the storm couldn't pull it from his grasp. He started moving again when she was a few meters away.

When she crested the cliff, she looked back at the beach. Three of the round heads had disappeared beneath the water, but one remained. He stared up at her. But there was nothing he could do. They knew the stories. She wouldn't want him to risk himself as well as her.

"Go," she whispered. He couldn't have heard her, but a moment later his head sank below the surface. She was alone.

Quinn choked on another sob, her breaths coming short and fast. The storm was ramping up, the clouds twisting above her and lightning flashing far out at sea.

"Hurry!" the man shouted. Quinn cried out in response but made her feet move again. She could hardly see through the tears and the rain, but she followed the pull on her heart. While the man had her pelt, she couldn't let him out of her sight. As the distance between her and the ocean grew, Quinn let out a yell that turned into a strangled scream. She sent a fleeting, painful thought to her mother.

The man was getting too far away. Wrapping her hands around her body, Quinn gathered her rage and followed him toward the human town.

Chapter One

QUINN COULD SEE A jagged piece of the ocean from the kitchen window, glinting a gunmetal blue like the pearlescent inside of an oyster. She would come to the window to gaze at this piece of sea when she wanted to remember her anger. Partially concealed by their neighbors' roofs, the water taunted and called to her. She longed to run to it, to feel the bracingly cold waves pull at her, and let the currents take her away. But it was the one place she could not go.

Quinn had been born a selkie, a shapeshifter, taking the form of a gray seal and living in the open waters of the sea off the coast of Scotland with her family and herd. Her mother had taught her how to peel away her pelt to reveal thin, uncoordinated limbs, and she had learned to prefer the safety and warmth of her fur. Wrapped in her pelt with the strength of her tail and her herd around her, the endlessness of the ocean stretching ahead, Quinn had felt invincible.

Now, in the kitchen with its creaking floorboards and

taunting window, her pelt stolen and hidden from her by the man she was forced to call husband, Quinn felt empty.

Her memories of the water had faded, despite her desperate attempts to grasp at the feelings and the images that became blurrier every year. She remembered the cold. She remembered the darkness, broken only by the weak light of the sun far above the surface. She remembered her family, though their faces were long lost.

She remembered the feeling of her pelt, pulled tight across her skin until she became a part of the ocean itself.

Gripping her elbows with opposite hands, Quinn dug her fingers into her arms. Nothing could make her forget her pelt. She had spent seven years on land thinking about her pelt every moment she was awake, and even while she slept.

Quinn was trapped in a human body. She resented her arms and legs, the nimble dexterity of her fingers, the fragility of her skin. Even after years of living on land, every step was a reminder of what she had lost. Of the life that had been taken from her.

Releasing her grip on her arms, Quinn turned from the view and began to clear the table of the dishes from her children's breakfast. Her two daughters had left for school a while ago, and their father long before that to his boat and the dawn catch. The house was quiet, barring the faint creaks and groans as the wood protested the wind.

After she put the dishes away, Quinn wiped her hands on the apron tied around her waist and went searching for her youngest child. Oliver, already four years old, could have started school and joined his sisters a few months ago. But his father worried about Oliver's lacking speech, as the boy barely spoke more than a few words each week. Quinn didn't think Oliver's quiet tendencies would have affected his ability to go to school, but she hadn't protested when his father decided he would start next year. She didn't protest much when it came to her children.

Quinn's husband and captor, Owen, believed in his grandfather's stories that selkies would bring good luck and fortune to any man able to make one his wife. He also believed the stories that warned of the dangers of a selkie's fury. But when Owen had had the chance to steal Quinn's pelt, he'd taken it, his eyes shining with the prospect of fortune and a family of his own. She was a perfect tool to help him achieve his dreams.

The issue was, Owen's grandfather had been a farmer, living far inland, where stories of the sea became diluted and clouded like muddied water. Quinn brought Owen everything but luck and fortune. He'd created the family he desired by force. Quinn had hoped that once Owen had his children he would let her go, but the stories of a selkie's rage and revenge were too ingrained in his mind.

"If I released you," he argued one night, standing firm as a dropped anchor against Quinn's raging currents, "I could never go to sea again without thinking you'd be waiting for the chance to pull me under."

His fear of her was a double-edged sword. It made Quinn glad to know he was frightened of her, but it also meant he would never willingly let her go.

She found Oliver in the small bedroom that the children shared. He stood on a chair that he had pushed up against the wall so that he could look out the window, his nose pressed against the glass. The view from here showed the road leading toward town and the docks. His sisters would have walked down the road to the schoolhouse.

"Oliver," she called, and he turned to look at her. All of her children had inherited her dark brown hair and fine features. But instead of eyes so brown they were almost black, which Quinn had passed down to her first two children, Oliver's eyes were a pale gray, like his father's. He was too young to have his father's cold, calculating look, which made Quinn's skin prickle, but seeing her features alongside Owen's was a constant, painful reminder of what Owen had taken from her. Oliver's nose had a small pink mark at the tip from where it had been pushed against the cold glass. "Come help me with the laundry."

He jumped down from the chair. They went back to the kitchen together so Quinn could take up the basket of freshly washed clothes she'd been working on before the children woke up. Oliver quietly raced ahead of her to hold open the kitchen door that led into the side yard.

Their home was high on a hill, which gave them the view of the ocean, but they were also surrounded by other houses that had crept up the hill as the town grew. Up here, the wind pushed off the lingering smell of salt brine and fish that lay over the town like a blanket.

Tramping through the thick grass, still green despite the fact that they were far into October, Quinn set the laundry basket beside one of the poles with the hanging line strung between them. Oliver bent over the basket and pulled out one of his father's shirts, holding it up for Quinn.

She dug through the pockets of her apron until she found the one filled with wooden clips. Taking the shirt, she hung it over the line, where it immediately began flapping in the wind. It was a clear day, the sky a reluctant blue, but the wind was as strong as ever. It pulled at her hair, which was braided roughly and fell down her back in a thick rope.

They worked silently, which was fine with Quinn. While Oliver's father worried about his reluctance to speak, Quinn knew it had nothing to do with any failing or delayed learning on Oliver's part. He could speak just fine. He simply chose not to.

When they had nearly finished hanging up all the laundry, with Oliver now racing back and forth between where Quinn stood beneath the line and the emptying basket, their neighbor came outside from her own kitchen door.

Quinn would have been more than happy to ignore her neighbors, and everyone in town for that matter, but they kept inserting themselves into her day anyway, particularly Mrs. Martin.

Mrs. Martin could hardly find fault in Quinn for doing her laundry, but Quinn hurried through hanging the final few pieces to try to get back inside quickly as her neighbor began to hang up her own linens a few meters away. Oliver had planted himself in front of one of the large, pale-yellow bedsheets hung up to dry and was making shadow puppets play over the fabric with the help of the weak sun. Fitting his fingers together in a way that made sense to him, Oliver produced a passable bird on the sheet, its stubby wings flapping against the breeze.

"Your boy," Mrs. Martin muttered suddenly from her yard, "ain't he old enough to be in school?"

Quinn clipped the last sock to the line. She met Mrs. Martin's gaze, unimpressed by the woman's hard stare and judgment.

Her neighbor found something new to gripe about every time Quinn stepped outside, and Quinn had lost the desire to snip back years ago. Mrs. Martin's apron was crisply white and tied neatly around her generous waist over a dress that fell to her ankles. Quinn's own apron had multiple stains, and she had tucked part of her skirt into the waistband, impolitely revealing her boots and some of her calf. She found it easier to move around with her skirt hitched up, but it was a scandalous breach of what the town wives considered proper. The sight always brought a furrow to Mrs. Martin's already wrinkled forehead.

Mrs. Martin continued, "Boys should be in school. Especially that one. No way he'll start talking more if he's stuck with you all day. He needs a proper education."

Oliver, who didn't speak but could always understand when he was being spoken about, dropped his shadow bird. With his wide, gray eyes focused on her, Mrs. Martin stiffened. Quinn knew her son was a little unnerving. Pale-eyed and silent, he made people like Mrs. Martin nervous. Quinn did little to prevent this. She knew it bothered Owen a great deal.

The small victory of seeing Mrs. Martin uncomfortable was instantly quashed when her neighbor sneered, bearing her yellowing teeth, and said, "With a mother like you, of course he'd be odd. I pity your husband. A woman should make child raising easier on the father, but your brood is fated to be just as outlandish as you were when you first came here."

Mimicking Oliver's silent stare, Quinn gritted her teeth against a waspish retort. Nothing good would come of bickering with Mrs. Martin. Besides, she had heard this all before. The townspeople didn't know Quinn was a selkie, but when

Quinn had first arrived trailing after Owen's heels, she hadn't known how to act like a human. She'd made mistakes, bulled through conversations, and made her resentment toward humans widely known. It was hard to recover from that initial impression in a small town with a long memory. They knew she was strange, and they quickly returned her anger with cruelty. Much to Owen's heartache, that treatment extended to their children.

"Oliver," she said, instead of snapping at Mrs. Martin like a feral dog. She waited for him to turn to her before holding out her hand. Oliver wound his way through the laundry lines and put his little palm in hers. Quinn led him back to the house, picking up the empty laundry basket on the way and balancing it on her hip.

Behind them, Mrs. Martin let out a dissatisfied snort. It was a sound Quinn was very familiar with.

She had settled into an uneasy life in the past seven years. She wore the clothes her husband gave her, but she wore them strangely. She went to town for groceries and supplies, but she never joined anyone for a conversation or gossiped about the neighbors, like they gossiped about her. She had brought three children into the world, but they were growing up to be unusual.

Quinn had considered what it would take for the town to accept her. Years and years ago, when she had given birth to her first daughter, she wondered if she should try to amend her disastrous reputation, just to make her life fractionally easier. Could she try to dress like the other women in the town, speak like them, act like them, long enough to make them believe she belonged there? Would it be easier than living at the edge of their lives like a mangy wolf, endlessly circling a herd of sheep?

No, she had decided. She would not change herself any more for these people. She was changed enough. And at this point, the town's opinion of her could not be changed either.

With the laundry hung out to dry, Quinn relieved Oliver of helping her with the other chores once they were back inside. He returned to the children's room, presumably to press his nose up against the window again.

Quinn pulled two fish out of the icebox and started removing the scales over the sink to prepare them for dinner. As she scraped her short knife against the fish's side, the translucent scales flecked her hands and forearms. The rasping noise and motion lulled her into a thoughtless trance. Her eyes swam in and out of focus, and the glittering scales seemed to become a part of her body.

A small noise made her look up. Oliver had come into the living room and was sitting on the rough wool rug, in view of the door to the kitchen. He had brought a little wooden toy boat and was making it sail across the uneven surface of the rug. Every so often, he would glance up at Quinn, as if checking she was still there.

This was how her days progressed. Her two oldest children and husband would leave early, and Quinn would be left on her own with her son tailing close behind. As Quinn moved through the house, putting the dry laundry away or sweeping around the front door, Oliver found somewhere to play that also gave him a good view of his mother. When she gave him lunch, they sat at the table together, and she watched as he ate.

While her children had all taken after her looks, Quinn had always kept a sharp eye out for anything else they could have inherited from her. She dragged a slow, assessing gaze over Oliver's head, his narrow shoulders and small hands. Nothing about him would make anyone think that he was a selkie's son.

Quinn looked after her daughters in the same way, but as her oldest was almost seven years old and had never shown any sign of selkie traits, Quinn was resigned to think that they were simply normal human children. Well, as normal as they could be with her as their mother.

Every so often, as if the thought was revealed by a tide washing out over the sand of her memories, Quinn would wonder how her own mother was doing. The pain of thinking about her herd had lost its sharpness as the years passed, but it was a deep hurt. She did not think it would ever disappear. She wondered if her mother had given birth to another selkie, one who listened to her warnings. Had she already forgotten Quinn? Or was she simply another story the herd whispered to one another?

In the early afternoon, her daughters came home. Oliver, knowing their schedule, had run back to his chair in the children's room to watch the road. Quinn joined him, and together they watched his sisters appear on the hilly street. Flora, her oldest, was tugging her younger sister, Evie, by the hand. The two walked quickly, and Quinn realized why when a group of children appeared on the hill behind her daughters. She couldn't hear what they were saying, but she could guess. Flora's mouth was set in a hard line as she dragged Evie up the road. Evie, shorter and a year younger, was struggling to keep up.

The moment he saw them, Oliver hopped off the chair and ran toward the front door. Quinn stayed in the bedroom, watching the group of children spitting and hissing at her daughters. They stopped at the edge of the yard but kept up their yelling. Quinn heard the door open and slam shut.

Her children came into their bedroom in a tight knot. The girls had on matching dresses, brown and plain against their fine features. Flora's hair was tightly braided in two plaits while Evie's hung loose over her shoulders. When Evie saw her, she immediately wiggled her hand out of Flora's and ran to hug Quinn around her waist, burying her face in Quinn's skirts. Quinn smoothed her daughter's wind-tousled hair.

Flora dropped their school things on the girls' shared bed and didn't look at Quinn. Her lovely face was pinched with anger. Of course, Quinn knew that the other children in town treated her daughters this way because of who their mother was. Flora was old enough to realize that, too. She found it difficult to seek comfort in Quinn like Evie did, knowing that Quinn was the source of the town's ire.

"Have you eaten?" Quinn asked her daughters. Still half buried in her skirts, Evie shook her head.

Flora led them to the kitchen and sat at the table with Evie while Quinn pulled out the remaining loaf of bread from Oliver's lunch, hard cheese, and some tart apples. Oliver pulled his chair around the table and pushed it up against Flora's, sandwiching her in between her two younger siblings.

Once the girls were eating, Quinn started peeling and dicing the potatoes that would go with the fish for dinner. She kept her gaze down to avoid the view from the window.

"Mama," Evie said, a piece of apple clutched in her hand.

"Do we have to go to school? Can't we just stay home with you and Oliver?"

Quinn put down her knife. Evie's dark eyes were wide and honest, like a mirror.

"Your father wants you in school," Quinn told her. *Away from me,* she didn't add.

Flora tore her piece of bread into small pieces, frowning.

"Father may," Evie said quietly, "but no one else wants us there."

Oliver stole one of the mangled pieces of bread from Flora's plate. His sister didn't notice, with her gaze trained on her mother like an accusation.

Once Quinn had decided she wasn't going to change herself to fit into this town, she had questioned that choice only a few times. The first had been when she took Flora out into the market once she began walking, and people had avoided her toddling daughter like she was a wild animal. Couldn't she have put up with the charade of her human life just enough to make her daughter's life easier? Or would it have been worse for her children if their mother lived a lie?

The second time she questioned her decision was when Oliver was born. Her husband, satisfied that she had finally given him a son, had run out to tell his fisherman friends and whoever else was in the pub the news. Left exhausted and alone with a still damp, blinking baby in her arms, Quinn held the image of her husband's pride and happiness in her mind. It was not a look she had ever seen on his face. Later, when the painful haze of childbirth had cleared, Quinn had realized Owen's pride was in reaction to seeing his desires come to fruition. He'd never questioned whether he could use Quinn to get what he wanted. He'd simply taken it. If she made herself smaller, fit herself into the box he'd designed, would she have less space to feel how much it hurt?

Every time, Quinn came back to the same answer. She would not change for them. Even as Flora's eyes turned hard when she looked at Quinn, she could not be any different than the way she was.

Quinn had no choice in the birth of her children. She cared for them once they came into the world, feeding them, cleaning them, and clothing them, but she could tell they needed more from her. If she could have loved them more, maybe she would have changed.

"Your father wants you in school," she repeated, but she came up and crouched by Evie's chair. Her daughter shoved the piece of apple in her mouth. "But it won't be for always."

Evie nodded, still chewing. Quinn glanced up at Flora and found her oldest already watching her. Something flickered in Quinn's chest, a brief wish that she could give her children the mother they deserved, even if it was someone other than her. But she was as much a part of them as they were a part of her. Nothing that the neighbors could say would change that.

OWEN RETURNED HOME JUST before the light completely faded from the sky. Quinn didn't move from her spot in front of the stove when she heard his heavy boots on the stairs leading to the front door. She recognized the sounds as he removed his oilskin coat, likely still dripping seawater onto the warping wooden floor, and shed his other layers before seeking her out in the kitchen.

She turned when he rounded the table.

Owen Melville was the son of farmers and had inherited the broad shoulders and hands of his fathers, along with their pale, dirty-blond hair, a straight nose, and wide mouth. Unlike his family, Owen had left the fields to seek work on the water. He had a boat and a small crew of fishermen who spent their days sailing up and down the coast following the shoals. Most days, his work ended in the afternoon, but then he would spend a few hours in the town pub with the other fishermen.

Quinn didn't mind Owen's delayed commute home. She would have preferred if he remained at the pub all evening and well into the night. But Owen always came home before the light was gone.

As he stepped around the table, Owen peered into the living room where the children were huddled on the rug. Flora had one of Evie's dolls in her lap and was sewing up one of her arms, which had begun to fray. Evie and Oliver were watching her deft fingers and the flashing needle intently.

"Heard the girls had some trouble on the way home," was how he greeted Quinn. It was an accusation as much as an observation, needling at Quinn, but she'd spent years dulling herself to the pain. She flicked a look at him and then back down at the skillet. Her silence was accompanied by the sizzling and popping of the fish skin as it fried in the pan.

Owen's hand darted out and gripped her wrist, squeezing hard enough that she could almost hear her bones creak.

She swallowed a gasp of pain and looked at him fully.

His eyes were hard and demanded an answer. Not trusting her voice, Quinn jerked her chin in a nod. Owen's frown deepened even as he released her arm. Quinn's fingers trembled as she reached for the skillet again, but it was not only fear that coursed through her blood at that moment; there was also rage. She wished she had claws to tear into her husband for grabbing her like that.

But killing Owen would mean she would lose her last connection to her pelt. Quinn settled for baring her teeth at him, eyes flashing, and felt a savage spike of pleasure when he took a hurried step back. His gaze flicked to the window, but there was nothing on the horizon save for a few small clouds. Quinn swallowed the rest of her rage and turned back to their dinner.

When Evie finally looked up from her sister's surgery on the doll and spotted her father, she scrambled to her feet and clung to his leg like she had done to Quinn. Oliver followed her and grasped Owen's other pant leg.

"How're my little ones?" Owen asked, and Quinn could hear the smile in his voice, any trace of his anger erased. Evie started rambling about what she and Flora had done at school, though she circled around their trip home. Owen nodded along as she spoke. When Evie finally released his leg, though she kept talking, Owen leaned down and picked up Oliver, one of his hands nearly spanning the whole width of Oliver's back. He followed Evie back to where Flora was sitting and dropped himself and Oliver into a chair. His face was angled toward his daughters, but Quinn could make out the grin pulling at his cheek and the light in his eye.

A strange, pinching feeling plucked at her whenever she saw Owen with the children like this. It was like they were inside a bubble, with a shimmering, transparent boundary encircling their joy, and if Quinn got too close, she would burst it.

Quinn was here because of Owen, trapped in her human body because of Owen, but he was also her only lifeline. She did not turn out to be the wife or mother he wanted, like the selkie wife in the old tales who had brought luck and fortune to her husband and his town, or the quiet, obliging mothers he'd known who bent to their husband's every whim. Quinn had turned out to be neither of those things. But Owen loved their children.

Owen was the only one who knew who Quinn truly was. The townspeople couldn't know she was a selkie, he had told her, or else they would all be demanding their part in the fortune she could bring. She must keep it a secret. That had been an easy order for Quinn to swallow. She didn't want anyone else to know about the selkies that lived on this part of the coast, lest they be dragged ashore and stripped of their pelts like she was. But with no other story to tell, her mysterious background and rough manner were left up to the town's gossip mill and quickly unfolded beyond Owen's control. His strange, dark-eyed wife who had appeared as if out of thin air one day, and the stories devolved from there.

Quinn knew that Owen had not kept her secret to protect her. He had kept quiet about his selkie wife because of his own selfishness, greedily hoping to keep all the fortune and luck to himself.

Resigned to let the townspeople talk all they wanted, Owen had only begun to worry when Flora arrived after months of forcing himself on Quinn. Now, with two daughters and a son, Owen was determined to make his children as much a part of the town as he was. His wife was a lost cause, but his children had time. Putting the girls in school had been the first step.

Evie eventually ran out of steam, her voice trailing off as she finished telling Owen about the end of the school day. He already knew what had happened when the girls walked home.

Flora pulled her final stitch tight and tied off the end. She handed Evie the doll, which Evie hugged tightly to her chest.

"They think we're strange," Flora said bluntly. "And they said their parents tell them not to get too close to us."

Quinn moved the skillet off the heat, wrapping the fabric of her apron around the handle so she wouldn't burn herself on the metal. She had done that many times when she was first learning to cook. The heat of the iron still leeched into her palm through the fabric until she pried her fingers away, stiff with shame.

Bracing her hands on the counter, Quinn finally looked out the kitchen window. The sun had set, but the orange glow of the town cast enough light for her to see the flat expanse of the ocean in the distance.

Behind her, Owen sighed.

"It's not your fault," he told Flora.

It's mine, Quinn thought, years-old anger bitter at the back of her mouth. She knew Owen thought the same.

"They'll come around," he said instead. "Once they get to know you, they won't be so mean. And one day you'll both make very fine wives for those boys."

Flora, with all the distinction of a six-year-old girl, made a noise of disbelief. Owen laughed, but the sound was clipped at the edges.

"Come," he said to Evie, diverting the conversation, "tell me more about this terrible lesson you've been subjected to."

With the dark shadows of the sea still swimming in her eyes, Quinn glanced over her shoulder. Oliver and Flora were looking at Evie as she mimicked her teacher's droning voice, but Owen had set his gaze on Quinn. She met it unflinchingly. They were stuck at an impasse, as Quinn would do nothing to change the town's opinion of her, and Owen could not cut her loose to free the children of her looming reputation. As long as Quinn was under his roof, he could keep her under his thumb, but she was like a barbed thorn, cutting deep and threatening even more pain should she be ripped out.

Turning her back on Owen's hard gaze, Quinn picked up the skillet with her apron and set it on the table.

"Dinner," she announced.

IT WAS MIDDAY, AND the girls had no school. After Quinn fed them their usual breakfast of cooked oats and honey, she waved them away from chores. Evie's laughter was bright and loud as they played a version of hide-and-seek where only Flora hid, while her younger siblings attempted to track her down in the small house. Oliver's quick, light footsteps went up and down the hall as he checked each room.

It was a bright, sunny day, the rare kind in autumn where she couldn't even see one cloud on the horizon. The ocean winked at her.

Pattering feet made her look around, and she watched as

Oliver made a circuit of the kitchen, checking under the table and chairs. He stopped by Quinn and pointed at her skirts.

Shaking her head, Quinn told him, "She's not here."

Oliver accepted this easily and set off toward the living room.

Quinn knew that she should have felt content in this moment, with her children happy and playing, but there was nothing there. She was glad that they acted like children, in spite of everything she brought down on them. She wondered if that would change as they got older. Flora had already begun to think along those lines, Quinn knew, but she was still young enough not to understand why.

Her children trampled through the house. Evie's teasing voice rose and fell, until she suddenly yelled from the hallway, "Ha!"

A pause, and then she asked, "Flora?"

With slow, careful footsteps, Quinn heard her oldest come into the kitchen. The old wood of the floorboards creaked as her siblings followed her.

"Mama."

Quinn tilted her head, not lifting her eyes from the dishes she was washing. "Yes?"

Evie whispered something too quiet for Quinn to hear, and Flora whispered back. Then, Oliver spoke.

"Mama, is this yours?"

This made Quinn finally look up. She opened her mouth to ask what was wrong, but when she saw what Flora held in her hands, the words died on her tongue. The plate clattered in the sink where she dropped it, her fingers losing their grip.

Flora held Quinn's pelt in her hands. It was as sleek and shiny as the last time she'd seen it, seven years prior. Not a speck of dust on it. Flora held it cautiously, like it could come alive at any moment. Oliver stood next to her with one small hand on the pelt. But his eyes were trained on her, as if he were seeing right through her. Evie was tucked slightly out of sight behind the doorway.

Quinn was speechless. She gaped at her children, and a rushing sound filled her ears, like the rumble of a wave crashing itself against a pebbled shore.

Through her daze, she heard Flora say, "I found it between the eaves of the roof, in your room. In yours and Father's room. I was trying to hide."

All this time, Quinn had been sleeping beneath her pelt. All this time, Owen had kept it right over her head. How had she never looked there? In the stories her mother had told her, the humans kept the pelts locked in chests or attics, not shoved into the dirty spaces of the house. Had Owen cared so little for it? Perhaps he had moved it there when her relentless searching had come too close to its previous hiding place. The thought of him knowing that she was so close to her pelt but unaware filled her with frothing rage.

Hand still dripping with dish water, Quinn reached out. The movement made Flora take a step back and draw the pelt closer to her body. Quinn met her daughter's gaze. She knew her eyes were wide and desperate, and she could see her reflection in Flora's dark irises. Her daughter looked at her, searching for something, and Quinn's heartbeat was loud in her chest.

Oliver spoke again. "It's hers."

Quinn didn't know how Oliver knew this, or how he'd realized what the pelt was in the first place, but his words dampened her anger. Somehow, her son recognized what she was.

Finally, Flora set her mouth and held out the pelt once again.

Quinn looked down at the pelt. In the seven years since she had lost it, she had dreamed about what it would feel like to hold it in her hands, to wrap it around her skin. She kept those dreams locked up tight in her chest where they couldn't hurt her. But now they spilled out, flooding through her veins and urging her to fulfill the desire that dreams could only imagine.

"Take it," Flora told her. Her daughter, having made up her mind, wouldn't let Quinn do anything else. Did she know what she was offering?

Flora held her arms completely extended. The pelt unfurled to its full length. In the sunlight, the gray and brown fur had a silver sheen to it, like the crest of a wave before it began to froth.

Quinn reached out and took the pelt. The moment her fingertips met the fur, tears pricked at her eyes. She gathered the pelt to her chest and held it tightly. It had been hidden in the dark, tight space between the ceiling and the roof, but it was warm to her touch like it had been lying in the sun for hours. The vise around Quinn's heart, which had been tightening for seven years, suddenly unraveled. She took a gasping breath, eyes flying open.

Her children watched her silently. She met each of their gazes, her daughters' dark, knowing looks and her son's pale, understanding one. Her lips moved soundlessly.

She had her pelt back, and with it she could be free again, free from Owen's control and the town's scorn. But it would also mean leaving her children behind. She couldn't take them with her, with no pelts of their own to brave the cold sea, but if she left them, would they fare any better than before?

Oliver watched as she struggled and then reached up to take Flora's empty hand.

"Go," he told Quinn. His voice was high and firm, and it strengthened her heart. Quinn blinked away the tears that welled in her eyes and tightened her grip on her pelt.

Then she bolted for the door.

Quinn ran madly down the road, her pelt clutched against her. People stared as she ran past, but it hardly mattered. Gripping the pelt in one hand, she yanked at the ties of her apron until it came loose and fluttered to the ground behind her. She could see the ocean in the distance.

When she made it to the main part of town, near the piers, shouts began to rise up as she dashed by. She paid them no mind. Her heart was dancing wildly in her chest, the dreams that filled her veins spurring her to go faster.

The smell of the ocean hit her, and she laughed, loud and unbidden. She steered clear of the pier and instead took the rocky path that led down to the shore. When she reached the rough, pebbly beach, she paused long enough to kick off her boots.

Just thirty meters away there were boats at the docks, bobbing in the high tide. Most of them were empty, but a few had fishermen idling around or unloading their hauls for the day.

By a stroke of luck or misfortune, Owen's boat was pulling into its spot on the docks just as Quinn reached the beach. She strode toward the water and reached back to get the laces of her dress undone and shoved the fabric down, taking her underthings with it. The day was sunny, but a biting wind skated off the water.

When her feet met the tumbling tide, she let herself walk into the sea until it came up to her calves before she stopped.

She searched the docks, waiting until she found Owen's pale head. It didn't take him long to realize something was wrong, as the other fishermen noticed her in the distance and began shouting and pointing. She let him see her for only a moment.

Then, with the joy of a bird taking flight, Quinn dove into the water. The chill dug straight to her bones. The pelt was instantly soaked, but she dragged the heavy fur around her shoulders and pulled it tight.

Quinn was holding her breath, but as her limbs twisted and fit themselves into the familiar shape, she felt her lungs expand, and the pressure on her chest eased. She closed her eyes to the gray-blue water, and when she opened them again, the sea was as clear as the sky above. Her body was warm beneath her fur. Fins tucked tight to her sides, Quinn kicked her tail and rejoiced in the speed and power as she shot away from the shore and into the depths.

Quinn was a seal once more.

Chapter Two

NOW

QUINN HELD HER BREATH for as long as she could, swimming as deep as she could bear the pressure. She wanted to be as far from shore as she could get before she surfaced.

Letting Owen see her on the beach had been foolish, but the shocked look on his face gave her a dented feeling of satisfaction. She could have let him discover her disappearance once he returned home and found the children alone, but watching him realize what was happening and being unable to do anything about it—in the exact place he had stolen her life all those years ago—had been worth it. To ensure that he could not chase her down, she remained far below the surface and swam into the open water away from the coast. She skimmed along the bottom until the ground dropped away and there was only the ocean stretching around her in all directions.

Before she had been trapped on land, Quinn had been able to hold her breath underwater for more than an hour. She estimated that only twenty minutes or so had passed since she dove away from the shore, but she was already feeling the strain on her lungs and body. Moving so quickly at such a great depth was pushing the limits of the body she had not inhabited in a long time. She needed to surface soon.

The midday sun was hidden behind lingering clouds and cast only a faint light onto the surface of the ocean. As Quinn rose, she used her flippers to twist in the water, scanning for boats or men cutting a path through the waves. There was nothing.

Her nose broke the surface first and she snorted to clear away the clinging water. She flicked her tail to bring her head all the way up, twisting again to look around now that she could see all the way to the horizon. The shore was far behind her, the cliffs and town merely an impression against the sky. Quinn rocked with the waves and took a few deep breaths to calm her racing heart.

What a human reaction that was. She had learned to slow her breathing on land when her pulse pounded loudly in her ears and her heart felt as if it would burst from her chest, because she had nowhere to run out the adrenaline. In those early months after Owen took her pelt, Quinn would find herself panicking without reason. She was scared of every human she met. She was angry every moment she lay by Owen's side. She missed her mother and her herd. If she sank too far into those emotions, her breaths would come fast and hard, and it felt as if a great boulder were weighing down her chest.

During those moments when her pulse pounded in her ears, Quinn would go outside and watch clouds gather on the horizon. A story her mother had told her once would glimmer in her memory until her breathing calmed and the sky would clear.

Even now, with nothing but space around her and her pelt made a part of her once again, something was pressing at her chest like an insistent hand. She filled her lungs slowly, blinking away the seawater streaming from her fur.

Owen's boat wasn't pursuing her. She kept watching, waiting for a shadow to appear on the horizon. Would he have sent the other fishermen away before coming after her? In all the years she had been trapped on land, Owen had never told any of the humans who Quinn really was. Would he tell them the truth now that they'd seen her escape?

But as the moments stretched with no sign of a boat headed her way, Quinn let out a sigh.

Blue-gray waves lapped at her face. Quinn broke her gaze away from the coast and resumed her swim, skimming right below the surface. The water beneath her was full of shadows, but she saw no creatures. Not even a small shoal of fish. She could have been the only living thing for kilometers.

Whenever she broke for air, Quinn twisted onto her back and checked the way she had come. She didn't know what was worse, not looking back and being surprised, or constantly looking to make sure no one could sneak up on her.

As she swam, her mind wandered. Owen may have chosen not to pursue her now, but when would he change his mind? Too many people had seen her running madly through the streets, leaving a trail of clothing behind her, and he would have to give them some explanation of why he'd kept a selkie under their noses for years. She had left quite a mess on his hands.

Not only did Owen have to manage his crumbling tower of

lies, but also the children. When she thought of them, Quinn's tail faltered for a second. She kicked herself back up to speed in the next moment.

Her children were the reason Quinn was free. Flora had handed Quinn her freedom herself, after Oliver had recognized the pelt as Quinn's. They could have left it hidden in the eaves. But they had brought it back to Quinn.

And Quinn had taken it and run without a second thought. She was here now, swimming in the open ocean, because of her children, because she had left them behind.

This was probably why Owen was not coming after her. Owen had gone to the children instead. She had let him see her before she dove into the water, let him know that the children were alone. He had chosen the family he loved over her.

This decision gave Quinn even more time to get away, far away from the shore. She should be glad, shouldn't she? That she had been right about Owen. She had been risking everything on the assumption that he loved their children more than he cared about keeping her trapped, and it had worked.

The children didn't need her. They would, in fact, be better off without her there, and with Owen's full attention. They would still be a family without her.

Quinn let herself pop above the water one more time to look back, even though she knew there would be nothing there. Then she inhaled and dove.

CUTTING THROUGH THE CURRENTS, Quinn felt like she was traveling down a path she had only seen in daylight but was now trying to navigate in the dark. The water was familiar to her, but strange and ominous at the same time. She had grown up in these seas. Seven years couldn't erase a whole childhood of experience. But it could certainly dull those memories.

The seal herd she was raised in never stayed in one area for too long. They moved up and down the coast according to the seasons and the migration of the fish shoals. It was late in the year, almost winter, and by this time the herd would have moved south to avoid the worst of the storms that ravaged this part of the shoreline.

Even knowing this, Quinn was heading to the last place she had seen her herd, on that small island beach. She had nowhere else to go, and a tiny part of her was recklessly hoping that she would find her mother there even after all this time.

On that fateful night when she and the four other seals had snuck away from the herd, the swim to the beach had only taken them an hour or so, barely long enough to warrant a pause to catch their breath. Now, Quinn had to come up for air constantly. And she was moving slowly, unsure of the direction and relying on her long-unused instincts. She couldn't rely on those instincts on land, so she had shuffled them to the back of her mind and done her best to ignore them. Uncovering them now that she was back in the water was like flexing a limb that had fallen asleep.

Eventually, the little island appeared in front of her. She dove low in the water until she found the seafloor again. The silty, rocky bottom offered little in terms of food, but that was never the reason her herd had stayed on this beach.

It was late afternoon now, and as she rose with the slope of the island's base, she knew that her herd wasn't here. There were no pups playing in the shallow water of the beach, no adults heading out for the evening catch. The water and the beach itself were empty. She stayed below the surface, with a few meters of water between her and the open air, slowing to a gentle glide as she swam parallel along the distance of the beach.

Quinn had known that this had been a foolish hope. Seven years had passed since she was taken from these waters; she couldn't expect everything to have halted in her absence. The herd and her mother had moved on. Perhaps the four who had returned had told the adults what had happened, and she became another warning for the next generation to stay away from the humans.

Or perhaps, after her loss, the herd had decided that this part of the coast was too dangerous to live near. But if they never came back to the island, how could she find them again?

Frustrated, Quinn snorted and twisted away from the beach.

If she couldn't find her herd, what could she do? She had her pelt and her freedom, but she was uncertain what to do with them.

Quinn fell back on her instincts. In her heart, buried beneath the fur and blubber and bone, what did she want to do?

A deep, unerring feeling rose up to answer her. She wanted to eat.

CATCHING FISH, LIKE HOLDING her breath, took some time to relearn. Without her dexterous hands and fingers, Quinn had to rely on her speed and teeth.

She had finally located a small shoal of fish a bit farther

south of the island. Their scales flashed silver and tempting in the last of the daylight. She managed to get a little one, barely a mouthful, before most of them scattered.

Quinn was much farther out at sea after her scramble to catch the fish. The ocean yawned beneath her like the mouth of a great beast. When she was younger, surrounded by her herd, the vastness of the ocean had not felt scary. Now, she could truly feel how small she was.

She came to the surface for a breath and a break. Her hunt had nearly sapped all of her strength, and she had still not eaten enough. Even after seven years, her pelt had held on to the fat reserves she'd had when she was young, but she would burn through them quickly if she did not manage to get more to eat. With the cold and the energy she spent searching for her herd, she would not last long without food.

As the sun set, the water turned inky and dark around her. She needed to find somewhere to spend the night that was safe from humans.

As she floated beneath the surface, Quinn cocked her head. She was listening and watching for the signs of another fish shoal and another chance at dinner, but what she heard was not fish. Straining her ears, Quinn ducked deeper into the water. The noise was farther out to sea, but it traveled far enough for her to make it out. Short, high-pitched squeals and clicks. Quinn tensed.

There were more than seals in these waters when she was growing up. Her herd had clashed with a pod of orca more than once, many pups lost to their clever tricks in the shallow water where the seals thought they were safe. Even full-grown adults could get swept up in a chase.

Quinn was in no shape to escape an orca pod. But she held still and listened a bit longer. She called back to her memories of the herd when they were traveling through open water, the slight differences in the calls that she had been taught to recognize. If she was wrong, she could die.

After listening to a few more calls, Quinn set her teeth. She stayed near the surface, where it would be easier to catch a breath in a dashed escape if she was mistaken, and headed in the direction of the sound.

Perhaps she was desperate, or maybe her instinct was still too weak to force her to seek shelter instead, but Quinn wanted to see another living mammal in these waters. The squeaks and clicks grew louder, and she knew that soon enough the emitters would know she was coming.

Her wide, dark eyes could only see so much in the dim water. She was relying on her hearing as much as these animals were.

Suddenly, the squeaks stopped. Quinn stopped, too. Her nose twitched.

Then, another sound came. It wasn't the rallying hunting cry of an orca. It was long and coaxing, curious. Quinn twisted, relieved, and began swimming toward the sound again.

At first the animals were only long, dark shapes cutting a slow path through the water. As she drew closer, she began to make out the short black fins, the rounded heads, muscular tails, and a dash of white on their chests. A pod of pilot whales. There were perhaps fifteen of them, with an older female in the lead who had been sending out the calls.

Scrambling for the lessons her mother had given her, Quinn slowed down. Once the pod was nearly upon her, she flipped upside down in the water, baring her belly to the matriarch. She needed to show them she meant no harm. In a pod this size, there was bound to be a calf. She didn't want them to think of her as a threat.

The matriarch let loose a series of fast clicks, and the rest of the pod dropped back. She continued toward Quinn. As she drew closer, Quinn could see that the whale's black skin was scarred, bearing years of experience and hard-won fights.

The whale stopped about a meter away. Quinn slowly righted herself, fins tucked close to her sides.

The matriarch turned her head to angle one eye at Quinn and clicked deep in her throat. The whale was wondering who she was and what she was doing out here, all by herself.

Selkies, while part sea animal themselves, did not speak as the other creatures in the ocean did. But they had developed a way to communicate with them. Through similar clicks and noises, they were able to convey simple phrases.

Whales see others, she asked the matriarch, *others like me?*

The whale turned to observe her with the opposite eye. Another squeak and some clicks.

Whales see seals, the matriarch told her.

Quinn's heart leapt. *Seals, like me?*

No, the matriarch said, *not like you. Seals made only of ocean. You are different. You are ocean, but also land.*

I'm not, Quinn snapped. The matriarch leaned away from her, and Quinn reined her anger in. The whale wouldn't know why that made her angry.

I'm sorry, she told the matriarch. *I was away from ocean for too long. I look for my herd. Have whales been in these waters before?*

For many seasons. This whale has led family on migration since mother whale died.

If this pod had passed by the coast during previous years' migrations, they would have surely seen Quinn's herd.

No others like me on your journey?

The matriarch let out a sad-sounding click. *No, child. No seal like you. This whale remembers. Seen your kind before, and made friends. But this whale has not seen my friends in many seasons. Now only seals with only ocean in their bodies.*

Quinn's heart, which a moment ago had been leaping at the hope, dropped to her belly. If the pilot whales had only come across regular seals for many years, then Quinn's herd was long gone. They had abandoned this area.

Or, she thought wretchedly, the rest of the herd had also been captured by humans in other towns. Surely if just a few of them remained, they would still travel the same paths? But if they had all been taken on land and had their pelts stripped from them, that could be the reason that the whales had not seen selkies in such a long time. Her herd had nearly three dozen members. What were the odds that seven years had been long enough to dwindle that number to nothing?

The pilot whale matriarch was still watching her. Quinn hung in the water, mind racing, and she felt as trapped as if Owen had taken hold of her pelt once more.

Is seal child all right?

Quinn grunted, tail flicking like it wanted to propel her far away, as if she could escape what she had learned by swimming from it.

Thank you for answering this seal's questions, Quinn said to the whale. She began to back away. The matriarch clicked at her, the sound coaxing and gentle. Behind her, the matriarch's family came to her side. A small figure broke away and circled under the matriarch's belly. A calf. Its squeak was even higher pitched than the others.

Quinn turned and dashed away, leaving the pod of whales behind.

WITH THE LIGHT GONE and only the cold, dark ocean around her, Quinn returned to the small island's beach. Her herd wasn't there, but at least it was familiar.

Feeling too unsteady to rely on her instincts, Quinn stayed near the surface as she swam back the way she came. Any human on a boat wouldn't be able to spot her in the water at this hour. But Owen wasn't foolish enough to try to chase her down once night fell, anyway.

She knew she would come up on the island soon and popped her head above water to get her bearings. The calm waves caught and reflected the moon back at her, like a flickering eye watching from every direction. Quinn turned in the surf, looking for the dark outline of the island.

Fortunately, she spotted it easily about half a kilometer away. Unfortunately, she was able to spot it because there was another light beaming through the darkness, softer and more yellow than the light of the moon. It flashed at her, then went dark, and then flashed again. A lighthouse.

Without the mouth to curse, Quinn grunted her frustration and let out a throat-trembling bark. There was a lighthouse built on the top of the island, which meant that the place her herd used to rest during their travels was no longer free of humans. They had taken this island from her, too.

Quinn grunted again and twisted her body in anger.

The sight of the lighthouse reminded her of something Owen had told her a few years ago. Something about the recent uptick in storms, and the dangerous rocks on the coastline claiming too many boats as of late, and how the fishermen and other sailors had gotten in touch with a board that controlled the country's lighthouses. Owen had told her they were constructing a lighthouse offshore. She hadn't asked where. She had barely been listening.

But this was the lighthouse Owen had been talking about, built right on top of the last place Quinn had seen her family. Even if the herd hadn't decided that this part of the coast was too dangerous after her disappearance, they would not have returned to the beach once humans had taken up residence at the top of the island. She'd been too focused on the beach itself when she came by earlier and hadn't noticed the building that sprouted out of the clifftop.

Against the evening backdrop, the lighthouse's beacon shone brightly as it swiveled in the tower. It would be a welcome sight for any sailor out on the open water. It made Quinn's heart clench.

Was there nowhere she could go that was free from humans? She had escaped the town that had been her cage for seven years, only to find that her jailers had spread and laid claim over what had been a safe place for her family. There would be no respite in the sea, since Quinn didn't have the stamina to keep swimming until she found a new island, *if* she could find a new island. Her memories of the coastline were lost like a shape traced in the sand before high tide.

As Quinn bobbed and swayed in the current, exhausted, her fury prodded at her, steadily building with every wink of the lighthouse beacon. The somber sky above her, laden with clouds, splintered and began spitting rain.

The downpour made Quinn blink. She peered up at the clouds, dark gray and churning like a hand had grasped them and twisted.

Don't, Quinn told herself. *The last thing you need right now is a storm.*

When she set off toward the island again, the clouds above her relaxed, but the rain did not let up. Quinn approached the island carefully, ducking under the water when the beacon's round, searching light passed over her, and began circling the shore for a place to rest. Her first pass around the island revealed a small wooden dock just big enough for perhaps two boats, but there was only one small boat floating in the water. Behind the dock, Quinn could barely make out a thin, winding path that led high up the island toward the lighthouse.

Quinn snorted at the dock and turned determinedly in the other direction, skirting around the island until she was on the opposite side. There was no beach there, just a towering cliffside with the lighthouse perched on top like a cairn. At least Quinn would be out of reach of the sweeping light at the base of the cliff.

A closer inspection revealed shallow divots and cracks in the cliffside, some of them large enough for Quinn to clamber onto. She searched for one that was deep and a little elevated out of the water.

The ledge was just deep enough for Quinn to wedge herself into the crack and get out of the rain. Lying on her stomach, Quinn tucked her fins under her and laid her chin down on the bare rock. Her nostrils fluttered as she caught her breath, and her whiskers twitched in the open air. The waves lapped at the cliffside, sometimes spilling onto the ledge.

Her mind was still racing with everything she had gone through, everything she had discovered in just one day, but her body was exhausted. She slipped into sleep as easily as if she had pulled on another pelt.

Chapter Three

A FEW DAYS HAD passed since Quinn's return to the sea, and she was uneasy in her freedom.

When the island had been free of humans and full of seals, Quinn and her mother often had to haul themselves quite far up the rocky beach to find a bare spot to settle down. With the herd around her and the sharp rise of the cliffs behind them, Quinn had slept soundly, knowing that she was as safe as she could ever be. The beach provided a little protection from the wind, too, and with an ocean full of fish only a few meters away, Quinn wondered why the herd didn't remain on this island all the time.

"It's just not our way," her mother had told her. "We must always be on the move. It is too dangerous for us to linger in one place for too long."

She had a far-off look in her eye when she told Quinn this, as if she was thinking about more than what she was saying.

Even when Quinn took this question to other adults in

the herd, she received similar answers. Grunting replies about moving with the tides and the fish, not sticking around one beach for more than a season, some murmurings from the herd's oldest members about following the route of their ancestors. And always there was that look in the adults' eyes, and Quinn was left with more questions rather than a satisfying answer.

Alone now and tucked on the opposite end of the island in her shallow cave, Quinn thought about how she had pushed for a reason for the herd's constant wandering. If they liked this island so much, why couldn't they stay all year long?

Quinn realized that she had answered her own question seven years ago. She and the other young seals had done just what the rest of the herd had feared would happen if they stayed put on the island. Quinn had become restless. When she had felt safe and protected, and she didn't have to swim hundreds of kilometers up or down the coast, her curiosity overtook her. She and the others had let that safety lure them into a sense of fearlessness. They had energy to spare on bravery, and they had let it coax them onto the shore and out of their pelts. And Quinn had paid dearly for it.

Quinn could also realize now that the herd had probably been on the move to avoid garnering human attention, since dozens of sleek seals would have drawn notice even if they had been the normal kind. Her mother and the older seals had most likely worried that a human might recognize their kind from the stories. Selkies were physically no different from normal seals, but Quinn had always thought there was a particular sheen to the coat of a selkie, an intelligence behind their wide, black eyes that gave them away.

But with the herd gone and not even a pack of regular seals to blend in to, Quinn would stick out in the waters around the island and near the town. She couldn't remember overhearing Owen or the other fishermen talking about seals hanging around these waters in recent years. If she stayed here and was spotted by the humans in the town, word would surely get back to Owen, and he would know that Quinn was still within reach.

Quinn's other option scarcely sounded more appealing. She could leave this island and the humans behind, and swim up and down the coast in search of any remaining selkies, even if they weren't her family. How long would that search take? Could Quinn stand to be alone for that long, as vulnerable as she was while she was slowly gaining back her strength and ability to feed herself?

With her pelt returned to her, at least she had the choice. She had spent seven years on land against her will, but the sudden return to freedom and realization that her life was back in her own hands—or in her current form, fins—was overwhelming. If she chose wrong, what good would it be that she had escaped Owen and the half-formed human life she had been living?

Quinn wriggled in the small space she had claimed in the side of the island. Her thoughts were making her agitated, and she shuffled to the ledge and slipped into the water to try to clear her head. The weather was cloudy but calm, and she began a slow loop around the island, a path she had started traveling to help rebuild her strength and search for food.

As she rounded the side of the island that faced the mainland, Quinn dove beneath the water as her thoughts wandered again. Quinn didn't miss Owen in any sense. She had slept in the same bed as him for years, but every night with him was a lance on a still-healing wound. There was no part of her that felt tugged loose by Owen's absence.

Quinn couldn't say the same for her children. She still believed she had made the right choice in leaving them behind. So far, that was the only choice in her newfound freedom that made sense to her. But Quinn's entire life on land had revolved around her children, even if she had kept them at arm's length as best she could.

She found herself wondering what Oliver was doing now that she wasn't at the house; would he have to go to school? She worried that, even with her gone, her children would still be outcasts among the other students. The tight grip of guilt squeezed her throat as she thought of sweet, silent Oliver withstanding the childish cruelties.

Or would Owen make all three stay home now, with Flora looking after her younger siblings even though she was still a child herself? It wasn't fair that Flora had to grow up so quickly. Quinn wished Flora's only concerns were playing hide-and-seek in their small house and fixing Evie's dolls. But by leaving them behind, she'd ruined any chance of Flora getting to live a normal childhood. She hoped the townsfolk would at least be a little kinder to them now that Quinn was gone.

Quinn had made a full loop around the island and was swimming at the surface, diving shallowly before popping back up at an easy pace that allowed her mind to wander. It was late afternoon or early in the evening and a good time to go fishing, if she could pull her thoughts together long enough to focus.

Her aimless swimming brought her close to the beach as she made another pass across the front of the island. The small boat was still docked to the pier. Quinn poked her head out of the water, taking deep breaths through her nose. Her whiskers twitched and trembled in the chill air above the surface of the ocean.

She was nearly past the stretch of beach when something caught her eye. The beach had been empty each time she had swum by in the past few days, but now the rocky shore held a dark shape, huddled close to the edge of the cliff and the water. Risking raising her head a bit higher out of the surf, Quinn inhaled deeply, nostrils flaring as she tried to catch a scent on the wind. The beach was protected, but the figure was close enough to the water that a breeze could carry a smell straight to Quinn.

The figure was a human. Instantly, Quinn tensed, her eyes locked on the hunched shape as if it were going to dive into the water and come after her.

Since there was still only one boat at the pier, Quinn figured this had to be one of the lighthouse keepers. From what she could remember of half-heard conversations and snatches of gossip in the market, there were three lighthouse keepers in total, all men.

Quinn narrowed her eyes. If she was staying on the island while she regained her strength and made up her mind about whether she was going to leave, it would be a good idea to know what kind of humans had taken over the island from the seals. She sank low in the water and moved soundlessly through the waves.

As she glided closer, Quinn gauged that the human was

barely bigger than her seal form, short, but stocky. He was crouched by the shore, a large oilskin coat making his shoulders broad and hiding his face behind the collar. The water rushed up the shore and lost its legs less than a meter away from the human's boots.

Quinn stopped as close as she dared. Still a few body lengths away from the beach, a thought occurred to her. With the human so close to the water, would she be able to sneak in close enough to set her teeth into the human's leg or arm, and drag him into the water with her? She had heard stories of selkies drowning people who got too close to the herd when seal hunting was a popular sport amongst the local humans, but she had never seen it done. While the selkies had only been protecting their herd, their actions had probably fed into the stories Owen heard from his grandfather, which had planted that seed of fear about Quinn in Owen's head. But she had never drowned a human. Could she do it now?

A strange feeling was filling her chest: her rage, which had been simmering ever since she had escaped but was still ready to boil over at any moment, gladly resurfaced at the sight of this human. Maybe he had done no wrong to Quinn directly, but his presence here reminded her of everything she had lost in the past seven years. Could she take this lighthouse keeper into the heart of the ocean and rid her world of one human?

Quinn was not an animal, but the violent urge to sink her teeth in this man's skin and drown him in the unforgiving sea came as easily as her other instincts. But just as quickly as her rage had risen, she felt horrified at the savageness of her thoughts.

The human would struggle, and Quinn didn't trust her heart to stay hard enough to kill him. She wanted her island back, but killing this human would not return the past seven years of Quinn's life to her.

The man didn't move in all the time that Quinn floated there, plotting and giving up on how to murder him. She wasn't going to learn anything about the keepers from the hunched figure, and Quinn began backing away when she heard a soft sound.

The keeper sniffled again, the noise nearly lost in the gentle waves breaking on the beach, but Quinn recognized the sound of crying.

The tide was rising; the water nearly reached the keeper's boots now, and as it stretched up the shore, the keeper finally raised his head. Wet tracks stained his cheeks, reflecting in the dim light. Quinn stopped retreating. She swam closer, staying low to the water.

The keeper's face was round and pale, with green, red-rimmed eyes and a pointed nose. A brown knit hat pulled low over his ears hid most of his hair, but a few ginger strands poked out of the front. The keeper took a shuddering breath as the tide rushed back in, and this time the water brushed the toes of the human's boots. At that moment, a few tears that had been clinging to the keeper's nose and chin shook free and landed in the water. The tears were nothing more than a few salty drops in a huge expanse, but they made Quinn's heart flip. Had there been three, or four tears? Quinn stayed right where she was.

When the water climbed up the beach again, Quinn watched the keeper's face intently. Another sob sent more tears dripping into the sea. When the seventh drop landed, Quinn felt a tug on her heart.

She stared at the keeper in disbelief.

She remembered another story her mother had told her, mostly to keep her entertained on the long journey up the coast one summer. She had told Quinn about one of their ancestors, a male seal, who had felt compelled to break away from his herd and head toward a human town. When other seals asked where he was headed, he could not explain, only that he knew he had to get there as soon as he could. He found himself at a rocky beach. He searched for what had drawn him to this place and came upon a human woman sitting on a rock in the water. She was crying. As he watched her, seven of her tears fell into the ocean, and again he felt that tug on his heart. He revealed himself to her. The woman, who was grieving the sudden loss of her husband, was shocked when the selkie rose out of the water and peeled back his pelt, revealing a very handsome man. The two fell in love, the selkie leaving the ocean behind to stay on land with his new wife.

Quinn had been puzzled at the end of her mother's story.

"Why did they fall in love?" she had demanded. "They just met! And how do human tears summon a selkie?"

"It's only a story," her mother said, soothing. "And not just any tears can summon a selkie. Only women seem to have such an effect on us, especially when they are feeling great grief or loneliness. Perhaps it is because at that moment we feel a great kinship to them. Some say that selkies were humans first, women who lost themselves in grief and asked the ocean to take away their emotions. The ocean, in a moment of tenderness, granted their wish and turned them into seals. But a few kept ahold of their human sides, which is why we can turn into humans, too."

This had confused Quinn even more, reminding her mother that she had told Quinn that selkies came from seals who became human, not the other way around. Her mother had laughed.

"We've many stories, love," she told her daughter.

But what Quinn could remember for certain was that only the tears of a human woman could summon a selkie. And even though she had never felt the call before, she knew that that was the tug she was feeling in her heart now. This lighthouse keeper was a woman.

Quinn flicked her tail to push herself a little closer to the shore. Ignoring the instinct telling her to turn back, Quinn let her curiosity take over and bring her close enough for her belly to scrape the rocky shoreline.

How had a woman come to be a keeper at the lighthouse? Quinn had seen the town's expectations of women, with only a few of them holding jobs outside of their homes. And hadn't she heard that the keepers were all men?

The keeper's eyes were closed, still leaking tears, but her hiccupping breaths were evening out. She tugged the brown sleeve of her sweater out from under the oilskin coat and wiped her cheeks. Now that Quinn was closer, she could make out a dense pattern of freckles across the keeper's face. However, if Quinn hadn't felt the pull toward the woman because of her tears, she wouldn't have figured out that the keeper was a woman. Her short, stocky figure was mostly hidden under the bulky coat, but a closer look revealed that the keeper's rounded face gave way to a squarish jawline. She was also wearing thick pants, which Quinn had never been allowed to wear when she lived with Owen.

If Quinn tried to get any closer, she'd be on the beach. Had she been able to hold her nerve, this would have been the moment to grab the keeper's ankle and drag her into the water.

The keeper sucked in a deep breath and sniffled loudly once more. She seemed to have gathered herself, and she wiped her face with her sleeve again. Blinking her eyes open as if unsticking them from a deep sleep, she met Quinn's gaze blankly.

Quinn had known this was coming. There had been time to duck back into the water and get away before the keeper opened her eyes. Instead, Quinn stayed. Perhaps it was the woman's tears calling to a deeper part of Quinn, tugging her closer despite the instincts telling her to run away, but Quinn also felt trapped by her curiosity. She needed to know more about this woman.

After a moment of staring at each other, the keeper shot to her feet. Quinn jerked back at the movement but didn't leave. Her flippers were tense, ready to send her flying through the water if the keeper made one wrong move.

But the keeper had frozen in place just like Quinn.

They watched each other, warily, and when the keeper remained stuck in place, Quinn raised her head out of the water a bit. She snorted, sending water flying, and the keeper took a step back. Feeling the opportunity slipping away from her, Quinn broke the silence.

"Why were you crying?" Quinn tried to ask, but what came out instead was a muffled, warbling bark. Of course, she couldn't speak to humans in this form.

Being barked at by a huge seal seemed to be too much for the keeper, and she turned on her heel and hurried up the beach toward the steep path leading up the island. She kept glancing back at Quinn, though. Maybe she was checking to see if Quinn was following her, but Quinn stayed right where she was and watched the keeper's retreating back.

Chapter Four

AFTER HER CHANCE DISCOVERY of the female lighthouse keeper, Quinn stayed away from the beach for a few days. She was curious how the woman had become a keeper in the first place and why she'd been crying alone by the water, but the memory of seven years of captivity put a damper on that curiosity.

Instead, she tried harder to recall anything she'd heard about the keepers while she lived in town.

She remembered a day in the first week of September, when the feeble summer gave way to the bitter winds of autumn, and she had taken her daughter Flora into town for the market. Quinn had led Flora to the pier in search of one of the fishermen who worked with Owen. There were two fishermen's wives already waiting and swapping stories they'd overheard from their husbands.

"A new keeper in October, that's what he told me," one of the wives said, bending her long, thin neck as she spoke to her shorter companion. "Mr. MacArthur's decided the lighthouse needs another keeper for the winter season. Too much work for only two men."

The other wife, who had a scarf tied tightly over her hair, pursed her lips. "Surely they could manage with just two; you've seen the size of James Donovan. Even if Mr. MacArthur is only half the help, with his arm and all."

This comment seemed to amuse the wives greatly, their laughs sharp and cold like the screech of a seabird.

Quinn hadn't understood what the wives found so funny, but she didn't know much about the lighthouse keepers. She knew they existed, and came to shore sparingly to restock their supplies, and she knew that rumors sprung up around them ever since the lighthouse was built five years ago and Finn MacArthur arrived to run it four years ago. James Donovan had joined him the previous summer. Since the town knew so little about them, the gossip among the wives and fishermen had run rampant.

Quinn tried not to listen to the gossip, partly because she simply wasn't interested in hearing what the town thought of the two lighthouse keepers, and partly because she knew if the gossip was anything like what the town said about her, there would barely be a lick of truth to any of it. She had never met the keepers, but felt a sort of solidarity with them as the town's favorite topics of rumor.

At least Quinn had given them much to talk about when she had first arrived in town. She had no idea how to live as a human, and she'd made every possible mistake and avoided everyone who tried to approach her. Her anger had been fresh and oozing, and the town, not knowing who she was, had responded to her mistrust in kind. Quinn had quickly learned human customs under Owen's instruction, but the damage was done.

"Any word on who the new keeper will be?" the scarf wife asked.

"No clue," her friend told her. "We'll have to try and catch him when he arrives next month."

She peered around as she spoke and realized who was in line behind her.

Voice dropping, she bent her neck even farther and whispered something in her friend's ear. They laughed, and Quinn took a deep breath.

When the wives finally got their fish and moved off, Quinn stepped up to the stall. Flora eyed the limp, open-mouthed fish with distaste.

The fisherman minding the stall looked up and let out a gruff, "I'll get Owen's portion."

The fishermen that Owen worked with would allocate some of their catch to each of their families. Quinn had been worried, in the early days of their marriage, that the fishermen would refuse to give her the fish. The men minding the stall always gave her great looks of distrust and handed over the catch like she would sprint off with it and leave nothing for Owen. Once their children came around, the men were a little less suspicious, but they were never happy to see her at the market.

The feeling was mutual for Quinn. She pretended not to hear a few fishermen discussing her in hoarse but audible whispers a couple stalls away.

Flora, not wanting to wait with the dead-eyed fish staring at her, had wandered to the cliff edge near the sloping path that led down to the beach. She crouched far enough back from the edge so that Quinn didn't worry, and began digging in the soft, sandy dirt for shells.

The fishermen a few stalls away ran out of steam talking about Quinn and switched to the only other topic of conversation that held the town's attention.

"Another lighthouse keeper coming—they must be expecting a rough winter this year," one of the fishermen said. He had a graying, unkempt beard that twitched as he spoke. The other fisherman, who was younger, with only a bit of stubble around his chin and a slightly crooked nose, like it had been broken in a fight, frowned.

"They can predict that this early?"

Twitchy Beard scoffed. "They can say whatever they like; they've got MacArthur out there staring at clouds and rainstorms like they're lines on a map. If he reckons weather'll be bad this winter, the board's sure to believe him. He's been head keeper there, what, four years? They've believed his predictions every time." He lowered his voice, and the crooked-nosed fisherman leaned in. "You ask me, it's all nonsense."

"Mr. MacArthur's predictions?" Crooked Nose asked, sounding scandalized.

"Aye," the old fisherman said. "No way he can track the weather that far out, unless he had some sea god whispering in his ear! When I was young, we never knew what kind of weather was coming until a few days before, when old Danny's knees started going stiff. Mr. MacArthur can stare at clouds all he likes, but weather ain't gonna follow a set pattern just 'cause he says it does."

The crooked-nosed fisherman glanced around, as if looking to see if anyone was listening to the old man, and Quinn made herself seem very interested in the stack of fish in front of her.

"But if he's been right every year, for four years," the young fisherman reasoned.

"That's the thing," Twitchy Beard declared loudly, but lowered his voice again when the younger fisherman went wide-eyed. "He hasn't always been right! Remember that great dirty storm, the first year MacArthur was there? Nothing about that storm was in his all-seeing report, and he was nearly wiped off that island 'cause he had no help. Took him another year to ask the board to hire a secondary keeper. I reckon he was worried another storm he couldn't predict would come and finish him off."

"But then, if he's asked them to send another keeper," the crooked-nosed fisherman reasoned, "wouldn't that mean he was predicting the storms correctly? He's preparing for something he thinks is coming."

"Ach," the older fisherman scoffed, "seems to me he just can't handle the work anymore."

The two fishermen kept discussing the lighthouse keepers, but Owen's coworker had finally returned with three fish strung together and held them out to Quinn. She took them without a word and called to Flora. Her daughter brushed dirt off her skirt and hurried back to her mother's side, clutching a fist to her chest. Quinn guessed she had found a shell or two to bring to Evie and Oliver.

As they made their way back through town, dodging barbed stares and the crowded stalls of the market, Quinn laid her fingertips on Flora's shoulder to keep her close. The market spilled them out onto the road in front of the town's pub, The Slippery Eel. It was too early in the morning for the bar to be open, but Ronnie, the widow of the Eel's previous owner, who now ran the pub with an iron fist and wooden spoon, stood in the doorway speaking to two men in low, serious tones. The men were dressed in smart black uniforms, nothing like what the local fishermen wore, and Quinn hadn't recognized them. One of them held out a piece of paper to Ronnie, and she took it with a frown.

"If anyone has any information," one of the men was saying to Ronnie, his thick mustache twitching with every word, "report it back to us."

"You're sure he's in these parts?" Ronnie asked skeptically.

"We've had reason to believe so," the man told her.

"Well," Ronnie sighed, propping a fist on her hip. She looked up and caught sight of Quinn. Ronnie was one of the few people in town who didn't grimace at the sight of Quinn, but wary of her business and Quinn's reputation, she never went out of her way in her kindness. As Quinn and her daughter walked by, Ronnie gave Flora a wave and a nod in Quinn's direction before turning back to the men.

The mustached man's partner had pivoted to look at Quinn. She didn't like the hard, assessing look in his eye, but he tipped his head and touched the rim of his hat in her direction.

"Ma'am."

In the early days of her captivity, Quinn would have hurried away without saying anything. But she had learned that her rudeness only encouraged the town to be more suspicious of her. She gave the man a quick nod in return and shepherded Flora up the road.

Quinn had felt that man's eyes on her back until they'd turned a corner.

She'd never found out what those men were asking Ronnie about. If Owen had seen them around town, he hadn't mentioned it to Quinn.

Tucked in the crevice of the island cliff, safe in her seal form, Quinn mulled over the memory. Thanks to the gossipy wives and fishermen, she actually knew quite a bit about the lighthouse keepers. But which one was the keeper she'd seen crying on the beach? She had to be the newest addition, the one the town had the least amount of information to build rumors on.

But knowing a little about the lighthouse keepers wasn't going to keep her safe if they ever discovered her. She'd let her curiosity overrule her sense when she let the crying keeper see her, and the keeper had been startled, but Quinn didn't know if the keepers believed in the same stories as Owen. Quinn couldn't risk her freedom again.

Twisting on the small ledge, Quinn squinted out at the ocean. It was a relatively calm day, and the horizon stretched for kilometers.

She didn't want to take any chances, but she also couldn't stand sitting still. She had to decide what was the better option: staying near the island and risking discovery, or leaving on the slim hope of finding the herd. For now, she laid her chin down on the slick stone and closed her eyes. The decision would still be waiting for her when she woke.

Chapter Five

NOW

As LATE AUTUMN SETTLED around the island, Quinn saw fewer and fewer boats venturing out into the water. She knew from her time with Owen that the fishermen spent fewer days on the ocean when the cold season set in. The added work of fighting bitter winds and sudden storms on top of their regular struggle to track and catch the fish made their trips exhausting and largely unsuccessful. Owen spent many of his winter days with the other fishermen in Ronnie's pub, piling through the door the moment it opened.

The fishermen still braved the waters a few days a month so that the town wouldn't go hungry, but it was understood amongst the people that they would depend on their preserved and hardier foods until the weather let up.

With fewer boats patrolling the waters, Quinn was able to swim more freely during daylight hours. She took advantage of the lack of competition to hunt the best fishing spots at sunrise, and again at sunset. But she was still careful to keep an eye out whenever she swam at the surface. Winter had not hooked its claws into the coast yet, and a handful of clear, sunny days encouraged the town's fishermen to set sail while they could.

On these days, Quinn kept close to the island. The fishermen never came close to the lighthouse's island, since the fish seemed to steer clear of it as well.

She had not seen the lighthouse keeper again. Quinn had begun checking the beach every night despite her initial caution, and sometimes even during the day she would pop her head above water to see if the keeper had ventured down the path, but the keeper had not returned.

On the morning a week after she had startled the keeper at the beach, Quinn slid off her ledge and into the water. The clouds were thick but sparse, casting huge shadows across the water as they glided in front of the sun and then past. Quinn forwent her morning hunt and circled the island. She skimmed just below the surface until the sloping, rocky shore of the beach came into view, and then she rose high enough to get her nose and eyes out of the water.

The beach was empty, the keeper's boat still tied to their small dock.

Quinn snorted, spraying water. She didn't know why she expected to see the keeper at the beach again, or what she hoped would happen if she did.

Perhaps it was because she, like Quinn, seemed to be alone in whatever struggle she faced. Whatever had made her come down to the water, she didn't want to share with the two other keepers. In that way, at least, she and Quinn were the same. Back in her seal form, Quinn had no one to depend on but herself. Her herd was gone, and her children were still on land.

This thought sent her spinning down a whirlpool of emotions. Should she have brought her children with her? Beyond their looks, Quinn had never seen them show any signs that they had inherited her selkie abilities. Then again, they had never been in the ocean. Owen had forbidden Quinn from returning to the water at all, and he had never taken their children to play in the surf on the summer days when the chill water was nearly bearable. If she had brought them with her when she fled, would they have been able to turn like her? They didn't have pelts to change them into seals, and she couldn't risk their fragile human bodies in the unforgiving sea.

Her mother, who had been full to bursting with stories, had never told her one about children born of selkies and humans returning to the sea. The selkies never took the children to the water with them when they escaped.

But if Quinn had brought Flora, Evie, and Oliver with her, she wouldn't be alone. She would be able to teach them, like her mother and the herd taught her, how to ride the currents and catch fish, tell them the stories of their ancestors, share the true story of how she had met their father. If they had come with her, she could have taken them far, far away from the town that had scorned them their entire childhood and started over. The wide, wild ocean would claim them as her own.

Quinn let this thought buoy her for a moment before she punctured it. She didn't even know if her children would have wanted to come with her. Why would they ever choose her, the mother who had made them outcasts among the town, above a father who loved them openly?

She sent another spear through her fanciful thought, asking herself if she really wanted her children with her because it was best for them, or if she wanted them there so she wouldn't be alone. The truth bubbled unpleasantly in her chest.

Quinn twisted in the water, barking in surprise when the sharp edge of a rock caught her in the belly. Irritated, she surfaced. The sun was a bit higher in the sky now, shining brightly off the water where the clouds' shadows weren't floating, and Quinn squinted around as she sucked in another breath through her nose.

She froze, her stiff tail jerking to keep her above the water, when she spotted two figures making their way down the island's path toward the beach. They were too far away to make out any details, but Quinn quickly decided it was worth the risk to come in close and see if the female keeper was one of the pair.

Letting the water swallow her back up, Quinn propelled herself quickly up the beach toward the wooden posts of the dock. The wood was covered in a thin layer of black, slimy algae, along with a few shiny barnacles suckered on near the surface of the water. Quinn wove in between the posts as she waited for the lighthouse keepers to descend.

Quinn popped her head out a few times, straining to hear the crunch of the keepers' boots on the rocky beach. When the sound of rocks shifting and clacking under the weight of human feet finally reached her, Quinn felt a spike of panic. What if the female keeper had brought the other human to try to catch Quinn? Had she told the keepers what she saw that night at the beach?

But then the keepers' steps echoed off the wooden planks of the dock, and it was too late for Quinn to dart away without being spotted. One pair of footsteps was heavy and tramping, like they carried a lot of weight, and the other was lighter and careful. Quinn tucked herself close to one of the posts and stayed in the shadows as best she could, listening.

The keepers didn't speak, but Quinn heard them grunting and the sound of ropes becoming untied and thrown into the belly of the boat. Then, finally:

"Mr. MacArthur reckons this'll be one of our last trips to town before the foul weather sets in. He's given me a list of things to get." Quinn didn't recognize this voice, and figured this was the second lighthouse keeper the town often spoke of, James Donovan.

If he was talking about MacArthur, then the second figure had to be Quinn's keeper from the other night.

"All right," her keeper said. Although Quinn knew that this keeper was a woman, she had lowered and roughened her voice to sound more masculine. She also spoke softly, as if to further mask the sound.

Some more clunking on the wood planks, and then the boat lurched away from the dock.

Quinn let them get about a dozen meters away from the beach before she followed them. It was clear that the keeper hadn't told the others about what she saw at the beach, or else they would surely have spoken about it when they reached the water. But if they were going into town, there was a chance they could cross paths with Owen. Quinn didn't know how much Owen had told the town after her public disappearance, but if he had finally revealed the truth about Quinn being a selkie, they would still be talking about it days later. Would the keepers overhear gossip about a local fisherman's missing selkie wife? Would the female keeper be able to put the pieces together and recognize Quinn as the selkie they all spoke of?

The simplest solution would be to swim as far away from the town and the island as she could get. She could put the past seven years behind her and get lost in the endless waters from her memories.

But without knowing where her herd was, where would she go? She wouldn't last long on her own with her rusty instincts and her worries weighing her down.

Quinn slowed and dove deeper in the water as the keepers crossed the wake of a fishing boat. The fishermen were headed far out to sea, and Quinn determined that it wasn't Owen's boat overhead—the hull had too many scratches—when she realized something.

The pod of whales had not been able to point her in the direction of her herd, but the pod itself would not have remained in these waters year-round to notice all its visitors. But the fishermen were always here. Maybe the whales hadn't seen any seals for years, but the fishermen could have. Owen would have made sure no word of seals in the waters could have gotten back to Quinn while she was on land, but there was a chance she could overhear them talking about it now, especially if the keeper brought up the strange seal she'd seen on the beach.

She was risking discovery by returning to the town so soon, but her days of aimless waiting on the island had left her desperate for the smallest bit of hope. She raced along behind the boat as it picked up speed, the sail full of wind, and pushed down her worries about what she would do if she was spotted. For now, she just needed to keep up with the boat.

It was a long, hard swim back to town, even with Quinn's steadily growing strength and stamina. As they came closer to the town's pier, Quinn was careful to stay deep enough in the water to avoid being spotted by a passing fishing boat or knocked about by a stray rudder, but she also kept an eye on the underside of the keepers' boat. There was a single long scratch on one side she used to identify it, as if it had been pushed up against the rocks at one point and nearly wrecked.

The town's pier had much longer posts that reached deep into the water so the boats didn't have to come as close to shore. Quinn circled around the post by the keepers' boat, questioning whether it was a good idea to surface. But she had come this far and needed to know if the keeper had said anything about her.

Quinn broke the surface of the water quietly, sticking to the post like a limpet and hoping its shadow was enough to conceal her.

This dock was much noisier, with many feet echoing off the wood and shouts filling the air. She listened hard to make out the voices of the keepers through the cacophony.

"I can go to the store and get the supplies. I'll know better what we're missing and what we'll need for the winter," James Donovan was saying. "You take Mr. MacArthur's reports to the post office and pick up any mail that's come in. You know where the post office is?"

"Yes," Quinn's keeper said quietly, if a bit hesitantly.

"Well, if you happen to lose your way, anyone can point you in the right direction," James said kindly with a laugh.

"Ho, Jamie!" a new voice shouted, and loud footsteps rattled up the dock toward the keepers.

"Mr. Dunwoody," greeted Jamie. "This is the dock foreman," Jamie told the other keeper. "Mr. Dunwoody, this is Tavis Murdoch, our new keeper. Met him yet?"

"Not quite," Mr. Dunwoody said. "You came and whisked him off before the town could get a good look at him!"

Good, Quinn thought. The less the town saw of the keeper, the less material they had to build rumors. She also noted the name, Tavis Murdoch. It had to be fake, to go with the keeper's disguise.

"Hello, sir," Tavis said. Quinn could barely hear the keeper over the bustle of the pier.

"Right, right," the dock foreman said distractedly, and Quinn wondered if he was busy taking a good look at Tavis to report back at the pub later that evening. "Anyway, making a supply run, are you? I've got that old cart up by the office if you need it, Jamie."

"That'd be great," Jamie said, and his heavy footsteps trod away from the boat. Quinn followed along below them, listening to the two other pairs of footsteps on the dock.

"Oh, and by the way, Jamie," Mr. Dunwoody called, "there's been two men poking around, police types, they ask a lot of questions but haven't caused any trouble so far. Just keep your nose clean around them!"

There was a sound like someone stumbling on the dock, though Quinn didn't know who it was. She waited for Jamie to respond. When he finally did, he sounded carefully casual. "What have they been asking about?"

Mr. Dunwoody, in a conspiratorial tone, told him, "Apparently they're hunting a suspect in a murder from one of the big cities down south. Think they came this way. Well, I told them just like everybody, there's no way a murderer would have gone unnoticed in this town, eh?"

Again, Jamie seemed to struggle to respond, and he walked

off without saying anything Quinn could hear. Tavis was still above her, and the dock foreman moved right along from the investigating police to the elusive new keeper.

"Work all right so far?" Mr. Dunwoody asked. "Even we in town know how Mr. MacArthur can be, though Jamie never lets a complaint slip when he's around us." He laughed, as if letting Tavis know he was in on a joke.

"It's been fine," Tavis said slowly, pointedly not laughing along.

"Has it?" The foreman didn't seem to believe the keeper, or was disappointed that Tavis wasn't any more willing to dig into Mr. MacArthur than Jamie was. But he let the conversation move on. "How many more times you think you boys will be in town?"

"Mr. MacArthur figures this may be the last trip," Tavis told him.

"Already?" Mr. Dunwoody grunted. "It'll be a long winter on that island, then."

"Mmm," was the only response.

"You been doing this work long? Grew up by the water?"

Mr. Dunwoody was pushing at his chance to get any details about Tavis Murdoch from the source, but it was like drawing blood from a stone.

"Not too long," Tavis told him. "I grew up inland. South."

"I guess you don't need sea legs up in that tower, but hope you're not afraid of heights." Mr. Dunwoody laughed.

At this point, Quinn ran out of space, swimming right up to the edge of the cliff under the docks. She strained to hear if the keeper said anything back, but their steps faded as they ascended the stairs that led up the pier and into town.

After a few moments listening to see if Jamie or Tavis returned to the boat, Quinn sank lower in the water.

Surely if Owen had let the town know that she was a selkie in the hope of widening the search for his missing wife and recapturing Quinn before she could seek her vengeance on him in the waters, Mr. Dunwoody would have been eager to spread the word to the keepers. Quinn didn't know who had seen her flight through town and escape into the water, but Owen must have told them something to assuage their questions. The keeper had no reason to mention spotting her off the island, at least for now.

Without the keeper to loosen the tongues of the fishermen, Quinn seemed to be out of luck in overhearing anything about the movements of the seal herds in the area.

Quinn decided to wait for the keepers to return to their boat before making the journey back to the island. It would be easier to slip away from the pier under the shadow of a hull. In the meantime she dove to the rocky ocean floor. The water muffled the sounds of shouts and calls of the humans above, and she surfaced occasionally to listen before diving back down.

Quinn looked up at the boat hulls and saw that Owen's boat was tied up a little farther down the dock. She hesitated for a moment, then pushed off from the ocean floor and swam slowly toward the post nearest to the boat. The water obscured the objects above the surface, slanting everything at an angle, but it didn't seem like anyone was peering over the edge of a boat or the dock and looking in the water. Quinn poked her head out as much as she dared.

There seemed to be three men near Owen's boat, though none of them were Owen himself. Relieved, Quinn tried to keep still as she floated in the shadows of the dock and listened to the men.

"No, give it here," one of them groaned, as if struggling under significant weight. "We'll put it up for the day."

"We done, then?" another asked.

"Yeah," the groaning one said, and a loud thud sounded on the dock right above Quinn's head. "Second shift can get a new one."

"Wonderful," said a third, very raspy voice. "To the Eel straightaway?"

"It's not even noon yet!" the second voice laughed.

"I would," the first man told them. "But Mary's been up my hide about getting the roof fixed."

"Oh, come anyway," the third voice said imploringly. "Get her a good bit of gossip about Owen's woman and she'll forgive you."

Quinn, who had begun drifting away when the fishermen's talk had seemed to lead nowhere, flinched, and then winced at the loud splash she made. She sank quickly beneath the water, eyes on the point where the men were standing on the dock. But the sound must have been swallowed by the hubbub of the pier, because no one appeared to look over the edge. She slowly broke the surface again, listening hard.

"—nothing new to talk about," the first voice was saying. "Owen's got no clue where she went, and won't let slip if he knows more than he's letting on."

Quinn let out a little huffing breath. She should have known that Owen's selfishness would hinder him in asking for help to search for her. Even now, he wanted to keep her all to himself.

"Come on," the third man said, and gave a hacking cough before he could continue. "Didn't you hear she was running full tilt down the main road, whipping off clothes as she went?"

"And how did a naked woman get through town unnoticed, after that, hmm?" the second voice asked.

The first fisherman let out a disbelieving noise. "I still don't think those people saw what they thought they saw. Sure, she ran through town, but she must have run off in the other direction, disappeared into the hills. With her dress *on*."

"Mary agree with you on that?"

"'Course not. Talked my ear off about it when she got home from discussing it with every other wife in town. They met up for tea at someone's house to really get in a flurry about it," the first voice said. "Told me she knew it was only a matter of time."

"Matter of time 'til what?" the second fisherman asked.

"'Til Owen's woman left him and the children. Mary and her friends always had it out that she wasn't the mothering type, you know. Doing worse by her kids by being there."

The third voice pipped up again. "Better off without her, then, ain't they? Those kids?"

"Been tough on Owen, though," the second fisherman said lowly.

"Wasn't any better for him when she was here," the third man declared.

The first fisherman sighed. "Mary and the wives seem to think that, too. She was all up in arms about how they'd been right about her ever since she arrived. That she was strange. I can't say if I'm with Mary on that, since Owen kept her all those years, but there was definitely something going on.

Why'd he let her stay, and have his children, when it was so obvious she didn't fit in?"

The second voice murmured something, too low for Quinn to hear, but then he spoke up. "Kate said a few of them were worried she was worse than strange."

"Worse how?"

The man, obviously wanting to lean into the rumors but embarrassed by his eagerness, loudly whispered, "They were wonderin' if she could have been a selkie."

Quinn's blood went cold.

"You remember those stories," the second man said, gaining steam, "about how selkies were beautiful, strange spouses meant to bring luck, but they'd abandon their families the moment they had a chance?"

Heartbeat pounding in her ears, Quinn strained to keep her panic in check.

Finally, one of the men burst out laughing. "The looks on your faces! You'd really believe those old wives' tales."

Another man chuckled awkwardly. "Right. To the pub, then? We don't have to worry about that kind of talk there. Owen hasn't been since his woman disappeared."

The three fishermen continued talking, but Quinn didn't bother to follow them as their footsteps trailed away up the docks.

The men's dismissal should have soothed her, but she should have known Owen wasn't the only one she had to worry about. The women of the island were gossipmongers, but they were also sharp as silver fishhooks and eager to dig into vulnerable, tender flesh.

Quinn didn't know if the wives would take their suspicions

to Owen, but their accusations had pierced her between the ribs. She'd known she wasn't the best mother to her children. She'd done what she could to separate herself from them to try to draw off some of the bad attention they got from town. But it seemed that had only made the town's opinion worse. The fishermen's wives thought she wasn't the mothering type? Maybe she wasn't, but she would have never been on land to give birth to her children if Owen hadn't trapped her there in the first place.

Flora's, Evie's, and Oliver's small faces flashed up in her mind, their eyes wide, like the last time she had seen them when Flora returned Quinn's pelt.

Something was bubbling up in her stomach like a frothing wave, and Quinn forced herself to duck beneath the surface before letting out a frustrated bark.

How could the wives judge her, when they were the ones who encouraged the rumors about her, they were the ones who made up lies about what kind of mother she was? How could they judge her when she had been fighting every day just to get to the next? When she had to share a bed with her captor, never knowing if she was ever going to be free? How could they judge her, when she raised her children so that they would not need her, if anything happened? When she had tried to give them a life that the humans could accept?

Quinn twisted in the water. The bubbling in her stomach had spread to her chest. With another angry bark, she resurfaced. The ocean, which had been decently calm and smooth on the keeper's journey to the town, was now rough and choppy. Rain pelted down from the sky, and far away, Quinn could hear the rumble of thunder. She edged out from under the dock and saw that the harmless, bulky clouds from this morning had grown and darkened, blotting out any bit of blue and all of the sun.

The dock above her was a flurry of motion, footsteps racing up and down the wood planks accompanied by panicked voices. The sudden storm had fishermen scrambling to secure their boats or their catches.

Quinn huddled in the faint protection of the dock, her anger still pulsing in her chest. She darted back toward the cliffs to see if the keepers had returned.

She only had to wait a few minutes, during which she swam short, pacing lengths in the water as her heart pounded away, letting out grunts whenever she thought of what the fishermen had said about her.

"Here!" she heard Jamie shout. When she recognized his voice among the crowd, Quinn stopped pacing.

"Where'd this storm come from?" Tavis shouted back. The wind had picked up, and it carried away Jamie's answer as it blew the roughening storm closer.

"Just get in! Here, grab that end," Jamie told him. The sound of the keepers readying the boat was also lost in the wind and panic on the dock. Quinn stayed close and waited for the boat to pull away. It did so jerkily, and she darted out from under the dock to dive beneath the hull.

Quinn raised her head to take a deep breath before she dove, but a sound amid the cacophony made her jerk to a stop. It was a small sound that could have easily been lost amongst the other shouts and calls. But Quinn recognized it at once.

Without pausing to think, Quinn turned and swam back toward the beach. She searched the shoreline, trying to find where the noise had come from.

"Papa!" the voice cried again, and Quinn kicked toward it. Her heart, already ragged from the wives' accusations and weak to the thought of her children suffering because of her, beat frantically in her chest.

She raised her head fully out of the water and searched the beach until her gaze caught on a small figure huddled near the shore right below the old, rotten staircase that led down from the docks.

The figure's hair, dark and shining, was achingly familiar. As the distance shrunk between Quinn and the beach, she recognized the green patterned dress, the worn brown boots. Quinn managed to make herself dip below the water as a boat passed over her on the way to the docks, but immediately surfaced again, her eyes zeroing in on the child who was now only a few steps from the water.

It was Flora. Quinn's eldest daughter was on the beach and caught in the sudden storm. Where was Owen? Why was Flora alone?

The conflicting thoughts that Quinn had been struggling with regarding her children and her choice to leave them behind rushed to the surface, and Quinn realized the opportunity before her. Her daughter was alone on the beach, away from the influence of her father, and Quinn trusted that Flora was old enough to make a decision for herself. If she revealed herself to Flora, would her daughter be able to recognize her like this?

Flora had been the one to find Quinn's pelt. She'd held it in her hands, her fingers digging deep into the mottled pattern of the fur.

Would she want to join Quinn, if Quinn gave her the option?

As if drawn in by a net, Quinn came closer to the beach. Flora had not looked up, shivering in the rain and waiting by the stairs as if she were stuck to them.

Quinn stopped right before the point where the tide broke and tumbled into a wave that washed up onto the beach. This close, she could make out the concentration on Flora's face. She looked healthy, Quinn was relieved to see, if a little untidy and beginning to get soaked. Her braid was messy, long strands having pulled free, and her dress looked as if it was on its third or fourth day of wear.

Seeing Flora again, even in such a tempestuous state, felt as if a splinter had been drawn out from beneath Quinn's skin. She came a little closer still, the waves pushing her toward one of the docked boats. She could make a noise to get Flora's attention so she wouldn't startle her.

What would Quinn do if Flora ran from her like the keeper had?

The thought didn't fill Quinn with dread so much as an anticipated disappointment. Her daughter was clever, and Oliver seemed to have realized the truth about Quinn with just a few clues, so she had to believe Flora would know her. If she saw Quinn and decided to run, Quinn could not blame her.

Still, she wanted to give Flora the chance to decide. But what would she do if Flora didn't run? Quinn was no good to her daughter as a seal, not unless Flora was able to become one as well. On the shore, the rain from Quinn's storm soaked Flora's dress until it clung to her like a second skin.

A *piece of the selkie, for a pelt for their love.* Her mother's voice echoed through Quinn's head like thunder rumbling in the distance. A part of a story she had once told Quinn, forgotten until just now.

A *piece of the selkie*, Quinn thought. How much of herself would she have to give for Flora to be able to make a choice?

But even as the faded memory of her mother's story came together, Quinn heard a sharp intake of breath above her. Twisting in the water, Quinn looked around wildly and felt a heavy stone drop in her stomach. She had lingered, indecisive, for too long. The tide had pushed her right up next to Owen's boat, and Owen himself was leaning over the edge and staring straight at her.

He recognized her. Quinn was frozen, her instinct stalling out at the sight of the man who had kept her trapped for so long. Owen had dark circles under his eyes, and his shirt was as unkempt as Flora's dress, but the startled look on his face hardened in a split second. Quinn remembered that Owen had kept her trapped on land long after he realized she had proven a useless wife and a regretful mother because he had feared what she would do to him if she ever returned to the water. How he feared that in this moment, Quinn could drown him.

The sky rumbled above Owen, and his face paled. Because he knew there was more to fear about Quinn than her teeth. He was not merely afraid of what she could physically do to cause him harm; he was afraid of what her anger could summon. And Quinn had summoned this storm.

She had realized her influence over the weather a short time after Owen had stolen her pelt. Fraught emotions could whip up a battering rainstorm like the one that had swept over the docks in a matter of moments. Quinn had never known she held this power until she came to live on land, perhaps because she had never felt so frightened and alone, so full of terrifying emotions, before she had come onshore. The first few storms that surged over the sea and coincided with her breakdowns in frustration seemed to be nothing more than chance. But when it continued to happen, Quinn started to pay attention. She would cry and watch as a cloud abruptly appeared in the sky and rain dropped over the town. She would feel rage, then instantaneously track a swirling storm sweep in from the ocean, nearly sinking the boats that had set out in fair weather.

Quinn had thought she was fighting on land alone, but the ocean listened, answering her call.

Owen had realized what she was capable of, too, though it had taken a little longer. She didn't need to say anything. He would come home after escaping sudden storms to find her raging in the house often enough to put the pieces together. He had looked at her with fear in his eyes.

When Quinn had given birth to Flora, a massive storm had blown over the town and nearly carried off every boat with it.

The storm that was currently assaulting the town had fed off of Quinn's anger at the wives and her own guilt over abandoning her children. Owen's appearance above her deepened that well of emotion, and he instantly recognized what she had done. He disappeared into the belly of the boat for one moment and then quickly reappeared, this time hefting a long fishing spear.

The sight of the spear sent an electric shock through Quinn's body, and she flipped in the water and dove, her tail making a frothing wave in her rush.

Quinn had regained her speed, but Owen had spent more than half his life on the water with his eyes on his prey. There was a splash above her and Quinn gasped when she felt her tail pierced by the starburst point of the spear. The line pulled tight, and Quinn struggled like mad as she was pulled back toward Owen's boat. Small clouds of red blood bloomed from the wound as she twisted.

Quinn had lost her breath when the spear pierced her and felt herself weakening against Owen's strength. Quinn let a jerking tug bring her back to the surface and sucked in a breath, her eyes rolling as she tried to see if any other fishermen had come to Owen's aid. But it was still just Owen, yanking on the rope, his jaw set. He hadn't called out for help.

Was he still trying to keep Quinn's true form a secret? How was he going to explain why he had speared and captured a seal, and what was he even going to do with her once he got her out of the water? Owen couldn't make her take off her pelt. Only she could remove it.

Quinn was panting as she struggled, but her mind started to clear of the panic that had overcome her when she first saw Owen. She tensed her body and whipped around like a spinning dolphin. The movement made the spear tip tear into her tail fin, but she bit back a bark of pain and kept going until she felt the spear begin to slip out of the wound.

Owen had stopped trying to reel her in and was holding on to the rope with everything he had. She wouldn't let him trap her again.

Quinn summoned every ounce of strength she had worked to regain in the past weeks and dove down, as if she would go straight through the ocean floor. With a great snap, the metal spear tip broke off from the wooden handle. The point was still lodged in Quinn's tail, but she darted away as quickly as she could, trailing blood behind her.

When she was a dozen meters from the docks, Quinn relented to her straining lungs and surfaced for a gasp of air. She looked over her shoulder to see if Owen had unmoored his boat to chase her down, but it was still tied to the dock. He was in the same spot at the edge of his boat, holding the useless rope in his hands and staring out at the water.

Past Owen's boat, Quinn could also see that Flora was rooted to the spot on the beach and was staring out into the ocean. She would have seen everything from where she stood. She would have seen Quinn, and seen Owen spear her, and seen their struggle.

Well, Quinn thought with grim satisfaction, *let him explain that to her.*

If Owen hadn't said anything about Quinn being a selkie to their children yet, he didn't have much of a choice now. Flora would ask questions. She would tell Evie and Oliver what she had seen.

Owen and Flora watched the sea for a few more moments, rain soaking their clothes, and Quinn watched them back. Then, Flora must have said something, because Owen turned toward her and put his back to the water.

Knowing that Owen wasn't going to try to chase her down, Quinn gave Flora and the beach one last fleeting look. Any hopes of approaching Flora were dashed, so she pushed her mother's story from her mind and turned her attention to the spear tip still lodged in her tail. There was no way for her to pull it out while she was a seal. Trying to catch the hooked end on something would only make it worse. She would have to leave it in until she had human hands again.

Quinn caught her breath for one moment and then began swimming toward the island. She stayed right at the surface since her progress with the spear still embedded in her was so slow, and she worried about trying to dive with her injured tail. The rain pelted down, and she blinked against the onslaught. She passed one boat as she swam away from the town, but luckily the fishermen aboard were eager to make it to the dock and get out of the storm and were not scouring the water for her dark, round head. They passed right by each other without incident.

The keepers' boat was long gone. Quinn couldn't even see it on the darkening horizon.

The ragged skin surrounding the spear tip stung in the salt water. The muscles around her fin seized whenever she moved them, and Quinn could feel her energy fading fast as the adrenaline from Owen's attack dried up.

Still, with kilometers of open water ahead and a town full of humans behind her, Quinn had no choice but to keep moving. Blinking through the rain and the sharp pain brought by every movement, Quinn swam slowly toward the island.

Chapter Six

Quinn was searching through Owen's things when someone knocked at the front door. Sweaters and pants were gutted from the dresser she'd been digging through looking for her pelt, and she sat back on her heels at the noise. Owen wouldn't have knocked. It was his house. But in the two months since he'd trapped Quinn on land and introduced her to the town as his wife, they had never had a visitor.

Leaving the mess as it was, Quinn stood and went to the door.

One of the fishermen's wives stood on the step. Quinn had met a few of them when Owen brought her to the market, when she'd still been uncertain in the heavy human clothes and overwhelmed by the number of people flooding the town's crowded center square. She remembered Owen introducing her as his wife and the women's short, polite greetings, which she'd returned with blank stares. The wives' faces had quickly closed off after that. Owen had pulled her away before they could say anything else.

She'd been to town a few more times since then, and each time she seemed to make her reputation worse and worse. A man had bumped into her, and she'd snarled at him. Two women had tried to chat with her at the produce stall, and she'd ignored them until they went away muttering things she couldn't hear. An older couple had stopped her on the street to ask how she was finding married life, and she'd been honest. But her honesty hadn't been what they wanted to hear.

Later, Owen had explained what expectations the town would have for her as his wife. He told the town that she was a woman from the small farming village he had grown up in, brought to him to be his wife when her parents could no longer support her. Her coarse manners were the fault of being raised in such an isolated community, and she would adapt to her wifely duties soon, or so Owen claimed. Quinn didn't understand why she had to pretend to like the life she was trapped in, but she did begin to pick up on the human customs that got her through each interaction without ending in disaster.

That still didn't explain why one of the fishermen's wives was at her door.

"Hello," the woman said after a long moment in which Quinn realized she should have offered a greeting.

"'Lo," Quinn murmured. She did not invite the wife inside.

"I was wondering," the woman said daintily, "if you'd like to join me and a few other wives in town for tea?"

"I would not," Quinn told her.

The wife blinked, the weak smile on her face slipping at Quinn's frankness. She wrestled it back up.

"Oh, come," she said with a little laugh. "Surely a few chores could wait? We'll have tea and some of Kate's scones, and you can finally meet some of the other women in town."

Quinn didn't like tea. Quinn didn't like the other wives. She didn't want to ingrain herself into this town any more than she'd already been forced to, and she especially didn't want to waste time she could be using to look for her pelt while Owen was away.

But her searches so far had turned up nothing, and as much as Quinn dreaded it, the odds of her being trapped on land with these humans for a significant amount of time looked ever more likely. Wouldn't it be easier if she had a few friendly faces to rely on?

Quinn stepped forward, and the wife took a hurried pace back so that she was one step below Quinn on the stairs, looking up.

"I'll come," Quinn told her.

"Oh! Oh, good." The wife smiled widely. "Dressed like that?"

Quinn frowned at her clothes, a short-sleeved dress and apron with the skirt tucked up so that she could walk freely. It was a warm day.

"Like this," Quinn told her. She didn't need a shawl when the weather was fine. The wife's smile twitched, but she nodded and held out her elbow for Quinn. She had seen the women walking around town linked at the crook of the arm. She had even seen devoted husbands and wives walk in such a way, but it looked completely asinine to Quinn. Wasn't it harder to walk weighed down by another?

But this was something the wife seemed to insist on. Quinn

reluctantly put her arm through the loop and suppressed a grimace when the wife clamped down on her tightly.

They walked down the road to a house much larger and grander than Owen's. The few people they passed on the street had odd expressions on their faces, but they didn't call out to the pair.

The wife ushered Quinn into the house without knocking and showed her through dimly lit hallways until they entered a wide sitting room. A dozen or so other women were already there, and they all went quiet the moment Quinn arrived.

She froze in the doorway. A creeping feeling of alarm tugged at the back of her neck, the same feeling she'd have when a predator was circling the herd.

"Come sit," an older woman told her. The wife who'd brought Quinn melted into the crowd.

She recognized a few of the women, though she didn't know their names. Her first month on land, all she'd thought about was getting her pelt back. She hadn't wanted to know the names of the humans that lived here.

Some of the women were openly staring at her. A few had their eyes on their cups, sitting stiffly amongst the others. How often did they gather like this?

"Sit!" the old woman commanded. Quinn frowned at her.

"No manners at all," one of the wives whispered to another, though it carried easily across the room. "You'd think she was raised by animals."

Skin prickling, Quinn walked slowly to the only open seat, which was isolated from the others by at least a meter on either side. She perched cautiously on the chair and attempted to mimic the way the other women were sitting, their legs tucked in and spines straight. There was no way she could know what to do to meet the humans' expectations, but she had best try to blend in. They didn't know what she was, and she wanted to keep it that way.

No one offered her tea.

"You have been Owen's wife for nearly two months, and still we know nearly nothing about you," the older woman began. "This is a small town. You are either a part of it, or a hindrance to it."

Quinn's heart sank. Her tentative hope in finding a friendly face among the wives was dashed as she looked around the room. She had not been invited to tea for the women to get to know her better. She had been invited to a confrontation meant to humiliate and temper her.

Even as she faced down what felt like every woman in town, Quinn's fear morphed into indignation. She bared her teeth like the animal they expected her to be.

"I never wanted to be a part of this town," Quinn spat.

A few wives gasped at her tone, others shaking their heads as if they'd known she was a lost cause all along.

"As Owen's wife," the old woman began, but Quinn let out a harsh laugh.

"I'd sooner be his wife than a fish would seek comfort from a shark."

The old woman's mouth was agape, and the wives behind her looked equally alarmed. One woman was looking at Quinn with eerie clarity, as if she'd recognized something in Quinn's ire, but offered no help.

"Have you no shame?" a different wife asked Quinn.

"I've nothing at all," Quinn told her honestly.

"You are wrong," the old woman quavered. "You have beauty, for which is the only reason I could understand Owen seeking a wife in you, and you have cruelty, which you wield without care. You do not wish to be part of this town? Fine. We will ensure you never find a place in it."

She turned from Quinn and faced the rest of the wives.

"Any who dare offer her kindness or help before she makes amends will receive the same treatment," she warned them. The younger wives wilted under her gaze. A pair of the older ones were already whispering fervently to each other, seeming to relish Quinn's humiliation. She recognized her neighbor near the back of the room, looking down on Quinn with disdain.

Quinn stood. She felt the rage building in her chest, lapping at the edges, and felt as though she were about to burst apart. The matriarch called out to her, but she couldn't hear anything over the rushing in her ears as she left the house. The previously sunny summer sky had darkened with quick-moving clouds. A warm rain showered down. Quinn marched away from the house and was nearly at Owen's door when she finally let her own tears mix with the rain on her face.

She had been foolish to hope for forgiveness from the humans. They were too selfish, too involved in their own assumptions about who Quinn was to see what she really needed. Quinn had to find her pelt and escape this town as soon as she could. Once she did, she hoped she never saw a human ever again.

Chapter Seven

QUINN FELT AS IF she had been swimming for hours, with each second marked by a twinge from her tail, when she finally spotted the lighthouse. The beacon had been lit and was swinging through the evening rain, flashing over Quinn like a spotlight.

As the island rose higher into the sky the closer she swam, Quinn grimaced at the thought of hauling herself onto the small, rocky ledge she had been sleeping in these past weeks. There was no room for her to move around and deal with the spear tip in the side of the cliff.

Quinn would have an easier time dragging herself up onto the beach. She'd seen for herself that the keepers rarely came down to the water, and it would be a relief to be up and away from the sea. Quinn headed toward the small, rocky beach where she had once slept with her herd.

She remembered when another seal in the herd had been injured, when she was only a few seasons old. A large male seal had been attacked and nearly caught by a pod of orcas, and there were long tears and teeth marks in the seal's hide. He had been swimming alone in open water but had managed to escape the pod and rejoin the herd, trailing blood. Older seals in the herd had scolded the hurt seal. He should have known better than to swim alone when the orcas were passing through their waters. He could have endangered the rest of the herd by leading the pod straight to them with the smell of his blood in the water.

The herd had immediately shepherded themselves to the coast and hauled themselves onto the closest beach for the night. Quinn, tucked in close to her mother's side, had watched the injured seal as he whimpered in pain while dragging himself across the rocky shore. Out of the water, his wounds bled heavily, the red color brighter and thicker without the ocean diluting it. Quinn's mother had nudged her away from the hurt seal, a look of concern staining her dark eyes.

"Will he be all right?" Quinn had asked her.

"I don't know," her mother said honestly. "He's lucky to be alive. We've lost many strong seals to orcas before."

"But his wounds," Quinn pressed.

"There's nothing we can do about them," her mother insisted. Quinn had seen smaller wounds from sharp rocks or too forceful bites heal among the herd, but this seal's injuries were much deeper. Her mother's nose twitched as the blood began to pool in the rocks where the seal had collapsed, his energy gone. "He may heal, but it's not up to him. He can only hope that the sea is kind and the herd is patient."

Quinn spent that night listening to the normal snores of the herd, broken up by the injured seal's pained grunts as he shifted on the beach. The herd had remained onshore, with only a few strong, fast adults risking the water to go catch fish, while they waited for the pod of orcas to move on. When the adults decided it was safe to begin their journey up the coast once more, the injured seal's wounds had stopped bleeding, but still looked raw and painful. Nevertheless, he limped after the herd when they entered the water. He made it through another season, but his wounds made him slow, and he was finally caught by another orca when the herd was moving down the coast.

Quinn didn't think her wound was nearly as bad as that seal's injuries, but as her mother had said, she had no way to treat her tail as a seal.

The island's beach was dark, the stones glistening with salt water and rain. She could make out the shape of the keepers' boat bobbing in the waves beside the dock and knew that the keepers had made it back to their island and already returned to their lighthouse. Quinn squinted at the path leading up over the cliffs and couldn't spot anyone coming back down to the beach.

She spent a moment hanging before the break in the tide, considering where she should try to haul herself out of the water. She eventually decided that the safest place would be the far side of the beach, away from the keepers' dock and boat.

Bracing herself, Quinn swam until her fins touched the ground and then began to haul herself out of the tumbling waves. There was a sharp, stabbing pain in her tail with every movement, and it made her clumsy as she crawled out of the water while keeping the spear tip from catching on the rocks. She tucked herself against the side of the cliff and lay still, panting.

When she'd caught her breath, Quinn gritted her teeth against the pain and shifted onto her side so she could lift her head and tail and get a better look at the wound. The spear had pierced her left tail fin, and Quinn's attempts to escape had widened the injury. It bled sluggishly.

Wincing, Quinn laid her tail back down.

In her seal body, there was nothing she could do to try to treat the wound. Her mother had led her to believe that injuries only healed over time and with luck. But Quinn had not been a seal for seven years.

Quinn had treated many small injuries in her time on land. Owen had taught her how to patch and bind wounds, how to stem blood flow, and how to treat against infection. He had done so for his own benefit, as he often came home with fishing hooks stuck in his skin and preferred her first aid over the brusque attention of his fellow fishermen. Quinn had been revolted at the sight of the barbed hooks piercing through Owen's fingers or arms, but she had learned to stiffen her jaw through it and eventually became very practiced at prying out hooks and patching the wounds.

She had no medicine or wrappings to treat her tail wound, but she couldn't leave the spear tip lodged as it was.

Quinn shifted to look over at the path that led up the island to the lighthouse. With the rainstorm, she figured the keepers would be busy with the beacon for the rest of the evening.

She gave herself a moment to breathe. She hadn't thought she would be parting with her pelt so soon, and her heart was pounding at the thought. But she couldn't leave her wound untreated. Quinn shuffled on to her back, blood flicking onto the rocks as she moved, though it was quickly washed away by the rain.

It had been seven years since Quinn had done this for the first, and only, time. The memory was still sharp in her mind. She started with her flippers like she did before, freeing her hands from the thick skin and regaining the use of her dexterous fingers. Her arms and chest came easily, and she pushed the pelt over her nose and eyes, gasping when her head was free.

Her hair fell down her back in a loose, wet tangle. She sat up, her pelt gathered around her hips like a rumpled skirt. Quinn pushed the pelt down over her thighs and then pulled her right leg free. Her right foot was uninjured, and she braced it against the rocky beach as she came to the worst part. Carefully freeing her shin, then ankle, and then her left foot, Quinn gasped as the pelt pulled free around the spear, and then the fur fell away, limp and lifeless beneath her.

Again, Quinn had to stop and catch her breath, the sound seemingly louder coming from her human lungs. Her bare skin had pebbled against the chilly rain. She drew her foot closer to her so she could peer down at the wound.

The spear was now lodged through her foot, the broken end of the spear sticking out from the top and the hooked tip pierced through the bottom. It looked worse this way. Perhaps because her tailfin didn't have bones to break, but Quinn thought that the wound was a clean slice through, even if the skin was ragged at the points of entry and exit.

Gritting her teeth, Quinn leaned forward and cautiously touched the exposed end of the spear. Even that light touch had her gasping in pain. She had her fingers and hands to grip the spear, but she wasn't sure if she would be able to pull it out on her own, knowing how much it would hurt.

A distant rumble of thunder matched the temperamental beat of her heart. Quinn had to pull the spear free before treating the wound. She could not let herself succumb to Owen's violence after surviving it for seven long years. She let the hatred she felt for him steel her nerves and wrapped her fingers around the hooked tip, which was slick with blood and rain.

"Uh," someone said behind her.

A cold hand seized Quinn's heart as she whipped around, releasing the spear and biting back the groan of pain. The smaller keeper stood behind her on the beach. She was wrapped in the large, oilskin coat, her damp knit hat pulled low over her forehead, and she was watching Quinn with wide eyes.

Quinn cursed her recklessness. It was too late for her to run. She could pull on the pelt and crawl back into the ocean, but it wouldn't change the fact that the keeper had seen her. Had she been here when Quinn was taking off her pelt?

"Uh," the keeper said again in a low, hesitant voice. She took a step forward but stopped immediately when Quinn flinched back. "Are you injured?"

Quinn gaped at the keeper. That was her question? She didn't ask who Quinn was, or *what* she was? Even if the keeper hadn't seen Quinn peel off her pelt, she had to be wondering what a naked woman was doing on the beach.

The keeper was waiting for Quinn's answer. Quinn tried to tuck her injured foot with its obvious bloody intrusion behind her, out of view, but that only resulted in a wince. She glared at the keeper, but the woman remained where she was.

Eventually, Quinn attempted a lie. "I'm fine."

"Are you in trouble?"

The keeper's face was serious, the skin between her eyebrows wrinkling as she looked down at Quinn. Her hands were loose at her sides, but there was a line of tension in her shoulders like she was waiting for a signal that it was safe to approach. Quinn was careful not to give her one.

"Trouble?" Quinn parroted back.

"Do you need help?" the keeper clarified. Her fingers twitched, the movement catching Quinn's eye before she focused back on the keeper's face.

Night had set in while Quinn had been struggling out of her pelt and dealing with the spear, and the layer of clouds let in only a sparse amount of light from the moon. The beach was spared the flashing glow of the beacon, and with her human eyes Quinn could only make out so much. The keeper was looking intently at Quinn's face, her gaze staying respectfully above her shoulders, not even glancing at the pelt beneath her. Quinn wasn't sure if the keeper had seen her remove her pelt, but her line of questioning was tinged with concern, rather than fear.

However, the keeper was still human.

"Not from you," Quinn said darkly, fisting one hand in the thick fur of her pelt.

The keeper cocked her head, a movement that reminded Quinn of a spaniel that one of the town's fishermen owned.

They stared at each other for a few moments. Quinn couldn't back down since she had no way to escape, and the keeper seemed too intrigued by Quinn to leave her alone. Quinn should have been more careful, but her struggle with Owen and resulting injury had stripped her of her common sense, and she had just wanted the comfort of a beach she had once claimed with her family.

Finally, the keeper moved. Not away from Quinn, but instead she raised her hands like a surrender and began to lower herself down. Quinn watched silently as the keeper crouched. When the keeper was level with Quinn, she paused, eyebrows raised as she waited for Quinn to react.

While Quinn didn't appreciate being treated like a wild animal that would lunge at any sudden movements, she couldn't deny that it was fitting for how she felt. She was trapped in a corner. If the keeper had rushed to her side, as she very obviously wanted to do, Quinn would have lashed out with everything her exhausted human body had left.

Now that they were face-to-face, the keeper lowered her hands. She tucked one into the space between her thighs and chest and used the other to brace her fingers against the rocky beach. Quinn was astonished by the number of freckles covering the keeper's face. They reached across her wide cheeks and pointed nose, even trailing up her forehead past fair eyebrows.

"You don't have to be afraid of me," the keeper told her. She was still using that low, masculine-sounding voice that Quinn had first heard her use when speaking with the other keepers. It was softer now, barely louder than the gentle rush of the waves on the beach, but still a lie.

Quinn narrowed her eyes. "I'm not afraid," she said. This was both true and not. She wasn't afraid that this keeper would hurt her. She was afraid of what it would mean if this keeper told others of what she had seen.

It didn't look like the keeper believed Quinn, so she blurted out, "I saw you crying."

Realization washed over the keeper's face slowly, in the way the moon pulled at the tides; gradually, until the shores were overcome. The keeper's green eyes darted between Quinn's face and the pelt beneath her, to the ocean where Quinn had floated as a seal and watched the keeper cry as the water crept up on her. With her chest rising and falling quickly, the keeper leaned into her braced hand, balancing on the tips of her toes as she stared at Quinn.

"Then it's real? You're real?" she whispered, as if worried someone would overhear. In her excitement, she let the low tones of her voice slip. "I mean, you're really a...a shapeshifter?"

Again, it wasn't fear that colored the keeper's voice. This time, it sounded more like wonder.

"A selkie," Quinn corrected her. If the keeper already knew about her, she might as well use the right name.

"A selkie," the keeper repeated, trailing off as she stared wide-eyed at Quinn.

Quinn knew she should have been more frightened. The last time a human had caught her with her pelt separated from her body, it had been stolen from her and left her trapped on land for seven years. Her memories of that night were sharp as urchins, and she remembered the look of awe that had shone from Owen's face when he had her pelt clutched in his hands. But the keeper made no move toward Quinn or her pelt. She wasn't leaving Quinn alone, but her attention didn't feel the same as Owen's possessive focus.

Quinn shifted, releasing her tight grip on the pelt and rearranging her injured foot.

This seemed to remind the keeper of her original questions.

"Are you sure you don't need help?" she pressed. "That

looks pretty painful. I could help you get it out, and bring some bandages for the wound, and maybe some clothes?"

"Why?" Quinn barked, tucking her leg in close to her again.

The keeper seemed baffled by her question. "Because you need help, and I can give it."

But Quinn had learned quickly that nothing was so easy when she was human. The keeper could help her with the spear to distract her while stealing the pelt when she wasn't looking. She could offer to get bandages to bind Quinn's wound, but return with the other keepers in tow. Quinn already doubted her ability to fight off one human, let alone three.

Quinn had also learned what the humans considered "help," in that the wives had tried helping her fit in by humiliating her into submission. They, like Owen, had only wanted to trap and confine her.

She kept these memories sharp in her mind as she stared the keeper down. But even as she did so, Quinn also remembered the feeling in her gut when the keeper's seven tears had fallen into the sea. She would have recognized the grief and pain in those tears even if she had been kilometers away. The keeper's weeping had drawn her in then and continued to do so now.

A sharp twinge in her foot reminded Quinn of the danger of getting too close to a human. But she could not deny that she doubted her ability to get the spear out on her own.

Quinn let out a pained sigh and met the keeper's gaze reluctantly. "If I let you help me, you'll do everything I say, when I say it. No quick movements. No questions. If you try anything, you'll regret it."

The keeper perked up like Quinn had offered her a great

favor. With her hands raised, she stood and took careful steps toward Quinn until she was at her side. Quinn's grip on her pelt was turning her knuckles white, but the keeper was only looking at her injury, her expression twisting with pity.

Quinn didn't want her pity. "I can't pull it out myself," she said roughly. "And I'll need something to stem the bleeding."

The keeper nodded and reached into her coat. She pulled out a slightly stained square of cloth from a pocket and Quinn said, "No. Gather some of that seaweed."

Looking as if she wanted to argue with Quinn's choice of bandage, the keeper pressed her lips together and put her cloth away. She scraped a few long pieces of seaweed off the surrounding rocks before returning to Quinn's side.

Quinn had turned so that she was facing away with the bottom of her foot and the pointed end of the spear angled toward the keeper. She twisted her head to maintain a line of sight on the keeper's hands.

"Pull it out all at once," Quinn told her.

The keeper, for her part, didn't grimace when she carefully wrapped her fingers around the bloody spear point. Her other hand hovered over Quinn's ankle.

"It'll be easier if I can apply a counterpressure," she told Quinn.

Bracing herself, Quinn nodded, and the keeper set her hand down. The feel of a human's hand on her skin made Quinn bristle, but she forced her muscles to relax as the keeper began to count down. The keeper met her eyes in the last moment, and the green of them was all Quinn saw before the keeper pulled and Quinn's vision went black.

She must have screamed or shouted, because her throat

was raw when she came back to herself. The keeper still had one hand on her ankle to keep her still, but in the other she held the spear, free of Quinn's foot and dripping blood onto the rocks.

"The seaweed," Quinn said weakly.

"Right." The keeper jerked, dropping the spear and reaching for the pile of seaweed by her knee. Her wrapping was clumsy, but Quinn didn't have the energy to do anything but watch as the ragged hole in her foot was bound up in strips of seaweed.

"You really should put some bandages on this, real ones," the keeper muttered, her gaze flicking between Quinn's wound and her face. "And medicine. There's some in the lighthouse. I could bring it to you—"

"No," Quinn told the keeper. She struggled up onto her hands and shifted her foot away. The keeper's fingers fell away from her skin and the wrapping she had just finished. "I can't trust you."

This response made the keeper grin for some reason, and perhaps it was a foolish thing for Quinn to say after the keeper had just helped her, though there was a flicker in the keeper's eye that didn't seem to match her smile. She was looking at Quinn with too much understanding.

"You've nothing to fear from me," she reminded Quinn.

"Because you're a woman?" Quinn asked.

Immediately, the keeper's face shuttered and closed. She swayed, as if she was going to tip over onto the rocky shore but caught herself just in time. Her eyes, still wide, were now tight at the corners.

Quinn stared back at her, unabashed. The keeper may have fooled the two men working at the lighthouse, and even the people in the town, but Quinn had seen past the illusion. This keeper knew Quinn's secret, but Quinn had stolen one right back.

"How," the keeper started, but then closed her mouth with a click of teeth. She stood sharply, legs unsteady as the blood rushed back in. Quinn raised her face to hold the keeper's gaze.

The faint moonlight illuminated the keeper's heaving, rain-soaked shoulders as she panted for breath. Her hands were clenched into fists, still coated in Quinn's blood and trembling. Now she was the one who was afraid.

If Quinn had gambled correctly, the keeper would not try to tell the others in the lighthouse of her presence. She would be too worried that Quinn would be able to spill her secret before they could get their hands on her.

Any words the keeper wanted to say seemed to have died on her tongue. She stood before Quinn, who was injured and couldn't even get to her feet, like she was the most dangerous thing to have ever crossed this beach.

Quinn raised her eyebrows. Then she held up her hand and made a shooing motion at the keeper.

That signal was all the keeper needed. The rocky shore crunched under her boots as she turned and hurried up the beach, leaving Quinn, alone but victorious, in the dark. With the last of her strength, Quinn reached out and picked up the spear tip from where the keeper had dropped it. She weighed it in her hand as the rain mingled with the remaining blood clinging to the metal, and then she drew her arm back and hurled it into the sea.

Chapter Eight

NOW

QUINN HAD SPENT LONG hours familiarizing herself with boredom. Her life as Owen's wife afforded few entertainments beyond the distractions her children provided. It felt like she was slipping back into the skin of her old life, wasting away hours at a time without accomplishing anything as she sat, foot propped up on a rock, waiting for something to happen.

She had moved from the spot the keeper had found her in. Tucked higher on the beach with the cliffs at her back, Quinn had situated herself so that it would be hard for anyone coming down the path to spot her before she saw them. This way, at least the keepers couldn't sneak up on her again.

Quinn had wrapped her pelt around her as best she could while still leaving enough for her to sit on and protect herself from the chill rocks. As a young seal, she and her herd would spend hours lying on beaches just like this one, comfortable as could be with layers of fat and thick fur making any flat surface a viable sleeping location. Her human body was not so forgiving. She had to shift often, rolling her weight from one hip to the other and cursing the sharp-edged stones.

A whole day had passed since the keeper had pulled the spear from her foot. All morning and afternoon, Quinn had kept an eye on the path, expecting that any minute the keeper would appear on the path with her two companions at her back. She had wondered, belatedly, if she should have kept the spear tip as a weapon in case the keepers did come for her. But it had felt good to toss the spear into the ocean and rid herself of any trace of Owen. There was no reclaiming it now.

Quinn had scared the keeper last night; she had obviously not been expecting Quinn to see through her disguise. Her revelation had had the effect Quinn wanted, sending the keeper running, but now she doubted if it would really be enough to ensure the keeper kept her mouth shut about Quinn.

With nothing to do but sit and worry, Quinn let every worst-case scenario roll over her. There was nothing she could do about it now. She had set herself up on the beach to spot any danger the moment it was within sight, and she could tuck herself back into her pelt as quick as a green flash. It would be hard for her to crawl back to the water from this high on the beach, but she preferred to stay dry while she was in her human body and didn't want the changing tide to swallow her up.

Quinn passed another night, this time without rain, and woke up after a few hours of restless sleep. Her foot ached, looking no better under its seaweed wrapping when she checked it a little after dawn. Her stomach ached, too. She wouldn't be fast enough to chase down fish with her injury, and the beach was bare of anything edible. She'd found rainwater pooled in the shallow divot of a boulder, and while it had tasted slightly salty, it sated her thirst but did nothing for her hunger.

Wrinkling her nose, Quinn crossed her arms over her complaining belly and willed her mind elsewhere.

The sky was scattered with clouds, but otherwise a bright blue sky and warming sun made the dreary gray beach shimmer with new color. The dark stones glistened under the gentle waves stretching up from the cerulean ocean, until the shore gave way to the gray and brown cliffs that towered twenty meters above Quinn's head. On the far side of the beach, the pale dirt path leading to the lighthouse cut through the cliffs like a scar. Following the path up the island, the rocky cliffs suddenly transformed into thick green grass, as if a blanket had been laid over the barren rock. Quinn had never been to the top of the island even before the lighthouse had been built. Her herd had never strayed from the beach, preferring to stay close to the water and reluctant to spend so much energy climbing to the clifftops.

From what she had seen of the lighthouse from afar, it was a bright white building that stood out sharply against the greens and browns and grays of the island it inhabited.

As a gentle breeze rolled off the water and kissed Quinn's face, she frowned at the bleakness of her situation. She was on the beach from her childhood, yet she found little comfort in the place. With no food or shelter, and an injury keeping her off her feet, Quinn let herself mourn for the security that her imprisoned life had provided. She had not had her freedom while she lived with Owen, but she had food every day and a place to sleep at night. It felt like she had traded one for the other, and now doubted whether the trade was worth it.

Quinn scoffed at herself. She slid down the cliff in a petulant slouch. Of course she preferred her freedom. It was simply her indecision that had led her to this point. She had hesitated to leave the island behind, and she had hesitated to approach Flora, leaving herself vulnerable to Owen again. She could not be so tentative in the future. Once her foot was healed, she needed to leave this place, and her human life, behind for good.

The issue now was that while she waited for her injury to heal, she was as vulnerable as a fish caught in a net.

THE SUN SET EARLY, dragging its fingers through the dusky sky and leaving trails of pink and orange on the scattered clouds. Quinn shifted for the dozenth time that day to try to settle in a position to sleep, but found herself wide awake hours after night fell. She listened to the rhythm of the waves hitting the shore, the faint accompaniment of the wind slipping across the craggy cliffs, and so she was instantly on alert when she heard the scratch of footsteps on a dirt path.

Keeping still and trusting her pelt to conceal her, Quinn darted her eyes across the path. A figure had crested over the cliffs and was making a careful journey down to the beach. She recognized her keeper right away. Though she had left the large, oilskin coat behind, she still wore the knit hat pulled low over her ears.

The keeper was scanning the beach before she made it all the way down the path. She paused when she didn't find Quinn in the same spot she had first found her in, but moved her search to the edges of the beach from the higher vantage point.

Quinn was pleased to see that it took the keeper a couple of moments to find her.

When the keeper finally did discover her hiding place, she started toward Quinn without hesitation. Quinn pushed herself up a little so that she wasn't lying flat on the ground and braced her back against the cliff for support.

She stared coolly at the keeper as she crunched across the beach. The woman wore a brown knit sweater with an intricate pattern around the collar and thick pants with patches on both knees. She was also carrying a bundle in her arms, and Quinn had a sinking guess as to its contents.

The keeper stopped before Quinn with the same distance that had separated them the other night.

"Hello," the keeper said. Her voice was different. The forced masculine notes were gone, and though it was still low, it was much gentler.

Undeterred by Quinn's stony silence, the keeper crouched down and laid out her bundle. Another pair of pants and a sweater had been wrapped around a roll of bandages, a small round tin, and a lumpy package wrapped in butcher paper.

"I know you must have expected the worst from me the other night," the keeper said, folding the sweater and pants into a pile and placing the butcher paper package off to the side. She held the bandages and tin in her hands, showing them to Quinn. "But I truly mean you no harm. I haven't told the others about you. I don't intend to. I just want to help you, if I can."

Quinn looked between the supplies in the keeper's hands and her earnest face.

"I don't understand why," she told the keeper. Quinn had seen how selfish humans could be, only doing things for others if they could get something out of it for themselves.

The keeper's mouth twitched in a smile, but her green eyes were somber. "I've been trapped before, with nowhere to go," she said. "I would have given anything for someone to give me a kind word, or a leg up on my way out. It seems to me that you're in a similar situation now, and I have the means to give you the help I desperately needed."

Quinn curled her fingers around her pelt, gripping it tight.

The keeper noticed and gave her another wincing grin. She set down the bandages and tin and picked up the wrapped package instead, picking apart the bit of twine keeping the paper together and revealed a chunk of bread and half a green apple.

Quinn's traitorous stomach gave her a sharp pinch, reminding her of how many hours had passed since she'd last eaten. She eyed the food with distrust and longing.

"I'm afraid it isn't much," the keeper told her, extending the handful of food between them, "but it has to be better than nothing. It's part of my breakfast."

The butcher paper waved merrily at Quinn as the wind flipped the corners up and down. The keeper's hand was steady. Whatever fear that Quinn had seen pass over the keeper's face the other night was gone, or at least well buried. Not only had she returned to Quinn, she had followed through on her offer and seemed intent on helping her, despite the fact that Quinn had threatened to reveal her secret.

With one hand tight on her pelt, Quinn reached out. The keeper was as still as a statue, but her eyes shone with excitement as Quinn plucked the chunk of bread out of the wrapping paper.

The bread was slightly stale, and Quinn had to dig her teeth in just to tear out a small bite. Her jaw ached as she chewed, but her stomach immediately settled.

The keeper watched her eat for a moment, with Quinn staring warily back. With a crinkle of the paper, the keeper leaned away and shifted into a seat, crossing her legs so she could rest the apple half on her knee.

"These are mine, too," she told Quinn, tilting her head toward the clothes. "The pants are old, but they should fit you. The sweater is a hand-me-down from one of the other keepers here, but I hardly ever wear it. The sleeves are too long on me. I'm sure they won't notice a difference in my wardrobe."

Quinn crammed the rest of the bread in her mouth and tucked her arms around her torso, holding the pelt tight. The keeper frowned and picked up the apple to offer to her again. Quinn didn't take it.

The keeper's arm wilted. "I suppose it is ridiculous to ask you to trust me," she said to Quinn. She wrapped the apple back in the paper and tied up the twine. "But you'll see that I don't give up easily."

The keeper set the packaged apple on the small stack of clothes. She leaned forward to gather up the bandages and tin, too. Quinn started, leaning forward off the cliff. The keeper froze.

Quinn regretted showing her hand like that, but she couldn't deny that a fresh bandage and medicine on the wound would be better than her nature-grown remedy. She didn't trust the keeper to apply them, but Quinn could manage it on her own.

"I'll leave these for you, too, shall I?" the keeper suggested, getting to her feet with a small smile on her face. "Though I'll need them back soon. Those will go noticed if they're missing for too long."

She glanced at the sky, which had faded from pink to purple as the horizon ate up the dusk.

"It shouldn't rain tonight," the keeper said. Then she turned and walked away. Quinn followed her path up the island until she was over the cliff, but the keeper didn't look back.

In the last of the light, Quinn finally reached for the bandages and the small tin. She shifted her leg out from under her and unwrapped the seaweed from around her foot. The top layer had already begun to dry and flake away, and underneath the damp inner layer of her wound was still red and irritated.

Quinn ripped off a small piece of the cloth bandage and gingerly wiped away the tacky blood, gritting her teeth as she pressed against the injured skin. Once it was as clean and dry as she could get it, Quinn reached for the tin. Twisting off the lid, she was relieved to recognize the slightly yellow salve inside—a salve she had used on her own children, and on Owen. He had taught her how to apply it to fresh wounds to help keep infection away and speed up the healing. She had applied it to many of his fishing injuries and used it liberally on her children when they came home with cuts or scratches.

Quinn knew it wouldn't completely heal her spear wound, which was pierced clean through her foot, but it would certainly help. She dabbed a little onto her finger and spread it across the inflamed skin on both sides.

The tin wasn't large, but this was a greater supply of the salve than Owen had ever been able to afford. Quinn had to be careful not to use too much.

Once done with the salve, Quinn shut the tin and unrolled a long strip of bandage. She laid the clean cloth flat over the top of her foot and lifted her knee so she could wrap it tight. She tucked the loose end back into the folds of the bandage and admired her work. The salve had a slight numbing effect, and Quinn let some of her worry of the injury becoming infected slip away.

She carefully rerolled the bandages and tucked it and the tin of salve in between the sweater and pants. The keeper had said she didn't think it would rain, but Quinn wanted to be cautious. As she slid them between the clothes, she jostled the apple half.

Quinn hadn't taken it from the keeper for a few reasons. The first was that she didn't want the keeper to have the satisfaction of seeing her eat it. The second was that she had felt guilt about taking what should have been the keeper's breakfast, and it had closed up her throat once she swallowed the last mouthful of bread.

And for a third reason, she had worried that this would be the only food the keeper ever brought her. She had followed through with what she had promised Quinn, but there was no guarantee of future visits.

She knew there had been a chance the keeper would have taken the apple back when Quinn refused it. The keeper could have taken Quinn's rude refusal and reclaimed the remains of her breakfast. After all, the townspeople had certainly been satisfied to return her rudeness in kind. Instead, the keeper left the food with Quinn, along with the medical supplies and clothes off her own back.

Quinn eyed the wrinkled paper package as she settled back

against the cliff and pulled her pelt back over her shoulders and chest.

She decided to eat it tomorrow morning. That way, if the keeper failed to come back, she would at least have something to satiate the gnawing feeling in her stomach, if only for a few moments.

THE KEEPER HAD SPOKEN truthfully. It did not rain that night, and the next day dawned cool and cloudless. Quinn waited for the sun to warm the dark rocks of the beach before relenting to the growling beast in her stomach. She unwrapped the apple and tucked the paper and twine into the folds of the clothes with the bandages.

The first bite of the apple, even though the white core of the fruit was slightly brown now, was immensely satisfying. The tart juice chased away the lingering taste of salt on her tongue. She savored it for as long as she could, tearing away small bites and sucking at the stripped core to get any remaining flavor.

The rest of the day passed slowly and uneventfully. She checked the bandage to make sure the wound hadn't bled through the cloth and was relieved to see that it was still dry. At one point in the afternoon, Quinn was certain she could hear voices caught up on the wind. She watched the point where the path crossed over the cliffs, but no one appeared. Perhaps the keepers were shouting to one another up near the lighthouse, the sound carrying easily over the empty island and down to the beach.

When the sun began to dip back toward the ocean, Quinn told herself not to get her hopes up. She knew the keeper would come back to fetch the medical supplies at some point, but she shouldn't hope for more food if it was all coming off the keeper's own plate.

The sun set, and Quinn lay down on the rocky beach, trying to leach any of the remaining warmth from the stones before the brisk evening wind could take it away. It was fully dark, with a vast scattering of stars appearing in the sky to wink distantly down at Quinn. Her herd had relied on the stars to direct them many times in Quinn's childhood, but they could not always depend on their appearance. She had learned to appreciate the cloudless nights when the herd swam straight and true through vast open water.

Quinn had not slept well since she had hauled herself onto the beach. The constant pain of her injury, her empty stomach, and the fear of discovery kept her awake. Even when she was able to fall asleep from sheer exhaustion, she managed only an hour or so before she would jerk awake again.

She was tired, but she lay awake, waiting.

At first, she thought she was imagining the sound of foot-steps. Maybe it was just the waves, slapping on the rocks. Or maybe it was the wind, buffeting in and out of the cracks in the cliffs. But then the sound grew louder, clearer. Footsteps on the dirt path. Quinn lifted her head.

Her keeper looked at the ground as she descended to the beach. When her boots hit the rocks, she finally looked in Quinn's direction and picked up her pace. In moments she was crouched in front of Quinn with a broad smile on her lips.

"Hello," she said, slightly out of breath. "I wasn't sure if you would still be here."

Quinn blinked up at her.

"I'm injured."

"Yes," the keeper agreed, and Quinn frowned at the laugh in her voice. Did she think that Quinn could swim, let alone walk, with a hole in her foot large enough to put her pinky finger in?

The keeper sat down, crossing her legs under her, and reaching into her coat. This time she not only had a paper-wrapped package, but a stoppered glass bottle of water, too. She lifted the water first.

"I realized I hadn't brought you anything to drink," she said guiltily. She set the bottle in front of Quinn with a soft clink of glass on the rocks. "And I've only got bread this time, unfortunately. Mr. MacArthur was worried I wasn't eating enough this morning."

Quinn levered herself up onto her elbows and reached for the bottle. Bracing her weight on one hand, she pulled the cork out of the bottle with her teeth and dropped it, setting the rim of the bottle to her lips. She swallowed the first few mouthfuls of water much too quickly and heaved for breath after the fourth. She wiped her mouth with the back of her hand, eyes closed.

The water seemed to course new life through her. It was lukewarm from being carried close to the keeper's body, but Quinn hardly minded. It was clean and plentiful.

She took another sip and held the water in her mouth for a moment.

When she opened her eyes, the keeper quickly looked away, but not before Quinn caught her rapt expression. A slight blush had settled across the keeper's cheekbones. Quinn swallowed again before setting the bottle down.

"Um," the keeper said, fiddling with the paper until it unfolded. She held out the bread, avoiding Quinn's gaze. "Here."

Quinn shifted her legs around so she could sit more comfortably before taking the bread. Again, she held her pelt to her chest with one hand while eating with the other. The keeper occupied herself by folding up the bit of paper and tucking it back into her pocket.

Her darting gaze snagged on the bright white bandage wrapped around Quinn's foot, and suddenly the smile was back. "Did the salve help?" she asked eagerly.

Quinn waited for the keeper to look at her again before nodding.

"I'm glad," the keeper said. She glanced around the beach. "Where did you put the tin? The rest of the bandages?"

Quinn bit down on her bread and held it in her mouth to free her hand. She leaned over and rooted around in the folded clothes, pulling out the bandages and tin together.

She offered them to the keeper, who held out her hands automatically to take them but then didn't pull away when Quinn did.

"Are you sure you don't need any more?" the keeper asked, eyeing Quinn's foot. "Enough to replace the bandage, at least?"

Quinn shook her head and waved the keeper off. She took the bread in her hand again and ripped off a piece with her teeth.

The keeper didn't seem convinced, but was just as reluctant to push the issue, and so she put the bandages and tin into some inner pocket of her coat as well. She sat silently for a while, waiting for Quinn to finish eating. When Quinn ate the last of the bread, she picked up the bottle of water again and took measured, careful swallows, so as to not upset her stomach.

Once Quinn set down the empty bottle, the keeper found the abandoned cork on the ground and re-stoppered it. She held the bottle in her hands, rolling it back and forth.

"So you'll accept food and medicine," she said slowly, "but are the clothes a step too far?"

Quinn, thirst and hunger abated for now, had slouched back against the cliffside and watched the keeper through lidded eyes.

"I don't need them," she told the keeper, lifting a corner of her pelt to show her meaning. It was plenty warm, and no one could take it from her as long as she was sitting on it.

"I suppose you don't," the keeper observed. "But if I may— and please believe me when I say this is merely a suggestion— if anyone else should discover you down here, won't it be much harder to explain a lone woman wrapped in a seal skin over a lone woman in a sweater and pants?"

"Do you think anyone else will discover me?" Quinn asked in return.

The keeper frowned, eyes flicking up to the point where the path crossed over the cliff. "Not in the near future," she said. "But Jamie wants to try to go to town again one more time before the season sets in. I'll admit that you blend in well with the beach, but Jamie's not that unaware. He'd notice."

It was odd for Quinn to hear the names of the lighthouse keepers from someone who actually knew them, instead of how the town spoke about them.

With the keeper this close, Quinn could see how she hid her feminine features; broadening her shoulders with bulky sweaters and her coat, concealing her hair under the knit hat, but she seemed to come by the squared off fingers and rough-worked hands naturally. With the false voice and name, the keeper could disappear into the male disguise as easily as Quinn could disappear into the beach.

Quinn was probably the only one who knew the truth about the keeper. The way she had reacted after Quinn unveiled her disguise gave Quinn the impression that she was seeing her ruse crumble for the first time, and it had frightened her. And yet, she had returned to Quinn's side and kept Quinn's secret to herself.

Quinn asked, "What is your name?"

The keeper, thrown by the sudden turn in their conversation, took a moment to answer.

"I'm known as Tavis here—"

"No," Quinn interrupted. "Your real name."

The keeper stopped rolling the bottle in her hands. Her fingers, a little red at the tips from the cold, turned white from the force of her grip. Quinn waited for the keeper to work out the inner struggle that was waging war behind those green eyes.

If she was going to trust this human, even to the smallest degree, Quinn needed the keeper to set them on a level field. They had secrets to dangle over each other's heads, like twin daggers linked by the same thread, but she needed a knife of her own to cut the rope.

The keeper pressed her lips together, then offered, "If I tell you mine, will you tell me yours?"

Quinn took a moment to consider, and then nodded. She was certain most of the townspeople didn't know her actual name; they only referred to her as "Owen's wife," and the few other than Owen who would know the name were no reason for her to worry. She risked very little giving her name to the keeper.

Once agreed, the keeper loosened her vise grip on the bottle and said, in a curious voice, "Maisie. My name is Maisie Garrow."

Quinn wondered how long it had been since the keeper—since Maisie—had used her own name. She certainly understood why Maisie had had to leave it behind when putting on the male persona; it was no man's name. And yet, Quinn thought it fit her.

Maisie was looking expectantly at Quinn now, eyebrows raised.

"Quinn," she said simply.

"Just Quinn?"

"Just Quinn."

Maisie nodded, accepting that for what it was. Then she smiled, and it lit up her whole face even in the weak, early moonlight.

"It's very nice to meet you, Quinn."

It seemed to be a genuine sentiment, but it was one Quinn could not return, so she merely nodded again. What she could say was, "Thank you. For helping me."

Maisie's smile flickered but remained fixed to her lips as she told Quinn, "It's like I said. I would have given anything to have help from someone else when I needed it most. Since I have the means to help you, I will."

Quinn knew that not just any woman could have made her way into the employ of the lighthouse under a false man's name, and wondered what Maisie had been through that was so dire to lead to such a choice. She seemed to understand the gravity of Quinn's situation, but had yet to ask any prying questions about how Quinn had gotten here, or how she had gotten her wound, or even any mention of Quinn being a selkie.

They each knew the basis of the other's secrets, and nothing more.

Quinn had given Maisie very few reasons to trust her, and very few signs that she was kindling a flicker of trust in Maisie, so she broached the topic herself.

"Why are you here?" she asked, and then added, "And why are you pretending to be a man?"

Maisie didn't respond right away. It was as if Quinn could see the torrent of thoughts flashing through her mind. The same worries haunted each of Quinn's answers, after all.

"Well," Maisie started, "the only way I am allowed to be here is if I am a man." She gestured at the island with the bottle. "The board, the lighthouse board, that is, would sooner hire a fish than a woman to work in a lighthouse."

Quinn made a scathing noise, and Maisie made one in return. This was a human misconception about women's capabilities that she had learned very early and very thoroughly in her years on land.

But Maisie paused before continuing. "As for why I came to be here, I will tell you, but I think in return you should have to answer one of my questions."

Quinn, who had been slouched against the cliff and heavy lidded, sat up taller and blinked herself to alertness.

She was curious now. This human who had voluntarily given Quinn food off her plate and took great joy in just learning her name, what had she been through that had led her to Quinn?

"A trade," Quinn said. "A name for a name, a question for a question."

Maisie nodded. "All right."

Maisie set the bottle down in the cradle of her lap and laced her fingers together. Her gaze slid away from Quinn and over the dark water, getting lost in the shadows of the horizon and the night sky.

"The truth is," she told Quinn, "I'm running away. My family had decided I was going to be married to a man who made a deal with my father. He wasn't kind, but he wasn't the worst man I've known."

Quinn thought of Owen, who was the worst man she'd ever known, but she also knew of men who had sanded down their rough edges and still took what they wanted. She shared a look with Maisie as she continued.

"The problem was I never thought of myself as someone who would be married. I've depended on my family for everything and had nothing for myself. And yet the only way out was to become someone's wife. I couldn't become someone on my own."

Maisie's voice faltered, and her brows drew together as she considered her next words. "My fiancé died, suddenly. I...I knew it was only a matter of time before I was trapped by another man, so I took the opportunity and ran away. It was easier to steal men's clothes and slip by that way than as a woman traveling alone. I wanted to get far away from the city where my family lived, and I heard that one of the remote lighthouses was hiring. I'd never done a day of work on the ocean or in a lighthouse in my life, but my father was a bladesmith and I knew how to work with my hands. I applied while I was halfway to the coast.

"It was either a miracle or sheer luck that the board accepted me. Or perhaps no one else wanted the job. Mr. MacArthur has a bit of a reputation among the lighthouse workers," Maisie explained. "But here I can make my own way. As Tavis, no one questions my ability to take care of myself. This island may be small, but it's given me more freedom than I've ever had in my whole life."

Quinn imagined what Maisie must have felt when she saw the island for the first time. For Quinn, it was a piece of her childhood, with memories preserved under every stone, but for Maisie, it was the promise of a future built by her own hands. A beacon and a refuge for each of them.

She understood Maisie's desperation for independence; she had craved it every day of the seven years she was on land, and Quinn could not fault her for going after the chance to seize it for herself. She could also imagine how difficult it would have been for Maisie to make it here on her own. Even if she had managed to get a little money before running away, every step toward the coast and the lighthouse must have cost her. She had said she would have done anything for a helping hand, which to Quinn meant that she had made it all the way here under her own will and stubbornness. Quinn admired her for it, but kept her face even. She didn't need to show Maisie that she was impressed.

Maisie sucked in a huge breath through her nose and released it sharply.

"Right," she said. "My turn." The question unfolded so quickly that Quinn knew she had been holding it on the tip of her tongue, perhaps ever since the first night. "How did you get injured?"

This was not the question Quinn expected. But then again, as she considered all she had learned about the keeper, she shouldn't be surprised. Maisie had done nothing the way Quinn expected her to.

Quinn could just tell Maisie that a spear had caused the wound. She hadn't promised Maisie as much detail as the keeper had provided unprompted. And it would be the truth.

But the more she knew about Maisie, the more she wanted to trust her. This was a dangerous thread Quinn was balancing on.

If she wanted Maisie to trust her in return, she needed to be more than honest.

Quinn met Maisie's eye as she told her, "My husband did this. He threw a fishing spear at me while I was trying to escape."

Maisie's eyes were round as coins. "Then your husband knows that you're a...a selkie?"

Quinn nodded. "He kept me trapped on land for seven years before I escaped a few weeks ago. The day you found me, I had seen my daughter on the beach and was distracted, and he was able to pierce my tail with a spear."

Mouth agape, Maisie seemed to process everything that Quinn wasn't saying within those few sentences. Then she asked, "You have children?"

"Three," Quinn said quietly. "Two girls and a boy."

"And they're all his?"

Quinn nodded again, a sharp, jerking movement of her chin. She hated remembering the nights that had brought her children to her. Her skin prickled, not because of the cold, and the look Maisie was giving her spoke volumes.

"Then," Maisie wondered slowly, "are your children human, or are they like you? I mean, can they also become seals?"

Quinn stared flatly at Maisie, feeling unmoored from having divulged so much. "That was more than one question."

"Right," Maisie said, looking sheepish. "I'm sorry."

"I get to ask two in return now."

"No." Maisie shook her head, leaning forward to place a hand on the rocks just a few centimeters away from Quinn's pelt. Stiffening, Quinn's gaze twitched between the keeper's hand and earnest face. "I mean, yes, of course, you can ask me whatever you want. But I also meant I'm sorry about what your husband did to you. Trapping you"—her eyes trailed down to Quinn's bandaged foot—"and hurting you."

It wasn't hard to guess what Maisie was thinking about as she looked at Quinn's injury, after she had unraveled the story of her late fiancé. Not the worst man, she had said, but also not a kind one. Perhaps she was imagining herself in Quinn's place, trapped in the town she'd grown up in, in a marriage that held her down like a chain on her ankle. Quinn's injury was like a shadow of the life she had narrowly escaped.

Quinn flexed her ankle and winced at the jolt of pain the

movement invited. Under the bandage, she could feel the ragged edges of her skin weeping again.

"Mmm," Quinn grunted. Maisie made a worried noise in return, but the look on Quinn's face seemed to quell her. "It's fine," she lied.

She didn't want to rely so heavily on Maisie to ease her pains. It had been years since anyone had truly been invested in her well-being, and it was going to be difficult for Quinn to relax her guard enough to bear it.

Sharing the source of her injury with Maisie in return for Maisie's story felt like tying a thread to the keeper's wrist and knotting the other end around her own. Instead of the daggers of each other's secrets, the stories were a connection given freely over a tenuous string.

"I'll keep my questions for another time," Quinn told Maisie. Seeming to realize that Quinn was ending their visit for the night, Maisie took her hand away from Quinn's pelt, curling her fingers on top of her own thigh. Thick clouds had rolled in overhead and blocked most of the moonlight. "You should go back up before they notice you're gone. Take your supplies, too."

"Okay," Maisie complied. Tucking the bottle beneath her arm, Maisie got her feet under her and gathered up the bandages and tin of salve.

"I'll be back as soon as I can," Maisie promised. She held up the bandages. "You'll let me know if you need this again, won't you?"

Quinn blinked at her a few times and then shuffled around until she could lie down, as she had been before Maisie came down to the beach. "It'll be fine."

If Maisie was unsatisfied with that answer, she only stewed on it for a moment before standing up, her face lost in the dim late evening. "All right," she sighed. "Good night, Quinn."

She turned away without waiting for a farewell in return. Her crunching footsteps were loud on the otherwise still beach.

"Good night," Quinn said softly, but Maisie's footsteps paused at the sound, and then continued. That thread that they had woven between their wrists stretched thin but held. Quinn wasn't certain if she should cut it now, while it was small and easily snapped, or let it grow thicker and stronger, until even the sharpest blade would have a tough time sawing through. She wasn't even sure if the connection could grow that strong, but she'd woven the first strand.

Chapter Nine

In autumn, Quinn and her family were usually already preparing to head down the coast toward calmer waters and follow the fish for the winter months. On land, Quinn's autumn was full of bracingly chill winds and morning sickness. Her mother had explained human birth and the cycles that tracked with the moon when she was younger after Quinn had asked how a human and a selkie could have a baby. She had been reluctant to share the information at first, but caved to Quinn's needling as she always did.

"You shall never need to use this knowledge," her mother had determined, "but I suppose it is best that you know more than nothing. It is not so different from how you came into the world."

Her mother had not known all of the symptoms of human pregnancy, of course; she could only guess on top of what she had heard from others' stories.

But as Quinn was sick into the scrap bucket under the

kitchen sink for the third day in a row after scaling a fish, she felt a pit growing in her stomach, or perhaps lower. Wiping her chin with the back of her hand, Quinn felt her abdomen with trembling fingers.

Was she imagining the small bump swelling there? She'd been on land nearly six months at this point, and she had bled for three of them. The first time she woke to see blood on her thighs, she had leaped from the bed, staring daggers at Owen, who had woken at her jolting movement. He saw the spots of blood on the sheets and her nightdress and held up his hands placatingly.

"It is natural for human women to bleed once a month," he explained. "It means she can bear a child."

Quinn's mother had told her of this, too. But she had not imagined that it would be so much blood. Her mother could not have known about the pain, either. Quinn had raged the second time her cycle came, cursing her human body, cursing Owen for keeping her trapped in it, cursing herself for being curious about human life. She was not curious now.

When her cycle did not come, Quinn had not said anything, but quietly enjoyed the respite. But then the next month, nothing again. She had taken over doing the laundry and had learned to wear the folded cloths between her thighs to avoid staining all of her clothes, so Owen did not notice the change. Now it was the third month with no blood.

She did not need her mother, or Owen, to tell her what had happened. Crouched over the bucket that she had already scoured multiple times that week to hide her sick before Owen returned home, Quinn felt the small bump beneath her stomach and let the dread overcome her. Owen wanted children. He had told her so, not even a month after he took her pelt from her.

He always seemed to get what he wanted.

Quinn, on the other hand, had never even thought of having children. In her herd, she was still considered a child in the eyes of the older seals.

But now she was going to be a mother, and her child would have a human father. Would they be like her, or like him? Or would they fall somewhere in between? She only knew what her mother had told her and shared from stories. Children born of selkies and humans were still a mystery to her and most of the herd.

When the nausea eased up its grip on her throat, Quinn heaved herself up using the sink and washed her mouth out with a handful of water. She spat into the bucket once more. Leaving the fish in the sink, she hauled the bucket outside and emptied its contents into the dirt around the side of the house, making sure to turn over the soil to cover the remains of what must have been her breakfast.

Through her small kitchen window, Quinn's old neighbor peered at her with a pinched mouth. Quinn turned back inside before she could say anything.

Storing the fish to cook later that day, Quinn waited for her stomach to settle a bit more. The weight of what was growing inside her seemed to press in from all sides. She was restless, moving from room to room in Owen's small house.

There were ways of getting rid of a child, she knew. But she did not know what those methods were. Would she be able to go through with them without Owen noticing, or wondering what she was doing? He had to be wondering when a child would come, too.

Quinn clasped her arms around her middle as she paced. She went over the stories her mother had told her about birth, about the pain of it, about the effort of bringing a living thing into the world. That reality was still months away, but would she have to sit here dreading it until the moment came? That almost seemed worse.

And once a child was here, what would she do with it? She did not want to be human. Her child would have no choice. Would they be trapped in the same way she was, without a pelt to give them safe passage into an ocean that would accept them with open arms? What did Owen even want with a child?

Quinn had no one to turn to and ask her questions. If she went to one of the other women in the town, word would surely get back to Owen within the day.

The tread of her pacing could have worn a hole in the floor. After an hour of spinning around and around in her thoughts, Quinn's stomach raised its voice. She wanted one of the tart, green apples she had tasted her first week on land. But there were none in the house.

Seizing the reason to be outside, Quinn wrapped a knitted shawl around her shoulders and went to the tin of money that Owen kept by his bedside. He gave her allowances for food, and surely he wouldn't notice if she took a little for the apples. He enjoyed them, too.

The walk to the town square was buffeted by strong winds and a glaringly bright midday sun. Quinn strode quickly down the side of the street, her chin tucked. She felt that if anyone got too close a look at her, they would notice a difference.

That was an absurd thought, given the bulk of her skirt and shawl covering her torso, but this town had sharp eyes for the next piece of gossip. Word of Owen's strange wife being pregnant would spread quicker than a thatch roof fire.

The market was busy, it being midday and sunny, but Quinn skirted around the edge until she spotted the produce stand that sold the fat, crispy green apples she craved. She hovered by the stall, eyeing the best apples as she waited for a few customers to pay for their groceries.

The next stall over had a small display of sheep's milk and cheese. A stout, pink-cheeked woman was minding the stall and talking with a tired-looking woman with a baby strapped to her chest. Quinn watched as the woman absentmindedly ran her hand over the baby's back and bottom, not so much a soothing gesture as a reassuring check that they were still there. Quinn didn't know how she could mistake the weight of a baby on her chest for anything else.

A throat cleared behind her, and Quinn glanced over to see the produce stall's seller frowning at her.

"You buy something or you leave," he told her.

Quinn plucked up three apples and dropped some coins in the seller's open palm. She pinched up the corners of her apron and set the apples in the pocket it made.

Unwilling to return to the house so soon, Quinn decided to take the long way back and exited the market on the road that led up and around the top of the town. She fished one of the apples out of her makeshift pouch and rubbed it on the front of her apron before taking a huge bite. The satisfying crunch and dribble of juice at the corners of her mouth gave her a moment of contentment.

She saw three women walking on the other side of the road stare at her and then lean in to whisper in one another's ears. Quinn ignored them and kept walking.

This path led her by the pub. It was already open, and a few of its patrons had spilled out to enjoy the sun with their full cups. There wasn't a crowd yet, but the ones who were there had gathered around a man who was gesturing wildly. Quinn guessed he was telling a half-true story about a huge fish that had just narrowly escaped his hook, stealing away his chance at fame.

But as she drew closer, Quinn noticed that the men around the storyteller were not grinning and gaffing as they usually were. Instead, every face was serious and trained on the man speaking as if he gave a sermon. With her free hand, Quinn tugged her shawl up and slowed her pace as she approached the pub.

The man was speaking quickly, as if he couldn't get the words out fast enough. "There was blood on the clothes. She was beating them with a stone, but they never got clean. It was a washerwoman, I tell you."

Quinn, having just come into hearing distance, felt her steps falter.

"You mean, just a lady washing?" one of the men asked, voice disbelieving.

"No, fool," the speaker snapped. "A washerwoman, a *bean-nighe*. I saw her up in the hills."

Silence fell over the group. Quinn felt like her heart was beating too loud.

Then, a loud, braying laugh from one of the larger men whose pint was already empty.

"You think you saw that old wives' tale?" He chortled. "Probably just some old nanny doing her daughter's laundry."

"It was not!" the storyteller said. "I'm telling you, the clothes were covered in blood—"

But the man hooted with laughter again, and a few around him joined in with weak chuckles. The men sitting closer to the storyteller did not seem to find the same amusement in his tale.

"Did you talk to her?" one of them, a younger man with curling brown hair, asked him.

"No," the speaker said, shaking his head. "I didn't dare get too close after I spotted her."

"Did you at least see how many clothes she had laid out?" another man, older and weather-beaten, asked him urgently.

The storyteller took a fortifying gulp of his drink. "Three shirts," he said. "I saw three shirts laid out in the grass, and she was washing one."

"So four," the weather-beaten man said in a low voice.

"Four?" the younger man repeated.

Their eyes shifted to the storyteller, but he seemed to have worn himself out of words and was staring into his cup.

"You know the tale of the washerwoman," the weather-beaten man said, and when the younger man shrugged, continued. "She is seen washing bloodied clothes in streams and rivers, and if you do see her, she is an omen of approaching death. The number of clothes she has laid out to clean harkens to the number of people who will die. The one who sees her is somehow related to the ones who will die, and if he is able to sneak up on her, she will tell him whose deaths were foretold in the bloody cloth."

"But if she sees you," another man piped up, "don't you lose your limbs?"

A few men scoffed but eyed the storyteller with concern.

The loud man was talking brashly about men who believed their grandmother's stories, but most of the other men were looking to one another, as if to find their belief or disbelief in another's eyes.

The younger man leaned toward the storyteller. "Where did you say you saw her?"

"In the hills," he said absently, "past the fifth road marker and by the twisting stream that empties into the river."

The men who seemed to believe the man's story continued speaking quietly, as if their hushed tones would keep the possibility of the omen from coming true. They debated what the washerwoman should have looked like, based on the storyteller's description, and argued whether she should be sought out again.

"Remember that merchant shipwreck, years ago, right up the coast?" one of the men whispered loudly, as if he were bringing up a ghost story. "Whole crew died except one in that freak storm? I heard from my uncle that the washerwoman was spotted before that happened, three baskets full of bloodied clothes at her feet."

"Do you remember who saw her?"

The man shook his head, a reluctant look on his face. More glances were exchanged as they tried to recall the night of the shipwreck.

Quinn, who had fully stopped in front of the pub to listen,

hurriedly began moving again when the younger man looked around.

The green apple, forgotten but still clutched in her fingers, was dripping juice from where she had gripped it so hard she had punctured through the waxy skin.

Quinn's quick footsteps brought her up the street and to the top of the town in no time. She pushed her shawl down, panting. If she craned her head, she could see the hills the storyteller had spoken of in the distance behind the cluster of houses.

Quinn knew what a *bean-nighe*, or a washerwoman as the humans referred to her, was. Her mother had told her the story of the creatures that called the land their home the same way selkies lived at sea. They weren't at odds with the nature around them, but they lived in humans' stories until they became reality.

As the weather-beaten man had said, a washerwoman brought humans warnings of approaching death. She would find a stream or river in the human's path and begin washing bloodstained clothes, the number of her load revealing how many would die from the omen. If a human was able to approach her without being seen and seized her, she would reveal whose death she had predicted.

Quinn's mother had also told her that a washerwoman, once caught, would grant her captor three wishes.

"But why?" Quinn had asked. "Why would she do what the humans want?"

Her mother had rolled onto her back with a sigh, but she could hardly get through any story without Quinn interrupting with questions, even though she told Quinn these stories to get her to go to sleep. So she said, "I suppose she finds purpose in it. Or perhaps to balance out the grimness of her omens. If she had nothing to offer the humans except portends of the deaths of their loved ones, they would never approach her. But if she could provide wishes, they might seek her out."

"But if they seek her out," Quinn pressed, "won't they get warnings of death anyway?"

"Some humans may value a wish over a life," her mother said. Quinn had frowned at that but let her mother continue.

The washerwoman had a few forms, she had told Quinn, which varied across the humans' tales of the *bean-nighe*. Some thought she was a squat, pitiful-looking woman, beating at the laundry with gnarled hands. Others thought she was rather rotund and always dressed in green. Some believed her to be tall. Still others spread tales that the washerwoman had breasts so long she was forced to throw them over her shoulders as she worked, lest they get in the way. Quinn's brow pinched at that, and her mother blew out a wet breath from her nostrils before continuing.

The washerwoman would often sing while she did her bloody laundry. Her songs were full of mourning and grief, but provided the watcher the opportunity to sneak up on the washerwoman while she was distracted with her task.

If the human came across a washerwoman with her long breasts thrown over her shoulders as she beat the clothes, they could sneak up on her, put one of her nipples in their mouth, and claim to be the washerwoman's foster child. The washerwoman would be compelled by milk kinship to believe the human was her own child, and she would tell them whose deaths she had seen laid out in the bloody laundry.

"But what if the washerwoman sees the human first?" Quinn asked.

"Then that human will no longer walk with their own legs or lift with their arms. To see death, and be seen in return, is not a feat any human body can bear more than once. Being spotted by a washerwoman as she does her laundry is like trying to glimpse through the veil into the world beyond our own. These bodies were not made for that place," her mother explained.

Quinn had scrunched her body up so she could flick her tail fins in the air, waving them like a piece of seaweed caught in a twisting current. She scooched closer to her mother.

"Are washerwomen born like humans? Or did they become that way like our ancestors?" Quinn asked around a yawn.

Her mother was quiet for a moment. "I'm not sure," she said. "I've never heard the tale of where the washerwomen come from."

"But you know everything," Quinn insisted as she wiggled her face into the crook between her mother's fin and body, the lull of sleep calling to her.

"Not everything," her mother whispered, like she was scared to admit it.

Still, Quinn thought, as she gazed at the distant hills. Her mother had known enough, and passed on her knowledge to Quinn, that she felt a small stab of hope pierce her heart. Even beyond her mother's reach, she found herself relying on her mother's wisdom to see her through.

If the storyteller was speaking the truth and there was a washerwoman toiling away in the hills, Quinn could go and find her and capture her to demand the three wishes.

Three wishes were enough for Quinn to fix the mess she was trapped in.

She wanted to tromp out into the hills that moment. A stream by the fifth road marker, she remembered the storyteller saying; she could search the hills until she found the washerwoman and wish for her life to be put back together before the day was over.

But it was already afternoon. Owen would be returning from the boat soon, and then to the house, where he would be expecting her to be preparing dinner. If she did go into the hills and wander every stream she came across and still not find the washerwoman, how would she explain her absence to Owen when she returned? Would the washerwoman even be there still for Quinn to find? Her mother had not said whether a sighted washerwoman could be found again. Perhaps because no human was foolish enough to seek her out on purpose.

The storyteller had seen four pieces of clothing near the washerwoman, meaning four deaths were coming to the town. As long as those deaths had not occurred, perhaps the washerwoman would still be at that stream, beating out the blood until her omen came true.

Quinn could go searching tomorrow after Owen left for work. She would leave as early as possible and scour the hills by the fifth road marker. If she could not find the washerwoman, she would have enough time to return home before Owen noticed she was gone.

With her plan decided, Quinn tightened her slackening grip on the apron pouch of apples and hurried in the direction of the house. She took a few anxious bites of apple as she went. Her craving had evaporated, but she wouldn't waste the food.

She kicked off the little bit of mud that seemed to find the bottom of her boots every time she stepped outside on the two steps that led up to the front door before going into the house. There were two large, worn boots set neatly just inside the door. Quinn froze.

"Quinn," Owen called from the kitchen.

Closing her eyes, Quinn took a few slow, quiet breaths to calm her rabbiting heart. She toed off her own shoes and closed the door behind her with a snap.

Owen was sitting at the kitchen table, his gaze set on the small window. Quinn said nothing as she came into the room and unloaded the two remaining apples onto the counter. She tossed the stripped apple core into the empty scrap bucket beneath the sink.

She could feel Owen's eyes shift and land on her back.

"You went to the market," Owen observed. "Just for apples?"

Quinn used a little water from the sink to rinse the tacky juice from her fingers and then wiped them dry on her apron. She turned, eyes down, and dug around in the pocket of her dress for the remaining money. The coins clinked hollowly as they dropped onto the table in front of Owen.

"Am I not allowed outside anymore?" she asked mildly.

"You don't like the market," Owen told her, which was true. "Is that all you did?"

Quinn nodded, once.

"Just for apples," Owen said again. Finally, Quinn lifted her eyes until she met Owen's face. He was staring at her with a blank, turned-up expression, as if his quiet disapproval would get her to speak more this time than any other time before.

Quinn gave him a blank look back.

It became clear early on in Quinn's life as a human that her stubbornness went far deeper than Owen's patience. She was lured into Owen's house and remained there due to the inexplicable pull toward her pelt that she couldn't control, but far be it that Quinn would meekly accept his treatment as long as she was here. Hiding the pelt from her did not make Quinn obedient to Owen. In fact, it did quite the opposite.

Quinn had considered killing Owen within the first week of being on land. He had already told the town they were married and explained away her oddness through some story of her upbringing that had snowballed into wilder and wilder rumors spreading around town. He had still believed that he could convince her to love him, at that point. He put his hands on her, and she knocked them away. He explained why he wanted her as his wife, and she laughed in his face.

"My grandfather told me selkies bring fair weather and good fishing," he said, stoically serious. She laughed again. Selkies did no such thing for humans, but her mother had told her about the superstition. Quinn was trapped here based on a lie.

Owen put his hands on her again, his grip tighter. He was slow and careful, and Quinn would not realize until later that he could be much worse, but as she kept her reactions compressed and her interest as dead as a windless sea, Owen finally told her, "I want children."

I could kill him, Quinn thought in response. She did not care if everyone in the town would suspect her; she didn't plan to stay here without him. But killing him meant she might never find her pelt again. Her artless searching of the house had turned up nothing. She needed him alive to reveal the location of her pelt. However long it took for him to slip up, Quinn would wait. In the meantime, however, she had to play into Owen's fruitless dream of their lives together.

After a few cool moments of silent staring in the kitchen, Owen sighed. Quinn took that surrender and turned to take the fish out of the icebox and began to prepare dinner. Owen remained at the table as she cooked, unflinching even as she took up their biggest knife to begin hacking at vegetables.

Quinn felt a prickle of unease in the back of her mind, though she hoped her slightly rageful cooking concealed it. Could Owen see that something was different? Had he noticed a change in the way she twisted like a fish in his net? How long until he put the pieces together?

With the fish sizzling in the pan and small puddles of oil hissing and spitting at her, Quinn pushed the thoughts down and resolved to worry about it when Owen wasn't watching her with pale, searching eyes.

THAT NIGHT, QUINN CURLED into a tight ball between the stiff white sheets of their bed. The house creaked and complained about the rush of wind outside. Owen was quiet beside her, lying flat on his back.

They were both awake. Quinn often spent many hours lying in their bed, her thoughts keeping her from sleep, but Owen was out like a light the moment his head hit the pillow. But not tonight.

He shifted, the sheets rustling, and put a hand on the point of Quinn's hip.

"When was the last time you bled?" he asked, sending Quinn's heart into a cold plunge.

She remained silent and still, hoping he thought she was already asleep, but he didn't take his hand away. He slid closer to her. His hand traveled forward and down until it rested right under her belly button.

"It's been a while, hasn't it," he said quietly. "Hasn't it?"

Quinn squeezed her eyes shut, tight enough that when the tears began to gather, they slipped down her cheek and over the bridge of her nose in a rush.

Owen set his forehead against the back of Quinn's neck, the hard press of his skull against the knob of her spine. She didn't want to know if he was smiling. He held her like that for the rest of the night, the weight of his arm over her waist. Trapping her.

QUINN WATCHED OWEN'S BACK as he disappeared down the hill the next morning on his way to the pier. It had dawned gray and foggy, and Quinn was resolved to head into the hills to find the washerwoman as soon as she was certain Owen was gone.

With her shawl around her shoulders and her hair braided away from her face, Quinn laced up her boots and set out into the chill morning in the opposite direction up the street.

The even path lasted only a mile outside of town before being reduced to a bumpy, uneven dirt track. Quinn was walking quickly, her cheeks warm and red from exertion and the cold by the time she came across the first stone road marker.

The hills were a hazy gray-and-green expanse. Quinn could only see perhaps twenty meters in front of her, but every step resolved more of the path. The murkiness of the morning and the dim awareness of her surroundings made her feel as though she were submerged deep underwater, where the ocean became nothing more than the few meters of water around her.

She walked and walked, and realized at the third marker that she had not eaten breakfast that morning. Still, she felt a weight on her stomach.

At the fourth marker, the fog began to lighten. She could see a bit farther off the road, where the green grass was broken up by small clusters of rock and short, hardy bushes. A tiny creek trickled under a stone footbridge, but Quinn kept walking, the storyteller's words replaying in her mind like a bird calling out the same dire note.

The fifth road marker was stone, like all the others, slightly grown over with moss as nature tried to absorb it back into the hills. Quinn stopped in front of it, chest rising and falling quickly.

The tips of her fingers were stiff with cold, and she flexed them before tucking her elbows into the shawl and pulling it tight over her hands as she crossed her arms over her chest. The path she had followed stretched on and on, the distance only determined by the markers, but in the fog she was certain she could have followed the dirt road to the end of the earth.

Instead, she stepped off the path, picking a side at random when she realized the storyteller had not given that detail when he spoke about the washerwoman's location. She would search the right side of the road first and move to the left if she found nothing.

She supposed she should feel nervous, searching the foggy hills for an omen of death. The storyteller had certainly conveyed the fear he had felt when spotting the washerwoman, and the other men had reflected the concern right back.

But Quinn felt more at ease than she had been in a long time. She was not frightened of the washerwoman any more than she was afraid of another selkie. Perhaps she should be a little more cautious than that, but she knew that nothing the washerwoman could do would be worse than Quinn being separated from her pelt, trapped on land, and pregnant with a human man's child. The washerwoman was her first bit of hope that she could escape this life.

The path was swallowed up by the fog behind her, her steps muffled by the thick grass, and Quinn shivered. She needed this to work.

She searched over the hills, following the current of the land to try to find the place where a stream cut through the landscape like a scar.

After perhaps an hour of fruitless searching, she felt a tug behind her breastbone. The direction it called her to follow revealed more shapeless, green hills, until suddenly she was a step away from putting her foot into a gurgling stream. No more than a meter across, the stream was shallow and quick moving, and Quinn turned to follow the current, hoping that the stream would widen as it hurried toward the ocean.

The stream did grow wider and deeper as she walked along its edge. It curved and wound its way around the hills. Quinn wondered what the storyteller could have been doing this far off the path, where it would be only fitting to find the subject of an old wives' tale.

Her instinct had not steered her wrong. Only a few minutes of walking later, Quinn heard a faint sound weaving its way through the fog. A woman's voice, low and eerie, beckoned Quinn closer to the purpose of her early morning search.

The fog gave up the washerwoman slowly, as if peeling back a curtain by unraveling the layers of the fabric. She knelt by the stream, which was now a couple meters across and at least a meter deep, holding a soaked white shirt. The shirt had a faint pink tinge, as if she was at the end of washing out a bloody stain. Behind her three more shirts lay spread out on the grass; two were clean, while the last one had a large red stain in the middle.

Quinn slowed, considering the washerwoman's back. She was fully invested in her task, singing her dirge absentmindedly, her head bent over the stream. She did not have breasts long enough to throw over her shoulders. Quinn got the impression that even when she was not kneeling at the edge of a stream, the washerwoman was rather short, but she was also wide of shoulder and stomach, her pristine gray dress and white apron stretched across a generous chest. Long black hair hung down her back.

Quinn did not think the word "pitiful" applied to the washerwoman at all.

She crept slowly up the grassy bank by the stream until she was behind the washerwoman. She would heed the humans' warnings and her mother's stories about being spotted by the washerwoman first and made sure her steps were silent as she approached.

When she was maybe a meter away from the washer-woman, Quinn lowered herself into a crouch before shuffling forward a bit more.

She carefully reached forward and laid her hand on the washerwoman's elbow.

Immediately, the washerwoman stopped singing, and her hands ceased beating the shirt in the water.

"It's been a long time since I've met one of your kind," she told Quinn. She did not turn around, and Quinn did not move.

"You know what I am?" Quinn asked quietly.

"Of course," the washerwoman said. "Just as you know of the creatures of the land, I know of the creatures of the sea. You are far from home, selkie."

Quinn's fingers twitched on the washerwoman's elbow. "In many ways," she agreed. "I've sought you out in hopes that you can help me."

Quinn held her breath as the washerwoman wrung out the shirt she was cleaning. The pink stain was now gone.

"Who told you of me?" she asked Quinn.

"My mother."

"She told you that those who capture me may ask things of me," she guessed. "That they make wishes to an omen of death."

"Yes," Quinn whispered, her chest so tight it was like she had the weight of the ocean on top of her.

The washerwoman shook out the clean shirt and held it up to inspect. "It's true, I can grant wishes."

Quinn sucked in a breath, her grip on the washerwoman's elbow tightening, but then she continued. "I can grant wishes to the humans who find me. I'm sure your mother's stories said nothing of what happens when one myth comes across another."

Not wanting to believe what the washerwoman was saying, Quinn whispered, "Please, I wish for this child to disappear. I wish to find my pelt. I wish to go home."

The washerwoman turned and looked at Quinn.

Her eyes were black. No, they were a deep, dark green. They caught Quinn's and held her there. The washerwoman's face was pale and shifting, and Quinn couldn't get a clear impression of what she looked like.

"I cannot grant your wishes, selkie," the washerwoman told her, voice laced with sadness. "I can only grant the wishes of the humans, since it is their deaths that I predict. You would never find me washing the clothes of someone you knew. Your blood is half seawater."

Quinn's hand had been dislodged from the washerwoman's arm when she turned, but it still hung in the air between them. She let her shoulder go slack, and her hand dropped to the ground. She curled her fingers in the damp grass.

Quinn curled her body, too, her head pressed into her knees. Her other hand was trapped between her legs and her stomach, where something small and helpless was growing that would forever tie her to the humans she despised.

The washerwoman placed a cool, damp hand on Quinn's shoulder.

"I'm sorry, young one," she told her.

Quinn sucked in a breath and let out a sob in return. All her fear, her rage, her loneliness flooded out, her hope dissolving with them.

The washerwoman kept her hand on Quinn's shoulder as she cried. She did not try to soothe her, which Quinn was grateful for. She did not want to be soothed. She wanted every part of her to bleed out with her tears until she was only a husk, until there was nothing for the little egg inside her to feed off of. Until she was as thin and lifeless as her pelt was once it was not a part of her.

When she was done, her throat ached. The skin around her eyes was tight and her knuckles were white from how hard she was gripping the grass.

She uncurled her fingers first. The washerwoman helped her sit up and back until she was no longer balancing on the balls of her feet. Quinn wiped her face with the hem of her shawl.

"Tell me what you want," the washerwoman said quietly.

Quinn shook her head. "It doesn't matter."

"It does," the washerwoman said. "Don't tell me what you wish for. Tell me what you *want*."

Other than her deep green eyes, Quinn still couldn't determine anything about the washerwoman's face. Her pale forehead, nose, and chin seemed to waver in every moment, as if Quinn were looking at her from underneath the ocean.

Remembering the conflicting stories of the men at the pub, Quinn wondered if the washerwoman could look like all of the figures they described. Perhaps she changed form to meet the expectations of the humans who crossed her path. But why? An omen of death had no reason to conform to human expectations.

"Can I ask a question of you, before I answer?" Quinn said, her voice hoarse. She swiped the back of her hand under her chin to wipe away the tears that still clung to her skin.

"Yes," the washerwoman replied. Her hands were folded in her lap, and Quinn realized that she could see them clearly.

They were fine hands with long, thin fingers, but they bore the weathering of years, perhaps lifetimes, of working bloody stains out of fabric. The streams in these hills were frigid, but the washerwoman's fingers were not red from being submerged in cold water.

"Do you predict the humans' deaths because you have to," Quinn asked slowly, "or because you want to?"

The washerwoman sat quietly for a moment, the stream burbling at her back. She tilted her head as she considered Quinn's question.

When she finally spoke, her voice was distant, though her eyes remained steady on Quinn's.

"I do not know how long I've been doing this. If I try to remember my life before I was roaming hills like these, collecting bloody clothes that needed cleaning, those memories are about as foggy as this morning has been. What I do remember is that I have met another washerwoman."

Quinn leaned forward. "There are others?"

The washerwoman inclined her head. "I've met only one. But she told me something, perhaps trying to help me as I struggled to recall anything about what I was like before I was like this, or perhaps just because she wanted to share the story.

"She told me that washerwomen were humans once; women who had died during childbirth. And somewhere between the loss of life and birthing new life into the world, we became trapped in it, though we were different than we had been before. We had held life and death in both hands. This is what gave us our ability to see human death coming before it arrived. We wash the bloody clothes as we would have cleaned the red-stained cloths of childbirth, and we warn the humans of approaching death since we could not predict our own.

"Sometimes humans who see me will claim to be my kin," the washerwoman said, looking to Quinn for confirmation that she had heard of this occurrence, so Quinn nodded. "Perhaps some time ago, some humans knew of how we washerwomen came to be and learned to take advantage of our grief and lost motherhood. The humans still find safety in claiming to be my foster children, though I think the knowledge of why it works has been lost in muddled human memory. I will not harm them if they claim to belong to me, even though I know that they do not."

Quinn felt guilt slowly climbing up her throat. If this story was true, the washerwoman had never gotten the chance to raise her child, and Quinn had come to her to beg to get rid of the one in her belly.

"I'm sorry," Quinn whispered, the words frail enough to be swept away by the stream's weak current.

"What for?"

Quinn tucked her knees up to her chest, feeling like a selfish child herself.

"You didn't get to be a mother," Quinn said, "and all the humans take advantage of your loss, even though they don't see the wound they're drawing blood from, and then I came to you to wish away this...this—" Quinn waved a hand in the direction of her stomach.

The washerwoman reached out and took hold of Quinn's hand, folding her fingers around Quinn's. The skin of her hand was rough and cool.

"Do not apologize for that," the washerwoman told her firmly. "You do not owe motherhood to me because I did not get it. You do not owe motherhood to anyone."

"But to ask you for this..." Quinn frowned.

The washerwoman squeezed Quinn's hand. "What happened to me has no bearing on your experience now. You did not know my story, nor do you owe me anything after having heard it. You are allowed to feel the way you do and hold those wishes in your heart. I am just not the answer you were seeking."

Her voice was kind, but it cut Quinn right to the core.

"To answer your question," the washerwoman continued, "I chose to do this for the humans. Bringing these warnings is something only I can do. No one forces me to clean the blood from these clothes, but the work gives me purpose, and on the rare occasions when a human does approach me searching for answers or wishes, I give them everything I can. It is my choice."

Her answer should have settled the uneasy feeling lingering in Quinn's chest, but it did not. Quinn plucked at the feeling until it unwound like a loose thread and revealed another question.

"Must all creatures like us," she asked, her voice as flat and cold as a river stone, "live under the expectations of humans, even when their stories about us barely scrape the surface of our existence? How can I be the selkie from their stories, when their stories are wrong?"

Around them, the fog was finally disappearing, and it seemed that the green hills stretched on forever in every direction. The washerwoman clicked her tongue and held fast to

Quinn's hands as she suddenly stood up. Her momentum dragged Quinn to her feet as well.

It was only now that Quinn could see how short the washerwoman truly was. She barely came up to Quinn's shoulder, but she had no trouble reaching up to grasp Quinn by her chin to make sure she met the washerwoman's eyes as she spoke.

"You live under no expectations but your own," the washerwoman declared. She released Quinn's chin. "If the story that was told to me is true, then I come from humans. I do not bear their omens for them because I believe I owe it to them. You yourself can become human, due to your ancestors' curiosity or need, but that is not all that you are. You do not owe them humanity simply because you are able to embody it."

Her dark green eyes could have swallowed Quinn whole.

"What do you want?" she asked again.

Quinn closed her eyes. With the endless rolling hills around them, the soft whisper of a breeze gaining strength as it dragged its fingers through the grass, and the lingering dampness of the air from the fog, Quinn could almost imagine herself standing before the ocean. The smell of the stream was too muddy to be confused for the sharp brine of the sea, but Quinn held tight to the ocean in her mind.

As a selkie, Quinn had felt strong enough to do anything. She was as untameable as a deep-sea current, as unstoppable as a wave crashing onto the shore. Her freedom was as inherent to her body as her fins or tail.

As a human, Quinn felt like she was bound in a net that was slowly tightening. The more she struggled, the tighter the net became. She could only do what Owen and the other townspeople expected of her.

If she could not wish herself out of this human life, what was her next best option?

"I want to make my own choices," she said. She had not chosen to be here in this body, to be with Owen or to fulfill his dreams of family and fortune. Her pelt, which gave her the choice to become human or seal, was taken from her. If she could not wish it back, she would learn to make choices she could live with until the day it was returned to her.

The washerwoman finally let Quinn's hand go. Quinn opened her eyes.

"Then start here," she told Quinn, "with this." She pointed to Quinn's stomach.

The braid in Quinn's hair had come loose, and the strands twisted in the wind like they were being tossed by an ocean current. She became disarmingly aware of her body, of the ache in her calves and feet from the long walk, of the tightness of her shoulders, of the way her skin prickled beneath her clothes from a feeling that had nothing to do with the cold. She had wanted to meet this body, to learn how it moved and spoke, and now she knew how it hurt and bled and fought.

She was terrified of seeing her body change again. To have to stand by and watch as she grew into something different.

Quinn laid a hand over her stomach, smothering the memory of Owen putting his hand in that same spot the night before with a soft press of her fingers.

"The humans will hate them, as they hate me," she told the washerwoman.

"Perhaps," the washerwoman said. "But the humans do not believe in me because they love me. Their fear is what makes them pay attention when they see me. It doesn't matter to me what the humans think about the washerwoman," she said, a thorny grin creeping its way across her mouth. "We live whether they like it or not."

The washerwoman turned Quinn toward the road and sent her on her way after that, the features of her face fluttering and shifting as she went back to the stream and picked up the remaining stained shirt. She began singing right where she'd left off.

WHEN QUINN HAD RETURNED to Owen's house, she spent an hour untangling the knots that the wind had spun into her hair. The last stretch of her walk into town had also soaked her to the bone, as a dense storm had rolled in from the water to replace the fog and drenched everything in its path.

From the kitchen window, Quinn could see that the ocean was tossing itself in sympathy with the storm. The huge, rolling waves would be difficult for even the most seasoned fisherman to handle. Quinn stood silently, pulling apart the knots in her wet hair, and waited for Owen to return.

When he did come back, he was even more soaked than Quinn, but the look on his face was the most weary.

"A boat capsized," he told her. "There were no survivors."

Quinn kept her face carefully blank. "How many men?"

"Four," Owen said. Quinn pictured four clean, white shirts, laid out on the thick green grass near a stream. "It was Barclay's boat."

Barclay was the loud, brash man who had laughed at the storyteller in the pub. The young fisherman who had seemed to believe in the washerwoman worked on the same boat. Quinn had scarcely even considered that it could have been Owen who was fated in the washerwoman's omen. She needed him alive.

Rain lashed at the kitchen window. She stood from her seat at the table and stepped into Owen's space. A rush of emotion passed over his face, confusion and wariness giving way to an eager hope. He gathered her to his chest, the cool, damp fabric of his jacket wrapped tight around her arms. His embrace didn't offer Quinn comfort, but she had never sought that in Owen. He used her like a fishing line to draw in the life he thought he deserved, one full of fortune and a beautiful family, and she had to stay close enough until she could sink her own hooks into him.

Chapter Ten

NOW

QUINN'S TENTATIVE REFUGE ON the beach came to an end as quickly as the weather turned. Two days had passed since the night she shared a piece of her story with the keeper, and while Maisie had returned each day to deliver more food and water, she could not stick around for very long.

"We've switched the shifts around," she told Quinn apologetically, cheeks flushed from her hurried walk down to the beach, "so now I'm up with Mr. MacArthur in the evening, and he's a lot harder to sneak away from than Jamie is. But here, look, I managed to get a whole piece of bread with some cheese this time."

Quinn took the food and excuse without complaint. Maisie was pleased by every bite that Quinn took, her expressions like an open book, but she did not try to bring up their divulgences, nor the two questions she owed Quinn.

When she was alone, Quinn had taken some slow, limping steps down the beach to relieve the aches in her body from lying on the unforgiving rocks. She tried not to place any weight on the ball of her foot, resulting in a staggering gait that did not allow for speed. But with Maisie's food and the salve, her injury was feeling better, moving from a sharp pain to a dull one.

Quinn had been waiting for the next storm to hit the island. The cliffs provided a little protection from the wind, but once a rainstorm rolled in, there would be nowhere for Quinn to hide.

Her worries came to fruition the next night. It had been gray and cloudy all day, the air thick with the weight of a coming storm. When the first drops hit Quinn's face, she sat up. Maisie had not come down yet today, but with the look of the clouds roiling in the sky, Quinn wondered if she would be able to make it down the path, or even leave the lighthouse at all.

Quinn tucked her knee into her chest and reached for the bandage around her foot. As she unwrapped the layers, she revealed a rusty stain that bled through the white cloth. When she pulled away the last piece of the bandage, she frowned at the injury. The skin around the hole was pink and tender, the edges irritated. It had only been a few days, but she was not healing fast enough.

The rain continued to spit at her, the drops cold and stinging on her bare skin. She did not want to sit through the storm unprotected on the beach. Quinn clasped her pelt around her shoulders and levered herself to her feet. She used the cliffside to balance as she hopped down to the water, injured foot tucked up.

Quinn was so focused on her feet and making sure she didn't trip and injure herself further that she didn't look up until the waves brushed her toes. The storm had gained strength and sent waves crashing against the shore. Quinn glanced up to try to figure out when she could slip into the water between a break in the tide.

But instead of an empty expanse of dark, roiling waves, Quinn saw a boat struggling in the water headed toward the island. The boat was already well within sight of the beach. Quinn's heart hammered in her chest as she recognized it as Owen's. He had come looking for her.

The wind whipped across the beach and nearly sent Quinn stumbling. Her wound ached as the strength left her legs and she lurched farther into the water, seeking protection in the riotous sea. If she could get her pelt on, she would be able to swim away before Owen made it to shore.

The stones under the tide shifted beneath her feet. She was unsteady, but kept going until water was up to her knees. The cold had numbed her toes. Her next step caught on a large, unseen rock beneath the black water, and sent her crashing into the waves.

The last time she had dove into the water with her pelt around her shoulders, Quinn had been elated. She had gotten her freedom back and found the ocean waiting for her with open arms.

Now the ocean was an unfamiliar beast. The cold, dark water was unwelcoming, caught up in the harsh storm as if bewitched. Quinn gripped her pelt tightly when she fell, worried that the sea would tear it away from her.

Quinn tried to kick away from the shore once she was submerged, but the waves were too powerful for her one working foot to compete with. She tried to kick with her injured foot and bit back a gasp of pain, keeping her mouth shut tight.

When she fell, she had instinctively sucked in a breath, but it had been too small and strained. She clawed at the water with one hand until she broke the surface.

She'd managed to swim out into two meters of water, but even here it was a challenge to stay afloat. The waves pushed and pulled at her and it took all her strength to keep her head above the surface. She twisted, trying to locate Owen's boat as she attempted to pull her pelt closed over her shoulders, but something was wrong. The fur wasn't becoming a part of her. It wouldn't wrap around her body. She couldn't turn into a seal.

Was it her panic that was stopping it from working? Or her injury? She kicked and gasped, mouth filling with seawater as a wave crashed over her head. The pelt was a heavy, water-logged weight on her back, but it felt as though any moment it would get snatched away in the pull of the current. What was wrong with her?

If she couldn't get her pelt on and she couldn't swim, then Quinn was stranded in the water. She had sought shelter from Owen and the storm, but without her seal form, she was as helpless as a newborn human. The ocean could not harbor her tonight.

Every kick was painful, but Quinn struggled back toward the beach. She found the shore with her hand first, feeling for the bottom to try to avoid kicking it. Another wave pushed her higher out of the water, and she jarred her knees on the rocks. With her pelt a clinging weight on her back, Quinn crawled up the beach and out of the water. Her arms and thighs shook from the cold and exhaustion.

Quinn only got a few meters up the beach before she had to

stop. She dropped her hips to the side and landed on the rocks with a wince. Braced on her hands, Quinn twisted around and searched the beach, terrified that Owen had made it to shore while she had struggled. But she was still alone.

Owen's boat was bobbing precariously in the waves, clearly trying to head toward the small dock, but forced back by the ripping tide. If he attempted to come too close to shore while fighting the waves, he could ruin his boat on the rocks. A shadowed figure behind the helm lurched against the wheel. Quinn could imagine the terrible look on Owen's face, his anger at being denied what he wanted, at being so close to getting her back. He might not have even seen her on the beach, but she knew he wouldn't have risked coming here for any other reason.

Finally, Owen turned the boat back into open water. He would have a hard time getting back to town on his own in such a storm.

Even as Owen's boat vanished into the dark horizon, Quinn couldn't relax. She risked a glance at her wound. The chill water had paled her skin, and the red gash looked even more stark. As she looked at it, a bit of blood welled up, quickly diluted by the rain and running in pink-stained streams down onto the beach.

Her foot was still numb, but she knew it wasn't good that the injury had begun bleeding again. It would hurt a lot more to walk, let alone swim.

While she gasped for breath and the storm swirled around her, Quinn wondered why she hadn't been able to pull the pelt on. Could she not turn back into a seal when she was injured? But she had been able to take off the pelt and become human with the injury; why would it be different the other way around?

She had felt panic when she hit the water. The sea had been unfamiliar and frightening, and without the body it knew so well, she could not fight against it. Had the ocean seen her as a human and not a selkie? It had not even been a week since she dragged herself onto the island's shore; how could the ocean forget her so quickly? She had been gone for seven years before, but tugging on her pelt for the first time by the pier had been as easy as breathing.

But something was keeping her stuck in this form now. Even with her pelt in her hands and her choices laid out for the taking, Quinn was trapped. Something in her chest squeezed tight.

Above her, the sky rumbled a warning. Lightning flashed. She blinked, searching for the beacon of the lighthouse. It swung high above her, sending light through the murk of the storm and far out onto the water.

Then, a voice: "Quinn!"

The beach was cloaked in shadow and blurred by rain, but Quinn squinted in the direction of the cliffs where she had been sleeping the past few days. A figure bundled up against the rain was staggering toward her.

"Quinn?" Maisie called again. She wore her big oilskin coat and a slick rain hat over her knit one, and she had one hand tented over her brow to keep the rain out of her eyes. Her sturdy boots made quick work of the soaked stones.

Quinn pinched her eyes shut, further dread pooling in her gut as Maisie crouched down next to her. She didn't want Maisie to see her like this. Embarrassment heated her cheeks even as the chill leached any remaining warmth from her body, which was sprawled out and shivering for Maisie to see.

Quinn balled her fists, her arms shaking from the effort to hold up her head and torso.

"Quinn." Softer this time. Quinn waited for a hand to land on her shoulder, or for a proprietary touch on her leg, but it never came.

Blinking against the rain, Quinn looked at Maisie. The keeper was huddled close but had her arms pressed against her own legs. She was looking back at Quinn with relief on her face.

"I was so worried when I couldn't find you," she told Quinn. "I thought that I was too late, or that something bad had happened…" She trailed off as her gaze finally flickered down to Quinn's feet. The wound was bleeding sluggishly now, the inflamed skin around the edge standing out starkly like a red warning flag.

"What happened?" Maisie asked.

Quinn pressed her lips together. She wanted to tuck her legs underneath her, hide the injury from Maisie's sympathetic gaze, and somehow convince her everything was all right. But she couldn't do any of that.

"Quinn," Maisie said for a fourth time, and this one had a weight behind it. "Were you trying to leave?"

Mouth still clamped shut, Quinn shook her head once. She would have hid in the water as a seal until Owen left, but the ocean had spat her back out like wreckage from a drowned ship. Without her pelt to protect her from the freezing water or her fins to propel her through the currents, Quinn was no different from a regular human, her arms and legs all but useless. The home she had been rediscovering since her reunion with her pelt had turned its back on her again.

She hadn't been trying to leave the island, but now she couldn't, even if she wanted to.

Maisie crouched nearby, waiting for Quinn to say something. If she told Maisie how close Owen had come to finding her, would she still want to help Quinn?

"Just," Quinn mumbled, and Maisie leaned in to hear her over the storm, "the rain."

Maisie's eyes flicked to the pelt still draped over Quinn's shoulders, waterlogged and clinging.

"I was worried about you," Maisie said quickly, "in the storm. It hasn't been this bad for a while, and there's nowhere to hide from the weather." She jerked her chin back toward the cliffs. "I came as soon as I could get away from Mr. MacArthur, but I have to go back soon. He'll wonder why I was out in the rain at all."

She shuffled a little closer, her knees almost touching one of Quinn's braced arms but stopping just shy.

"You shouldn't be out here with that injury," Maisie told her, voice gentle. The embarrassment that was swirling in Quinn's chest peaked, hot and sharp, in opposition to Maisie's kindness.

"I'm fine," Quinn spat. It was such an obvious lie, but she couldn't help it. She didn't want Maisie to see her like this, so helpless, and think that she couldn't take care of herself. Maisie had brought herself here, to this island, against all odds. Quinn could barely last a week on her own before she had her feet knocked out from under her, any independence she'd worked toward crumpling under a limp, useless pelt.

"Your wound isn't healing," Maisie pressed. "You can't swim with an injury like that before the skin heals over. This rain won't help it, either. You need more than just a salve and some bandages."

"I don't want your help," Quinn gritted out, leveling Maisie with a stubborn, burning look that she had used on Owen very often. Maisie didn't back down.

"You don't want it," she said, "but you need it. Come up to the lighthouse with me."

At this, Quinn could have laughed. She didn't, but her voice was laced with sharp humor. "Right. No, thanks."

"You can't stay out here in this," Maisie pressed. "And you can't leave either, it seems." Quinn glared at her, daring her to ask why she was stuck, sprawled on the beach like a bit of discarded seaweed. But Maisie bulled on. "At least in the lighthouse you'll be dry, and your wound will be able to heal."

Quinn scoffed. "You do not live up there alone. What are the other two keepers going to think when you drag me through the door? I have seen how men react to finding selkies. I have only just escaped from humans, after which my husband put a spear through my foot, and yet you would have me seek shelter with them."

She was hurling the words at Maisie in a flurry just like the storm surrounding them.

"I'll deal with them," Maisie said, her voice hardening in response to Quinn's ire. "They won't do anything to hurt you."

There was a determined set to her mouth and a steadiness to her eyes, her early fear swallowed up by a new resolve.

"I don't trust men," Quinn told her flatly.

"You don't have to," Maisie said. "You can trust me."

Quinn stared at her.

Maisie had brought her food and water, left her clothes

even when Quinn didn't wear them, and shared her story on just a promise that she would get to hear Quinn's in return. Maisie had learned her secret and kept it. But was it trust that she had with Maisie, or something else?

Whatever it was, did she really have the choice to refuse it at this point?

As much as she didn't want to admit it, Quinn knew Maisie was right. Her foot wasn't healing, and until it did, she wouldn't be able to leave the island, let alone avoid a massive storm. Owen had come too close to finding her. If Maisie could get her into the lighthouse, where it was dry and hopefully warm, she would probably heal faster, and she would be out of sight if Owen came looking again.

"They don't have to know who you are," Maisie said with a pointed look toward Quinn's pelt. Perhaps she could see Quinn wavering as they sat there under the torrential downpour.

"Who would I be, then?" Quinn asked. "Do they have many naked women showing up at their door in the middle of a storm?"

Maisie's stubborn face broke into a grin. "None. But you won't be naked."

She stood, leaving the space in front of Quinn suddenly cold and empty, and hurried back toward the cliffs where Quinn had been hiding. She returned to Quinn's side carrying the clothes she had brought down days ago.

"Here, I hope these actually fit you," Maisie said, unfolding the sweater first. "Can you sit up?"

Maisie had seemed to take Quinn's question as an agreement to go to the lighthouse. She eyed the thick sweater in Maisie's hands and reached up to touch the corner of her pelt.

Seeing this, Maisie pursed her lips, then blinked.

"You need to keep that with you?"

Quinn nodded.

"Okay," Maisie said, and she dropped the sweater and pants in a soft pile over Quinn's legs before undoing the fastenings of her coat. Beneath the bulk of the oilskin, Maisie revealed a worn cloth bag with a long strap held crosswise over her chest. Heedless of the rain, Maisie freed one arm from the coat so that she could unhook the bag from over her shoulder. She stuffed the wet sleeve of her sweater back into the coat and crouched down.

Flipping open the top of the bag, Maisie drew out the bottle of water and a hastily wrapped piece of bread. She held the bag out to Quinn.

"Is this big enough?"

Quinn took the bag with one hand. It was limp and the fabric was thin, with messy, overlapping stitches holding the strap to the body of the bag where the seams had given out. Had Maisie brought this with her when she ran away from home?

Quinn laid the bag down with the top flipped open and carefully peeled the pelt from her back. She folded it, fruitlessly brushing water off the fur as she went, as small as it would go, which was still rather bulky. But once it was flattened and folded tightly, she was able to fit it into the bag and close the top. She gripped the strap of the bag with a white-knuckled hand.

"No one will take it from you," Maisie told her. Quinn wished she could believe her, just like she wished all she felt between them was trust, but that was too risky. She wouldn't let her pelt out of her reach for a second.

Without its comforting weight around her shoulders, Quinn was very aware of how bare and vulnerable she was. She shifted her arms to attempt to cover her chest with little success.

Maisie, either blind to Quinn's sudden shyness or ignoring it, reached over and picked up the sweater she had dropped on Quinn's legs. She held it up, looking off to the side but still watching from the corner of her eye.

Quinn shifted, getting her balance under her, and then raised her arms.

With a small, funny smile on her face, Maisie fitted the sweater over Quinn's head and tucked her hands into her sleeves. Quinn felt like a child. This was how she dressed her own children. Or this was how she had dressed them before Flora grew up a little and insisted on dressing herself and her siblings.

The sweater was heavy with rain and smelled of briny, wet wool. Compared to her pelt, the sweater was scratchy, but it was loose on her shoulders and comfortable enough. Quinn frowned when Maisie held up the pants.

"I'm afraid there are no skirts to be found in a lighthouse," she told Quinn with a smirk.

Of course there wouldn't be. Quinn sighed and then braced herself to stand. When she got to her knees, Maisie's hand appeared in front of her. She considered it—square and calloused—for a moment before sliding her own frozen fingers into its grip. With Maisie's help, she was able to stand and keep most of her weight off of her injured foot.

Maisie held out the pants for Quinn to put in one leg at a time, eyes averted. She helped tug them up over Quinn's hips and then let Quinn do up the buttons.

Maisie considered her, mouth pursed and cheeks a little red. A few strands of hair had escaped her hat and were plastered to her forehead with rain.

"It'll do for now," she decided.

"What will you tell them?" Quinn asked. She leaned over to pick up the strap of the bag, looping it over her head so that the comforting weight of it rested on her hip.

"Something they'll believe," Maisie said, coming around to Quinn's side and offering her shoulder. "That you need help."

Quinn hoped Maisie had a bit more to offer to the lighthouse keepers than that, and seeing her incredulous expression, Maisie chuckled, the sound light and airy in opposition to the crashing thunder and roiling sky above them.

With one last squeeze of the bag's strap, Quinn accepted Maisie's shoulder and looped her arm over the keeper's head. They were nearly of a height, Quinn a little shorter, but Maisie easily bore some of Quinn's weight so that she could take a few testing steps up the beach.

"Come on," Maisie said, "it's going to be a long walk."

Chapter Eleven

QUINN'S FOOT WAS THROBBING, but she clenched her teeth against the pain and continued to take step after step, Maisie's shoulder a steady point of support.

Finally, they were standing at the top of the island. The storm felt even stronger up here, with the wind ripping at Maisie's coat and Quinn's borrowed clothes. They kept their heads ducked, and Maisie led them the rest of the way to the lighthouse's front door.

Quinn looked up only once to catch a glimpse of the lighthouse, the massive three-story tower stretching high into the storm-swept sky. The beacon was a thick beam of light from this close, slicing through the darkness like a sharp knife through a fish's belly. A whitewashed building huddled at the base of the tower. Yellow light gleamed through the small second-floor windows, like a secondary beacon for those lost on the top of the island.

This was all Quinn was able to make out through the rain

before they were at the doorstep. Maisie reached for the brass knob and shoved through the door without hesitation, dragging Quinn in her wake.

The door deposited them into a narrow vestibule. On the right, a long piece of driftwood was nailed to the wall with two coats hanging from round pegs. A couple scarves and hats were also piled up on the coatrack pegs, in various states of wear.

Maisie didn't stop to remove her coat. She tugged Quinn forward into an even narrower hallway with a threadbare rug thrown over the wooden floor. Maisie's boots were loud compared to Quinn's near silent footsteps. She didn't seem concerned that they were dripping rain, and in Quinn's case, seawater, all over the floor.

They passed a few closed doors and pictures hung up in the hallway, though it was too dark for Quinn to really see what the pictures contained.

"Mr. MacArthur?" Maisie called suddenly, pausing by a stairwell that led off to the left, her voice shockingly loud now that the din of the storm was muffled. She had dropped into the low timbre Quinn had heard before, the one she used to sound more masculine.

"Murdoch?" came the reply from farther down the hall.

"Well, at least we don't need to haul upstairs," Maisie muttered, and led Quinn forward to the last door.

Maisie shouldered this door open as well and brought Quinn into a brightly lit kitchen.

The kitchen was warm, with a large, scrubbed wooden table and two benches on either side in the middle of the room, a cabinet on one side filled with mismatched plates, bowls, and cups, and a coal-burning stove and counter on the other. There was also a sink with a deep basin and what looked like an ice-box tucked in the corner by the counter. Shining pots and pans hung from hooks on the wall above the stove.

A low fireplace on the other side of the table held a bright, crackling fire, but Quinn focused on the man standing before it, his back to the door.

"Murdoch," the man said, a reprimand in his voice, "where have you been—"

He turned as he spoke, and stopped at once when he saw Quinn draped, soaking wet, over an equally damp Maisie.

The man, who had to be Finn MacArthur, the head light-house keeper, had close-cropped black hair, dark eyes, and very fine features that were sharpened by his stern expression and clean-shaven jaw. He frowned at them as he turned all the way around, the backlight of the fire throwing shadows across his face. Like his hair, his clothes were very neat, all sharp angles and pressed edges. He was not wearing the work-ready pants that Maisie had on, but a pair of fitted trousers and a starched button-up shirt under a thick, but clean, sweater. The stark per-fection of his clothes drew Quinn's eye to the shortened sleeve on his left arm, which was pinned up where his elbow should have been.

Quinn blinked and suddenly recalled the whispered gos-sip she had heard in the market about MacArthur. Of course, the arrival of a one-armed man to run the lighthouse would have sent every fisherman, fisherman's wife, and the like into a flurry of rumors.

MacArthur was observing Quinn in the same way she

was looking at him. She kept her face as placid as possible, but she was sure that a good chunk of her wariness was shining through.

"Explain this, Murdoch," MacArthur commanded.

"Sir, please," Maisie began. "She's injured; can I sit her down first?"

MacArthur's stony face didn't change, but he nodded once.

Maisie led Quinn to the table and pulled out one of the benches by hooking her ankle around a leg and dragging it forward. Quinn twisted and Maisie helped lower her to a seat on the bench, the bag with her pelt squashed in between her and the table.

"Elevate your foot," Maisie told her softly, voice low. Quinn grimaced but brought her leg up to stretch out on the rest of the bench.

MacArthur rounded the table to stand in front of Quinn. She looked up, returning his stare. She was placing her trust in Maisie by coming to the lighthouse, but she knew nothing of the men Maisie shared a roof with. MacArthur noted her bristled reaction but didn't comment.

"I was outside checking on the toolshed," Maisie started her story. "I couldn't remember if Jamie and I locked it up this afternoon before the storm. When I was out there, I heard someone calling out on the beach. Calling for help."

Maisie had taken a step back when Quinn sat down, but she hovered near Quinn's shoulder as she spoke.

"I went down to the beach and found her washed up, half drowned, with a giant hole in her foot," Maisie explained, and while Quinn was affronted to have someone believe she would do something as human as drown, the memory of the ocean spitting her out after her pelt didn't work was a sharp stab to her pride. "I couldn't leave her down there."

MacArthur considered this, his dark eyes trailing over Quinn's soaked clothes down to her wounded foot. It was still leaking blood, although much slower than before. She hated to be so vulnerable in front of him.

"And how did you end up here?" MacArthur asked, directing the question at Quinn this time, "on an island with thirty kilometers of open water between us and the mainland?"

Quinn sucked in a breath, leaning into the fear-soaked adrenaline flooding her veins. "I was on a boat, with my husband. We were caught in the storm. I had to get away from him," she said shakily. She glared up at MacArthur. "He hurt me, and I needed to get away. I jumped overboard and swam here."

"You swam with that injury?"

Quinn let a touch of her rage simmer through. "It was better than the alternative."

MacArthur's frown deepened. "He did this to you?"

"Yes."

MacArthur let out a slow breath. "I see."

He tapped the toe of one shoe on the floorboards, a hollow sound.

"Sir," Maisie said, "shouldn't she stay here?"

"Do you mean until the storm is over, and it is safe to return to the mainland?" MacArthur asked in return. "Or longer?"

Maisie was stiff at Quinn's side, her hands worrying the pockets of her oilskin coat.

"She's injured," Maisie said. "Could she stay until she's healed?"

MacArthur's gaze was sharp as it moved between Quinn and Maisie.

He told Maisie, "Go and fetch Jamie."

Maisie stopped fiddling with her pockets. She took a breath, then hesitated. It was apparent to Quinn that she didn't want to leave her side, and Quinn was hardly ready to be alone with MacArthur. But Maisie—*Murdoch*—worked for MacArthur.

He raised an eyebrow at Maisie. She quickly nodded and left the room, not bothering to pull the door shut behind her.

With the crackling fire and the house creaking in complaint of the storm's blustering winds, it was hardly quiet, but the room felt still with tension. Quinn kept her gaze up and trained on MacArthur's face.

"Why are you here?" MacArthur asked her. Perhaps he thought she would crack under the pressure of being alone in a room with him, but Quinn had perfected staring down the only man in a room.

"It was better than the alternative," Quinn repeated.

"This husband," MacArthur said, "he lives on the mainland?"

Quinn paused before nodding, figuring it was all right to admit that much.

"He would be looking for you, if you returned there, then," MacArthur guessed.

She nodded again.

"This is not a shelter house," MacArthur told her. "This is a place of work. A place of order."

Quinn didn't say anything. There was nothing she could say to him to convince him to let her stay. She was not going to beg protection from a human.

They waited in silence until Maisie's footsteps returned, followed by an even louder set of footsteps.

Maisie came right back to Quinn's shoulder when she reentered the kitchen, and Quinn looked around her to see the man who had entered behind her. Jamie, or James Donovan, was a very large man, with short hair and a beard trimmed close to his face. From the state of his rumpled clothes, he looked to have been woken from a deep sleep, though how he could sleep through such a storm was a wonder. His hazel eyes widened when they landed on Quinn.

"Murdoch has found a castaway of sorts," MacArthur told him bluntly, "who would like to treat the lighthouse as a way-station and stay here until her injury heals."

Jamie blinked and scanned Quinn, searching for her injury. When he spotted the hole in her foot, he let out a surprised grunt.

"W'kind of injury is that!" he boomed, a little slurred from sleep. He turned on his heel and left the kitchen, steps shuddering through the house like an echo of thunder. Quinn glanced up at Maisie for an explanation, but before she could even ask, Jamie was thudding back into the room. He held a metal box with a red cross painted on the side.

Jamie dropped to his knees beside Quinn, and she flinched away.

Each of the keepers caught the movement, and while Maisie pressed her lips together and sidled a little closer to Quinn's side, MacArthur watched silently with his arm tucked behind him, and Jamie leaned back on his heels.

"I've something that can help," he told her, his booming voice softened.

Quinn eyed him, wary of his broad shoulders and easy strength—just like Owen's.

"Can't he do it?" Quinn asked, jerking her chin in Maisie's direction.

Jamie and MacArthur shared a look that made Quinn's blood boil. She hated how close Jamie was to her, hated how MacArthur was looking at her like a problem to solve, hated that she'd had to stoop so low as to get help from humans.

Maisie gave her a regretful look. "Jamie's better at first aid. If you want it done right, he's the best one for it."

Quinn sucked in a sharp, angry breath through her teeth. But her injury hurt, and she'd told Maisie she would trust her, even if she didn't trust these men. She nodded at the keeper to continue. Jamie set down the box and flipped the latch to open the lid, revealing a tidy pile of medical supplies. He pulled out a familiar roll of bandages and round tin, as well as a small, stoppered bottle and a square rag.

"This'll sting," he told her, apologetic. He pressed the rag to the open mouth of the bottle and swished it a few times. He looked up at her, a warning, and she braced herself.

The antiseptic stung a lot, like she was being stabbed all over again, but Quinn didn't cry out. She refused to make a sound and instead gripped the edge of the bench with one hand, fingernails digging into the wood as Jamie wiped the edges of the wound. He was surprisingly gentle, the delicate motions at odds with his large, rough hands.

"Looks like you were stabbed by a spear," he said, peering at her foot.

She bit out, "Fishing spear."

Jamie paused, a complicated look flickering over his face,

and Quinn saw something shift in MacArthur's expression, too. He quickly shut it down when he saw her looking.

"Hmm," was all Jamie said, and he finished cleaning her injury before applying the same salve that Maisie had brought her a few days ago—which now felt a lifetime away—and then wrapped it tightly with the bandages.

While Jamie tucked away the end of the bandage, MacArthur finally spoke again.

"She cannot stay here."

Maisie made a noise of protest, a complicated look passing over her face. She'd made Quinn believe that she could convince the keepers to let her stay, but now that she was actually facing MacArthur's refusal, the monumental effort it would take seemed to be dawning on her. Quinn watched quietly.

"She has nowhere else to go!" Maisie said quickly, pitch rising. "We can't send her back into the storm, and there's no way she can make it back to the mainland!"

"It is a nasty wound," Jamie reasoned, clicking his box of supplies shut and getting to his feet, "but with a few days' healing she could at least manage to walk on her own. We can take her back on our last trip to town."

"But—" Maisie started, and then paused when MacArthur raised an eyebrow at her. Jamie, too, seemed surprised by her insistence. Quinn had the feeling that Maisie had spent a lot of her time at the lighthouse proving her loyalty by being agreeable and even-tempered. But if Maisie backed down now, these men would return Quinn to Owen's waiting arms.

"Sir, I'd ask you to reconsider," Maisie pressed on. She tilted her chin up, but Quinn could see how her fists were clenched with nerves. "What's wrong with her staying here, at least until she's fully healed? Her husband did this to her, and you would have us send her back to him while she's wounded?"

Jamie, who had missed that part of Quinn's story, looked wildly between Maisie and Quinn. He eyed the fresh wrapping he'd just completed on Quinn's wound and frowned, his forehead wrinkling with suspicion that he didn't bother to conceal when he caught Quinn watching him in return.

"She cannot stay," MacArthur repeated, "because we have nowhere to put her."

"She can have my room," Maisie offered quickly.

"And you will sleep where?" MacArthur asked, and Maisie hesitated. She, like Quinn, was hiding something from the other keepers. It would be hard to keep a secret like that without a closed door to rely on.

"On the floor," Maisie said instead. "She can have the bed. I'll sleep on the floor."

"I can't have you staying in the same room with a woman you just met." MacArthur shook his head. "It's not proper."

"Sounds like her husband's not proper," Jamie grumbled, but he didn't push back on MacArthur's decision. MacArthur shot him a look. Quinn also gave him a sideways glance, surprised by the comment. In town, when a wife showed up with a strange bruise or mark from her husband's hands, it was ignored or explained away as something she was responsible for. Quinn's injury was much worse than anything the fishermen's wives had endured, but it shocked her to hear a man laying the blame on the right shoulders.

Maisie turned to Jamie. "You saw the wound. Surely you can't think of sending her away before she's better?"

Jamie's mouth twisted as he considered her and Quinn.

While MacArthur seemed undeterred by Quinn's situation in favor of maintaining the integrity of his lighthouse, Jamie's hesitance was steeped in suspicion. Quinn felt for the weight of the bag at her hip to ground her as dread filled her throat.

But there must have been some worth to the trust Maisie had placed in Jamie, because he let out a sigh and flapped a hand at Maisie. "Murdoch can bunk with me, we can split time on the floor."

Quinn risked a glance at Maisie and saw her mind working very quickly behind her green eyes. She had taken off the rain hat at some point, and her freckles stood out sharply on her pale face.

While Quinn's thoughts raced, Jamie joked, "You don't trust us, Mr. MacArthur? You really think we'd try anything? I'm hurt, I am. I thought you knew me better than that."

MacArthur seemed to repress rolling his eyes at Jamie's tone. "It is not about that. It is about what is proper."

"Ain't much proper about living in a lighthouse," Jamie said. "Society can't see us here." He said "society" with heavy disdain. It made Quinn's lips want to twitch up, but she forced them to be still.

"That is also not the point," MacArthur said.

Jamie kept bickering, as if needling at MacArthur was going to change his mind, but Quinn had seen statues with less rigidity. However, every so often, Quinn could see Mac-Arthur's eyes crinkle at one of Jamie's jokes.

Beside her, Maisie sucked in a steadying breath. Quinn looked up at her and saw a wave of determination settle over her face, as if Jamie's decision to side with her had boosted her conviction. Quinn wanted to ask what decision she had come to, what she had planned, but Maisie spoke before she could ask.

"She can stay with me," Maisie said. "It won't be improper."

MacArthur took a step to the side so that he could see Maisie from around Jamie's bulk. "I disagree."

"It is improper for a lone woman to stay in a room with a man she just met," Maisie summed up, and waited for Mac-Arthur to nod. Jamie turned to look at Maisie, too. "Then it would be fine if she stayed in a room with another woman?"

Quinn stared at Maisie, unblinking. What was she doing? Quinn couldn't believe that this was Maisie's plan, to give up everything she'd worked for on the unlikely chance that it would convince the keepers to let her stay. But in what world would they let Maisie stay, let alone Quinn, once they knew the truth? She made a tiny motion with her head, trying to stop Maisie without saying anything. The keeper caught the motion but didn't back down.

MacArthur was looking at Maisie steadily. Jamie looked confused.

"You know me," Maisie said, though her voice wavered. Jamie nodded at her, and it seemed to spur her forward. "Do you trust me?"

Quinn marveled at the way Maisie laid her foundation in trust. Maisie's whole life, the life she had struggled and fought for, was dangling on the edge. And she would topple it for Quinn, for these men.

Jamie nodded again, no hesitation. MacArthur considered her for a handful of long moments, before telling her, "I trust the worker you are. I respect the person who I've labored beside for two months."

"I need you to trust me now, then," Maisie said.

"Trust you with what, Tavis?" Jamie asked.

"My name," Maisie said steadily, reaching up for her knit hat, "is not Tavis, nor Murdoch. My name is Maisie Garrow."

She took off her hat and ran a hand through her chin-length, bright red hair, rumpled from being tucked away.

Maisie kept her gaze on MacArthur as she spoke.

"I applied for this job under a false name, but I meant to do it well. I have learned quickly, and I would not trade this life for anything. I would have never been able to find this life as a woman. But I am just as well suited for it as any man," she declared, the look on her face daring the other keepers to defy her. "Murdoch has earned your trust, but he and I are the same."

Jamie's mouth had dropped open, and MacArthur's eyes were darting quickly up and down Maisie's body as if he could spot anything that should have given her away. Quinn was hardly breathing.

"I'm asking that you trust me," Maisie finished, "and that you allow her to stay here until her injury heals."

A huge gust of wind rattled the glass windowpanes, but none of the lighthouse's inhabitants flinched at the sound. Quinn thought that the whole wall could have been torn away by the storm and the keepers wouldn't even look around to find the cause of the noise.

MacArthur and Jamie stared at Maisie. She kept her eyes on MacArthur, firm, but braced for whatever could come. Quinn looked between all of them in slow, shifting glances, though she lingered on Maisie the most.

How could Maisie risk herself like this? Just to get Quinn a place to stay in the lighthouse? She had already seen a piece of Maisie's selflessness in the bits of food she shared from her own plate, in the readiness to spill her secrets before asking Quinn to lay out her own. This, however, this was more than a kind gesture to a wounded stranger. Maisie was risking everything for Quinn's safety. And she was risking it with two men who had all the power to make Quinn's situation infinitely worse.

Quinn's fingernails were pressing indents into the underside of the wooden bench from how tightly she was gripping it, waiting for someone to speak. She wished this body had claws or something she could use to intimidate these men, and to protect herself, if necessary, but she also didn't want to ruin Maisie's trust by lashing out like an animal.

Jamie had managed to close his mouth at some point after Maisie's revelation. He crossed his arms over his broad chest and reached up to run a hand over his beard. MacArthur was motionless at his side, arm still tucked behind his back like a soldier. Behind them, a log cracked and dropped in the fireplace.

"You applied for this position under a false name?" MacArthur finally asked.

Maisie blinked at him. "Yes. I knew they wouldn't even look at an application under a woman's name."

"They would not," MacArthur agreed. His tone was not angry, Quinn thought, but it did not inspire confidence. It felt like a building wave, the pressure mounting to a peak before it finally broke and flooded the shore.

"Well, this fixes things, doesn't it?" Jamie asked loudly.

He still had a hand on his beard, and he didn't flounder

when all eyes swung to him. He gestured between Maisie and Quinn.

"She couldn't stay because we were all men, right? Now there's another woman. It's even." He nodded to himself. "She can stay in Murdoch's—I mean Maisie's—room. Not against the rules for two women to share, right, Mr. MacArthur?"

MacArthur, though he had to tilt his head back a little to look Jamie in the face, somehow managed to appear like he was looking down his nose at him. A wrinkle had formed between MacArthur's eyebrows.

"There is no rule against it," MacArthur admitted slowly, "because there have never been women in this lighthouse."

"Then it's not against your 'proper' rules," Jamie said, satisfied.

"As usual," MacArthur sniffed, "the real issue seems to be flying over your head. The problem is no longer that this woman needs to share a room in the lighthouse, but rather that one of its keepers is not who she said she was. Namely, that she is female."

Jamie tucked his hand into the crook of his elbow, fully crossing his arms. A considering look flashed behind his eyes as he looked at Maisie, at her defensive stance, the determined set to her mouth. He'd been reluctant to disagree with MacArthur on Quinn's behalf, but he rose to Maisie's defense without hesitation.

"She's right, though, isn't she?" Jamie asked.

"About what, Jamie?" MacArthur asked tersely.

"She's well suited for this job. You admitted it yourself, not three days ago."

Maisie's eyes widened as she looked from Jamie to Mac-Arthur.

"Be that as it may," MacArthur said, shifting his weight, "the matter of her employment here was produced through obscure means."

Jamie made a *tsk*ing sound, as if Maisie lying on her job application was hardly consequential. "She does the work, don't she? Us knowing she's a woman now won't change the fact that she's good at this job."

"The board would not agree with you," MacArthur told him.

"But they're not here, are they?" Jamie shot back. "You are."

This time, all eyes swung to MacArthur.

Maisie had been quiet the entire time they were arguing, and she seemed ready to vibrate out of her boots with the nervous energy rolling off her, but she kept her mouth shut. Quinn had been getting the impression that within the walls of this lighthouse, MacArthur's word was law, and while the keepers had the jurisdiction to test the limits of his flexibility, he would have the final say. But he seemed to be wavering under Jamie's argument.

Quinn was shocked by how quickly Jamie had sprung to Maisie's defense, his reasoning so simple it evaded any doubt that he really meant what he was saying. But was the support of another keeper enough to save Maisie's place here?

MacArthur tapped his foot on the floor.

"Ms. Garrow," he tested out, and Maisie stiffened. "I admit that you have been an exemplary addition to the lighthouse. I would be hard-pressed to find a replacement for you who could do the job even half as well. I'm sure you noticed during the application process that this is not a much sought-after position." His words were crisp and to the point.

"The board would not approve of you working here," he told her. Now Quinn stiffened, and she saw Maisie's shoulders climb up toward her ears, but Jamie stared calmly at Mac-Arthur's profile, waiting for the rest. "However, at this point, the board does not know. And as I see it, they do not need to become aware of the fact."

A pause, as if the room itself did not believe what it had heard.

"You mean," Maisie started, her voice finally her own. It was small and nervous, but the layer of fake masculinity was peeled away. "You'll let me stay?"

MacArthur nodded, then, shifting his weight to his left, added, "I of all people shouldn't judge someone's ability to do this job based on perceived physical capability, especially since you have already proven yourself capable."

Jamie's face broke into a wide smile.

While Maisie's shoulders dropped in relief, she tilted her head toward Quinn and asked again, "And she can stay, too?"

"As we have established," MacArthur said, "I trust you." Quinn heard the unspoken, *Even if I don't trust her.* "However, our current rations were decided when only three people were going to be occupying the lighthouse for the winter, and while we have settled the issue of where she should sleep, I will not tolerate any distraction from your duties."

Jamie cut in, "No worries on the food front, Mr. Mac-Arthur. Murdoch, I mean Garrow—"

"Maisie's fine," she told him, a wobbly smile on her lips. He grinned back at her.

"Maisie and I managed to get a bit more than you'd planned on our last trip, despite having to dodge that storm and those two investigators—" He ground to a halt, eyes widening at his slip.

MacArthur frowned. "Investigators?"

Maisie, like Jamie, had gone rigid at the mention of the two men Quinn remembered the dock foreman talking about, the ones who had been asking questions around the pub and town about an escaped murderer. Quinn wondered why they hadn't told MacArthur about it before. They seemed as cautious about the outsiders as Quinn was about most humans.

Jamie quickly recovered, though his eyes shifted nervously to Quinn for some reason. "Just some busybodies that Dunwoody warned us about. We should have enough supplies for one more s'long as we don't need seconds."

MacArthur's jaw twitched. "Fine, then. Still, I will not stand for any lagging on lighthouse duties while she is here. This is not a hospital, nor is it a social club."

Jamie looked around, eyes comically wide. "Are you sure? Could have fooled me, what with the isolated island and all."

Maisie let out a laugh, though she tried to smother it in deference to the look on MacArthur's face. Quinn, however, wanted to hear her laugh again.

Slowly unpeeling her fingers from the bench, Quinn considered the three humans before her. Who were these men, who so easily accepted Maisie when she finally shared the truth with them, against everything that Quinn thought she understood about humans? Maisie had asked them to trust her, but it was obvious that she had had enough faith in them in return that the risk was not unfounded. Miraculously, Maisie's plan had worked.

Jamie continued to needle MacArthur until the head keeper

raised his voice and declared, "Since the matter has been settled, we should end this discussion. Ms. Garrow, you will see that—" He stopped, turning back to Quinn with furrowed brows.

"Quinn." She saw Jamie tilt his head when she said her name, like he was trying to remember something after hearing it. Too late, she wondered if it was wise giving the keepers her real name. Knowing that Jamie was the keeper who came to the mainland to resupply, he would have come across the fishermen at the docks or the pub and perhaps heard the rumors swirling about Owen's strange wife. Quinn pressed her lips tight. She had no last name to give them and would never claim Owen's as her own. She hoped they wouldn't press her for more.

"You will see that Ms. Quinn is settled," MacArthur continued smoothly. "And then return to your post. Jamie, back to bed."

"You say this ain't a hospital," Jamie grumbled, "but it sure feels like a military post sometimes." He flicked a final glance at Quinn but said nothing as he gathered up his box of medical supplies and left the kitchen, throwing a jovial, "See you in the morning, then!" over his shoulder as he went.

As his thundering footsteps faded down the hall, MacArthur turned to Maisie.

"I'll be in my office," he told her, and with a nod to Quinn, left the room.

The moment they were alone, with the kitchen door shut between them and the rest of the house, Maisie collapsed onto the bench next to Quinn.

"I can't believe that worked," she muttered.

"Neither can I."

Maisie leaned forward, her head cradled in her hands as

she balanced her elbows on her knees. She let out a long, tense breath. She peeked at Quinn, her damp red hair parting like a curtain.

"I told you it would be fine, though, didn't I?"

"It seems you did not believe yourself," Quinn said. "Though we've established you are very good at pretending."

Maisie sat up, a grin on her face. "I'm very good at being a keeper, too. MacArthur can't deny it now that Jamie's let it slip."

This seemed to remind her of what else MacArthur had to say about not slacking on the job, and she hopped back to her feet.

"Here, I'll show you to my room," she said, holding out a hand to Quinn. "I've got a towel and some clean water you can use to wash up, though it's going to be cold."

"I don't mind cold," Quinn told her as she carefully lifted her leg off the bench and let Maisie help her to her feet. The bag with her pelt swung against her hip.

"Yeah, I noticed," Maisie replied blithely.

Maisie's room was the second door from the kitchen, though she stopped at the small stairwell on the other side of the hall to tell Quinn, "This leads up to Mr. MacArthur's office."

Still dripping water from their clothes and hair, Maisie led Quinn into her room. It was small, with only a single, iron-framed bed, a three-drawer dresser, and a cramped table with a chair wedged underneath it. The table held a pitcher and a large, blue-patterned bowl. A towel was draped over the back of the chair.

Maisie propped Quinn up against the wall before hurrying

over to light the two oil lamps mounted on the walls. Then she pulled the chair out from the table and moved the towel to hang over the bedpost instead. Before Maisie could reach her, Quinn shuffled along the wall, taking tiny steps and using the heel of her foot to keep her bandage off the floor, and set herself down in the chair. She gathered up the bag and set it in her lap.

"Right," Maisie said, still clutching her ragged knit hat. She pressed a hand to her chest. "I should put my coat away. Use all the water you need, and if you want to take off those clothes and trade them for anything dry in the dresser, I'll hang the wet ones by the fire in the kitchen."

Quinn nodded.

Maisie didn't move immediately, hesitating as if she was worried about leaving Quinn alone. Quinn lifted a hand and made a shooing motion.

That made Maisie smile. "Okay," she laughed, and left, pulling the door shut behind her.

There was a window by the bed, but with the soft glow of the lamps and the storm outside, Quinn couldn't see anything through it. Instead, the window showed her bedraggled reflection.

With no one else in the room, Quinn finally pried her fingers from around the bag's handle and set her pelt down next to the table. There was no way to completely wash off the smell of the ocean, and the brine clung to her hair, but Quinn stripped, and she used her wet fingers to untangle the largest knots and braided it back. When she was satisfied enough, Quinn carefully got to her feet and hobbled over to the bed to fetch the towel.

After some cursory swipes to dry her body, Quinn went to the dresser and poked through the drawers. She found a pair of loose drawstring pants that did not look like they got much use and another oversized sweater, green and thinner than the one Maisie had brought to the beach for her, but good enough for now. She searched the top drawer for a pair of socks.

The socks she unearthed from the drawer were also thin, with a hole in one of the heels, but Quinn didn't want to take one of the thicker pairs. The clothes fit her, in the loosest sense of the word. She was tying a knot in the drawstring to keep her pants on her hips when Maisie knocked on the door.

"Are you dressed?" she whispered, loud enough to be heard through the wood.

"Yes," Quinn answered.

Maisie stuck her head in. If she had anything to say about Quinn's choice of her clothes, she didn't share it, and instead pointed to the wet ones dripping from the chair.

"I'll take those to the kitchen?"

"They're yours," Quinn said, shuffling back toward the chair. "You don't have to ask me for permission."

Maisie made a face as she came all the way into the room to fetch the clothes before Quinn could try to bring them to her. "I gave them to you to keep. They're yours now."

Without her coat, Maisie's shoulders were rounder, but still broad. Her sweater was dry and had a pattern of little fish around the neckline.

Quinn made a noncommittal noise in return, and Maisie left with the wet clothes.

Replacing the towel on the back of the chair, Quinn took her pelt out of the bag and kneeled to lay it out on the floor on top of the woven rug by the bed. Unlike the borrowed clothes, Quinn's pelt was already nearly dry. She ran a hand through the fur.

The feeling of it beneath her fingers was comforting, but Quinn pressed her lips together as she thought about how her pelt had failed her, how it hadn't wrapped around her when she was struggling in the waves.

Before she could dwell on it for too long, Maisie came back, knocking again before cracking the door open.

"I have to stay up with Mr. MacArthur," she told Quinn. "With the storm and all, he needs someone to be able to go up and take care of the beacon in case anything happens."

Quinn nodded and started to lay down on her pelt.

"You," Maisie started, then paused. "You can take the bed?"

"I don't need a bed," Quinn told her. "This is fine."

Maisie narrowed her eyes at Quinn.

Quinn rolled her eyes right back. "I've slept on rocks for a week. This is already much better than that."

"Fine," Maisie relented. "But at least take this." She went to the dresser and pulled a blanket out of the bottom drawer, holding it out to Quinn. She took it, if only to appease Maisie.

"The door doesn't lock," Maisie told her, "but I've taken to wedging the chair under the door when I want to make sure no one can come in. Not that they would!" she said quickly, eyes wide. "Jamie and Mr. MacArthur wouldn't do that; they're very respectful of privacy, and they're good people."

"I believe you," Quinn said, spreading the blanket over her legs. She believed that Maisie trusted these men, enough to tell them about who she really was and bring Quinn to them, and that would have to be enough for now.

"Right," Maisie said, and Quinn looked up at her earnest tone. In the low lamplight, a blush had spread underneath Maisie's freckles. "Well, good night, then. I'll try to be quiet when I come back."

The door snicked shut behind her a final time. Quinn sat there for a few moments, staring at one of the flickering flames on the wall. Eventually she got back to her feet and doused the lamps, throwing the room into darkness. She lay down on her pelt and pulled the blanket up to her shoulders.

She was warm and dry, with her pelt beneath her and her injured foot wrapped in fresh bandages and a sock. And yet she was still uneasy. Quinn didn't even attempt to sleep as she stared at the window, which flashed at regular intervals as the beacon from the lighthouse swept around the island.

Chapter Twelve

NOW

IT WAS STILL RAINING the next day, though it no longer felt like the storm was trying to blow the lighthouse off the island. Maisie had snuck into her bedroom sometime in the early hours of the morning, and Quinn pretended to be asleep as she listened to the rustle of clothes and the bedspring creaking when Maisie slid under the covers. At the same time, Quinn heard Jamie's heavy footsteps in the hallway, moving toward MacArthur's office and the kitchen.

A couple hours passed, and with the soft sound of Maisie's breathing, Quinn managed to fall asleep.

Sometime around midday, Quinn blinked awake. The room was dim, rain pattering on the window beneath dull gray clouds. Shifting onto her elbow, Quinn peered up at the bed where Maisie was still sleeping, the covers pulled over her face so that only her closed eyes and tangle of hair were visible.

Quinn wouldn't wake her. She got to her feet as quietly

as she could and paused, glancing between Maisie and her pelt. Was it worse to take her pelt with her or leave it in the room? She listened hard, trying to pick up any sounds of the other keepers in the hallway. When she heard nothing, Quinn steeled her nerves and folded her pelt, storing it behind the dresser so it was at least out of sight of anyone in the doorway.

When she stuck her head outside, the hallway was empty, and even darker than Maisie's room since there were no windows, but Quinn felt along the wall toward the bathroom that Maisie had pointed out to her the night before. Her foot throbbed dully as she shuffled around.

On her way back to Maisie's room, the front door opened, letting in a bluster of rain. And Jamie.

He kicked the water off his boots as he sloughed off a huge oilskin coat. Spotting Quinn braced and frozen against the wall, he stopped.

"Hello," he said slowly, stepping into the hall. "How's your foot?"

"Fine," Quinn told him, edging closer to Maisie's room. "Better. Thank you," she said haltingly, the words stiff on her tongue. "For your help."

"'Course." He nodded, though his eyes hardened when he noticed the way she was hugging the wall. "Nasty one you have there; no surprise you could barely walk. Good thing Murdoch—I mean Maisie—found you when she did."

The way he stumbled over Maisie's name, but then easily corrected himself, the way he was standing a few steps back so that he wouldn't crowd Quinn with his bulk in the already narrow hallway, the seemingly thoughtless gestures that Quinn should have appreciated, put her on edge. Something about

Jamie was too calculated. She should be thankful that he had sided with Maisie so quickly the previous night, but it made her wonder what his reasoning could have been. He certainly didn't seem to trust Quinn.

"Your name is Quinn?" he confirmed after a few moments of her studying him.

She nodded.

He pointed at himself. "James Donovan, but everyone calls me Jamie. Realized we didn't really get to introduce ourselves, what with everything else going on. Though maybe Maisie told you? And our boss is Finn MacArthur, Mr. MacArthur to us, and to you as well as long as you're under this roof." It wasn't a command so much as a good-natured warning.

Quinn, of course, would not be telling him that she knew their names already, as well as what the entire town thought about them. But she also knew that the town was very often full of rumors based on lies. Jamie and MacArthur had already proven that they were not what she had expected by letting her stay at the lighthouse.

"Fine," she said instead. It came out colder than she'd intended, but she still hated that she'd had to seek shelter in the humans' lighthouse. However, Maisie had risked so much while convincing the other keepers to let her stay, and Quinn should try not to undermine her work by raising her hackles every time one of the men spoke to her. She tried to soften her shoulders.

Jamie jerked his chin at Maisie's room. "She's got the day off till dinner. It's her turn to cook. Wake her if she's not up by then."

Quinn nodded again. Jamie flashed her a small grin and

then squeezed past her, turning his shoulders so that he wouldn't brush against her as he passed. Still, Quinn went rigid again, breath caught in her throat at the feeling of him so close to her.

It wasn't like Owen. It wasn't. And Quinn had learned how to fight back against a man like Owen when she lived as a human, but now with the hole in her foot from Owen's fishing spear, and without her pelt wrapped around her, having a man so close was a shock.

But then Jamie was past her, either without noticing the effect he had or pretending not to. He continued down the hall and up into MacArthur's office. As she reminded her lungs to inflate, Quinn wondered if MacArthur had been up there all night and through the day.

She hurried back into Maisie's room before Jamie came back down. Maisie was still asleep. Quinn's pelt was behind the dresser where she'd left it. Quinn paused by the table to drink a few handfuls of clean water out of the pitcher before unfolding her pelt. She sat down, crossing her uninjured foot under her and reaching for the sock on her other one. The bandages were still clean, no spot of blood, though it still hurt. She carefully maneuvered the sock back on.

Though it was still raining, Quinn could finally see out the window, which showed her a stretch of grass that sharply dropped off into a cliff. Beyond the edge of the island, the ocean was a mess of whitecaps, the waves huge and churning even from this far above the surface. Quinn watched the water, fingers digging into the fur of her pelt.

Maisie woke before dinner. Quinn wasn't sure how long Maisie had been awake before she croaked, "Hey," breaking Quinn's gaze from the window.

Maisie's eyes were bleary, but she grinned at Quinn.

"Jamie says it's your turn to cook," Quinn informed her.

"Ugh," was Maisie's reply, and she tugged the covers over her head. Only a few red tufts of hair poked out on her pillow.

"You don't like to cook?" Quinn asked.

"No, it's fine," Maisie said, voice muffled. "They've been going on about how I'm a better cook than either of them, but they'll probably make me do it all the time now that they know I'm a girl."

As this was what Quinn had been taught while living with Owen, she didn't say anything. These keepers may be more accepting than most that Quinn had met, but they were still men.

Maisie sprang up after a few moments buried beneath the covers. Her hair was a mess of red and gold, a bright spot in the otherwise pale room.

"But you're probably starved!" she exclaimed, and threw herself from the bed. Quinn sat in the chair while Maisie dug around in the dresser for fresh clothes. She began pulling on another knit hat, tucking away the ends of her hair, but then paused. After a long moment, she stuffed the hat back into the drawer.

"Come on," she said, voice a little odd as she offered a shoulder to Quinn. It was faster to let Maisie help her walk, Quinn reasoned, and she slid her arm around Maisie's shoulder, her fingers brushing the back of Maisie's warm neck.

As she hopped down the hallway, Quinn managed to catch

a glimpse of the framed paintings hanging on the whitewashed walls. A few were of the lighthouse itself, perhaps done right after it was built, and another was of a fine-looking ship on a choppy sea. She squinted at the boat, trying to make out the small script on the bow, but Maisie tugged her forward before she could read it.

The fire in the kitchen was still burning, but it had simmered to little more than a few flames and smoldering coal. The clothes Quinn had borrowed from Maisie were hanging from a rack below the window. Neither of the men were in the kitchen when they entered. Maisie set Quinn down at the table and pointed at her foot. "Up."

Quinn rolled her eyes but propped her foot up on the bench all the same.

"Is it feeling all right now?" Maisie asked as she bustled around the stove and countertop. She took a glass down from one of the cabinets and filled it with water from a pitcher, setting it on the table and sliding it over to rest near Quinn's hand.

"Better than it was," Quinn allowed. She curled her fingers around the glass when Maisie turned back to the counter.

"I'm glad," Maisie said. She took down a huge, gleaming pot from a hook on the wall and placed it on the stove. Moving a tarnished kettle out of the way, she also pulled out a large cutting board and a knife. "I wish I could have gotten to you sooner, but at least you're here now."

Quinn watched silently as Maisie moved around the kitchen, crouching by the corner and pulling up a trapdoor to a root cellar and gathering up a handful of onions and potatoes. Her hands were quick and capable as she began the process of making what Quinn thought would be a very potato-heavy stew. Soon the kitchen was full of the wonderful aroma of onions cooking in a small amount of butter from the icebox, and the sound of Maisie cutting the potatoes into small, bite-sized pieces.

Maisie had none of the hesitation Quinn had around cooking. It was clear to Quinn that she had grown up working in the kitchen, and she wondered if the other keepers hadn't been able to spot it before because they had not grown up that way.

Just because Maisie was good at it didn't mean she enjoyed it, Quinn reminded herself.

Once Maisie had tossed the potatoes into the pot along with a couple cups of stock, she began sweeping the small pieces of potato skins into a bucket with other food scraps. Jamie walked into the kitchen as she pushed the bucket back underneath the sink with her foot.

"Hello, hello," he said through a yawn. He looked significantly more worn than he had been when Quinn saw him that morning. Quinn wasn't sure what kind of business lighthouse keeping entailed, but she was beginning to realize that there was more to it than she had assumed.

"It's not ready yet," Maisie told him, pointing at the table with a wooden spoon. "Sit."

"Aye," Jamie muttered, but he sucked in a big breath as he sat down and released it in a contented sigh. "My favorite nights are the nights you cook."

His back was to the stove, so Jamie didn't see the way Maisie's shoulders tensed. Quinn did, meeting her gaze when Maisie looked over.

But Jamie left it at that, crossing his arms on the table and leaning in toward Quinn. She returned his attention, getting a closer look at the keeper. The skin around his hazel eyes was crinkled like the eyes of a fisherman, worn from constantly squinting against the glare of the sun off the waves or from spitting rain. His trimmed beard was thick and dark, but Quinn could see a bare line where a thin scar curved up from below his jaw into his right cheek.

Quinn herself could attest to seeing many injuries inflected by fishing gear, including her own, but the one on Jamie's jaw looked too clean to have been caused by anything but a blade.

"Quinn," Jamie said, barely above a mutter like he hadn't meant to say it out loud. She raised an eyebrow at him. "I feel like I know that name. You live in the fishing town on the main island?"

Quinn's stomach clenched, but she didn't let her face change. She knew Jamie likely would have heard of her, but she hoped that the town's predilection for calling her "Owen's wife" would mean that infrequent visitors of the town would not know her real name.

Was there a chance Jamie knew Owen? He had been friendly with the dock men, but there were dozens of fishermen in that town.

"Not anymore," she answered.

"But you did before, yeah? Or else why would you have been out on a boat nearby?" Jamie pressed, though he made it sound like he wasn't searching for information, just making conversation. Quinn shifted nervously under his stare.

Maisie wasn't fooled by Jamie's nonchalance either, and she turned to meet Quinn's gaze over Jamie's head. "Jamie," she asked, trying to draw his attention away from Quinn, "did you remember to change—"

"Yes," he said, eyes not leaving Quinn's. "So what was your boat doing so close to the island?"

Maisie spun around fully and implored him, "That's none of our business!"

"You made it our business bringing her up here."

"I couldn't leave her down there! Jamie, you were on my side about this last night; what's with the interrogation now?" She stomped over to the table and crossed her arms, the spoon sticking out at an odd angle, staring angrily down at Jamie.

"Not an interrogation," Jamie told her, though his eyes didn't leave Quinn's. She resisted the urge to bare her teeth. "I'm not about to change my mind. I think she should stay until her wound heals." Maisie relaxed a fraction. "But I also think that if she is staying here, we should at least know a little about what brought her here in the first place."

Maisie threw up her hands. "You heard why! You treated that hole in her foot yourself!"

"Yes," Jamie said calmly, finally looking up to meet Maisie's eyes. "And any man willing to do that to his wife is someone we need to know about."

"He is from the fishing town," Quinn cut in.

Both Maisie and Jamie turned to her. Jamie leaned forward. "And wouldn't it make sense that the first place he would search would be this island? This lighthouse?"

Quinn pursed her lips. Owen had already tried to come by the island once. Would it be better for her to be honest about the close call she'd had on the beach, or try to ease Jamie's suspicions about her?

The storm outside rattled the kitchen window, the rain an unending downpour that seemed to be steadily growing in strength again. Quinn tried to calm her frantic heartbeat. If she could not temper her reaction, the keepers would be finding out more about her than she wished for them to know.

"He'll think I've drowned," Quinn reasoned. Owen had come to the island to look for her, but his search wouldn't reach past the beach. There was no way for her to explain that Owen would never expect her to seek help in a lighthouse full of humans, that he would think she was more likely to remain a seal and hide away to wait for her wound to heal. Owen would be looking for a round head in the waters, and he wouldn't want to alert the keepers to anything strange. And besides, with the winter season settling in, Quinn didn't think that Owen would risk his boat sailing out to the island again with how close he'd come to wrecking the last time.

Jamie frowned at her, rubbing a knuckle along his jaw.

"Is it better if he thinks you have?" he asked.

"Yes," Quinn said immediately.

Eyes flinty, Jamie nodded. "Fine," he relented, "I can infer enough from the bloody hole in your foot that your husband wasn't much of a husband. But if there's any chance he'd come here looking for you, you need to tell us. Maisie brought you here, but we've all got a hand in this now that we've decided to let you stay."

At that moment, MacArthur pushed through the door of the kitchen and paused on the threshold when he saw them all braced around the table.

"What's this?"

"An interrogation," Maisie said, scowling, at the same time Jamie said, "Dinner."

MacArthur sighed, closing the door behind him.

"Ms. Garrow," he said, "your pot is boiling over."

Maisie swore and dashed over to the stove, the wooden spoon clanking as she brought the heat down.

"Have we learned anything?" MacArthur asked, rounding the table to sit down next to Jamie.

"Enough for now," Jamie told him. Quinn narrowed her eyes at him, and he grinned sharply back at her.

"Good," MacArthur said. "And Jamie is correct, Ms. Quinn, in that your presence here will impact us all, should anyone come looking for you. I've allowed you to stay in my lighthouse on Maisie's word, but I would appreciate your cooperation while we make sure your continued presence won't harm the rest of us."

It wasn't a threat like she'd heard from Owen before, but Quinn could still pick up the underlying *or else* in MacArthur's words.

Maisie muttered something over the stove, her back turned, but Quinn thought she could make out the words, "stupid thin walls."

Quinn, sitting stiffly with both men at the table now, nodded once to MacArthur. In truth, she didn't care if Jamie or MacArthur was troubled by her presence here, as long as Maisie didn't suffer. Owen's boat had failed to reach the island, and he could try to return another day and search the beach, but now there would be nothing for him to find.

He also had the children to consider. Quinn wondered what he was doing with Flora that day, and why she had come to the beach with him. How much had Flora seen through the water? She had to have seen Owen throw the spear, but Quinn hoped she hadn't seen the way it pierced her tail, the way the blood pooled around her in red clouds.

Quinn didn't know what Owen would say to explain himself. Flora would have certainly told Evie and Oliver about it, but she wondered if her children would put together the seal Owen had attacked was their wild-eyed mother who they'd last seen fleeing the house with a fur pelt.

As Maisie brought down four bowls and began ladling stew into them, Quinn's thoughts again wandered to what her children had been eating. Without her there to put three meals on the table every day, she hoped they had figured out a way to keep themselves fed if Owen was still devoting his time to searching for her.

Maisie carried the bowls to the table, the contents steaming. It smelled very good. Quinn moved her leg off the bench, and Maisie sat down next to her.

Jamie made an excited noise and looked prepared to shovel as much into his mouth as he could.

"It's hot," Maisie warned flatly, just as the first bite hit Jamie's tongue. He yelped.

MacArthur stirred his stew absently, eyes on the window. There were ink stains on his fingers, and his face was drawn from lack of sleep, and yet his clothes still looked as if they had just been pressed. His posture, in complete opposition to Jamie's hunch over his bowl, was straight-backed and stiff.

Maisie swirled her spoon in her bowl and brought a bite up to her mouth, blowing on it before eating.

She looked at Quinn from the corner of her eye.

Quinn picked up her own spoon and ate. The stew was

delicious, miraculously so since Maisie had only used a few ingredients.

Jamie made an appreciative noise, already scraping the bottom of his bowl. "I'm serious, your nights to cook are the best nights. I wish it was like this all the time."

Maisie stopped eating. So did Quinn, teeth pressed together behind her lips.

"We share the responsibility of cooking," MacArthur reminded Jamie, finally taking a bite of his own food. "Though I also believe Ms. Garrow has the best skills for it."

"Makes sense now," Jamie said through a mouthful. "Never knew a man who could cook so well as Murdoch."

Maisie's smile was brittle and false. "That's a shame for your stomach."

"Forgot what I was missing," Jamie said. "You grow up cooking with your mother, then? Mine never let me come near the kitchen, always shouting about the dirt under my nails even after she'd scrubbed them clean."

Still wary, Maisie replied around a spoonful of stew, "Yeah."

Jamie brought his bowl to his lips and tilted the dregs into his mouth. He gave another contented sigh. "You're sure we can't have this *every* night? Your cooking, I mean, not stew."

He laughed, but Maisie seemed to have reached the end of her patience and set her spoon down with a rough *clack*. She met Quinn's eyes with a meaningful look that didn't go unnoticed by the two men. Jamie's smile slipped from his face.

Quinn had a feeling that Maisie had been harboring similar uncertainties about MacArthur's and Jamie's acceptance of her the previous night, and while Jamie may have meant nothing by his comments, Maisie's frustration reminded Quinn of the anger she had felt all throughout her time as Owen's wife. All she knew about being a woman had been taught to her by Owen and the town. She had no power over her own life. She had no one who believed she could be more than what was expected.

But Quinn was not a woman. She was a selkie. Being defined by only one part of her existence had infuriated her. This was what Maisie must have been feeling now. This was what Maisie must have been feeling for a long time, and what drove her here under a false name.

Across the table, Jamie was wide eyed, his bowl hovering between the table and his mouth. MacArthur had also stopped eating when Maisie's spoon hit the table. His lips were a thin line.

This silence of the kitchen was roughly shattered by a crack of lightning outside the window. The keepers all jolted at the noise, and Quinn closed her eyes, fisting her hands in her lap. She attempted to soothe the snarl of emotions in her chest that had gotten the storm's interest, but it was like trying to comfort a cornered predator. Her inability to control the storms she summoned just added to her frustration. What good was this power if she could not dispel the storms as easily as she called them?

"This storm," MacArthur muttered, and the bench scraped against the floor as he stood. "Right, I want no further discussion on this. The duty of cooking is split equally amongst all keepers. My expectations of your work have not changed. Jamie, be sure that yours have not altered, either."

Jamie's bowl clattered against the table, and Quinn opened her eyes. He was leaning forward, slanted crosswise on the table to speak directly to Maisie. "I didn't mean anything by it, whatever it was I said."

Quinn's lip curled at the apology, but he seemed sincere. From what she had seen of him in just a day, Jamie was the blundering honest type that raised more hackles than it soothed. Maisie, who knew him better, accepted his apology with a stiff nod.

MacArthur tipped the remaining contents of his bowl into his mouth and set it down with a final-sounding *clack*.

"Jamie, the dishes. Ms. Garrow, with me."

Maisie stood immediately, but then shot a glance at Quinn. Quinn waved her off. She could get back to Maisie's room on her own, and she still had some stew to finish.

As MacArthur left the room at a clipped pace, he spoke to Maisie over his shoulder. "Get your coat. I want to check the beacon room—"

The kitchen door closed behind them before Quinn could hear the rest.

Even though Jamie had been prying into her story the moment he had sat down across from her, and Quinn should have been worried that he would take advantage of them being alone to poke at her even more, she felt resolved, her spine hardened from Maisie's determination to stand her ground.

Jamie rubbed his eyes in a way that looked like it could have hurt.

"Made a right mess of that, didn't I," he said, though it wasn't clear if he was talking to Quinn or himself.

"Yes," she grumbled, and then turned back to her stew.

While she ate, Jamie let his hands drop and began to gather up the abandoned bowls. He carried them to the sink and placed them in a large bucket, splashing a bit of clean water into it and picking up a stained rag to start washing. He was so large he had to spread his feet quite a bit apart to be able to reach into the sink. The sight of him, back hunched and legs cocked out, made Quinn snort despite her anger.

Jamie glanced at her over his shoulder, and she quickly went back to finishing her meal.

"I really didn't mean to upset her," he said quietly, though his low voice carried easily through the kitchen. "I don't think she should cook all the time 'cause we now know she's a woman."

Quinn set her spoon down in her empty bowl.

"It's just that MacArthur and I can't cook for shit," he said bluntly.

"Neither can I," Quinn conceded. She shifted nervously when he turned to face her and excised the basic truth. "I learned, but never got further than passable."

Jamie came to the table and collected her bowl. "Aye, well, I just don't want you to think that I'm thinking of Maisie that way. I'm glad she's here as a keeper. And I know what it's like, having other people's expectations weighing you down."

His gaze was far off, as if lost in a memory. Outside, the rain continued, but there was no more lightning.

Jamie blinked, seeming to drag himself back to the kitchen from wherever he'd gone, and looked down at Quinn.

"Let me take a look at your wound before you go back to Maisie's room," he offered.

Her heart kicked anxiously, aware of the distance between the beacon room and the kitchen, but she just said, "Okay."

Quinn propped her foot back up on the bench and removed

her sock as Jamie finished the dishes, scouring out the pot and putting everything away. He left for a moment and returned with his box of medical supplies.

"Still hurt?" he asked her as he knelt by the bench.

"I've felt worse," she told him.

"So, yes," he surmised, clicking the box open to remove a new length of bandage and the tin of salve. He held his hand over her foot. "All right?"

Quinn twitched her ankle. "Go ahead."

She watched his every move closely. He was as gentle as the previous night, and unflinching as he revealed the wound and examined it. Seemingly satisfied that it wasn't any worse than before, he applied more salve and began rewrapping it with the new bandage.

"You're good at that," she told him, then bit her cheek.

He grinned up at her. "Years of practice."

"On other people? Or yourself?"

Jamie's grin faded, and his fingers stalled. "Both, I suppose. Me and my brother got hurt a lot growing up. I learned to treat us when no one else could."

Quinn could tell that this admission had layers of truth she couldn't see. Jamie had mentioned his mother when he was asking Maisie about cooking—wouldn't she have been able to take care of her sons' injuries? Then again, mothers weren't always there for their children, whether they wanted to be or not. She felt a pang of guilt.

"There," Jamie said.

"Thanks," Quinn murmured, fitting her sock back on her foot.

"You good to get back to Maisie's room on your own?"

"I can manage."

"Then I'll go see if Mr. MacArthur and Maisie need any help," he said, getting to his feet. "G'night."

Quinn's trek back to Maisie's room was slow, and once she shut the door behind her, she leaned against the wood, her hands trapped behind her back. The bedroom was dark without the lamps lit.

Quinn watched the rain through the window.

She hadn't expected for Jamie's thoughtless comments about Maisie to affect her so much. It had dredged up the tangle of emotions that Quinn had tried to leave behind with the remains of her life as Owen's wife, but obviously she hadn't been able to cut herself free.

She was a selkie, but now she was trapped back in the human body that she had waited seven years to escape. She was a selkie, but her life as a woman, her children, haunted her every thought. She was a selkie. If she could not control her emotions, she would be a danger to each of the keepers, even Maisie.

Quinn was a selkie. When her heart called out, the ocean called back.

Chapter Thirteen

THEN

THE HOUSE WAS TORN apart. It looked as if a hurricane had swept through, upending both the kitchen table and the couch, crumpling the rug into the corner of the room, leaving a wake of disaster through the hall. But a storm had not passed through the house. Quinn had.

She was looking for her pelt again.

The baby, Flora, was asleep in the smallest bedroom, which remained undisturbed. Quinn didn't quite know what to think whenever she laid eyes on her daughter. It was obvious that she was going to take after her in looks, but Quinn couldn't be sure if she would be like her mother in any other way. In the ways that mattered.

Quinn laid a hand to her stomach and wondered if any of her children would be like her. If this next child would know anything about where its mother came from.

After she had laid Flora down for her nap, Quinn had gone into the kitchen and stared out the window at the ocean. Her stomach was uneasy, her body already bracing for another pregnancy. Owen was long gone, already out on the water, and Quinn was trapped in the house. So she got to work.

She'd started in the living room, pulling up the thin couch cushions and blankets, though she should have known that he wouldn't hide her pelt in such a simple place. But the anxious feeling in her belly grew and grew, and it wouldn't listen to reason. She shoved the rug out of the way and tried to pry up the floorboards with her fingers.

Outside, gray, threatening storm clouds began to gather.

Quinn tore through the kitchen blindly, upending the table and trying the floorboards again. Then she opened all the cupboards, rattling through their contents as if she could have missed seeing her pelt in all the times she had searched through here looking for a pot or a pan.

The house creaked as she made her way to the bedroom she shared with Owen. Rain splattered against the windows.

Breathing hard, Quinn ripped the sheets off the bed. Then she flipped the mattress itself. She went through the dresser, pulling out clothes and tossing them aside until there was nothing in the drawers. She went to Owen's side of the bed and stared at the chest shoved against the wall.

Kneeling in the pile of bedsheets and clothes, Quinn curled her fingers around the chest's lid and tugged. It didn't budge. Her heart stuttered beneath her ribs.

Beyond the house, lightning flashed, the sudden storm that seemed to have swept in out of nowhere chasing all of the fishermen's boats back into dock. The waters had turned choppy and dangerous, itching to topple a boat in the waves.

In the house, Quinn ran to the bathroom and searched the

small cabinet for a hairpin. She had seen Owen do this when he had lost the key to the house once. He'd taken the hairpin from her hair and poked around in the lock until it opened.

Quinn had worried about the flimsy nature of human locks, and why they placed so much trust in them if they were so easily fooled, but now she was grateful.

Fitting the pin into the small hole at the front of the chest, Quinn wiggled it around, unsure what exactly she was looking for or how it should feel. Her heart was pounding in her ears. She kept fiddling with it until something in the lock clicked.

Dropping the pin, Quinn ripped open the lid. It was a small chest, perhaps less than half a meter wide and tall. Quinn dug through a stack of papers—sealed and official documents such as the deed to the house, their marriage license. Digging further, Quinn's fingers touched fabric, and her heart stuttered, but when she pulled it free it turned out to be an old cloak.

Old, but very fine. Small stitches embroidered the edges, depicting long, elegant creatures riding through the ocean waves. Seals.

There was nothing else in the chest. Quinn's pelt wasn't there.

Outside, lightning crackled across the sky, splintering the dark clouds. The rain was falling thick and heavy, obscuring nearly anything that wasn't an arm's length away. The town shuttered itself against the deluge. There was no fighting a storm like this.

Quinn didn't know how long she sat in the wreckage of the bedroom with the embroidered cloak clutched in her fingers. It could have been an eternity, or a few heartbeats. The baby had slept through it all.

Somewhere in the house, a door opened, and the roar of the storm grew before it was muffled by the door again. She heard heavy footsteps pause and then continue into the house.

"Quinn," Owen shouted from the bedroom's doorway. "What did you do?"

She turned and took in his drenched hair, dripping coat, and pale face hardened with shock.

"Where is it?" she asked him, voice strained as if she had been yelling for hours.

He knew what she was asking for. It was the question she had hounded him with for weeks after he had first brought her here. In the beginning, she asked for her pelt multiple times a day, and he would brush her off with a few words and some coaxing. Then she only asked once a day, springing the question on him in the most unsuspecting moments, as if she could startle the answer out of him. This caused him to frown at her and abruptly change the subject.

After weeks of denying her every attempt, Owen's answer remained the same, but he began to lash out at her in turn. If she was careful, she could ask him once a week and get a growled response. But if she caught him at the wrong moment, he would reach for her with rough hands and leave bruises on her skin as a warning. Eventually, she stopped asking.

The last time she had asked had been right after Flora was born. His answer had been the same.

And so it was now. "I can't tell you," he snapped.

Another crack of lightning flashed in the window, illuminating Quinn's stricken face in pale light.

Owen flinched, just a minute twitch of his face and his

hand clutching the doorframe, but Quinn caught it. Tearing his eyes from hers, Owen searched the room.

"Where's the baby?"

"Asleep."

"You shouldn't be acting like this, with the baby here," he said.

The anger barely contained in her chest flared.

"Where is my *pelt*, Owen?" she demanded. She slowly got to her feet, dragging the cloak up with her.

"I can't tell you," he repeated, an edge to his tone. As if she was being tiresome.

"Then I will keep looking," she fired back.

"Quinn," he warned. But she pushed past him, shying away from his considerable bulk, the cloak held in her fists as she strode down the hall, past the room with her sleeping daughter, and back into the overturned living room. The large window in the back provided a framed view into the heart of the storm.

"Think of your daughter," Owen tried next as he followed her, dripping water everywhere.

"I am," she bit back. "I am thinking of how to explain to her that her mother is kept prisoner by her father."

"You aren't a prisoner."

"I'm not *free* to leave!" she shouted.

"You are my wife," Owen argued back. "You are my child's mother. You belong to me. If you refuse to bring me luck, you will at least take care of my family."

"The only reason I remain here is because you took my pelt." She was breathing hard again, and her hands flexed around the cloak, wanting to rip it apart. "Why are you still keeping me here?"

Owen pushed his wet hair out of his face and dragged his hand over his eyes. They were bloodshot, as if he had been crying, but Quinn knew it was more likely that he had been splashed with salt water while fighting to get his boat back to shore.

"Why keep me here," she asked again, "when we make each other so miserable?"

"You are my child's mother," he said again. But he didn't deny the accusation that they made each other miserable.

"*Before* I was that," Quinn countered. "Before I bore a child, why did you keep me here? Why did you bring me here in the first place? Don't tell me it was because you loved me," she warned. "I know that is not the truth."

"I did love you," he said anyway, and she scoffed.

"You were the most beautiful thing I'd ever seen," he told her. "The night I saw you on the beach, I couldn't believe you were real. I'd heard stories from my grandfather, things he passed down from his own grandfather, about the seals who could walk on land as humans. I made him tell me those stories every night. I grew up hoping that one day I'd see the fantastic creatures from his stories. I moved from my parents' farming village to the coast to learn the water trade." He took a few cautious steps toward her, and she bristled, but he simply laid two fingers on the cloak in her hands. "I brought my grandmother's cloak, which was threaded with the stories I loved. And that night, my wish came true. You were real. And your pelt was right in front of me. I wanted to hold on to you with everything I had, and to do that, I needed your pelt."

His fingers slid over one of the embroidered seals.

"My grandfather told me stories," he continued, "about you, about what you could do in human form. He told me that your kind could bring luck to a fisherman, that you could bring favorable seas and weather."

She glared pointedly at his soaked frame and then at the deluge outside.

"I do no such thing," Quinn retorted.

"I know that now," Owen conceded.

He had been searching for a good luck charm. Instead he had found a curse.

"So why keep me here?" Quinn asked.

Why hadn't he sent her away the moment he realized that Quinn brought nothing but severe weather and an unhappy household? Why hadn't he given up on her?

Owen's pale gaze slid over her.

"I will not be made a fool," he muttered, his tone dark. "I will not have the town think my wife got the best of me and left me to raise my child alone. I may have no fortune from you, but I will keep my pride."

Quinn said nothing. That her life on land was ruled by Owen's selfishness came as no surprise, but his insistence to prolong both their suffering just to save face with the other humans was almost laughable. Were men made of so little?

His use of Flora as a reason to keep Quinn around made her think of the second child growing in her belly. Owen didn't know about it yet, but he had already tightened the trap around Quinn.

"And I can't let you go," Owen continued when she remained quiet. "Because I've seen what you can do even without your pelt." He gestured to the window.

Quinn's head snapped up. There were moments in her time on land when Owen seemed to be scared of her, but he had never said it out loud.

"And you're frightened of me," she breathed. His face twisted at the accusation, but he could not deny it. He was afraid of what she could do to him with her pelt on her back and the full power of a storm bending to her anger. If she was ever free, Owen would never be able to step one foot in the ocean without dreading her revenge.

"If I returned your pelt," he asked slowly, "would you spare me?"

She could lie and feed his pride, ease some of his fear in the hope that he would become more relaxed in his caution. But even if she did, even if she could convince him after all this time that she was finally giving in to his fantasy life with her as his grateful wife, he would never let her go. She knew he would never willingly return her pelt. So why pretend? Quinn took in a trembling breath through her nose and let the embroidered cloak slip from her hands, pooling at her feet. She turned to face him straight on.

"No," Quinn answered.

She could imagine the feel of her thick pelt in her hands, the reassuring weight of it over her shoulders, and the taste of freedom. If she had her pelt back, Quinn would be able to do anything. Owen wouldn't be able to stop her. If this weak, human body could still summon the rage of the ocean, she wondered desperately what she could do with her full strength behind her.

Owen nodded at her answer, confirming his own suspicions and closing the door on any chance that he would reveal the location of her pelt, and stepped back. When he began to turn away, Quinn spoke again.

"I was never your story," she told him. "And I will never belong to you."

He paused, a complicated look passing over his face. Then he waved a hand at the creaking house around them, at the room she had torn apart. "Then I suppose we are both trapped."

Chapter Fourteen

NOW

QUINN SAT IN THE dark bedroom and waited for Maisie. She didn't know if Maisie was going to be pulling another long night with MacArthur, but she didn't feel tired enough to lie down after an entire day of resting, and she was still trying to get her emotions in order.

The storm that swirled around the island was not Quinn's creation, but it had certainly responded to her tight-lipped anger in solidarity with Maisie's outburst in the kitchen. Or had she summoned this weather, what felt like a lifetime ago on the beach, when she was alone and hurting? A week of no rain while Quinn sat numb and shocked on the rocky shoreline, waiting to be discovered, and then as the first bit of rain rolled in, she had tried to escape into the ocean and was roughly turned away. Quinn could still feel the unfamiliar, cold embrace of the water, and remember the fear that had flooded her body.

Perhaps the storm started naturally, but then Quinn had

gotten hold of it. It cried out and called to her through rattling windows and flashes of lightning while she placed her life in Maisie's hands and the keeper had risked everything to convince the others to let Quinn stay.

And then tonight at the table, while Maisie had faced her worries that the keepers would think less of her now that they knew who she was, Quinn's heart had rumbled in response. Maisie had built a life she loved against all odds, something Quinn had never been able to do in seven years with Owen. And Quinn needed to make sure she was not the reason Maisie lost it.

But now Maisie was dealing with the storm that had barely stuttered since Quinn's arrival at the lighthouse. Had she noticed it surge at the kitchen table? Quinn thought it was unlikely, since Maisie had been preoccupied, but she needed to be more careful. The keepers of the lighthouse were more attuned to the weather than even the fishermen who lived and died by it. Owen had put the pieces together about Quinn and the storms that came to her like unruly dogs to heel, which meant that others could, as well.

The issue was, once Quinn summoned the storms, she had no further control over them. She might as well have tried to tell her heart to stop beating. While she had been in Owen's house, she hadn't minded watching the weather churn and thunder when she felt her anger slipping to the surface. The storms had comforted her. They were a reminder that even though she was alone, she was not helpless.

Now, however, an untethered storm was a threat to the humans who harbored her.

The door creaked open.

"You didn't light the lamps," Maisie said, a tentative question buried in the statement.

Quinn tore her gaze from the window and watched as Maisie struck a match and filled the room with a soft, yellow glow. Maisie's hair was windswept and a bit damp but she wasn't wearing her coat.

"All's fine with the beacon," Maisie told her, shaking out the match after lighting the second lamp. "I'm on call with MacArthur, but it should be fine tonight."

"Does that man sleep?" Quinn asked.

"I think he does"—Maisie grinned—"though I've never seen proof of it. There's a camp bed in his office, and he does have his own room. Jamie might convince him to at least sit on a horizontal surface long enough to be considered a nap, but Mr. MacArthur's always nervous when a storm's coming through."

"You aren't?"

Maisie crossed the room, skirting around Quinn's pelt with care, and picked up the towel to scrub it roughly over her hair.

"This lighthouse is made to withstand a little weather, and we're here to help it do so," Maisie told her. Quinn thought a multi-day storm strong enough to make the most seaworthy of vessels think twice about setting sail was more than just "a little weather."

"Could you show me?"

The question caught Quinn off guard as much as it did Maisie. Quinn wasn't sure what made her ask, but she was interested in seeing what the keepers did at the lighthouse, and she especially wanted to see what kind of life Maisie had fought so hard for. Also, she didn't want to sit around in Maisie's room waiting for her foot to heal.

Maisie sat up a little straighter. "You want to see the lighthouse?"

"And what you do in it," Quinn said quietly.

"Of course you can!" Maisie glanced out the window and tilted her head in consideration. "But maybe after this storm has passed. It's a much easier job to appreciate when the sun's out."

$$\ast \quad \ast \quad \ast$$

QUINN DIDN'T NEED TO wait long for the last of the lingering storm clouds to fade into the horizon. By the next morning, a weak sun shone down on the rain-soaked island. She followed Maisie to the kitchen for a quick breakfast of a shared loaf of bread, a handful of dried fruit, and a cup of very strong tea.

"MacArthur makes it every morning," Maisie told her when Quinn winced at the first sip. "Lectures me or Jamie if we make it any weaker."

While they were in the kitchen, Quinn retrieved the borrowed clothes still hanging on the line by the now banked fire and changed into them in Maisie's room.

"I'll be outside this morning, helping Jamie with the cleanup," Maisie told her, eyes averted as Quinn shrugged the sweater over her head. "Storms like that always throw stuff around."

"Okay," Quinn said. She folded the clothes she'd slept in and placed them on the chair, and then knelt to carefully roll up her pelt before fitting it into the bag.

"You can leave that in here," Maisie told her, her voice gentle. "No one will come in or try to take it."

Quinn froze. She didn't know how much Maisie knew about selkies, and she certainly hadn't discussed how her husband had kept her trapped on land for seven years before her escape. Owen had known to steal her pelt because his grandfather had passed down the story. Had Maisie heard the same story?

She had felt resigned to leave her pelt in Maisie's room while she was elsewhere in the lighthouse. When she was only a few rooms away and had a good idea of where the other keepers were at the time, she was not worried about Jamie or MacArthur discovering her pelt. But leaving it inside, far out of her reach, made her nervous all over again.

Even though her pelt had failed her, it was Quinn's only connection to freedom. She couldn't stand for it to be in the hands of another ever again.

"Here," Maisie said suddenly. She moved to the dresser and crouched to open the very bottom drawer, pulling out the remaining linens to leave an empty space. "Would this be okay?"

A closed drawer was better than leaving it out in the open, but still Quinn hesitated.

"I just think," Maisie told her softly, "that you would draw more attention to yourself, and the bag, if you carried it around the lighthouse. Jamie will probably ask about it. MacArthur will wonder."

And Quinn would have no good answer. Her fingers tightened around the strap. But she could see Maisie's point.

She shuffled over and crouched next to Maisie, carefully

fitting the bag and her pelt into the empty drawer. Maisie handed her a few of the linens to layer on top.

Quinn laid a hand over the hidden pelt and met Maisie's eye. "It's all I have."

Maisie nodded, her gaze sincere. "I understand."

Pulling her hand away took great effort, but Quinn managed to push the drawer shut and stand. Maisie stuffed the leftover linens in the top drawer and then offered Quinn her shoulder.

When they were at the front door, Maisie paused to put on her coat and boots, and then jerked around.

"You don't have shoes!"

"No," Quinn agreed.

"But your foot…"

"I wouldn't want to try and stuff this in a boot anyway," Quinn told her. "I'll be fine. I made it up the island barefoot, if you remember."

"I suppose so." Maisie sighed. She fitted herself under Quinn's shoulder again, and they stepped outside.

It was a chill, damp morning, but the sun was doing what it could to warm the air, and Quinn was just glad to be outside again.

Maisie led her around the base of the lighthouse, where a storage shed was built into the side of the building. There was also a large, flat space of cleared land in the shadow of the lighthouse tower, where Jamie was currently crouching over some supplies. Beyond the clearing there was a low stone fence that did not encircle the entire lighthouse building but seemed to serve as a buffer between the rear of the building and the short stretch of grass before the island dropped off into the steep cliffs. Somewhere far below them was the crevice that Quinn had slept in when she had first escaped.

Maisie brought Quinn over to the low fence and set her down. The stones were still cold with rain, but they were out of the shade of the lighthouse and in the path of the sun.

"We have a spectator?" Jamie asked.

"If that's all right?" Maisie asked in return, eyes flashing.

"No bother to me," he said easily.

Maisie made sure Quinn was settled before finally stepping away, and Quinn suppressed the urge to roll her eyes.

"Checking for damage?" Maisie asked Jamie as she crouched next to him.

"Aye," he told her. "Water or otherwise."

With a nod, Maisie began helping him sort through the supplies.

Quinn watched them for a while, but it was a boring, monotonous job that was even more so for an observer. A glance at the surroundings gave her little more entertainment. The top of the island was mostly grass and cliff, the scene barely disrupted by the human's whitewashed building. The clear sky gave her an unobstructed view of kilometers of open ocean in every direction she could look. Eventually, Quinn set her restless fingers to the sad excuse of a braid that remained in her hair and began unwinding the strands. She put the strip of cloth she'd used to tie off the end between her teeth. Her finger combing searched for every knot, gently pulling them apart, until she could brush through from head to end without obstruction.

Then, with nothing better to do with it, she put her hair back in another braid.

When she looked back at the keepers, Maisie held a hose and funnel from the shed and Jamie walked one of the large barrels through the doorway, and then rolled it over the gravel.

"Paraffin," Maisie explained, noticing Quinn's attention. "To fuel the beacon."

They filled the canister, the liquid's sharp smell quickly swept away by the wind. "How do you get the barrels up here?" Quinn asked.

"With a wheelbarrow," Jamie said, closing the barrel once the canister was full. "And a lot of breaks."

"A *lot*," Maisie agreed. She was rinsing out the hose and funnel with some rainwater that had collected in a squat bucket by the lighthouse. Jamie rolled the barrel back into the shed.

Maisie asked, "Wash the windows?"

Jamie appeared in the doorway and made a face at her.

"Wash the windows," Maisie said again.

Grumbling, Jamie disappeared back into the shed, during which Maisie shot Quinn a conspiratorial grin, which quickly fled her face when Jamie appeared again with an armful of mop handles, rags, and smaller buckets.

"Cursed windows," Jamie declared, dumping one of the mops into Maisie's waiting hands. He stormed off.

Maisie shot Quinn another look, and Quinn couldn't help but grin back.

"It's more boring work," Maisie told her. "Do you want to head back inside?"

"I'll stay out while it's sunny," Quinn said.

Maisie nodded. "Can't blame you. Yell if you need anything. I'll come get you when we're going to head up to do the beacon room."

With that, Maisie disappeared around the side of the lighthouse.

Quinn took a breath. If she closed her eyes, she could imagine that she was at the bottom of the cliff behind her, tucked into the safety of the crevice, out of sight from keepers or fishermen. But then she heard Jamie call out from the other side of the lighthouse, his voice carrying but the words lost in the wind, and Quinn's illusion slipped.

But the memory of how Maisie had found her clung to Quinn's mind like a piece of wet seaweed. She'd been chewed up by the tide and summarily rejected when her pelt failed her, but she still didn't understand why. She'd been panicked, sure, and scared, but she had been panicked and scared when she had dove into the water for the first time in seven years after Flora returned her pelt to her.

She'd tried to pull on her pelt the previous night before Maisie returned. Breathing evenly, she'd wrapped the pelt around her shoulders on the floor of Maisie's bedroom and waited for the familiar feeling of the fur closing over her skin, molding her into another form. But it had never come. She'd lain on the floor, still human, for many moments before she'd flung the pelt down again, tears pricking her eyes. Maisie had come back to the room shortly after, and Quinn feigned sleep to keep her from noticing.

Now Quinn considered her injury, still wrapped tight in Jamie's bandages. She'd been able to remove her pelt with the wound, but was there something wrong with trying to reverse it? The wound had been inflicted on her tail fin, and was reflected on her foot, so surely if she put the pelt back on the injury would still be on her fin.

Quinn thought hard, trying to remember if her mother had ever told her a story about a selkie's pelt refusing to allow its owner to shapeshift. But no memories rose to the surface. Her mother, and the rest of the herd's elders, had been firmly against removing their pelts at all, and thus wouldn't have encountered the problem. If her mother had ever heard stories about this happening to other selkies, she had not shared them with Quinn. Likely she had hoped Quinn would never be in such a situation, and Quinn wished she could go to her mother now and seek her forgiveness for not listening to her and the stories she did share.

Far below her, waves crashed against the cliffs. Quinn twisted around, bracing one leg against the wobbly fence, to look out over the water.

There was little she could do but hope that her injury was the issue and that she would be able to pull her pelt over her shoulders once her foot was healed and find her way back to being a seal. She didn't dare consider that she would never turn back. After seven years of waiting, she would not accept defeat after only a week.

A while later, Maisie found Quinn in the same position, her eyes lost in the horizon.

Maisie gave her a tight smile and a knowing look.

"We're going inside," she said, holding out her hand. Jamie was behind her, the full canister of paraffin clutched in one hand. He was also giving Quinn an odd look.

Quinn blinked the image of the ocean from her eyes. Then she took Maisie's hand and let her help Quinn off the fence and back into the lighthouse.

LIGHTHOUSE WORK, QUINN CAME to discover, was a series of mostly boring, laborious jobs to fix something, clean something, or prevent something from getting broken or becoming dirty. At least, this was what took up the majority of Maisie's and Jamie's time. Quinn did not see MacArthur again until dinner that evening—it was Jamie's turn to cook, which resulted in a great deal of clanging pans and a worried wrinkle in his brow as he peeled potatoes—and the lead keeper looked as worn as the other two, though he showed it more in the shadows under his eyes than in rumpled, stained clothes.

Being in the room with the two men still put Quinn on edge. But she reasoned that if she was going to be staying with them until her injury healed, she should know more about their routines, how they moved around the lighthouse and when she needed to worry about her pelt. However, she needed to be careful how she went about it. She remembered how her sharp mistrust and social blunders early on in her life as Owen's wife had quickly turned the town against her. MacArthur already saw her as an inconvenience, but she hoped his faith in Maisie would extend far enough for her to grab the end of that thread.

"Can I ask what work you do here?" Quinn asked MacArthur as they waited for Jamie to finish cooking.

MacArthur considered her, seeming wary. The sun had set about an hour previously, and the clean window reflected the bright light of the fire and gas lamps back into the room, along with the three figures at the table. Maisie was lying slumped over the table but her head tilted, betraying her attention.

"I keep our records," MacArthur told Quinn finally. He

continued, growing more relaxed when he saw she wasn't feigning interest. "Weather logs, predictions, travel charts for passing ships. I also record all of the events within the lighthouse, which is reported to the board along with everything else. I've just finished writing the report on the latest storm. There was quite a bit to explain since it did not concur with my most recent prediction based on previous years' weather patterns."

The unruly storm having been Quinn's fault, she carefully kept her face still as she nodded.

"Lighthouse keeping's not what most people expect," Jamie piped up from the stove. "Mostly grunt labor and clerk work."

"Which is not suitable to everyone," MacArthur said stiffly.

"And why there's more than one of us," Jamie agreed readily, lifting the lid off his pot and peering at the contents with great distrust. "I for one, can't predict weather for anything. No chart's going to help me see a storm before it's hitting me in the face."

"As I've explained," MacArthur said pointedly, shooting Jamie a look, "there is more to it than charts, there are calculations, and records—"

"And weather patterns, yeah, yeah," Jamie said, delivering the pot and four bowls to the table. Tonight's dinner was a thick potato soup, not unlike Maisie's stew from the night before. Jamie accompanied it with hearty slices of bread for each of them, toasted over the open flame of the stove.

MacArthur pursed his lips and turned to his meal.

"We're almost out of bread," Jamie said to the table.

"I will start another batch tomorrow," MacArthur responded.

Quinn swallowed a bite of rather bland soup. "You make your bread here?"

Maisie, who had managed to lift her head once food was in front of her, nodded at the kitchen storage, where Quinn could see bags of flour stacked in the corner.

"Can't make a trip to the bakery when we eat through a loaf every couple days, and we'd clear them out trying to stock up between trips to the mainland," she said. "MacArthur's a fine baker."

"To say nothing for his cooking," Jamie muttered into his spoon.

"Coming from you, Jamie, that means nothing," Mac-Arthur said primly. "But yes, I make the bread."

Quinn had never tried making bread herself, with easy access to the bakery and a staunch resistance to learning more human customs than she had to. She was confused as to why MacArthur would have picked up such a homely skill.

"How did you learn?" she asked him.

MacArthur set down his spoon and fiddled with his piece of toast. Jamie, having slurped down his portion between breaths, turned to listen expectantly. Maisie was still eating, but was doing so quietly so she could also hear. Quinn could have been surprised that the two keepers hadn't asked about MacArthur's skill with breadmaking, but she found she wasn't surprised at all. For as much as they trusted one another, they seemed to know very little about one another's personal lives. Maisie herself was proof of this.

Perhaps part of the strategy of getting along in such close quarters under a toiling workload was by keeping their lives private. Quinn had no such reservation. She wanted to know more about the people who harbored her.

MacArthur was still fiddling with his toast, spinning it in his fingers by the crust. Then he seemed to realize what he was doing and put it down.

"I picked up the skill after I lost my arm," he said matter-of-factly, the shoulder connected to the shortened limb twitching up. "I needed to practice motor control and build up strength in my remaining hand. I had very few options at the time, but I had access to a kitchen with flour and yeast. It was practical."

Maisie was nodding. "Kneading's a workout, even when you're not making a baker's dozen."

"Indeed," MacArthur said, picking up his spoon again.

"Maisie can cook, Mr. MacArthur makes bread." Jamie ticked off each point with his fingers. "I need to get a skill that's as useful as those before I become obsolete."

"You did not acquire this job by being unskilled," MacArthur said.

"No, I *acquired* this job by being able to lift heavy things and put up with dreadful weather for months on end," Jamie replied. "Though I was also warned that temperatures inside the lighthouse could be dreadful, too."

He was grinning as he spoke, and it widened at MacArthur's glare. Quinn flicked her gaze between them. She was sure Jamie respected MacArthur, and MacArthur certainly commanded it without concentrated effort, but Jamie's persistent joking kept throwing her off. The relationship between the two men seemed to ebb and flow like a tide, though she wasn't certain which direction it was heading. Maisie, too, respected the head lighthouse keeper, but something about him had allowed her to feel confident in revealing her true nature.

"Perhaps you ought to get another skill," MacArthur said, eyes glinting, "since Maisie is also able to lift heavy objects and puts up with all sorts of dreadful things. And as you say, she can cook."

Maisie snorted, then shot Jamie an apologetic look while covering her grin with one hand.

"Aye," Jamie muttered, sending the keepers narrow-eyed glares. "Tell me, we have any need for a chorus of one?"

"Oh, god," MacArthur groaned, and quickly spooned the rest of his dinner into his mouth with as much dignity as he could preserve.

"You can sing?" Maisie asked Jamie, eyes wide.

"God," MacArthur repeated emphatically, and shoved the rest of his toast between his teeth as he stood from the table. He did not get very far before Jamie launched into a boisterous, booming melody.

Jamie had a nice voice, a little wobbly from disuse, but it firmed up as he continued. She'd heard the drunken belting of more than a few fishermen on their way home from the pub, and the layered chanting of a crew preparing to set sail, which did more to set her on edge than mesmerize her with song. Jamie could hold the tune, which was more than what most of the fishermen could claim.

Quinn didn't recognize the song, but it had all the familiar elements of the fishermen's chorus: something about a woman, the sea, and a man's longing—whether it was toward the woman or the sea was unclear. Maisie banged a fist on the table in time with the beat.

She didn't seem to know the words either, but her smile was wide, and Quinn couldn't help but grin back. Was this what nights at the pub were like for the townspeople?

Jamie finished with a great flourish, and Maisie clapped for him.

"How's that?" Jamie asked broadly, twisting on the bench to look at MacArthur's back, which provided no reply.

"Where'd you learn that song?" Maisie asked him instead, leaning forward on the table, her earlier tiredness forgotten. "I haven't heard it before, though it sounds familiar."

"Picked it up when I left home, couldn't tell you when or where," Jamie said, scratching under his chin. "Seems like every town has their own version with the same contents."

"Makes sense, I suppose," Maisie said. She leaned over to catch a glimpse of the still silent MacArthur and shot Jamie a conspiratorial look. "I take it Mr. MacArthur's heard your singing before?"

"Often," Jamie told her. "Till he so kindly reminded me that it was not a requirement of my role."

"Which is still true," MacArthur informed him from the sink. But he had done nothing to stop Jamie from finishing his song, Quinn noticed. Jamie sent MacArthur's back a cheeky grin.

"Cooking wasn't a requirement for me," Maisie said. "Nor baking for you, and you can't deny it's a skill. I certainly don't share it."

"The usefulness of each is debatable," MacArthur said, wiping his hand on the spare dishcloth.

"Perhaps Jamie may take the night off to consider other, *practical* skills he may acquire," MacArthur declared. "With the weather settled and fine for now, I will be taking the evening to catch up on sleep. Ms. Garrow, please do the same. Nothing in the charts for tomorrow, as it stands."

He dipped his head at Quinn. "Good night."

Maisie waited for the door to snap shut behind MacArthur before knocking her knuckles on the table, in the same rhythm she had followed while Jamie sang. "You really don't remember where you learned that song?"

Jamie turned on the bench to stretch out his long legs, wincing as something in his back popped at the motion. The light from the fire played over his beard and thick eyebrows, which drew together in thought. His teasing grin had faded once MacArthur left the room.

"Must have picked it up from someone," he said. He scratched a hand through the bristly hair on his throat. "But can't remember who, or where, really. Probably in a pub."

"Did you travel a lot before you came here?" Quinn asked him. She wondered what other songs or stories of the sea Jamie could have picked up.

His eyes flickered toward her, then away again. "A fair bit. Never went anywhere worth the time it would take to talk about it until I got the job here."

"But you made sure to visit the pub wherever you went, hmm?" Maisie ribbed, eyes light.

"Of course," Jamie said. "Best place to go when you're new to a place. Can always find someone willing to lift up the town's skirts and show you its secrets."

"That's a horrible comparison." Maisie frowned. "You're not in a pub now, remember."

She turned to Quinn while Jamie sucked his teeth. "Did you ever visit the pub in town? Had a slimy name, didn't it?"

"The Slippery Eel," Quinn offered. "And I never went."

Maisie nodded. "I never got to go when I was home either. Managed to stop in a few on my way to the coast, though." She grinned. "Should have known they'd be full of men."

Quinn thought of Ronnie, and then remembered the last time she'd seen the town's barkeep.

"There were some policemen at the Eel a while ago," she said. "Seems like they know where to look for town secrets, too."

She'd spoken only in the hopes of relating one piece of her human life to the keepers, but it was like she'd dropped an anchor on the conversation. Maisie went still. Jamie's eyes sharpened, all the teasing joviality gone from his face. The feeling was similar to Quinn's first interactions with humans after Owen had stolen her pelt—she'd said something wrong and suddenly everyone was looking at her with scorn in their eyes.

"That so," Jamie muttered, the glow of the fire making his pupils flicker. "Did you hear what they were asking about?"

Quinn curled her tongue behind her teeth. "Not really."

But she also remembered when she had followed Maisie and Jamie to the docks, what now seemed like a lifetime ago. Before Owen had struck her with his spear, she'd been listening as the dock foreman warned the keepers about some men poking their noses in the town's business. Looking for a murder suspect, Quinn recalled. Jamie had gone oddly silent that day, too, as well as when he had accidentally mentioned the investigators to MacArthur the night Maisie brought Quinn to the lighthouse.

But who was she to press him for answers? Her secrets were shoved into Maisie's bottom dresser drawer, and she wasn't about to pull them out at the slightest prodding. He'd questioned her about living in the town but hadn't pushed the subject since MacArthur firmly cut off that conversation. While he seemed to have his suspicions about her, he had tended her wound and made no objection to her staying in his home.

Perhaps he, like Maisie, was trying to sink his past in the waters between the mainland and the lighthouse's island.

Maisie was running the edge of her thumbnail along the wood grain of the table.

"We're cut off from all of that here. This lighthouse is like nowhere else," she said absently, seeming to agree with Jamie's earlier statement.

Jamie hummed. Quinn looked between the two keepers, wondering what these two humans would have run away from to make this isolated island so desirable. Humans, like selkies, preferred to live in herds, large social groups that depended on one another for protection, food, and care. But these three humans had left that all behind.

After a few quiet moments with only the fire crackling in the hearth, Maisie shifted to look at Quinn.

"Well," she said, "sleep, then? Best follow MacArthur's orders. If he says it'll be calm tonight, it'll be calm."

Quinn nodded at her, swinging her leg over the bench to take Maisie's proffered shoulder.

Maisie bid good night to Jamie, who mumbled something in return, but he stayed seated at the empty table while Quinn and Maisie were swallowed up by the dark hallway.

THE FOLLOWING AFTERNOON, AFTER Jamie checked Quinn's wound again and found whatever he saw satisfactory before applying more salve and a new bandage, Maisie brought Quinn up to the lighthouse's beacon.

The lighthouse tower was echoing and hollow from the ground level, and Quinn craned her neck to stare up into the empty space. Narrow, slit-like windows let in the weak sunlight to illuminate the twisting iron stairs, but the light did little to warm the space. The swept floor beneath Quinn's bare feet was cool.

"Are you sure you're up for it?" Maisie asked her for the second time.

"I want to see it," Quinn said, also for the second time. "From the inside."

"All right."

Maisie led her to the base of the stairs, and Quinn reached out to grip the iron railing. The metal was even colder than the floor.

Maisie and Jamie had done more work outside that morning, and Maisie had abandoned her coat at some point and rolled up the sleeves of her sweater to bare her pale, heavily freckled forearms. Quinn kept hold of one of Maisie's hands as the keeper started up the stairs, and she kept shifting her gaze between her feet on the steps and Maisie's arm. The bone of

Maisie's wrist jutted out prominently in a way that made Quinn want to touch her fingers to it, though she wasn't sure why.

With Quinn taking the stairs one at a time, their progress was exceedingly slow, but Maisie kept pace with her easily. When they were perhaps halfway up the tower, Maisie started chattering, as Quinn had come to notice Maisie often did when a silence laid on too thick for her taste.

"The lighthouse has only been operating for about four years," she told Quinn. "Mr. MacArthur was the first person the board hired to work here, and he's been here ever since. From what Jamie's told me, he had a bit to say to the board when he first arrived, bothering them to get the most recent machinery for the beacon, reporting every little issue with the building. Seems that if this was to be his lighthouse, he wanted it operating as best it could. Even when Jamie got here, I think it'll be just over a year and a half now, MacArthur was very specific about who he wanted working in his lighthouse."

They were nearing the top of the stairs, but Quinn's foot was beginning to cramp from the stiff position she was keeping it in. She squeezed Maisie's hand, and Maisie stopped at once. She gave Quinn an assessing look, and Quinn shook her head.

"Keep talking."

"Okay," Maisie said, letting Quinn rest for a moment. "So, MacArthur was very specific about his keepers, right? Except his specifications had nothing to do with background, or experience, like you'd think. He wanted people who would dedicate everything to the job. He didn't want you to have a wife back on the mainland, distracting you from your work. He wanted people who could come out to this chunk of rock in the middle of the ocean and give everything to the lighthouse."

Maisie paused again when Quinn drew herself up and put her foot on the next step. They walked quietly for a few moments as Maisie made sure Quinn wasn't pushing herself too hard, and the stairs creaked beneath their feet.

"But MacArthur got what he wanted," Maisie said, checking over her shoulder to see how many steps were left. "He got Jamie, who's built like an ox and works just as hard, with nothing tying him to the mainland. And then me."

Quinn, who was trying to focus on her breathing to distract from the spiking complaints from her foot, flicked Maisie a glance. A weak smile stretched over Maisie's lips, but her eyes were somber.

"I left my old life behind and needed somewhere to start anew. This lighthouse was the perfect place."

They had finally reached the top of the stairs. A trapdoor was already propped open, and Maisie helped Quinn navigate the final few steps into the beacon room. When she was sure of her footing on the wooden floor, Quinn looked up.

They were surrounded by windows on all sides. Quinn had been imagining the view from the little kitchen window in Owen's house, her small escape to the ocean for so many years, but this was worlds apart. The late afternoon sun beamed into the west bank of windows and warmed the small space. Squinting against the brightness, Quinn turned on her heel to look over endless stretches of ocean spilling out in every direction. With a nearly clear sky, the water was a magnificent blue, the color shifting with the movement of the waves. The sight made Quinn's breath catch in her throat.

Maisie heard the noise, and this time her smile was broad and genuine.

"Gorgeous, isn't it?"

Quinn nodded. She couldn't find the words to tell Maisie how overwhelmed she was by the sight of her ocean surrounding her. She gripped Maisie's fingers tightly instead, and Maisie squeezed back. The warmth of Maisie's palm against hers was so starkly different from how Owen's hands had felt, and instead of shying away from the touch, Quinn found herself leaning into it. As she blinked against the brightness of the sun and Maisie's smile, something sparked in her chest.

"We so rarely get to see it like this," Maisie told her. "With a clear sky and sun."

They stood like that for a few long minutes. Quinn tried to soak in every bit of it.

When her heartbeat finally slowed—from the view or for a different reason, she wasn't sure—Quinn looked around the rest of the room.

The unlit beacon sat in the middle of the circular room like a mechanical beast, just waiting to be woken. There was little else in the room. With just enough space for Maisie and Quinn to stand shoulder to shoulder between the glass and the beacon, it was smaller than Quinn had thought it would be.

"Come this way," Maisie said, tugging on Quinn's hand. She helped Quinn around the beacon, the wooden floor sounding off a hollow thump every time she let her weight fall on her good foot, until they came to a section of the windows that was actually a door. Maisie unlatched it and stepped out onto a small deck surrounded by a thin railing.

Quinn hesitated in the doorway.

The lighthouse's beacon room was very high in the air, on top of an already very steep cliff, and the distance between Quinn and the ocean suddenly loomed.

Maisie squeezed her hand again and shifted her head so that Quinn was looking at her instead of the water.

"It's all right," she said softly. The wind's fingers found their way into Maisie's hair, sending the red strands fluttering around and across her face, but her bright green eyes caught and held Quinn's attention. "I've got you."

And Quinn knew this was the truth. She had placed her trust in Maisie and found herself saved over and over again. Quinn inhaled sharply through her nose and stepped outside.

It was significantly colder outside of the beacon room, with the full force of the wind and the winter chill easily cutting through Quinn's thick sweater and nipping at her bare feet, but she hardly noticed. Without the protection of the glass, the sounds and smell of the ocean welled up around her.

She reached out and gripped the rail with her free hand to steady herself.

"I remember when I first got to see this," Maisie told her, the words registering to Quinn as if they were spoken far away. "I never wanted to go down."

Quinn was filled with a feeling she had only experienced a few times in her youth, when she had grown into her fins and had been able to swim freely with the other young selkies in the herd, darting through open water with nothing to stop them. She remembered how they had leaped above the surface just for the sheer joy of the feeling of being weightless for a mere second.

Quinn felt a glimmer of that weightlessness now. If she let go of the railing, she thought the next breeze could pick her right up off the balcony. Perhaps it would be enough to bring Maisie with her.

Maisie curled her free hand around the railing as well.

"It's funny," she said. "We're on an island with no way to leave except by boat, and even standing here, there's nowhere to go except back down those stairs, and yet, looking out at all of this, it feels like freedom."

Something in Quinn's chest stuttered.

"I had forgotten what freedom felt like," she told Maisie, who tore her eyes away from the horizon to look at Quinn while she spoke. The afternoon sun made her freckles burn bright gold. "For seven years I was trapped in a life that wasn't mine to live. Even the parts I came to care about were only momentary flashes of light through the bars of the cage. But then my daughter handed my pelt back to me. She handed me my freedom."

Quinn blinked, the words catching in her throat.

"I don't want to ever give it up again."

Maisie released Quinn's hand, and Quinn swayed, suddenly untethered, but then Maisie slid her arm around Quinn's shoulder and cupped Quinn's head with her fingers. Quinn allowed herself to be pulled into a half hug, eyes wide, her forehead resting on the curve between Maisie's head and shoulder. She could see the hollow of Maisie's throat over the neck of her sweater.

"We won't let them take it from us," Maisie told her. "Our freedom is in our hands now."

She spoke the words as if they were carved into stone. Her confidence, and the steadiness of her breath that Quinn could feel when she was tucked in close to Maisie's chest, made Quinn believe her.

Quinn closed her eyes and let the feelings warm her like the afternoon sun.

Chapter Fifteen

NOW

THE ROUTINE OF THE lighthouse was dictated by how favorable the weather was that day. When there was no rain, Jamie and Maisie worked outside and cleaned up from previous storms or prepared for the next one. When it did rain, the long night shifts kicked in so that someone was always awake to mind the beacon.

But no matter what the weather was, Quinn scarcely saw MacArthur outside of mealtimes. She had felt his considering, analytical gaze on her during dinner, but whenever she looked back at him his eyes were focused elsewhere.

The way he observed her was not like the way some men in the town had watched her, even though she was known as Owen's wife. It didn't leave her with the prickly feeling that those other men's stares had left on her like a rash.

She wished MacArthur would just ask the questions he had on his mind. Maybe her answers could resolve any remaining reservations he had about letting her stay.

Maisie had no reservations about asking Quinn questions. Quinn had told her the names of her children, at Maisie's request, and a little about what it had been like for Quinn to raise them. This had occurred two evenings ago when a clear night released Maisie from beacon duty and she had propped her head on the edge of her bed to gaze down at Quinn on her pelt, the moonlight just strong enough for Quinn to make out the shine of her eyes.

In return, Maisie had told Quinn about her two brothers. How she had grown up jealous of all the things they were allowed to do, while she was made to stay at home and help their mother. How they had once helped her sneak out of the house and into their father's workshop where the boys apprenticed, and they had shown her how they worked with their hands, and her clever fingers were just as deft with iron as they were with a paring knife.

She told Quinn how all three of them had been told off by their mother when Maisie came home with soot from the furnace on her clothes, a burn on her pinky, and a grin on her face.

Maisie had seemed glad to be able to talk about her family. She had kept her past quiet while working at the lighthouse under a false name, but now she shared it with Quinn, and Quinn felt compelled to talk about her family in return.

She told Maisie about her mother. How she had told Quinn stories and warned her about the dangers of humans.

"If only I'd listened to her," Quinn said, shifting on her pelt to run her fingers through the fur.

Maisie was silent for a moment, then said, "I know you've suffered a lot since you've been human, but I'm glad I got to meet you. Maybe"—she yawned—"in another life, I could have found you first."

Quinn let that settle over her like a second blanket, and took a long while to fall asleep after Maisie finally dozed off.

MacArthur was not so easy. Jamie was open, and still a bit thoughtless sometimes but quick to apologize, in his conversations with Quinn. She could see the way Jamie sidestepped around giving details of his own family with jokes and toothless biting remarks. It was hard to fault him, when Quinn did the same. She was glad at least that Jamie seemed to be softening around her.

But MacArthur continued to hold himself at a distance. Quinn would have been glad for this when she was living in town under Owen's roof, but now, while she had to seek shelter amongst humans, MacArthur's distance made her nervous. It reminded her of the way a pod of orcas would hunt, observing their prey from afar before closing in.

Quinn would not be an unsuspecting victim.

The days in the lighthouse stretched, and December enveloped the island with little fanfare. The next time a storm rolled in—this one not caused by Quinn—and the heavy clouds on the horizon promised to last through the night, Quinn caught MacArthur before he could leave the dinner table.

"Could I see how you track the storms?" Quinn asked.

Half out of his seat, MacArthur appraised her. He wore a thick sweater over his collared shirt tonight in deference to the chill that seeped into the building despite the huge fire at their backs, and he had rolled the sleeve up to lay flat against his upper arm.

Jamie and Maisie, who had been arguing over who got

the larger half of the last piece of bread, looked between Mac-Arthur and Quinn with open curiosity. Maisie had told Quinn about the long nights she had spent in MacArthur's office, though she'd been quickly confused by his rapid calculations and mapping of charts. She preferred the physical work, as did Jamie.

"I could do it, if need be," Maisie had told her. "But I don't get the same satisfaction from it as Mr. MacArthur does."

The kitchen window shuddered against the torrent of rain as Quinn waited for MacArthur to respond.

"You're interested in my weather mapping?" he asked finally.

Quinn nodded. "I'd like to see how it's done." She'd seen how MacArthur had relaxed when he spoke about his work. And it was the only reason she could come up with to give her an excuse to get into MacArthur's office. Years of living with Owen and searching for her pelt had made her suspicious of closed-off rooms.

"You trying to steal all of MacArthur's secrets?" Jamie prodded jovially, though his eyes were calculating. Maisie rolled her eyes at him but Quinn worried the inside of her lip at Jamie's attention.

"It's rather tedious work," MacArthur warned her, his eyebrows drawing together and forming a wrinkle on his forehead.

"So's watching me and Jamie put a fresh coat of paint on the walls," Maisie piped up, having snatched the larger piece of bread while Jamie was distracted and grinning in victory. Jamie stuck his lip out at her. "But she sat and watched us do just that yesterday."

"I see your point," MacArthur told Maisie, stepping away

from the table. He came around and stood beside Quinn. "You are certain? I'll need Maisie with the beacon tonight."

Quinn realized that he was asking if she would be all right being alone with him while Maisie was working.

"Yes," she told him. Her only concern was her pelt, but it was tucked away in Maisie's room, where it had been undisturbed except when Quinn retrieved it each night to sleep.

MacArthur nodded once and held out his hand. After a moment's hesitation, she gripped his forearm and allowed him to help her to her feet. Her injury was healing under Jamie's constant assessment, but he still advised her to be careful about putting weight on the wound.

MacArthur's arm was stiff under her fingers, but he was carefully considerate with her as they left the kitchen and headed toward his office.

"Night, Quinn!" Maisie called through a mouthful of bread.

The short stairway up to MacArthur's office was too narrow to go up side by side, and when MacArthur seemed to second-guess what he should do, Quinn released his arm and motioned him up.

"I can use the wall," she told him.

"Right," he said, and climbed up with light footsteps. The stairway cut to the left at a sharp angle, and she heard him open a door that flooded the hall with light.

She followed as quickly as she could and found herself in a surprisingly spacious office. A large wooden desk was pushed up to the wall beneath a wide window that gave Quinn a clear view of the swirling storm. The organized papers, tools, and books on the desk were illuminated by an oil lamp.

Two other oil lamps hung from the wall and shone brightly

over a towering bookcase that contained rows and rows of bound, title-less volumes, an open cabinet that contained intricate metal tools and spyglasses, and a large map pasted over the wall opposite the window. There was one chair pushed under the desk and, as Maisie had promised, a camp bed folded in the corner.

MacArthur went to a corner of the room and began shifting handfuls of books off a second chair that Quinn hadn't seen. Once the books were cleared off, he carried the chair over to the desk and motioned for her to sit.

"Well," he said when she was seated, "I suppose I can just explain what I'm currently working on and go from there."

He pulled out his own chair and sat, pulling apart his neat stacks of papers and unfolding more maps. Quinn tilted her head to better see the maps and saw what looked to be the coastline of the mainland in varying distances, with the lighthouse's island circled and noted with coordinates in even, tight handwriting.

"Tonight's storm follows the pattern of weather that I've been tracking for this season," MacArthur began. His speech was carefully controlled, as was every other part of his person, but Quinn could hear a bit of excitement behind the words. "It's based off past weather records that I kept from every year since I came to work at this lighthouse, as well as the path of the ocean currents and other natural factors."

He tugged a book out from under a stack and found the marker with a finger, flipping it open. Squinting at the page, he opened a shallow drawer and took out a pair of wire-framed glasses, placing them on his nose.

Quinn could make out a cramped *21ˢᵗ November, 1898,* in

the same handwriting as that on the maps. The journal was full of that tidy handwriting, with each day receiving at least one large paragraph describing the weather conditions. Days with severe weather could warrant three paragraphs or more.

"These are thorough," Quinn remarked.

MacArthur nodded. "I include everything, as anything could be useful when trying to predict weather patterns in the future. I also have journals that have notes on the status of the island and the lighthouse," he told her, flicking his fingers at the bookcase packed tight with bound books. "When my predictions are correct, like they were for this storm, I also record that, now, so that I will know what worked."

He slid one of the maps out and laid it in front of Quinn, smoothing his hand over the yellowing paper.

"The storm is moving this direction," he told her, drawing a line with his finger. "We can expect the heaviest rainfall in the early hours of the morning, and to see the tail end of the storm tomorrow night at the earliest."

MacArthur talked her through his methods for tracking the storms, using his one hand to fiddle with the metal tools and showing her how to measure distances on the map, then how to anticipate the amount of time that the storm would take to pass.

Even while he was speaking, MacArthur would consider the storm outside the window and reach for one of his many sharpened pencils to make a note in the current log.

Quinn barely had to say anything to prompt MacArthur to keep going, a few hums or an inquisitive noise enough to convince him that she was listening. And she was listening. It was interesting to hear how the humans had devised strategies to follow the patterns of nature, which her herd had been able to figure out through instinct and the passed-down knowledge from their elders.

It was not, however, giving her any indication that Mac-Arthur had something to hide. His speech, the office, and the voluminous but orderly collection of journals only showed Quinn that he was a man dedicated to his work. Owen, who had become a fisherman despite growing up as a farmer, had not spoken of his job this way. It was only a means to an end, a step he had to take to achieve the life he dreamed about, with another step including Quinn's capture.

At one point, MacArthur went quiet as he stood and went to the bookshelf to retrieve another journal, and was quickly skimming through the days. Quinn took the opportunity to study one of the maps a bit more closely without the tools.

The map showed not only the island and the mainland, but the rest of the country as well, which included dozens of islands of varying size that emerged from the ocean in jagged pieces. Quinn leaned forward, placing tentative fingers on the paper, and traced the path she remembered following in her childhood. As she dragged her fingertip down the line where land met water, she counted how many human towns she ran across. There were many. Humans populated so many places on the coastline, Quinn was amazed that the herd had been able to find safe places to rest during their journeys.

Of course, years had passed since Quinn traveled with the herd. This lighthouse was only four years old. Some of these towns could have been built in the time she was trapped on land.

"Are you looking for something?"

Quinn quickly drew her hand back from the map. MacArthur

was watching her again, in the way that made her think he was seeing more than he let on.

"No," she said, "I've just never seen it like this."

"The country?"

"Any of it," Quinn said. She paused, considering how to phrase her next words. "I traveled a lot as a child, but I wouldn't be able to point to the places I've been on this map. And when I was living in the town"—she flicked him a glance—"it seems like everything changed. Maybe I wouldn't even recognize the places I grew up in."

MacArthur settled back in his chair. He nudged his glasses up his nose with one finger.

"I also traveled when I was younger," he said. Quinn's pulse jumped, but she kept her face steady as MacArthur finally divulged something to her. "I worked on a trading ship that traversed oceans. I did navigation, and weather prediction, much as I do now, and it seemed that every few months we had to update our maps. I'd seen so much of the world, and yet it continued changing, so I could return to a place I'd visited a year before and it would be completely new. It was wonderful," he said. "But it was also frightening."

Lightning crashed outside, illuminating the window with a bright white light that flooded over the crowded desk and MacArthur's face.

"Frightening?" Quinn asked.

MacArthur's hand was balled in his lap, but he uncurled and flexed his fingers, seemingly unconscious of the movement.

"I was frightened to learn how inconsequential I was in the world, I suppose," he said softly. "Everything keeps changing, with or without you there."

"Is that why you don't travel anymore?" Quinn guessed. "Why you started working here?"

MacArthur, who always held himself rigidly, as if he were bracing for a fierce gale to try to knock him off his feet, tensed further. Had she pried too far?

"No," he eventually answered, "that is not why. I found my situation drastically changed and needed a new type of work to dedicate myself to."

Quinn didn't look at MacArthur's missing forearm, but she was very aware of its absence.

"I can understand the need for a drastic change," Quinn tried, shifting her injured foot meaningfully. "I was trying to leave even before my husband did this to me. If it wasn't for Maisie, I don't know if I'd have the choice to walk away again. But I'm glad I did."

MacArthur met her gaze steadily.

"Can I ask," Quinn risked, "how you lost your arm?"

She was playing a bit unfairly, levering her history with her husband for a piece of MacArthur's past. But she wanted to understand more about the head keeper and hopefully learn what made him different from the humans she knew in town. She wanted to know that Maisie's trust in MacArthur was earned.

MacArthur flexed his fingers again. His chair creaked as he adjusted his seat, and Quinn let his silence draw out, not willing to break it before he did.

"I don't speak of it often," he said. "I've told Jamie the bare bones, and perhaps he's passed that on to Ms. Garrow, but otherwise—" He flicked his fingers, as if shooing away a pest.

"I could ask Maisie," Quinn said, "but I'd rather hear it from you."

"Why?"

"It's your story," she said. "You should be the one to tell it."

MacArthur removed his glasses and set them on the table, rubbing at the slightly red, twinned indents they left behind on his nose.

"It is not much of a story," he warned her. She waited him out again. Trusting her with his past was more than an inconvenient guest would warrant, but she had to let him make the choice.

"But all right," he began, and Quinn quickly smothered a victorious grin. "As I said, I was a navigator for a trading ship. We were making a return journey after many months abroad, and delays in our schedule meant that we were arriving in spring, and I instructed the captain that we should take a longer route to avoid the rains sweeping up from the lower coast.

"He trusted my predictions, as did I, and we set a course to sail straight up and around the outlying islands so that we could enter in protected waters. I stayed up that night, at the helm."

MacArthur paused to write something in the logbook before continuing.

"My predictions were wrong. Suddenly, a storm swept in, sending our ship heaving through towering waves. We could scarcely see a meter in any direction. The crew were scrambling from the sleeping quarters to get the sails under control. Our cargo was weighing us down.

"I didn't know it at the time, but we passed right by this island," MacArthur told her. "The storm carried us across kilometers of rough ocean until the mainland got in the way. We wrecked on the cliffs. The crew and the captain all drowned, and I nearly with them. I'd been thrown from the ship when it struck the rocks and was crushed against the cliffs. I don't remember how it happened, but when I woke, I was in a hospital, my entire body was a bruise, and my arm was gone."

He lifted his left upper arm, eyes glazed, staring at a forearm and hand that weren't there.

"I recovered as well as I could, and searched for work. But of course, few ships can offer jobs to men with only one arm, even if most of my work is on paper. Then, a few years later, I heard that they were installing a lighthouse here, on this island. I applied immediately. I thought that if there had been a beacon shining that night, perhaps I could have done something sooner, turned us away before we wrecked…"

MacArthur trailed off. There was nothing Quinn could say in response to his story. She was startled at how willingly the words flooded out of him after so many days of seeing MacArthur as an unbreakable dam, but it was as if he had simply been waiting for someone to ask and be patient enough for him to answer. She could understand his protectiveness of the lighthouse now, and of the people who worked there. He saw the lighthouse and its beacon as redemption.

MacArthur cleared his throat. "Well, that is the story. It occurred seven years ago, and I'm very used to only having one hand to work now."

Quinn blinked a few times.

"You said this happened seven years ago?" she asked.

"Yes," MacArthur said.

A sudden storm in spring, he'd said. Something that hadn't been predicted in his charts. And they'd wrecked on the cliffs beyond the island, near the town.

"Do you remember what month?" Quinn asked, leaning

forward. It was her turn to curl her fingers into a fist, trying to ignore the thrashing wind and rain outside.

"It was April," MacArthur told her.

Quinn remembered a dark, cold beach, the feeling of taking her first steps with her human feet. She remembered the sharp anger at the sight of her pelt in a man's hands. She remembered the hot tears sliding down her cheeks, mixing with the rain of a storm that cried out to her in response.

Sitting in MacArthur's warm office, Quinn felt a chill grip her spine.

There was a chance she was wrong. She had no way to be sure of the exact day that Owen had taken her pelt, and MacArthur hadn't been specific about it either. In those first few weeks, Quinn had summoned all kinds of storms as she struggled to adapt to the weight of her human body and the weight of Owen's entrapment.

But deep in her heart, Quinn knew this was no coincidence. MacArthur had said the storm had come out of nowhere, and it was strong enough to throw his ship against the cliffs and smash it to pieces. The mainland didn't see storms like that every day.

It had been Quinn's storm that resulted in the ruin of MacArthur's ship. Her storm, responding to her despair at losing her pelt, had wrecked his ship and resulted in MacArthur losing his arm.

MacArthur was watching her again. He didn't have to look hard to notice how stiff Quinn had suddenly become, how she was curling her fingers in her lap, desperately trying to seize the roiling emotions that were bubbling up like a geyser.

She couldn't let him figure out that she was responsible for the storm that overturned his life and took his hand from him. Quinn couldn't let him figure out the effect she had on the weather.

He had already warned her that sheltering her in the lighthouse put each of the keepers at risk. If he knew just how dangerous she really was, he would have every reason to change his mind about letting her stay there.

And Maisie—she couldn't let Maisie know, either. She already knew too much about who Quinn really was, and Maisie cared about MacArthur. He had offered Maisie the shelter she needed to leave her old life behind. If Maisie found out that it was Quinn's fault MacArthur had suffered so much, Quinn didn't think that Maisie would be able to forgive her. Maisie would side with the humans she had placed her trust in. Quinn was just a selkie who wielded her trust like a tool.

"Ms. Quinn," MacArthur said, the words swimming in Quinn's ears. "Quinn, are you all right?"

Quinn sucked in a sharp breath. She couldn't control the fear that had flooded her at the thought of losing Maisie's trust, of losing the safety that these three humans had strung up around her because of her own actions. The thought of facing Maisie's anger, of MacArthur's scorn, frightened her more than Owen ever had.

Outside, the storm felt her fear, and responded.

A deafening crash made MacArthur leap to his feet. The thunder crack was louder than anything Quinn had ever heard, and it raised goose bumps along her arms.

"My god," MacArthur exclaimed. "That could have hit the tower."

He started to step away and then paused.

"Quinn, I need to go up and check on Maisie," he said, speaking loudly to be heard over the racket of the storm. "Are you all right? Should I get Jamie?"

Trying to control the rapid rise and fall of her chest, Quinn pressed her lips in a tight line and shook her head.

"I'm fine," she gasped unconvincingly. The last thing she wanted was to have Jamie watching over her as she spiraled. "Go. Help Maisie."

MacArthur hesitated. Uncurling her fingers, Quinn made a shooing motion at him.

Obediently, MacArthur took one step toward the door, but his face was still full of calculated concern.

"I'll send Maisie down to help you once I'm certain the beacon is all right," he told her, and then turned away and hurried out the door before she could refuse.

Quinn shut her eyes and tried to slow her breathing. If she could calm down, maybe the storm would too.

The chair creaked under her weight as Quinn leaned forward, gripping her knees. The thick fabric of her pants creased under her hold. Except they weren't her pants, they were Maisie's. Everything she wore she had borrowed from Maisie. She had given Quinn so much, and Quinn had provided only pieces of the truth in return.

How could Quinn stay here, knowing the pain that she had inflicted on MacArthur, and the further pain she could inflict on Maisie, and Jamie, by association? She pressed her hand to her chest as she remembered all of the hatred she'd felt for Owen, for the wives of the town, for all the humans who had made her life miserable while she was trapped on land. She had never been in a position to hurt them back. But now, with MacArthur's story laid in her hands like a curse, Quinn ached at the thought that her storms had hurt someone who was innocent in her suffering.

She'd had thoughts of taking her vengeance out on any human, but like the moment on the beach when Quinn quailed at the idea of taking Maisie by the ankle and dragging her to the depths, in her heart she knew that she could not be so purposefully cruel. But she had caused harm even before she knew she had the power to do so.

Jamie had been right to be suspicious of Quinn. Even if her influence over the storms wasn't enough, Owen would still be looking for her. If Owen came here looking for her again, he was a risk to Maisie's life, and Jamie's and MacArthur's for harboring her.

But then again, how could she leave now? She couldn't put on her pelt and become a seal. She was injured and had nowhere to go.

And, she thought desperately, she didn't want to leave Maisie. She'd pushed down the feelings that had been steadily building, like a wave gaining strength from underwater currents, but she wouldn't be able to stop it from breaking over her.

Her feelings for Maisie scared her more than anything else. How could she care about a human that way, after everything she'd gone through? How could she even consider it? Her place was in the ocean, with her pelt around her. She was a selkie. Like her mother told her, she needed to stay as far away from humans as she could. Caring for one was out of the question.

But Quinn had already failed her mother once.

Long minutes dragged by, and neither MacArthur nor Maisie came to the office for her.

Quinn eventually steadied her breathing and set her jaw. She stood, using the desk for support, and shuffled out of MacArthur's office and down the hall. It was nearly pitch black in the windowless hallway, so Quinn felt along the wall.

In Maisie's room, she knelt by the dresser and unearthed her pelt. She didn't lay it out on the floor, instead curling up with her back leaning against Maisie's bed and the pelt tucked into her chest with her knees pulled in tight. The fur glinted in the flashes of lightning through the window.

Maisie found her like that, moments or perhaps hours later. It was still dark outside, but the storm had lessened, and it seemed that MacArthur had finally sent Maisie to come looking for her.

Quinn didn't move when the door opened or when Maisie's soft footsteps came to stop in front of her. She didn't look up when Maisie crouched down. Only when Maisie placed a hand on Quinn's knee, her fingers impossibly warm even through the fabric, did Quinn drag her gaze up from the floor.

"Quinn?" Maisie asked, perhaps after multiple tries.

Quinn searched her eyes for something that would tell her what to do. Should she tell Maisie everything, and hope that her honesty was enough to redeem the destruction Quinn had wrought? Or did she keep quiet, and hold on to the little bubble of safety that Maisie had made for her for a little while longer?

"I'm tired," she told Maisie.

Maisie nodded, accepting this as all she would get out of Quinn.

"Do you want—" she started, then stopped, and tried again.

"You could sleep on the bed, if you want. It's better than the floor."

Quinn was exhausted, and she could feel every bit of resistance crumbling beneath her fingers. She was very aware of Maisie's hand on her knee.

"With you?" Quinn asked.

It was a terrible idea. Her heart was pounding loudly in her ears again as she waited for Maisie's answer.

"If you want," Maisie said again, and Quinn thought her voice held just as much emotion as she was feeling.

Quinn nodded. She unfolded from her cramped position, her legs stiff and protesting, and climbed onto the bed with her pelt.

The bed was not very wide, and Quinn took up quite a bit of room. But Maisie didn't seem to mind. She was staring at Quinn with her mouth slightly parted. Quinn wondered what words had gotten lost on their way past her lips.

Then Maisie blinked and stood, stripping off her outer layers. When she joined Quinn, the mattress dipped, and Quinn rolled onto her side so that she and Maisie were facing each other.

Maisie's hair was slightly damp, the strands clinging together and scattering across the pillow like thin tendrils of seagrass. Quinn clutched her pelt tighter to stop herself from reaching out to twine the hair around her fingers.

Maisie didn't try to ask Quinn anything, though Quinn was sure MacArthur must have mentioned something when he sent Maisie to her.

"The beacon?" Quinn asked instead.

Maisie shook her head slightly. "It's fine. The storm calmed down enough that MacArthur wasn't concerned about it going out before morning. We're safe for tonight."

Quinn wished that were true. She wished that all Maisie had to worry about was an unpredictable storm and keeping a lamp lit for passing ships.

With the way they were lying, on their sides, facing each other, and Quinn's pelt trapped in her arms, this was the closest Maisie had ever been to it. In all this time, she had never touched it.

When Quinn shifted, she drew Maisie's eyes down to the fur tucked against her chest. Maisie started to draw back, but Quinn stopped her by reaching across the small space between them and taking one of Maisie's hands in hers. Quinn curled her fingers across Maisie's and nudged her forward.

Maisie's eyes were wide, and she resisted a little until Quinn pushed her again. When Maisie's fingers brushed the fur of her pelt, Quinn sighed. This was something she could give to Maisie. It was an apology and a plea, though Maisie didn't know of either.

Maisie sank her fingers into the thick fur. It was nothing like what Quinn had felt when she had seen Owen holding her pelt on that cold beach. The wrongness of it, the unnatural feeling at the sight of her pelt in the hands of a strange human, none of that came over her now. Perhaps it was because the pelt was still in Quinn's arms. Or perhaps it was because Maisie was not just any human.

Combing her fingers through the thick fur, a frown creased Maisie's brow.

"I thought it would be softer than this," she whispered. Then she blinked up at Quinn. "Sorry, is that rude?"

And Quinn laughed. The fist around her heart loosened, a feeling she had come to expect when she was around Maisie. It was a dangerous feeling to depend on.

"It keeps me warm," she told Maisie. "It may be rough on the outside, but that is what keeps me safe."

Maisie smiled. "How fitting."

She continued to pet the fur of Quinn's pelt for a few moments, despite her claim, and Quinn relaxed with the motion.

There was nothing she could do about her situation right now. She could face it tomorrow.

"Thank you," Maisie told her belatedly. When Quinn raised her eyebrows, she clarified, "For trusting me with this."

Even if Maisie didn't know what Quinn was trying to give her, she was grateful for every bit of trust that Quinn spared. It should have made Quinn feel worse, made the guilt bubble back up to the surface, but Quinn stubbornly set that aside and let herself be content in that moment. She'd wanted to give Maisie a piece of her, and she had. Maisie had proved, over and over again, that she was worth Quinn's trust. Quinn would need to do the same if she wanted a chance to keep the bubble of this life in the lighthouse safe.

But the problem with bubbles, Quinn thought as she watched Maisie fall asleep with her hand still buried in Quinn's pelt, is that they were fragile. Even the slightest pressure could cause one to burst.

Chapter Sixteen

WHEN QUINN SAW MACARTHUR again the next afternoon, she passed off her panic from the night before as a result of poor sleep and stress. He accepted her excuse reluctantly but allowed her to change the subject to the lighthouse and how the beacon had held up against the storm.

"I've decided that we need to replace some of the gears in the beacon," he told her. "If we're going to have more nights like last night this winter, we need the beacon operating on fresh hardware."

"I see," Quinn said, though she didn't really know what he meant.

Maisie had gone to help Jamie after lunch, and Quinn hadn't seen her since. When MacArthur retreated back to his office, Quinn headed toward the lighthouse.

It was still raining lightly and the tall, echo-ridden stairwell was dimly lit by gray light.

Quinn ascended one step at a time. Her foot was healing

and feeling better with each passing day, but the wound still couldn't take her weight for longer than a second. She gritted her teeth and pushed onward even when her calf started cramping halfway up.

At the top of the stairwell, the trapdoor into the beacon room was closed. Quinn pushed it open with one hand and peered into the room.

Jamie and Maisie were crouched, heads tucked together, next to the beacon. A panel was open near the bottom of the machine and Maisie had her hands buried inside it. They were both intently focused on whatever she was working on.

Using both hands, Quinn pushed on the trapdoor until it creaked as it swung open on its hinges.

Jamie looked up and around at the noise.

"Quinn!" he exclaimed, and quickly stood to help her with the door.

"What are you doing?" Maisie asked, sitting back on her heels. "Did you come up the stairs by yourself?"

"Yes," Quinn said, pretending not to see Jamie's offered hand as she pulled herself up into the beacon room. He closed the trapdoor behind her.

"You shouldn't be using your foot that much," Jamie muttered.

"I'm fine," Quinn told him, then repeated when Maisie shot her a look. "I'm *fine*. Look, it's not bleeding."

"Right, 'cause that's the only thing we need to worry about," Jamie said, eyes narrowed. When Quinn just stared back at him, unashamed, he held up his hands and returned to his crouch next to Maisie.

Even with the trapdoor closed, there wasn't much room

for three people to be huddled around the beacon, especially if one of them was Jamie. Maisie pointed at an empty crate on the other side of the room.

"You can sit there," she told Quinn.

Quinn skirted around the keepers and the beacon, her fingertips resting on the glass walls for balance. Rain beaded against the glass and rolled down in tiny streams. Outside, the sky was an endless field of gray clouds sitting atop an equally dreary sea.

Flipping the crate upside down, Quinn sank down and turned back to the keepers.

Every so often, Maisie would make a soft noise and shift aside for Jamie to look at the machine, or she would ask Jamie for a different tool or pick up a new gear after extracting a dull one.

Quinn liked seeing the look of intense focus on Maisie's face and the way her eyes brightened when she finally got a new gear to fit into the machine. Maisie had told her how she loved working with her hands, and Quinn was getting to see that joy happen in real time.

When Maisie was finished, Jamie leaned back with a contented sigh.

"So, Quinn," he said, "how was your evening as MacArthur's assistant?"

Maisie flicked a glance at Quinn out of the corner of her eye, but she didn't stop her fiddling. Quinn knew she was still curious about what had happened last night and why she had been so rattled.

"Fine," Quinn said, and Maisie choked back a laugh. Quinn

pursed her lips. "It was interesting to see MacArthur's strategy for tracking the storms. His weather logs are very detailed."

"Incredibly detailed," Jamie agreed. "And extremely dry, for reporting on rain."

"They're for the board and for his future reference when charting next season's storms," Maisie said. "They're not his diary."

"Are you sure? Seems like we could track his mood based on whether there was a storm that day or not."

"What, like he's sad whenever it rains?"

"No, the opposite. He's happy because it means he gets to do his job." Jamie grinned.

Maisie scoffed but a small grin pulled at her mouth, too.

Quinn knew Jamie was only joking, but after what Mac-Arthur had told her last night, she didn't find MacArthur's obsession with tracking the storms and making careful predictions to prevent others from getting caught up in their wake as humorous as she had before.

"MacArthur told me about the night he lost his arm," she said flatly.

Maisie and Jamie stopped smiling. She put down her tools and turned toward Quinn.

"He what?"

"He told me how he lost his arm."

"Why?"

"Because I asked him," Quinn said, looking between the two keepers' wide-eyed expressions. "He said you knew already."

Jamie's jaw worked, his gaze shifting between Quinn and

Maisie. He said, "I've guessed most of it from what little he's told me. I've never had the full story out of him."

"Me either," Maisie said. "But he told you?"

Quinn nodded, and watched as the keepers shared a heavy look. Why had MacArthur told Quinn the full story when he hadn't even told his keepers? Quinn had gone into his office with the intention of digging around in MacArthur's secrets, but she hadn't expected to succeed.

Quinn had been searching for a reason to trust MacArthur. Giving her the whole story of losing his arm was the most valuable thing he had to offer, and it was apparent from Jamie's and Maisie's reactions that he had held it close to his chest all this time.

Perhaps he told Quinn because she was meant to be temporary. She wasn't meant to stay on the island and work for MacArthur for the rest of her life like Jamie and Maisie. Then again, he had assumed, correctly, that Jamie and Maisie had worked it out already. But it was a very different beast to face down the truth head-on rather than letting others piece it together while you're out of hearing range.

And hearing MacArthur's story had cost her. Quinn knew it was her storm that had sent MacArthur's ship crashing into the cliff. By trusting her with his story, MacArthur had brought her face-to-face with the realization that she could not remain around the humans without fear of ruining the lives they'd built.

Quinn clenched her fists in her lap, her knuckles pale.

She studied Maisie's expression. The keeper had known something was wrong with Quinn last night, and now she knew what Quinn and MacArthur had discussed. But Quinn hadn't told her about her influence on the weather. Maisie wouldn't be able to put together the fact that MacArthur's lost arm was her fault unless Quinn was honest with her about everything.

Quinn wanted to be honest with Maisie. She wanted Maisie to trust her. But if she did reveal everything, she knew she would lose Maisie.

"He told you about the storm, then?" Maisie asked, and Quinn flinched. Jamie was watching her steadily.

Quinn nodded, pressing her fingernails into the soft skin in the middle of her palm and willing her heartbeat to slow down. "The storm, the ship, everything."

"Well," Jamie sighed, rubbing a hand over his beard. "Ain't that something."

"I'm glad he told you," Maisie said firmly, shifting around on her knees so she could face Quinn directly. "If he trusts you with that, it's almost like he's accepted you as one of us. Like one of his keepers."

Quinn kept her face tense to keep from flinching again.

"I don't want to be one of *his*—" she snarled, a hot spike of anger lancing through her chest at the thought of belonging to another man. Even if MacArthur wasn't the same as Owen, Quinn didn't want to be just another man's possession.

Maisie's eyes went wide. "That's not what I meant! Not like that."

Quinn shook her head, pressing her palm against her throat as if she could slow her breaths by pressing down on the thin skin there.

"I just meant," Maisie said quickly, her hands flexing like she was trying to pull the right words from the air, "that you have a place here."

"And that's nothing to take lightly," Jamie added. He said it gently, but Quinn knew that he valued MacArthur's trust immensely, and wanted to make sure she knew how precious it was.

Not trusting her voice, Quinn nodded.

Maisie, unsatisfied but perhaps not willing to push her further in front of Jamie, turned back to her work on the beacon. After a moment, Jamie moved to join her, his dark head and her red one again bent toward the beacon's metal guts.

Quinn should have figured that Maisie would be happy to hear that Quinn and MacArthur were building a semblance of a relationship, as it meant that she and Quinn were no longer struggling alone in Maisie's endeavor to keep Quinn safe. But that meant it would be even more painful when Quinn eventually let her down.

Jamie, on the other hand, seemed to have dug up some of his previous suspicions. Was he wondering why MacArthur would trust the full story with Quinn, before he told Jamie? There was no way for Quinn to ask Jamie about it without causing him to raise his guard even higher.

Beyond the rain-slicked glass, Quinn could see darker clouds gathering on the horizon. For the first time, she hoped that the storm that was coming at her call wasn't stronger than the man-made tower she was sheltering in.

LATER THAT EVENING, QUINN sat at the kitchen table watching MacArthur's focus bounce between whatever he had cooking on the stove and the storm outside the dark window. Quinn had tucked her injured foot up on the bench and was toying with the end of the bandage. She'd been able to walk down the stairs of the lighthouse on her own after Maisie had finished with the beacon. Her foot ached dully, but she thought she'd be able to start walking on it without worrying about causing more damage soon.

Quinn had been restless all day. MacArthur's story hung over her like a looming predator. She wondered if it would be better for her to make the first move and tell Maisie the truth about her storms, rather than wait for the moment to strike unexpectedly.

She didn't know if Maisie had picked up on the new conflict tormenting Quinn's thoughts. After finishing her work, Maisie had gone to her room for a nap in preparation for a long night shift and had been dead to the world when Quinn poked her head in to check that her pelt was still in its place in Maisie's drawer.

The kitchen window rattled against a huge gust of wind. MacArthur glanced worriedly outside, abandoning a pot full of mostly potatoes at the stove to go peer into the dark evening, though any view the window could have offered was blurred by the storm. This one was the worst Quinn had heard since she arrived. The wind screeched and howled as it tore through the air, like a wild thing on a rampage. Quinn wasn't sure if the storm was all her doing but she worried that her turmoil had only made it worse. MacArthur hadn't seemed surprised by the arrival of this storm, but his nerves were rolling off him in waves.

Jamie was currently out in the rain, checking over the lighthouse's supplies at MacArthur's direction.

Every few moments, the steady light of the beacon would swing through the dark, a sword of light sliding through the storm. At one point MacArthur seemed to be counting quietly under his breath to make sure the beacon's rotations were consistent.

Eventually, MacArthur retreated to the stove and half-heartedly stirred at the pot.

"Was this in your charts?" Quinn finally asked.

MacArthur glanced at her over his shoulder. "It was," he said, and Quinn's shoulders relaxed a fraction. "But it's much stronger than what I would expect this early in the season."

"Hmm," Quinn mumbled in response.

MacArthur continued to check on the window as he prepared dinner, his movements careful as he switched from minding the pot on the stove to slicing open a new loaf of bread. Quinn still wanted to see his process for baking. At that thought, she pinched her ankle, sharply reminding herself that her place here was precarious.

The front door opened, the sound of the storm rising as it echoed down the hallway, before it was muffled again. Rather than hearing the shuffle of Jamie removing his coat and sodden boots, however, Quinn heard his heavy footsteps come quickly toward the kitchen. She and MacArthur were already turning toward the door when Jamie came in.

Beard dripping rain, Jamie searched the kitchen. "Where's Maisie?"

"Asleep," Quinn told him.

"What's wrong?" MacArthur asked, stepping toward Jamie with the bread knife still clutched in his hand.

"I'm worried the boat'll come loose," Jamie said quickly, already backing into the hallway. "Caught sight of the water, and it's the most unruly I've ever seen it. I need her help to secure the lines."

He disappeared just as quickly as he arrived. Quinn heard a loud knock on Maisie's door, a pause, and then the door creaked open. Jamie repeated his concerns to Maisie, and she said something in return that Quinn couldn't catch. A moment later, two sets of footsteps headed down the hallway, and the front door opened to let in a swirl of screeching wind before slamming shut.

MacArthur stood eerily still, eyes fixed on the kitchen door. He raised his hand, the handle of the knife resting in his curled grip. An aborted movement of his left arm made Quinn frown. He'd told her that the loss was years old, but Quinn was sure that MacArthur would give anything right now to have two hands to be able to go and help his keepers.

"Should we wait for them?" Quinn asked softly, but MacArthur still jerked. He nodded, returning to the counter to set down the knife and turn off the stove.

Rather than joining her at the table, however, MacArthur began to pace in front of the fire. His anxiety was bleeding into the room, and Quinn could hardly escape it, since she had her own worries. It felt like her heart had been replaced with a spiny urchin, its needles punching tiny holes in her chest with each breath.

Long minutes dragged by. Once or twice, MacArthur

made an aborted movement toward the door, but always stopped himself. She didn't know if he was attempting to go outside, or go seek solace in the journals he had so carefully constructed to help him predict moments like this, or perhaps head up to the lighthouse to watch the beacon turn himself. Each time, however, he resumed his pacing.

"Has the boat come loose before?" Quinn asked, a desperate attempt to distract him.

"Once," MacArthur told her, spinning away from the window and treading up the floors toward the door. "Jamie wasn't able to secure it by himself. There was nothing we could do but wait for the storm to die down so he could row us out on the dinghy and retrieve the boat. It wasn't this windy when that happened, so she hadn't floated too far. A few kilometers."

"A long ways to row," Quinn observed.

MacArthur spun back toward the window. "It was."

The front door banged open. MacArthur twisted around as Jamie burst into the kitchen.

"It's Maisie," he shouted, and Quinn's stomach dropped. "She's gone off the side of the cliff! She's in the water!"

Quinn thought she heard MacArthur say something to Jamie about the dinghy and the rescue line, but she was on her feet the moment Jamie had said Maisie's name. She was through the door of the kitchen before he'd finished speaking.

She heard her name among Jamie's and MacArthur's shouts behind her, but Quinn didn't hesitate. She ran flat out to Maisie's room and ripped open the bottom dresser drawer. Her pelt, dry and neatly folded, was waiting for her.

Quinn didn't let herself think. Maisie was already in the water. The storm screamed.

She ran out of the room and found Jamie and MacArthur blocking the front door as MacArthur struggled into his coat, giving Jamie hurried instructions. He turned as she came toward him, and his words died off. Her pelt was thick and warm in her hands, in plain sight.

Quinn darted around the men and ran out of the open door.

The rain instantly soaked through her clothes, licking down her hair and getting in her eyes as she sprinted down the dirt road that led to the beach. Jamie had said Maisie had gone over the side of the cliff. The path carved a scar down the island and ran along the edge of the cliff close to the beach. Even at its lowest point, it was a ten-meter drop to the water.

Quinn ran faster. Rain slid off her pelt like a hand grasping at the tide.

She remembered how she had been chewed up and spat out by the ocean when she'd tried to pull on her pelt before. She'd been terrified of the place she had used to call home. She hadn't understood why her pelt rejected her.

Quinn needed it to work this time. Maisie needed her. It had to work.

She didn't feel the path under her bare feet, the dirt slicking to mud under the downpour, she didn't feel Jamie's carefully wrapped bandage coming loose, she didn't feel anything except her heart beating loudly in her ears, her breaths fast and panicked as she sprinted to the cliff's edge. The beach was another few dozen meters down the path, but Quinn skidded to a stop at the cliff. There was something crumpled on the ground in the sodden grass.

Bending to pick it up, Quinn's heart leapt from the edge. It was Maisie's knit hat.

She searched the gray-and-blue water, the froth of the waves kicking up into the storm. It was too dark. Quinn dashed rain out of her eyes and squinted at the sea, trying to make out a shadow, a black spot in the water, something.

There! Maybe twenty meters from the dock where the keeper's boat was swaying dangerously on waves that boomed and crashed when they broke on the beach, Quinn saw something moving in the water. It rose on a wave, and Quinn could make out the shape of a head, a hand, reaching out before it was swallowed by another mountain of water.

Quinn couldn't spare the time it would take to run the rest of the way to the beach. She dropped Maisie's hat and quickly pulled off her sweater and pants, leaving them in a crumpled heap. She stepped up to the edge of the cliff with her pelt in her hands.

The wind whipped around her, tugging, pulling at her, watching as she edged forward, like the storm was curling its fingers around her and preparing to toss her into the sea. Quinn sucked in a breath and let it fill every bit of space in her lungs.

She should not be afraid of the storm. This storm had come for her. She had summoned these rains, the wind that shrieked through the sky. It was answering her call.

She did not need to be afraid. She needed to save Maisie from the storm she had created.

Quinn threw the pelt around her bare shoulders. She threw one more glance at the point where she had seen Maisie struggling in the waves, and then looked at the drop before her. Over ten meters of sheer cliff, the rocks slick and dark with rain, and then the turbulent water waiting for her below. She knew these waters. She had grown up playing in the shallows of this beach. She knew how deep the water was at the point below her; deep enough for this.

The waves slammed into the cliff side, the water clawing its way up the rocks as if reaching out to her.

Quinn jumped.

As she plummeted through the air, Quinn shut her eyes. She held the pelt tightly around her shoulders even as the wind threatened to pull it from her grasp. She imagined the feeling she'd had when she'd hit the water with the pelt around her shoulders for the first time in seven years. She remembered the joy, but she also remembered the fear. Her emotions had been tangled together, but that had not stopped her from finding her freedom again.

The moments stretched as she fell and the sounds of the screaming wind, the thundering waves, they all fell away. It was like she had already put her head underwater. The noises dulled, and she breathed deeply, feeling her heart beat confidently in her chest.

When she hit the water, her eyes flew open. It was impossibly cold. She plunged a few meters down into the inky sea, which swallowed her up like the bright sky swallowed a star.

Her limbs seized in the cold. Her fingers were stiff as stone around the edge of her pelt. She held the ends tighter. Kicking her feet, Quinn pleaded silently to the sea.

As Quinn kicked, propelling herself through the roiling

tide, a sudden warmth spread across her back. Her fur stretched and molded itself to her body, enveloping her torso, shortening her limbs to flippers, and finally slipping over her head and eyes.

Quinn was a seal again.

She didn't have time to revel in having her body back. Angling in the water, Quinn shot in the direction she had last seen Maisie. Her fin ached, the injury not totally healed, but she pushed through it.

With the waves crashing and slapping the surface, Quinn struggled to listen for Maisie. Was she calling out? Had she already slipped under the surface? It was hard for Quinn to see even with eyes made for seeing beneath the water. The gloom was full of twisting shadows and shapes, and none of them were Maisie.

She fought through the water as her muscles and lungs strained. She kept the image of Maisie thrashing at the surface in her head. If Maisie was still fighting to stay afloat, Quinn could fight just as much to get to her.

Finally, she saw movement ahead of her. Something big, waterlogged and moving against the current as she tried to keep her head above water.

Quinn put on a burst of speed. She surfaced as close to Maisie as she could get, the rain and ocean spray stinging her eyes immediately.

Maisie was gasping for breath. Her heavy clothes were weighing her down, and though she seemed to be trying to swim to shore, the waves tossed her around like she was a piece of driftwood. Quinn swam in close until Maisie's hand bumped into her fur.

Jerking in the water, Maisie gasped, "Quinn?"

Quinn barked.

"Help me," Maisie pleaded, spitting out a mouthful of water.

Quinn ducked under the surface and swam beneath Maisie, avoiding her thrashing feet, and aligned herself with Maisie's body. Maisie had been wearing boots when she left the lighthouse but she must have kicked them off in the water. Giving Maisie her back, Quinn popped her head above the surface again.

Maisie wrapped her arms around Quinn's wide neck. The additional weight was considerable, but Quinn didn't think Maisie could keep swimming for much longer, her already pitiful strokes hindered by her clothes and oilskin coat.

Once Maisie had a secure grip, Quinn kicked them toward the beach. She wished she could tell Maisie to try to keep her body near the surface, and they kept colliding when Quinn moved her tail to propel them through the water, but she settled for trying not to dislodge Maisie as she moved. Perhaps she was imagining it, but now that she'd gotten Maisie back, the storm wasn't as frightening. The waves were still tumultuous, but Quinn sliced through them like an arrow.

Maisie had tucked her face behind Quinn's head to try to avoid the spray of water that washed up in her wake. Quinn could hear her shallow breathing, feel the rapid beat of her heart even through all the clothes and fur. Her fingers, pale with cold, were locked tight around Quinn's throat.

High above them, the lighthouse swung its bright beacon in its roving circle. Had Maisie been looking at that light while she was trying to swim to shore? Quinn used it to edge her way back toward the beach without getting too close to the cliffs.

Quinn had never felt more relieved at the sight of the familiar shoreline. It was rain-soaked and barely more inviting than the storm, but Quinn felt a final burst of adrenaline at the sight. She let a whuff of air out of her nose to try to get Maisie's attention.

"Nh?" Maisie asked, keeping her mouth closed against the salt water. She shifted against Quinn's back. "Oh, thank goodness."

The waves were strong enough to push them nearly all the way up the shore. When Quinn's flippers could reach the rocky bottom, she twisted in Maisie's grip. Maisie slid off her back but kept a hand on Quinn's fur. She helped Maisie climb out of the surf, heaving herself up the beach with the last of her strength.

When she was just out of the reach of the waves, Maisie sank to her knees, then sat down. She was still breathing heavily. Her face was drained, lips pale and her freckles standing out starkly against her skin. But she was all in one piece.

Quinn shuffled forward and set her nose against Maisie's trembling thigh. Maisie dug her fingers into the thick fur of Quinn's pelt.

"You saved me," she whispered, voice fragile, but Quinn hung on every breath.

A *name for a name*, Quinn thought, her black eyes wide and unblinking on Maisie's face. A *life for a life*.

"Can you come back?" Maisie asked shakily. Her fingers were tight in Quinn's fur, almost to the point of being painful, but Quinn couldn't find it in herself to be bothered by it.

She was a seal again. Her injury throbbed, but she was back

in the body that could withstand the ocean's beatings, that could carry her far from this island, farther away from Owen and everything he represented. If she took off her pelt again, would she struggle to put it back on if she needed to?

Maisie was safe, for now. If Quinn took off her pelt and stayed here, if she returned with Maisie to the lighthouse, she would be risking putting Maisie in danger again. The storms, the not-so-distant threat of being discovered by Owen, and the truth of what had happened to MacArthur seven years ago; could Quinn really push that all aside, just to stay with Maisie?

A low, rumbling whine built in Quinn's throat.

"Please," Maisie whispered, rain dripping down her cheeks and chin, "come back."

If Quinn left, what would she find out in the dark, lonesome expanse of the sea? She didn't even know if her herd was still living in these waters. She could leave and end up alone for the rest of her life. She would have her freedom, but that would be all. A month ago, that had been everything Quinn could ask for.

The clouds above them were dark and heavy, twisting through the sky and turning dusk to midnight, but the rain lessened. The wind softened to a sigh. The cliffs surrounding the rocky beach held them close, like a mother encircling her children in her arms.

Maisie's fingers softened their grip.

"If you want to leave," she said, like she was dragging out every word from deep inside, "I understand. I shouldn't... shouldn't ask you to stay, when I've known all along that you were waiting for this moment. For the chance to be free again."

Giving Quinn a wobbly smile, she let her hand slide from Quinn's back.

This was Quinn's choice. Maisie knew it, and she could have said more to try to get Quinn to stay, but she knew what it was like to face a path laid by someone else. She knew what it was to live and fight to make her own choices.

And it wasn't a simple choice, but Quinn found herself making it quite easily after that.

When Maisie moved to stand, Quinn hefted a flipper up and laid it over Maisie's leg. Maisie froze. She watched Quinn through wide eyes.

Quinn freed her other hand first. The pelt peeled away slowly, and Quinn's bare skin quickly pebbled against the chill rain. When her shoulders were free, Quinn lifted her remaining flipper and pried away the fur so she could use both hands to push the pelt over her head. She met Maisie's gaze with her pelt still wrapped around her legs, her tail lying heavy beside Maisie's legs and her torso propped up by a hand on the rocks.

"I'll stay," she told Maisie. "For now, I'll stay."

Even though she was exhausted, a smile split Maisie's pale, rain-damp face. She let out a half-laugh, half-sob, and brought her hands up to frame Quinn's face. Quinn swayed into her hold, putting her other hand down in the rocks beside Maisie's hip and caging her in between her arms.

Maisie ran her thumb across Quinn's cheekbone and laughed again, softer. Quinn leaned forward, chasing the sound, and Maisie closed the rest of the distance between them. Their mouths bumped and slid apart, rain and salt water making their skin slick, but then Maisie adjusted her grip on Quinn's face and tilted her jaw, and Quinn parted her lips, and they found each other again. Maisie tasted like the ocean. When she opened up to Quinn, every thought, every worry fled Quinn's head. She only knew Maisie's fingers in her hair, Maisie's freckled nose pressed into her cheek, Maisie's breath stuttering against her mouth.

They broke apart and Maisie gasped for air. Quinn stayed right where she was, cradled in Maisie's hands.

They were both breathing hard now. Quinn felt her chest rising and falling rapidly, but this time, it wasn't due to fear. The rocks she was leaning on were biting into her palms, but she didn't dare move. She was entirely entranced by the look in Maisie's eyes.

A sharp call from the cliffs finally startled them apart. Maisie twisted around, Quinn already searching for the source of the noise, and her heart leaped to her throat when she saw Jamie halfway down the path to the beach. MacArthur was close behind him.

Maisie snapped back around, her eyes on Quinn's tail.

"Quickly," she said, voice stronger now. "Take it off, all the way off."

But it was too late. Jamie's footsteps hit the beach as Quinn pushed the pelt down her hips and kicked her feet free.

"Hey," he called, "are you—"

He cut off abruptly. Quinn and Maisie both sat with their backs to him, but Maisie had turned her chin so she could watch him coming, and Quinn felt her gaze slide to her face, waiting for Quinn to decide what to do.

Quinn had made her choice. Now she'd deal with the consequences.

Gathering her pelt in her arms, Quinn turned to Maisie and gave her a nod. Lips pressed together, Maisie returned it. They helped each other to their feet. Maisie leaned heavily on Quinn's shoulder, a mirror of the way Maisie had supported Quinn when she'd first helped her off this beach. They turned and faced Jamie and MacArthur, who had finally caught up, together.

Quinn's pelt was draped over her arm. She was otherwise bare, except for where Maisie's bulk and coat hid her from view.

She met Jamie's eyes and then MacArthur's.

For a moment, no one said anything. The rain continued to patter down, and Maisie was shivering from the cold, but her gaze was steely on her fellow keepers.

Then, Jamie spoke. "You're a selkie."

She'd been right to be suspicious of what Jamie knew. He knew the word for her kind, which meant he'd heard the stories. From the way his shoulders tensed with caution and his eyes hardened, he must have heard the savage tales of selkies who drowned unsuspecting victims and abandoned their children without a second glance. How much of those stories did he believe?

"Yes," Quinn answered him. There was no use denying it.

His gaze shifted to Maisie. "You knew."

"Yes," she said.

"Your injury," Jamie continued, swinging back to Quinn. "What you told us about your husband, did he know?"

"Yes," she said. "He knew. It was why he did it."

"Why?" MacArthur asked. His neat hair was plastered

down by the rain, but his posture was strict as ever, his eyes calculating.

Quinn let a fraction of her contempt for Owen slip over her face, knowing that they would see it. "He kept me trapped on land for years. I escaped. He saw the chance to trap me again and he took it. It didn't work out the second time."

"But you didn't make it away unscathed," MacArthur remarked. They'd all seen Quinn's foot.

"You really swam here, then," Jamie said. "Not from a boat, like your story, but from the town."

Quinn tilted her head at his tone.

"I thought I recognized you," he admitted finally. "When you first arrived, I thought I knew you. I've been to the town. I know the fishermen there. I've heard about the man with a strange wife, seen her from afar as she avoided the towns-people."

He paused, assessing, then added, "I heard about her kids. How the town thinks they're strange, too."

"They're not," Quinn snapped. She took a step forward without thinking about it, and Maisie swayed forward with her. "They're not like me."

Jamie, with all his strength, tensed at her approach and searched her face. Was he afraid of her? Or was he afraid of the stories he'd heard about selkies, and reckoning with what he knew about her against what he thought he knew about her kind?

"You said your husband kept you trapped," MacArthur broke in again, then paused for a long moment. "Your children?"

Quinn could feel Maisie stiffen since she was draped over

her shoulders. Jamie's face shuttered, and he shot MacArthur a look. Quinn wasn't sure if MacArthur was asking whether her children were trapped, too, or asking how they had come to be when her husband was keeping her against her will.

"He wanted them," she told MacArthur. "He loves them. I—they were a piece of me that I could give without losing the rest of myself."

Maisie's fingers tightened on Quinn's arm.

MacArthur took a step forward so that he was closer to Quinn and Maisie, Jamie quiet as he watched from over Mac-Arthur's shoulder.

"So you escaped," MacArthur said. "And, injured, you came here. Maisie found you and helped you." He was studying the way that Maisie was leaning on Quinn for support, the closeness of their bodies. Quinn didn't dare twitch under his gaze. "You told us a fraction of the truth and accepted our shelter."

He took another step forward so that he was within arm's reach. Maisie was holding her breath.

"And you saved Maisie."

Quinn blinked, startled.

"I saw you," MacArthur said quietly, though Quinn was sure Jamie could hear every word. "You did not hesitate for even a moment. The second Maisie's name left Jamie's mouth, you had decided to save her, despite the fact that it could very well end this way, with us discovering your secret. You saved her."

He held out his hand. He had a large, square palm with thin fingers, much better suited for delicate occupations than the tasking labor of a lighthouse. But when Quinn laid her hand in his, she could feel the calluses of hard work rough against her skin. MacArthur squeezed her hand.

"Thank you," he said.

Maisie reached out and laid her other hand on MacArthur's shoulder, his left shoulder. She gripped his arm tightly.

"A life for a life," Quinn said softly, and Maisie turned her fragile smile on Quinn, eyes lighting up.

"Name for a name," she echoed, and Quinn smiled back.

Jamie finally moved. He came to stand right beside Mac-Arthur, but his eyes were on Quinn.

"Thank you for saving her," he said, his voice low. He was looking at Quinn's and MacArthur's joined hands, at the way Maisie was propped up on Quinn's shoulders, and the corners of his mouth twisted sharply. "I can help you back to the lighthouse, Maisie."

With a sinking feeling in her gut, Quinn let go of Mac-Arthur's hand. The way Jamie was looking at her was not so dissimilar to how Owen had looked at her when he had figured out she could control the storms that threatened his livelihood.

Maisie curled her fingers into Quinn's arm. "It's all right. Quinn's got me."

"She's still healing," Jamie said flatly.

"She was well enough to rescue me," Maisie argued back. But even she glanced down anxiously at Quinn's feet.

"I'm fine," Quinn told her quietly. She had released Mac-Arthur, but she didn't want to let go of Maisie, even with Jamie's attention sharp against her skin. Could he still think she would hurt Maisie after everything she went through to save her?

MacArthur, assured that Maisie was all right and ever the devoted keeper, took Quinn at her word and got back to business. "Jamie, the boat?"

Even with his hackles up, Jamie let himself be swayed by MacArthur. "I can tie her down myself, now the waves have died down. Unless you want to help?"

MacArthur nodded, and Quinn caught the pleased smile at the corner of his mouth. The men broke off and made for the dock, leaving Maisie and Quinn still stacked together. When MacArthur and Jamie were out of earshot, Maisie asked quietly, "Do you think they saw us? You know, before."

She gestured to Quinn, her bare legs and the pelt draped over her arm. It took Quinn a moment to put together that Maisie was asking if she thought MacArthur and Jamie had seen their kiss before Quinn's transformation had distracted them.

"I'm not sure," she said honestly.

Quinn herself had been a little distracted in that moment.

The look Maisie shot her was still tinged with concern, but the sly, satisfied glint in her eye made Quinn's heart kick in her chest.

"Let's go," Quinn told her, adjusting Maisie's weight across her shoulders and tightening her grip around Maisie's waist. "You need to get warm."

"I sure do," Maisie muttered back, her grin twisting the words in a way that made Quinn fight to keep her breathing and steps steady. She glanced over their shoulders and spotted Jamie and MacArthur on the dock, Jamie reeling in the loose line hand over fist while MacArthur crouched by the dock cleat and wrapped the rope in a new knot. She thought she could see Jamie's mouth moving, and while she worried what he could be saying to MacArthur about her, there was nothing she could do about it now. It wouldn't take them long to catch up.

Pushing the thoughts dredged up by Maisie's grin aside, Quinn jerked her chin toward the top of the cliffs.

"I need to get my clothes," she told her, instead of everything else she wished she could put to words.

Chapter Seventeen

DARK CLOUDS LOOMED OVER the frozen town, and Quinn was heavy with Owen's third child. Every part of her ached, but with no one to comfort her and two daughters to take care of, Quinn moved through life like a puppet on a string.

She sat at the kitchen table, her chair angled to the side to make room for her swollen belly, and watched as Flora picked at the simple lunch Quinn had managed to prepare. Evie was asleep in the kids' bedroom.

This next child would come soon. She dreaded its arrival, knowing she would have no one but herself to rely on through the birth. Owen had stayed by her side a few minutes into Flora's birth before turning a sick shade of green and leaving to wait outside the house until he heard the baby wailing. Quinn had never dared ask any of the midwives in town for help, knowing that they had been poisoned against her by the reputation she had amassed. The only thing that had gotten her through Flora's and Evie's births had been her mother's stories.

Selkie mothers gave birth alone, just like seals. Quinn could rely on the assurance that generations of mothers before her had struggled and fought on their own and been rewarded with their children.

But Quinn had not felt worthy of reward after birthing Flora and Evie. She had felt exhausted, alone, and sticky with blood. That was what awaited her with this third child.

She knew what kind of pain to expect, and the signs that would tell her the baby's arrival was imminent. She also thought she had at least another month before the birth.

Quinn grimaced when another lancing pain shot up her lower back. She laid a hand over her stomach and tried to control her breathing, but then a tidal wave washed over her and she bit back a scream. Her skin bulged and shifted beneath her fingers. The baby was moving. It was coming early.

"Mama?"

Quinn opened her eyes just enough to see Flora watching her with concern folded into her forehead.

"Flora," she panted, "go to your sister."

Her daughter's brow crumpled even more. Quinn fisted her hand on the table and tried to focus on the feeling of her nails biting into the soft part of her palm, but she couldn't conceal the next wave of pain as it washed over her. Flora's eyes began to swim with tears.

"It's okay," Quinn told her. "Go take a nap with your sister. It's okay."

Flora climbed down from her chair and walked slowly

toward her room, tears dripping down her cheeks, and she kept checking over her shoulder to look at Quinn. Flora had been too young to remember Evie's birth, but she'd cried along with Quinn when her sister came screaming into the world.

"It's okay, baby," Quinn managed to tell her with a pitiful smile.

Flora closed the door behind her. Quinn let out a pained exhalation the moment she was alone. She took a moment to remember her mother's stories and let that ground her.

Flora's and Evie's births had not been easy, but as Quinn moved through the familiar motions of laying down linens and finding the positions that reduced the effort of childbirth, she grew more and more concerned about the third baby. The pain would flare and then settle, but all of her effort seemed to go nowhere.

Perhaps an hour in, Flora tried to open the door and stick her head out.

Quinn knew she was making noise. Her hairline was damp with sweat, and she'd peeled off her outer layer so she was only in a rucked-up white shift. She was on her knees clutching the table for support, her chest rising and falling rapidly, but she looked up at the noise.

Flora was still crying silently.

"I'm sorry," Quinn told her. "Just wait a little longer, okay?"

"Mama needs help?"

Quinn pressed her forehead into the edge of the table. "No," she bit out. "I'm okay." There was no one she could send Flora to ask for help.

As another wave of pain rolled over her, Quinn wished for her mother. Memories and stories could only do so much. She wanted her mother's comforting presence, her steadfast assurance that everything would be all right. Even if her mother had never given birth as a human, Quinn knew that it would be easier with her mother there.

"Help," Flora insisted, now at Quinn's side. Quinn rolled her head, trying to push the agonized look off her face, and then stilled when something touched her forehead. She blinked her eyes open to see her daughter's face pinched in concentration as she pressed her small hand to Quinn's skin, as if she could push the pain away. Quinn was hot and clammy, and Flora's hand felt marvelously cool in comparison.

"Okay," she said after a moment, feeling the next wave coming on. "Thank you. You can go back in your room."

"Better?" Flora asked, pressing more insistently until Quinn reached up and replaced Flora's small hands with her own.

"Better," Quinn agreed. She swiped her thumb across the hot skin under Flora's eyes. "Don't cry. Mama can do this by herself."

After a little more insisting, her daughter finally retreated back to the kids' room.

Even while she was overwhelmed with pain, Quinn was touched by her daughter's care. However, once she was gone, and there was nothing for Quinn to focus on but the never-ending cycle of strain and effort and failure, Flora's moment of kindness exacerbated Quinn's loneliness.

Why did she have to suffer alone to fulfill a dream that didn't belong to her? Why was she going through a near-death experience over and over again just so Owen could build a family that Quinn wanted no part in? How could the other women of the town who had been through the same suffer-ing leave her to bear it alone? She had felt like she'd proven something with Flora's birth; proven that she could withstand even the worst pain of being human. But then she was forced to endure it again, and again now, and Quinn didn't know if the cycle would ever end.

If this child was a boy, would Owen be content? Or would she have to continue bearing his children until his dream was fulfilled? Was this punishment for not bringing him the luck and fortune he'd desired from her in the first place?

Her building anger powered her through a few rounds of fruitless pushing. Outside, the darkened sky grew thick and swirled with energy.

Quinn wasn't even sure Owen was out on the water. The fishermen took their boats out only rarely during the winter months, but the town still needed to eat. But if he wasn't on the boat and he hadn't returned home yet, that meant he was at the pub. He was drinking while Quinn was on her knees in the kitchen digging half-moon indents into her palms.

Thunder rumbled over the town like a great herd of wild animals were stampeding through the streets.

Quinn was gasping for breath, feeling too tight in her skin, like this human body would come apart any moment. She needed fresh air. She needed to be outside. She could barely keep her eyes open from the heat of her tears and the pain, but she looked through slitted lids toward the door off the kitchen. It was maybe a little over a yard away, but it felt like an infinite distance. Uncurling her hands, Quinn lowered herself to the floor and crawled.

When she pushed the door open, the first spray of rain on

her face was almost as comforting as Flora's cool hand. The storm was too heavy to carry the smell of the ocean on the wind, but having the open sky above her allowed Quinn to take a deep breath. She shuffled herself down the steps and lay on her back in the patchy green-and-yellow grass.

She didn't have the energy to worry about the neighbors seeing her. The rain was falling in gray sheets, and she hoped it was enough to conceal her should anyone care to look out their window. No one in their right mind would go outside in this weather.

Quinn knew she should be cold, but as the rain washed over her and the ground seemed to soften beneath her like it would swallow her whole, her anger heated her chest.

If she could summon a storm like this, why was she still trapped in this life? How could she be so powerless without her pelt that even when she changed the world around her, she couldn't change the things that mattered the most? She never felt in control of the storms. They only came in response to her anger or fear.

She laid her hands over her heaving stomach. The child surged beneath her touch, but she still wasn't able to deliver it.

How long could she go on like this?

Pain and rage swirled beneath her skin, and Quinn wished she could inflict just a fraction of this onto Owen. Maybe if he could feel what she felt, he would finally let her go. But he had seen her go through this pain before and left her to bear it alone. He had listened to her cries, her screams, her pleas to return her pelt to her, and he had ignored them. He had only been afraid of her when she'd leaned into the vicious selkie legend and threatened to take everything from him.

Could she do it now? The storm twisted around her, as if waiting for her signal, and she wondered if her rage could grow large enough to wash this whole town into the sea. She could end Owen's dream here.

"Quinn!"

Owen had finally returned home. She didn't know how he'd made it through the deluging rain, but she opened her eyes to see him stumbling toward her. The wind picked up and buffeted him from side to side, but he leaned into it, as if forcing himself upriver against a fearsome current.

"The baby?" he cried. Was he asking if this storm had come because of the baby's arrival? Or did he think she'd already lost it, and the weather had turned so aggressively because she was mourning?

Even in circumstances like this, Owen was more concerned for their unborn child than he was for her.

Quinn let out a guttural scream. She'd been holding it back in the house, not wanting to scare her daughters, but she released it now. The storm responded in kind.

She couldn't hear if Owen was still calling out to her. The wind and rain kept him back, and she could hear the house creaking alarmingly beside her. How much more did the storm need? If she tore out her heart, would that be enough?

Something touched her shoulder, and Quinn flinched. When she opened her eyes, she thought the pain was making her hallucinate the figure crouched beside her. But the touch on her shoulder became a firm grasp, and the face of the woman who lived next door swam into view. Quinn wasn't sure of her name.

Her neighbor had kept her distance from Quinn, obviously

wary of the order the matriarch of the town had given to the wives after Quinn had failed to meet their expectations, and this was the closest she had been to another wife since then. Face drawn tight, the woman leaned in to be heard over the storm.

"How long has it been?"

Quinn was dizzy with agony and couldn't make sense of what her neighbor was asking. She hiccupped a sob and shook her head.

Shielding her eyes from the spitting rain, the woman looked around them. Owen was nowhere to be seen, and there was no one else out in the storm. Mouth set in a hard line, Quinn's neighbor released her hold on Quinn's shoulder.

Before Quinn could cry out, the touch reappeared on her bent knee. Quinn lifted her head to see the woman kneel between her legs, moving the bloody hem out of the way and meeting Quinn's eyes.

"Push," she commanded.

"I can't!" Quinn cried.

The woman wrapped a hand around Quinn's calf and squeezed. The touch was not possessive, as Owen's would have been, or searching like her children's; it was a touch meant to comfort.

"You must," the woman told her. "Push."

Quinn dropped her head in the wet grass and sobbed. Despite this woman being ordered to leave Quinn alone or fear the same outcast treatment, she was risking the storm and ostracism from her own community in order to help Quinn.

At a loss to understand the bounds of human kindness, Quinn cast aside the thoughts she'd had about dragging this town, Owen, and herself into the sea. If her neighbor was willing to risk her life to help Quinn, she couldn't subject this woman to such a fate. She thought of Flora and Evie inside, innocent of all that caused Quinn's rage. For them, she released the storm.

Grounding her feet in the grass and letting her neighbor's commands wash over her, Quinn tried again, and brought her son into the world, bloody and wailing.

Chapter Eighteen

NOW

QUINN WAS BRACED FOR further interrogation by MacArthur and Jamie when everyone was back in the lighthouse and she and Maisie were in dry clothes by the fire, and she was not disappointed. MacArthur gathered them around the kitchen table with four cups of strong tea after lighting a few more lamps to illuminate the room in a soft glow. The dark window shuddered against the storm.

Quinn had expected that Jamie would dig into her at once, now that he had an opening to justify his suspicions, but it was MacArthur who took the lead. He was studying each of his keepers in turn. Jamie was hunched in his seat on the bench beside MacArthur, though he'd grabbed an apple at some point and was spinning it in his fingers. Maisie was swaying slightly on the bench beside Quinn. She wished that she could take Maisie straight to bed to rest, but she needed to know what the men thought of her before spending one more night in the lighthouse. Quinn waited until MacArthur's gaze eventually settled on her.

"You are a shapeshifter," he prompted her.

"A selkie," she agreed.

He tilted his head toward Jamie. "That's the word he used. It is accurate?"

"It is."

"I don't know much about selkies," MacArthur admitted.

"You spent your life at sea before coming here," Jamie said incredulously. He had rolled his sleeves up over his forearms and was carefully peeling away the skin of the apple with a paring knife. MacArthur shot him a flat look that lost its edge when it skidded over his bare arms and hands. Quinn pressed her tongue against the back of her teeth as MacArthur quickly swung his gaze away.

"And if I listened to every bit of superstitious nonsense some sailor nattered on about during the night watch, I'd never sleep again," MacArthur shot back. "I know the basics."

"Which are?" Jamie prompted him.

Now MacArthur shot Quinn a look, as if she would stop him, but she just stared expectantly and felt Maisie do the same at her side.

Straightening up in his seat, MacArthur cleared his throat.

"Selkies are shapeshifting seals who can take human form by taking off their pelts. As animals, they are not noticeably different than regular gray seals. As humans..." He hesitated, mouth working as he figured out how he wanted to phrase it. "As humans, they are often exceptionally beautiful and coveted for their looks."

Quinn raised an eyebrow at him, and Maisie snorted.

"We've got proof of that now, don't we," she offered. Quinn turned her incredulous look on Maisie instead, but MacArthur bulled on.

"Selkies' pelts are incredibly important to them," he said, and Quinn quickly looked back at him. "If a human is able to steal a selkie's pelt, the selkie will have to remain on land with them until it is returned. From the stories I've heard, it's been inferred that it is during this time that selkies and humans can have children together."

Quinn was aware that all three of them were trying very hard to not stare at her in a way that made it very obvious they wanted to stare at her. Jamie had paused carving off the skin of his apple. Maisie's laughter had died.

Quinn asked, "Is that all?"

MacArthur's eyebrows pulled together as he tried to think of anything he'd forgotten, but it was Jamie who spoke.

"No," he said. "That's not all. I've heard stories of what happens to the people who steal a selkie's pelt, or try to and fail. I've heard stories about selkies dragging men into the ocean depths." He spoke softly, but his eyes were hard on Quinn. "Stories about how selkies take their revenge in blood and water."

Quinn sat rigidly, forcing herself to take measured breaths. She'd known that something had been sitting on Jamie's mind since he saw her pelt. But it still hurt her to see the caution in Jamie's eyes because he saw her as a creature capable of such violence.

Owen's fears had never come true, but a part of her was always aware of her ability to take revenge on the humans she hated. She'd thought about when she saw Maisie for the first time. Quinn had wondered if she could drown Maisie and rid her world of one human. But she hadn't been able to, and instead, she'd met Maisie, been helped by her, befriended her, and now sat next to her on a kitchen bench in the human's lighthouse after saving Maisie from being claimed by the sea.

Maisie herself responded to Jamie. "Even if that is true, she hasn't hurt us!"

"She's been injured," Jamie pointed out.

"Have you forgotten that she saved me from drowning not even half an hour ago?" Maisie yelped, leaning so far forward she came off the bench.

"She saved you, yes," Jamie said. "But that doesn't mean she wouldn't hurt one of us. Or that she hasn't hurt anyone already." He tilted his head, as if listening for a far-off sound. "How can we even be sure she didn't get that wound while dragging her husband under?"

"I didn't kill him," Quinn answered throatily. "But I've thought about it. Many times."

Maisie sat back heavily with a pained look on her face.

"Would you?" Jamie asked.

Tiny moments from each of her seven years on land flashed through Quinn's mind, each of them little hurts that built and built like icy raindrops until they became a fierce, overpowering storm. Quinn clenched her hand, fingernails digging into the grain of the table. She blinked away the memories until her head cleared.

"No," she admitted. "Because then my children would be alone."

Jamie let out a sound like he'd been struck in the chest. MacArthur held up his hand before Jamie could speak again.

"Because you left them with him?"

Quinn's skin prickled as she recalled the way the wives had spoken about how she had abandoned her children, how there were probably stories about how selkies were uncaring, selfish mothers who left their children behind the moment they had the chance. She had left them, and she would have to live with that decision every day. But it would have killed her if she stayed.

"He loves them," she told them. "He loves them more than he ever bothered to care for me, and I knew if I left, he would choose them. *You* don't get to question why I did it. *You* have no right to judge me for what I've done or not done, when every day all I've fought for is to be able to make a choice about *my* life." Quinn's voice rose as she spoke, her last words ringing out in the lamplit kitchen.

"You're right," MacArthur said.

Jamie made a noise of protest, but MacArthur kept going. "The part about your pelt is true, isn't it? That if someone takes it from you, you're unable to leave their side?"

Quinn ached all over, but she nodded.

She didn't look at Maisie. Maisie had seen the way Quinn acted around her pelt. She'd been able to put enough together to know that Quinn needed a safe place to put it if it was ever out of her sight.

Quinn had also let Maisie put her hands on it. Perhaps it shouldn't have mattered so much now that she had felt Maisie's mouth against hers, but now Maisie would really understand just how much Quinn trusted her.

"Then anything you could have done in return to free yourself from that man was well deserved," MacArthur said, drawing Quinn's focus back. "Don't you agree, Jamie?"

Jamie tilted his head back. "I suppose," he mumbled.

"Well, then, now we know what to believe about selkies," MacArthur said, nodding as if they'd come to an agreement on something. "At least, the basics, right?"

Quinn unclenched her hand from the table and curled it around her cup of tea instead, the ceramic making a gentle sound against the wood of the table, and agreed. "Those are the basics."

The storm was still making itself known on the other side of the window. She wasn't lying to them, but she wasn't being completely honest. Owen hadn't known about Quinn's ability to control the weather until she threw a storm in his face, and it seemed easy to assume that word of that selkie talent had not infiltrated the existing stories that passed between fishermen. Even Quinn's mother had not told her about it. Perhaps it wasn't common, and in that case, it was not a basic quality that Quinn needed to divulge.

Quinn knew what the next question should be, and since Maisie already knew the answer, she offered it to MacArthur and Jamie for free.

"My husband took my pelt from me and hid it for seven years. I was only able to leave when my daughter found it and gave it back," she said.

"Your daughter?" Jamie repeated, setting down the knife for good and seeming to immediately forget his peeled apple. "Your daughter gave it back?"

"Yes."

"Did she know what it meant?" This was from Maisie, and it was softer than Jamie's startled question.

Quinn felt her shoulders pull up a little bit, but she forced them back down. "Maybe not entirely, but my son seemed to have an idea. They brought it straight to me. They didn't ask what it was." Quinn remembered the steady look in Flora's eyes, though her hands had trembled around the weight of Quinn's pelt. "She just gave it back."

"And you left," Jamie said.

Quinn slid her gaze over to him, expecting scorn and judgment, despite what MacArthur had said. Here she was, admitting that she was just the kind of mother the town had always accused her of being.

"I left," she said.

"We're not all made to be mothers," Maisie said, and she was looking at Jamie, too, repeating the sentiment she had already shared with Quinn. "Even when forced."

That soured whatever else Jamie had wanted to say. He nodded.

Quinn swallowed the rest of her tea in a large mouthful, though it had gone cold. Maisie snuck a hand across the table and tried to steal Jamie's peeled apple. He pushed the whole plate of skinned pieces toward Maisie, and she blinked at him in surprise.

"Eat it," he told her. He had the same look on his face as he did when attending to Quinn's wound. She could clearly remember the fear on Jamie's face when he'd told them Maisie had fallen over the cliff, and the relief when he'd found them on the beach. Jamie may not have trusted Quinn, but they shared a concern for Maisie.

"Well," MacArthur said. "Then I suppose we had better talk about what happens now."

Quinn blinked at him. Talk? If he was going to tell her to leave the lighthouse now that he knew what she was, she'd rather he got to the point. She risked a glance at Jamie, remembering that the two men had spoken while they tied up the boat and Quinn was out of earshot.

"You are still healing," MacArthur explained. "We promised you shelter while your injury healed. We knew that you had escaped your husband, who inflicted the wound, and now we know why you had to come here. You did not lie," he said, chin dipping as if to recognize her efforts, "but you were not entirely truthful."

"Bit of an understatement, I think," Jamie said gruffly.

"I wasn't honest when I came here either," Maisie tried to argue, a section of apple forgotten in her hand.

"But you aren't a damn selkie, are you?"

"Jamie," MacArthur warned.

"No, listen. We can pretend everything's well and good, but you can't deny that the situation has changed. We didn't know what we were dealing with, and now we do. How can we know that's all she's hiding?" Jamie turned in his seat to look imploringly at MacArthur as he spoke, but it was as if he were shining the lighthouse's beacon directly in Quinn's face.

MacArthur at least had the grace to meet Quinn's eyes. "If she meant us harm, I'm sure she could have accomplished it by now, injured or not."

"Exactly!" Maisie jumped in, frowning worriedly at Jamie. "She doesn't want to hurt us; she just needs help. Right?"

Now Maisie turned on the bench toward Quinn.

"Right," Quinn agreed, not taking her eyes off Jamie. She did not want to hurt the keepers any more than she already had, and while she had agreed to stay at the lighthouse since Maisie asked her to, Jamie was not wrong to question her place amongst them. He was right that she still hadn't told them everything. Quinn was certain if Jamie found out about her ability to summon storms and the fact that she had caused MacArthur's past misfortune, he would consider her too much of a threat to be allowed to stay—or to leave alive.

MacArthur made his decision and directed it at Jamie. "I do not think we have anything to fear from Quinn. She can stay here until she is healed, as we originally agreed."

While Maisie's face lit up, Jamie's darkened. He seemed to be considering what he could possibly say to convince Mac-Arthur to see his side, but couldn't get the words out.

"Jamie," MacArthur said softly, and the sudden change of his voice took Quinn aback. This was not a head keeper commanding his employee to heed his command. This was a gentle nudge from someone he trusted. Jamie, too, seemed surprised by MacArthur's evocation of his first name. Something passed between the two men that made Quinn risk a glance at Maisie, whose brow was raised, before Jamie finally sighed.

"I see your point," he mumbled. Quinn tensed when he finally looked at her. "We were doing you a favor, then you did one for us." He nodded at Maisie. "We're square. For now."

It was a better outcome than Quinn had dared hope for. Jamie still didn't trust her, that much was obvious, but he trusted in his fellow keepers wholeheartedly.

That was enough for Maisie. Jamie looked like he wanted to say something else, but after glancing at Maisie's still pale face, he kept his mouth shut. MacArthur sent Jamie to check on the beacon one last time before he could turn in, so Quinn waited for Maisie to finish her apple, taking a few bites of fruit at Maisie's insistence, before they helped each other down the hall. Maisie was shaken, but otherwise uninjured, and Quinn's injury was only now kicking up a fuss at her rough use.

Quinn's pelt was still soaked, so she hung it over the frame at the end of Maisie's bed instead of tucking it into the sheets with her. Maisie quickly fitted herself into the free space in between Quinn's arms when they lay down.

She grinned up at Quinn, the whites of her eyes flashing in the low light.

"You nearly drowned an hour ago," Quinn reminded her.

"But I didn't," Maisie shot back, her breath warm on Quinn's chin. "Because of you."

Maisie's arms were wrapped around Quinn's waist, and she watched Quinn's face as she slid her hands slowly up and down Quinn's back over her borrowed nightshirt.

When Quinn's face betrayed nothing, Maisie slid her hands down again and slipped one under the shirt so her rough palm could press against the skin of Quinn's back. Quinn sucked in a breath.

"Just this," Maisie said. "Okay?"

Quinn's skin must have still been chill from the rain, because Maisie's hand felt like a hot brand on her back.

"Okay," she managed to say. Maisie grinned at her once more, sleepily, and then her eyelids slid shut. The rain was scarcely more than a gentle tap against the window. Quinn studied Maisie's face, which was a bit difficult with how close Maisie was tucked into Quinn's chest. She settled for curling her hand around the back of Maisie's head until she could press two fingers behind Maisie's ear and feel her pulse beating, strong and sure, beneath her skin.

THE SKY WAS REMARKABLY clear the next few days after the gloom that had instigated Maisie's unplanned evening swim. Quinn used these days to finally get her foot fully recovered. There was a large scar where the wound had been, but she could finally walk normally, if slowly. She even managed to climb to the top of the lighthouse with Maisie one afternoon without needing to stop once. However, neither of them seemed to be in a hurry to share Quinn's progress with Jamie or MacArthur.

She and Maisie spent every moment together. This was hardly different from how they had been before that night on the beach after Quinn pulled her from the water, but how they spent that time together certainly was.

Maisie touched her whenever she had the chance. She would take Quinn's hand in hers and study her fingers like she'd never seen them before. She would rest her forehead against the back of Quinn's neck when they slept, her breath soft and tempting against Quinn's skin. When Maisie left Quinn in a room to go work outside, she would trail her fingers down Quinn's cheek before gripping her chin and placing a kiss on her lips.

Of course, she only did this when they were alone. But she was taking chances, hooking her ankle around Quinn's while they ate at the table with Jamie and MacArthur. She'd hastily thrown herself away from Quinn when Jamie had rounded the corner of the lighthouse unexpectedly. Quinn wasn't completely sure that Jamie hadn't seen them, but he hadn't said anything beyond asking Maisie to come help him fix one of the windows.

Every moment felt stolen. Quinn could hardly believe that Maisie gave herself so willingly, on top of everything she had offered Quinn already. She tried to give as much in return.

After a quick breakfast on the third day of sunny skies, Maisie and Jamie went outside to fix the stone fence that ran along the back of the lighthouse, as the storm had knocked quite a few rocks loose and it needed patching. Quinn cautiously followed them out and found the driest bit of grass to sit on and observe.

While the sun was bright and glinted off the sea below like a winking, iridescent shell, Quinn shivered in her thick sweater and borrowed jacket. The sun could do its best, but winter had come.

She watched as Maisie and Jamie fussed over the fence. Quinn was glad Maisie was feeling well enough to work, like being thrown from the cliffs into the water was nothing more than a chill to be shaken off. She studied Maisie's face for concealed wariness, or fear, but found none.

You saved me, Maisie had told Quinn. But Quinn hadn't said that it was her storm that put Maisie in danger in the first place. It was Quinn's fear that had nearly dragged Maisie beneath the waves. She had seen what her storm had done to MacArthur. She refused to let it hurt Maisie, too.

And MacArthur had thanked her.

Quinn pressed one hand to her mouth and fisted the other in the chill grass, the blades brittle beneath her fingers. MacArthur had thanked her for saving Maisie, Jamie had called them square, and Quinn had let it slide between her ribs and settle somewhere in her chest where it burned steadily like a candle. How long could she keep using their kindness before the candle burned out?

In all her years on land, she had scarcely seen the goodwill that the keepers had shown her in a few short weeks. Owen had been kind until it became clear that nothing would sway Quinn from her hatred. The townspeople had turned against her almost immediately. Even the few who came close to kindness, like Ronnie the pub owner, had done so from a distance. They would offer smiles and conversation, but nothing more.

How were the lighthouse keepers so different from the other humans she'd met? Maisie had quite literally given Quinn the shirt off her back and expected nothing in return. MacArthur accepted her into his home on Maisie's word. Even before she pulled Maisie from the water, they had offered her safety simply because she needed it.

The candle in her chest flared, burning white hot. Quinn inhaled shakily and forced herself to take steady, calming breaths.

Maisie wanted Quinn to stay, so she had. With that choice, Quinn had put her freedom on the line. She hoped it was worth it.

"Quinn," Maisie called suddenly, and Quinn looked up. Maisie was standing with a large, flat rock clutched in her hands. Jamie was half hidden by the wall. "You okay?"

"Fine," Quinn called back, lowering her hand. "Just trying to warm up my fingers."

Maisie's brow furrowed. "Do you want to go back inside?"

"No," Quinn said, "but maybe I'll go on a walk. A slow

one." She added the last part with a put-upon sigh at the look Maisie gave her.

"Don't push your foot," Jamie warned curtly, the top of his head moving along the line of the fence. She made a noise of agreement. Even if Jamie had his reservations about her, he still cared about her injury. Perhaps it was only because he wanted her to heal faster and be on her way, but it was more than she could have expected. She walked slowly, as promised, and let her eyes skip from the ground in front of her to the ocean, to the horizon, and back. She wished the wind would lift her worries off her shoulders and carry them off into the distance.

As she rounded the other side of the lighthouse, her gaze trailed along the ragged cliffs and the winding path down to the beach. She missed her next step and nearly tripped on a clump of grass.

There was a boat pulling into the dock alongside Jamie's.

In an instant, all her worries, all her fear, welled up like a geyser. Was it Owen's boat? No, it was too small. But hadn't Jamie said that the waters were too dangerous to cross from the mainland during winter? Who had traveled all the way here despite that?

Distant male voices calling out over the wind finally sent her hurrying back around the island.

Maisie must have seen her out of the corner of her eye, because she grumbled, "I thought you said you'd go *slow*."

"Someone's here," Quinn said.

Both Maisie and Jamie jerked to their feet.

"It's not…" Maisie asked, wide-eyed, and Quinn knew who she meant right away. It had been her first thought, too.

"It's not my husband. At least, not his boat," she said, gritting her teeth as she wheeled around to follow Jamie and Maisie back to the lighthouse. Jamie's face was closed off, shoulders stiff.

They paused long enough for Maisie and Jamie to confirm what Quinn saw, and to see three men heading toward the path, before piling into the lighthouse. Jamie shouted for MacArthur.

"What?" came MacArthur's reply from his office.

"Someone's here!" Jamie repeated. There was a pause, and then MacArthur's hurried footsteps descended the stairs, and they all gathered in the kitchen.

"Who?" was MacArthur's first question, his eyes swinging to Quinn.

"It's not my husband's boat," she told him. "I'd recognize it."

"I didn't recognize it, either," Jamie said, rubbing a hand over his beard.

"Who would need to come here so bad they'd risk the water in winter? Especially after that last storm?" Maisie asked, voice a little higher than normal. Quinn flinched and tried to pass it off by sitting down as if her foot was hurting her when Jamie flicked a glance at her.

"Whoever it is," MacArthur said, his spine straightening, "they can't see Quinn. She's not meant to be here."

"Should she hide in my room?" Maisie asked.

Jamie shook his head. "Closed doors are more suspicious."

MacArthur glanced around the sparse kitchen, then strode to the still open window. He leaned out a little and looked down.

"Here," he said, waving Quinn over. The window was about three meters up from the grass, but there was a stack of crates settled against the wall.

"You want her to go out the window?" Maisie asked, incredulous.

"It's the best option we have," MacArthur decided. "Jamie, come help me. Maisie, you need to go get one of your hats. Your hair."

Maisie cursed and dashed for her room. She hurried back in, stuffing her hair in the knit hat as MacArthur propped open the other windowpane, then gestured for Quinn to come forward. She leaned out and then turned back to MacArthur.

"I'm sure you're strong, but you hired Maisie for laborious jobs. I'm no tiny thing."

MacArthur's jaw clicked, but he nodded. Stepping away from the window, Maisie and Jamie took their places behind Quinn. She swung one leg over the sill to straddle the window.

There was a knock at the front door. Quinn, Jamie, and Maisie all twisted their heads toward the sound. MacArthur stood in his best impression of a soldier, or perhaps a captain.

"Hurry," he told them, and strode from the kitchen, shutting the door behind him.

Quinn brought her other leg out so that she was seated sideways on the sill, gripping the frame with both hands. Maisie laid her hands over one of Quinn's.

It really wasn't a far drop, Quinn reasoned to herself, but her heart refused to slow its beating despite this logic. Jamie's fingers brushed her other hand. She met his eyes and felt that despite his hesitance about her, she could trust him with this. She had to.

Quinn twisted around so that she was facing the wall as she slid below the window. She unpeeled her fingers long enough for Maisie to grip her right hand with both of her own, and then did the same on the left with Jamie. They each had a double grip on her hand and wrists and slowly lowered her out of the window. The rough wall tugged at her clothing as she slipped down, and Quinn stretched her toes out, reaching for the crates. She gasped when she suddenly dropped, but she landed on her feet, the crates creaking beneath her.

"Sorry," Maisie whispered, "they're in the hallway."

"I'm fine," Quinn whispered back, and they released her. Jamie disappeared back into the kitchen, but Maisie lingered for a moment. Quinn met her gaze steadily, and then raised a hand to shoo her away.

Quinn turned and put her back to the wall as she heard Maisie close one of the windowpanes again, leaving the other open so Quinn could listen as the door to the kitchen creaked.

"These are my employees," MacArthur said, his voice steady but tight. "Mr. Donovan and Mr. Murdoch."

"Donovan and Murdoch?" a new male voice repeated.

"Yes."

"Right," the man said, and there was a pause. "Full names please, gentlemen."

"James Donovan," Jamie answered, gruff and wary. Quinn had never heard him sound like that, even when he'd been questioning her.

"Tavis Murdoch," Maisie said, and she'd remembered to lower her voice, though she spoke slowly, as if uncertain.

"As I told you," MacArthur said, in a tone that belonged to the uptight, controlling keeper that the town believed

MacArthur to be. "And I'm Finn MacArthur. Would you mind explaining why you've come all this way now? We don't often receive visitors this time of year. And you are not from the board."

"No, we're not," another voice, again male, said. "We apologize for interrupting your work," he said, not sounding apologetic at all, "but I'm afraid we couldn't wait until the winter season was over."

"What couldn't wait?" MacArthur asked.

"We're part of a task force," the first man said. "Searching for a murderer."

The wood floor of the kitchen creaked.

"Excuse me?" MacArthur said. He'd only heard Jamie mention the investigators on the mainland once, by accident, and Jamie hadn't explained anything further. What would bring those men to their door?

"Really, George," the second man said with a sigh. "They gave us a whole script. Listen," he said to the keepers, "there's been an ongoing manhunt spread across nearly the whole damn country, starting from Glasgow. They've hired men in nearly every town from coast to coast. Your village was too small to warrant its own force, so we've been sent to investigate since we were the closest jurisdiction."

"A manhunt," MacArthur repeated.

"Aye," the second man said.

"Well, I'm not sure if we can make your trip worth it," MacArthur said. "Hard to hide on an island this small."

"Aye," the second man said again, "but even so, we're being paid to ask, so we'd better ask."

The first man ran through a list of questions about how

long MacArthur, Jamie, and Maisie had been working at the lighthouse, and where they'd been before that.

When they came to Maisie, she hesitated, and then said, "Edinburgh."

"Long ways to travel for a job," the second man observed.

"There aren't many lighthouses hiring in Edinburgh," Maisie responded.

When they turned the question on Jamie, he gave the name of a town that Quinn didn't know. The men moved on without note.

MacArthur answered the questions readily, but both Jamie and Maisie remained cautious as the men continued. Quinn knew that Glasgow was a large human city, many times bigger than the little coastal town Owen called home, and she wondered how its problems could spread so far.

She was just beginning to relax when another voice called out from the hallway, "Excuse me, I hate to interrupt your investigation, but was that seal fur I saw in the other room?"

Quinn's heart jumped into her throat, and she scrabbled for a grip on the wall, pressing herself flat as if she could disappear into it. That was Owen's voice. He was here. He'd found her. She cursed silently, thinking of the pelt she'd left out in Maisie's room when she'd been distracted by Maisie waking her up with warm, curious hands.

"Who are you?" Maisie asked, and Quinn's legs trembled.

"This is a local fisherman, who volunteered to be our guide," the first man said. "Owen?"

"Yes, sir," Owen replied. Quinn had told Maisie Owen's name during one of their story trades, and she heard Maisie make a muffled noise.

There was a pause. "In the other room," Owen explained. "There was a pelt on the bed. Very fine looking."

"Yes." Maisie's voice was strangled.

"Do you hunt?" Jamie asked quickly. Of course, he'd recognized Owen's name, too.

"Only once," Owen said, low. "But it was a fine catch."

Dark clouds had begun gathering far off in the distance. They rolled and built just like the turmoil in Quinn's chest, and she wondered if she should lean into it to summon a storm that would chase Owen and these men off the island. But such a drastic change would be too suspicious for MacArthur to ignore. She couldn't reveal herself yet.

Quinn took a few slow breaths and forced herself to pay attention to the humans. The clouds remained but didn't advance on the island.

"My grandfather was a fisherman and warned me to leave the seals alone," the second man added cautiously. "Some superstition he had about bringing bad luck. Herds have thinned around here, though. Most of the seals moved up and around the coast to the east, according to the men he used to sail with."

This caught Quinn's attention through the panic. This man had provided Quinn the first real clue to where her herd may have gone.

"Fascinating," MacArthur drawled.

"That pelt you have," Owen continued, trying to regain control, "would you consider selling it?"

"No," Maisie said flatly, before he'd even finished speaking. The silence in the kitchen pressed on Quinn's lungs.

"It has," Maisie said roughly, "sentimental meaning to me."

"Right," Owen said, and Quinn's heart dropped from her

throat to her stomach. He knew it was Quinn's pelt. Would he think that Maisie had taken it from Quinn and trapped her on this island, that Maisie would be able to claim the fortune Quinn had never brought to him? Now that he knew where it was, he would know Quinn wasn't far off.

"Well," the second man said, "thank you for answering our questions, gentlemen. We appreciate your cooperation."

There was a shuffle of footsteps as MacArthur impressed on the men that it was important for them to return to their boat and the mainland before the weather turned.

"Owen," one of the men called. Was Owen still in the kitchen trying to figure out how to ask where Quinn was without giving anything away to the two investigators? He must've been furious, knowing that she was so close but still out of reach. And his pride wouldn't be able to stand the thought that Maisie was claiming the selkie luck and fortune that he himself had never obtained.

Finally, slow footsteps made the floors creak as Owen left, calling back to the men. Quinn worried that he would still try to take her pelt on his way out, but he couldn't do anything with MacArthur watching.

Quinn stayed pressed against the wall even as their voices faded. If Jamie and Maisie were still in the kitchen, they didn't make a sound either.

The bright, sunny day that Quinn had preserved seemed too cheerful, too far in opposition to the dread settling in Quinn's belly. She didn't want to move yet, for fear of Owen seeing her as the men left the island, but she was also frozen in place from what she'd heard.

How could she have been so careless to leave her pelt in plain view? Maisie's room had become a safe place for it. This was only true so long as it was only the lighthouse keepers around. She'd leaned into the comfort and safety the keepers offered, and this is what her carelessness had cost her.

Hearing Maisie claim her pelt had made Quinn's heart jump, but Quinn needed to be able to protect her pelt herself. Now Maisie was in danger because of Owen's attention, too.

Still, she remembered what the man had said after. If the humans had noticed that the seal population that used to live in this area moved to the east, there was a good chance that her herd was a part of that migration. And perhaps her mother was among them. How long would it take her to travel all that way on her own?

But even as Quinn's blood sang for her to go in search of her herd, she felt as if her feet were caught in a muddy bog. Could she leave this island to go searching for her family on the small chance that she'd find them again? Could she stay here and live with not knowing? Could she stay at all, now that Owen knew where she was?

"Quinn."

Maisie had appeared around the side of the lighthouse, her mouth a tense line and the skin around her eyes tight with worry. She offered Quinn a hand to help her down from the crates.

"I'm so sorry," Maisie said. "Your pelt, I should have moved it, but I didn't think—"

"Neither did I."

"He's gone now," Maisie told her, hand still outstretched. "They've all gone." Quinn slid her palm into Maisie's and stepped off the pile of crates, Maisie easily supporting her weight as Quinn leaned into her.

Quinn kept her eyes on the water as they circled back to the front door, scanning for the retreating boat, but Maisie hurried her inside before she could find it.

As they walked back toward the kitchen, Quinn paused by Maisie's open door. Her pelt was draped over the end of Maisie's bed like an invitation. What good would it do to stuff it away into a drawer now? The damage was done.

In the kitchen, Jamie was standing by the window with his back to the wall, a far-off look in his eyes. MacArthur was seated at the table, his elbow resting on the scrubbed wood so he could pinch the thin skin at the top of the bridge of his nose. His eyes were pressed shut.

"You said he wouldn't come here," Jamie rumbled at Quinn. "Didn't you?"

MacArthur blinked at Jamie and looked at Quinn. "One of those men was your husband?"

"The fisherman," she confirmed.

She was ready for his next words to be a dismissal from the lighthouse, but instead MacArthur let out a large sigh. "Right, that'll have to be first then. Jamie," he said, and Jamie immediately cut his gaze to MacArthur. "Maisie. Sit, if you would."

Quinn and Maisie moved to take up their usual bench across from where MacArthur was seated, but he held up his hand.

"Ms. Quinn, if you wouldn't mind sitting beside me. I'd rather my keepers sit together."

Quinn glanced at Maisie, but did as MacArthur asked,

maneuvering herself onto the bench beside him. Maisie sat directly across from her.

Jamie unpeeled himself from the wall slowly and shuffled into the remaining seat.

MacArthur took a few slow breaths before lowering his hand and opening his eyes.

"He wanted your pelt."

Quinn had to grit her teeth to keep reacting too sharply. "He knows how it works."

"And he knows we're hiding you," Jamie cut in. "He led those men here."

"It seemed to be the other way around to me." MacArthur frowned. "He was able to get here because they needed a guide. My question is, now that he knows where you are, how safe is it for you to remain here?"

Quinn clenched her hands in her lap. She'd known the moment she'd heard Owen's voice that the lighthouse could no longer shelter her. Her gaze shifted painfully to Maisie, who looked like she was barely containing herself from breaking down in tears, her freckles stark against her pale face.

"If she stays, she ruins us all," Jamie declared in a deadened voice. "If her husband came here once, he'll come again, and I reckon he'll bring more men next time to ensure he can take what he came for."

"But those men weren't here for Quinn!" Maisie cried. "Owen used them to get to her!"

"It doesn't matter now," Jamie said. "They'll come back, and she can't be here when they do."

Something burst in Quinn's chest. The night he'd learned

her secret, it seemed like Jamie was frightened of what she could do to them as a monstrous selkie. But now, Owen was the danger. He was still ruining her life and any sense of safety she'd been able to cobble together. Quinn opened her mouth to speak.

"They weren't here for her!" Maisie yelled. "They were here for me!"

Quinn let out a startled gasp instead.

"What?" MacArthur asked, face pinched. Jamie turned to stare at his fellow keeper.

Maisie touched her fingertips to her lips, like she was also shocked by what had passed through them. She met Quinn's eyes again and gathered her nerve.

"Maisie," MacArthur said, soft but stern.

"They came for me," Maisie repeated.

Fingers trembling slightly, Maisie dropped her hands to the table. Although her breaths were unsteady, she set her chin and confessed.

"I didn't become Tavis just to get this job. I mean, I knew I needed a man's name to even send in an application, but I'd already been using the name Murdoch before I'd ever heard of the lighthouse. It's easier for a man to slip through a town alone than a woman." Quinn remembered what Maisie had told her about her journey to get here, the struggles she'd had. Maisie had told her it had been worth it to leave her caged life behind. "And I knew they would be looking for a woman."

She rubbed at the bare skin of the fourth finger on her left hand.

"I was engaged. An agreement my parents made with a man who wanted to invest in my father's business. My father is a metalworker. Tools, knives, things like that. Both my brothers were apprenticed under him, and they needed the work. I was just part of the deal," Maisie recited, and Quinn frowned. "I met the man I would marry the day my parents told me.

"I begged them not to make me marry him. I didn't want to be married. I wanted to work in my father's shop. But of course"—Maisie laughed hollowly—"that wasn't proper work for a lady. We were engaged, and there was nothing my parents could do unless they wanted to lose everything.

"We were allowed to be left alone together, since we were engaged, and while he wasn't what you would call charming in public, he was downright awful in private. He was used to getting what he wanted without asking twice."

Maisie rolled her shoulders, as if throwing off unseen hands.

"It must have been only a week or two until our wedding, he came to our house. Father and my brothers were at the shop, and my mother left us alone to go to the market, or maybe he told her to leave, I don't remember," she said. "But he didn't want to wait a week or two. He would have what he thought was his."

Her voice was cold and biting like a north wind.

"We were in the kitchen when he grabbed hold of me. I screamed, but he covered my mouth with one hand. He tasted like iron. He was much bigger than me and angry that I was fighting back. He pinned me against the counter next to my mother's knife block. My father made my mother those knives for her cooking. He sharpened them every season. One of them was for carving, for butchering an animal." Maisie's eyes had glassed over, and while Quinn desperately wanted to reach out and take her hand, she worried that if she touched Maisie now, she'd shatter. "I took it from the block and aimed for his neck."

The lighthouse's kitchen was dead quiet as Maisie searched for her next words.

"I knew—I couldn't stay there. I couldn't wait for my family to return. I left him on the floor and ran to my room to grab some clothes and the little bit of money I'd been able to save." Her mouth twisted. "There was blood on my dress so I stole a pair of my brother's pants instead. Then I took my coat and left."

Maisie spread her hands, palms up, on the table.

"There would be no question about guilt," she told them. "But staying there as his wife would have been just as bad as being locked up for his death. I became Tavis Murdoch in the next town. Odd jobs got me further and further from Edinburgh, until I saw the advertisement for the lighthouse."

"Edinburgh," MacArthur said, finally breaking the silence. "But those men only mentioned Glasgow."

Maisie nodded slowly. "His family, my fiancé's family, is originally from Glasgow and his parents still live there. His father's business there is what gave him his credibility in Edinburgh. It's not hard for me to believe they would pay for a manhunt for their son's murderer."

"It was self-defense," Jamie whispered. He was hoarse, like he'd been screaming, but it was his words that finally made Maisie look up and meet his gaze.

"Self-defense," Jamie said again. "He forced you."

"I killed him," Maisie said plainly.

"You were trying to protect yourself," Jamie amended. "He was in the way."

Maisie stared at him, mouth parted. Never, in all Quinn's time living as a human, had she heard a man defending a woman for fighting back against another man.

Remembering what Maisie had originally shared with her on the beach, Quinn wondered if Maisie hadn't told her this part of her story right away because she had expected Quinn to be shocked or repulsed by her actions. Her story certainly seemed to stand in sharp contrast with the kind, selfless human she had begun to deeply care for, but if anything, Maisie's confession strengthened Quinn's feelings toward her. Quinn knew what Maisie must have been feeling at that moment. She recognized the lines that had been crossed, the limits that Maisie had been pushed to, and she knew she, too, would have lashed out like Maisie had.

Quinn did not expect the two male keepers to understand this. But Jamie's gaze was steady. She risked a glance at MacArthur.

The lead lighthouse keeper was looking between his employees, mouth pressed in a tight line as he considered what Maisie had shared. Quinn let herself feel relieved that MacArthur was not immediately appalled by Maisie's actions or her honesty.

"Those men didn't say anything about a woman," he observed. "In a case such as yours, I would think that would be their leading question."

Shuffling in her seat and sitting up a bit straighter, her shoulders uncurling, Maisie swiped the back of her hand under her eyes to wipe away the tears that had sprung up there.

"I know," she said. "But when they said Glasgow, and Owen was asking about Quinn's pelt, I panicked."

MacArthur made a disbelieving gesture. "And yet somehow, you are a proficient enough liar to convince Jamie and me of your identity as Tavis Murdoch."

Maisie gave him a weak grin. "I only had to prove I was a good worker. You didn't care about the rest."

"True." MacArthur sighed. "When I requested additional keepers, I didn't care about pedigree or history. I only wanted people who would work hard and support the unforgiving demands of the lighthouse. You have done exactly what I asked."

Maisie looked relieved to have finally unraveled her story, but then MacArthur continued. "This does not solve our current problem, however. Those men may not be looking for you, but this fisherman will certainly return for Quinn."

Jamie leaned forward, arms braced on the table. He had been studying Maisie with a pained expression, though Quinn wasn't sure if it was from the horror of her past or the thought of his fellow keeper being taken away, and now he slid his gaze over to Quinn. Everything he'd said the night of Maisie's rescue was still weighing down Quinn's chest with guilt.

But instead of the sharp, vindictive glare she'd been expecting, Jamie's eyes were full of pity. It startled her to see such an expression on his face after he'd questioned her place in the lighthouse. Had Maisie's story softened him? He seemed ready to believe what Quinn had said about her own past, and perhaps seeing that reality so close on Quinn's heels undercut his remaining reservations about her.

"He will come back," Jamie said, echoing MacArthur.

"I know," Quinn said. And when he did, he would bring the men who could be searching for Maisie. If Quinn stayed, she would risk being captured by Owen again, and she would bring an end to Maisie's freedom. She turned to her keeper.

Maisie's mouth was slightly parted, cheeks pale under her freckles as she arrived at the same conclusion that Jamie and Quinn had already realized.

"I'm sorry," Quinn told her. "I can't keep my promise. I'll have to leave before Owen returns."

Chapter Nineteen

LUCKILY FOR QUINN AND the lighthouse keepers, the winter weather prevented any more boats from coming to the island the next day. The sea was rough with choppy waves and gusts of wind strong enough to tip a five-man boat. The rain was less consistent than the wind. Clouds would suddenly spit down like they were aiming for Jamie or Maisie as the two scrambled around the lighthouse like worker bees protecting the hive. Then, just as suddenly as the rain started, it would stop.

The storms were mostly natural, but Quinn had pushed her influence onto them to ensure the water was completely unsailable. She knew she was only delaying the inevitable.

Part of her had already begun drawing away from Maisie the moment she'd seen the three men's boat at the dock. She kept remembering Owen asking about her pelt and how close she'd come to losing it again. Her pelt was still on Maisie's bed, but the anxious tug in her chest whenever she left it alone in the room had returned.

Her foot was healed. Quinn's original deal with MacArthur had been that he would let her stay at the lighthouse while she recovered. But then Maisie had asked her to stay. Not until she was healed, or until the winter weather cleared—she had simply asked her to *stay*.

As much as Quinn wished she could remain at the lighthouse in the bubble of safety the keepers had created for her, she could not stay and risk Owen capturing her again or risk Maisie's future to the manhunt. She also remembered what one of the investigators had said, and it pulled at her like an insistent wind would pull at her at the cliff's edge.

The seal herds from this area had moved east. Her family could have migrated with them. Now that her wound was healed and she was gaining her strength back, she could go searching for them. It had been seven years since she saw another selkie, and the thought of being with one of her own kind again made her feel like her lungs were full of water.

The following morning, two days after the men had come to the island, Quinn woke with her nose pressed into Maisie's shoulder. She'd slept fitfully, her mind racing the whole night with thoughts of where her herd could be, how many of her family were still alive after all this time. Even with Maisie breathing steadily beside her, Quinn couldn't relax.

The room was lit weakly from a gray dawn. She'd listened to the sporadic fall of rain all night, but the clouds seemed to have let up for the time being.

Moving slowly, Quinn slid out from under Maisie's sleep-heavy arm and dressed in the half-light of the morning. She had figured out by now that Maisie was not easily woken, but she was careful not to disturb her anyway.

Quinn pulled Maisie's old coat on top of all her other borrowed clothes and slipped from the room.

The wood floorboards creaked beneath her steps. She tiptoed past Jamie's room and unlatched the front door, immediately greeted by the bite of a chill winter morning when she stepped outside.

The clouds were ever present these days, but as Quinn walked slowly around the lighthouse, she spotted a break in the sky, far off on the horizon. The clouds had split apart to show a pink-and-yellow sky, dyed brilliantly by the rising sun that was hidden from Quinn's view. It illuminated the sea below.

Quinn was barefoot. With her wound healed, she should have borrowed a pair of boots, and her toes were feeling the bite of cold in the damp grass, but she wanted to feel the earth beneath her feet.

On top of the island, staring out at a far-off patch of ocean, Quinn could remember how it had felt to be trapped in Owen's house. She had broken free of that cage. Could she close herself into another?

A life with Maisie wouldn't feel like a cage, but if she stayed, she would be closing off a future without seeing if it was possible.

Quinn had to know. She would have to leave this island and search for her herd, and she would have to leave Maisie behind. The thought made her feel as if her heart were being wrenched in two.

But even if she left and escaped Owen's reach, how could she be sure that Maisie would be safe? Owen could still come back to the island searching for Quinn and her pelt and bring the investigators with him. Without Quinn there, Owen's search would come to nothing, but the men could close in on Maisie, even if it was just to realize that she was a woman disguising herself as a man. If Maisie was discovered, would the other keepers be in trouble, as well?

If she left now, Quinn would be too far away to help. She didn't think she could leave Maisie on the island without knowing that the life she'd built at the lighthouse was secure. But could she convince Maisie to leave with her and abandon the lighthouse to ensure she kept her freedom? Quinn thought of another story her mother had told her, a story that seemed so fantastic that Quinn had hardly believed it. A story she had remembered when she'd seen Flora soaked and alone on a beach, but Quinn had worried that she had nothing left of herself to give to make it come true.

After her years with Owen, Quinn had dreaded the thought of giving up another piece of herself. She was already so fractured, so desperate to hold on to any part of her that had made it out of that town. But Quinn no longer felt like she was clinging desperately to keep herself whole. Because of Maisie. At every turn, Maisie had given and given and given to Quinn, her kindness, her home, her love, and it had never made her any less. Maisie had shown Quinn that she could give a piece of herself and get just as much in return.

Quinn let her mother's story fill her with hope. It was possible she could bring Maisie with her when she left, but she'd have to tell Maisie the truth about what she could do. She would have to let Maisie see every part of her.

QUINN WENT TO MACARTHUR first. He had risked so much letting Quinn stay in his lighthouse, and she didn't want to leave without being completely honest with him. Quinn knew there was a good chance he would not be as accepting toward her after she told him the truth, but it wouldn't matter once she was gone, and MacArthur deserved to know.

MacArthur was, of course, in his office, updating his weather log. It was still early in the morning, but the rest of the lighthouse had begun to wake up. She knocked softly at his door, which was unlatched and swung open slightly at her touch.

"Yes?" MacArthur asked, head still bent over the paper as he scratched out a few more lines.

"I need to tell you something," Quinn said.

She hesitated by his desk, the second chair in the room again buried by a stack of books and some paper tied together with a thick string. He glanced up at her, glasses perched on the tip of his nose so he had to tilt his chin down to look at her over the top of the rims.

"All right," he said. "Just let me finish this."

He waved his pen at the chair. "You can move all that."

She did, looking around the orderly room for a place to put everything. MacArthur finished his last few notes and blew on the ink to make it dry quicker.

"Weather log," he told her unnecessarily. "Not much to say, but this cloud cover is different from last year."

Quinn, responsible for said clouds, nodded absently. She waited for him to put away the pen and remove his glasses, and then he turned his attention on her.

"So," he said, "you're leaving, then?"

"You allowed me to stay as long as my foot was healing, and now I'm healed. So yes, I am leaving," she confirmed. "But I have something I need to tell you first."

MacArthur frowned but gestured to her to go on before tucking his hand in his lap.

Quinn took a breath.

"The morning after Maisie fell into the water, we talked about who I am," she started.

"A selkie," MacArthur said.

"Yes, and we spoke about what you all knew about selkies, about what stories you'd heard," she said. "The basics."

MacArthur nodded curtly and didn't ask why she was bringing this up again. Perhaps he was picking up the slight urgency in Quinn's voice or the focused gleam in her eye.

"There is more," Quinn told him. "More that you should know about me. I did not tell you then, because I did not want to leave."

"Quinn—" MacArthur began cautiously.

She cut him off. "I know I must leave. Nothing can change that now. But after everything you've done, I figured you deserved to know who you've been protecting all this time..."

The oil lamp on MacArthur's desk crackled, making the flame shiver and throw strange shadows across MacArthur's face.

Quinn told him, "There are stories that I heard as a pup that I hardly believed, because I couldn't understand them. Stories of my kind being filled with unwieldy emotions, rage, grief, fear, enough that the feelings could consume them like a whirlpool. But instead of drowning in these emotions, these selkies could send the feelings outward. All that rage or fear, they could send it out, where it would take another form.

"When I was young, I could hardly imagine ever feeling such a way. But then when my pelt was stolen, when I was forced to remain on land with a man who saw me as a tool, I understood. I knew what that rage felt like. I felt it wash over me, and I let it suck me down."

Quinn leaned back in her chair, fingers flexing in her lap as she remembered the moment she gave in to the feeling.

"That rage could have ruined me. Without my pelt, it was like a piece of me was carved away, leaving a gaping wound. The rage only widened it. But instead of tearing me apart from the inside, I remembered what my mother told me. I let it go. I forced it out into the world."

Trying to explain the feeling with words felt unsubstantial. Quinn could see the confusion on MacArthur's face. She needed to make him understand in a way he couldn't deny.

Getting to her feet, Quinn went to the bookcase and swiftly scanned the spines, which were labeled with dates. The lighthouse hadn't been around when she had first come to shore, but there were years of records going back since MacArthur had been placed in charge. She tried to remember times in the past four years when she had given in to the storm.

MacArthur already had the most recent journal spread out on the desk, so Quinn searched through the dates, trailing her finger along the spines of the packed shelf until she found a few journals with dates that stood out. She pried them out of the bookcase and brought them to the desk.

"Depending on which story you believe," Quinn told him, "selkies are creatures of the sea. We come from the water and live at the mercy of the ocean. But selkies are also part human, and in the other stories, we wished to be part of the water, and the sea listened. It turned us into creatures that could swim the depths just as we could walk on land."

Quinn opened the oldest journal on the desk and began flipping through the pages, slowing down and turning them with more care when MacArthur made an aborted motion to try and take over. She kept talking as she scanned the pages.

"No matter what our origin was, the ocean heard our wish and granted it. She listened to us. But selkies are not just connected to the water. We know the tides, the wind, even the rain that falls on us from above," Quinn said quickly as the dates in the journal came closer and closer to what she was looking for. "And they listen, too."

Finally, she turned the page and an entry with tight, slanted handwriting caught her eye, the script a bit messy as if the writer had been in a hurry.

March 17, 1896

Sudden storm trampled in from the south, not in charts or predictions. Heavy rain with winds from south and southwest, pushing clouds into a collision path with the mainland. Passed over island in late afternoon. Minimal lightning.

She shifted the journal toward MacArthur and pointed at the date.

"My oldest daughter's second birthday. Owen left me alone in the house with her, my one-year-old daughter, and my infant son. When my daughter realized he was gone, she broke down crying, and nothing I could say could calm her down. Her sister got caught up in it. I felt so helpless, and angry at Owen for leaving me there," Quinn recalled. "And angry that it was already so obvious that I was useless to my children as a mother."

Quinn pushed that journal aside and pulled the next one forward, thumbing through the pages. She found the next one quickly and put her finger on the date.

"My son's birthday. He came into this world reluctantly, and nearly killed me on the way out."

Huge storm from the west, not part of the chart predictions, the journal reported. *High westward winds and frequent lightning made it impossible to sleep, concerned about the beacon but all operated smoothly until morning.*

She went through the next journal and found a few more before glancing up from the pages at MacArthur. He was sitting still and straight in his chair, but a crease had formed between his eyebrows. He was studying his own writing but looked up at her when she paused.

Quinn waved her hand at MacArthur's desk and at the towering bookcase stuffed full of journals with pages and pages of similar information.

"You track the weather," Quinn said. "Your predictions are accurate nearly to the last drop of rain. How do you explain these storms that seem to come out of nowhere?"

"There are always margins of error," MacArthur said, his voice barely above a whisper.

Quinn inhaled and nodded, but she pushed aside the older journals and brought the most recent one back to the front of the desk. Careful of MacArthur's last entry, she flipped back a few weeks until she found the day Owen had pierced her with the harpoon.

"This is the day my husband tried to spear me like a wild animal," she told him.

Terrible storm rolled in with little warning. Pushed in by winds from the west and northwest, strange for this time of year.

She turned a few pages forward and gestured to another entry.

"When I tried to put my pelt on after Maisie found me, and the ocean spat me out like a bone."

Storm overwhelmed the island, heavy downpour rolling in from the west. Predicted rainy weather but not to this degree.

Quinn tilted the journal until the pages fell open to the most recent page, which included MacArthur's notes from the last few days. His entry the morning after Maisie fell into the water was clipped but just as informative as the others.

Predicted storm much worse than expected, high winds from north and visibility obscured beyond ten meters. Keeper Murdoch taken over cliff by winds, rescued.

Seeing Maisie's fake name in MacArthur's reports made Quinn's chest twinge. He was protecting her even in his journals, knowing that he would have to submit them to the board.

When he noticed what date she was looking at, MacArthur finally spoke.

"The storm that nearly took Maisie?"

Mouth thin, Quinn said, "Not at the beginning. It was in your predictions, wasn't it? But you said yourself that it was stronger than it was supposed to have been. That was me. When Jamie told us she'd fallen in…"

She trailed off, figuring that MacArthur would be able to recall his own emotions in that moment quite well.

A few moments ticked by in silence. MacArthur took his hand from his lap and laid it over the journal, his fingers spread wide over the neat writing.

"So what you are telling me," he said softly, "is that you can control the weather."

"I don't think 'control' is the right word," Quinn said. She had never been able to call a storm into existence with just a thought or stop one from approaching just because she wanted to. She had as much control over the storms as she did over the blood flowing in her veins. The storms simply listened for her call and responded in their own way.

"Then what is the right word?"

MacArthur lifted his gaze from the desk and met Quinn's. He was giving her the same attention he had given to Maisie when she'd divulged her sordid past, and her skin prickled under his sharp eyes.

"I can influence it," she relented.

"And you are telling me this because…" he prompted her.

"Because I need you to believe me when I tell you another story," she said, her chest constricting with each breath.

Was this still the right thing to do? MacArthur and Maisie had laid their stories bare in front of her, but that did not mean she owed them her stories in return. It would be so easy to let the keepers think they knew everything about her there was to know. Quinn could slip from their lives like a story that faded as it was passed from person to person, until she was only a piece of a mismatched legend.

But, no, Quinn thought. That wasn't at all fair to Maisie or MacArthur, or even Jamie. Quinn knew what it was to be taken advantage of by someone who couldn't recognize the pain they were inflicting. Quinn didn't want to be the person who hurt them through her inaction. What if Owen returned and revealed the truth about what Quinn had wrought with her storms? It wouldn't take long for someone like MacArthur to work out what Quinn had hidden from them.

She needed them to hear the truth from her own mouth.

Quinn took a shaky breath and told him, "There was another storm, long before the lighthouse was built. Far before you started recording the weather around this island. Seven years ago."

MacArthur's sole hand flexed on the journal, and the page made a soft crinkling sound as it crumpled under the pressure. His gaze was fixed on Quinn's face.

"Seven years ago," she continued slowly, "I had never set foot on a human beach. I grew up in this area with my herd, and our parents warned us away from the occupied shores, but I wanted to know. I wanted to know what it was like to walk on two legs. I wanted to see what it was my mother was so frightened of.

"My wish was granted. I came to shore. I walked on two legs. And the man who would become my husband stole my pelt from the beach and forced me to follow him back to the human town."

Quinn stretched her legs out straight in front of her, eyeing the thick muscle of her thighs, the curve of her calves beneath the thick pants, the delicate structure of her ankle.

"It hurt more than I can describe," she whispered. "Having my pelt taken from me was like having a limb peeled away layer by layer. I screamed and cried, but he wouldn't listen to anything I said. I was forced to follow him or else I felt I would have been torn to pieces.

"That was the first time I called out, and the storms called back."

The oil lamp sputtered on the desk before finding a steady flame once more. The wind picked up, and the lighthouse creaked in response.

Quinn looked up. "I don't need to describe the storm that came to shore that night," she said. "You told me about it your-self."

She didn't dare glance at MacArthur's shortened left arm. The room, already small and further crowded by Mac-Arthur's note keeping, seemed to shrink under the silence that stretched out between them. There was only a handspan distance between their knees.

In her time at the lighthouse, MacArthur never gave Quinn the impression that he was a violent man. Owen had been cruel, and grown violent, and Quinn had quickly learned to recognize it amongst the men in town. MacArthur was too collected to let his temper show on his face let alone in his fist, and she had seen how he had reacted to bad news by treating the problem as something that needed to be fixed, rather than something that needed to be addressed with anger.

Quinn couldn't tell if MacArthur was angry now. He was

tense, his posture stiff, but was it because of shock or rage, or something else?

"I am glad the storm came that night," she whispered, the words loud in the bubble of the office. "It showed me that I will never be powerless. But in my hurt, I caused more pain than I could have ever imagined."

The storm had been a battering, vengeful thing that night seven years ago, even far above the beach in the town where Quinn had been led. She could imagine what it would have been like on the water. Lesser boats would have been swallowed whole. Anything sailing nearby would have been caught unaware in the dark, with no lighthouse to lead them safely away from danger.

MacArthur's chair creaked as he leaned away from her.

"This is what you wanted to tell me?" he asked flatly, eyes closed. The wrinkle between his brows had smoothed away, but he was far from calm.

"Yes."

"Why? Why would you tell me this, when I would have never found out if you had not?"

Quinn hesitated, the tightness in her chest coiling around her heart. MacArthur's proper speech was carefully conceal-ing his true reaction, but a bit of his unease was slipping out between the words. Quinn had known revealing the truth could cause this pain, but seeing it happen in front of her was still difficult to swallow.

"Because I wanted you to know," she told him. "You'll never see me again, but I wanted you to know who I was."

This made MacArthur's careful mask crack, and his face twisted with emotion. He curled his arm around his middle, hand clutching the crisp fabric of his shirt and wrinkling the clean lines.

"Go," he said. The word was barely above a whisper, but to Quinn, it was as good as an order. Her time in the lighthouse was up. She stood and walked quickly to the door. She paused with her hand on the handle.

"I will not forget your kindness, even if you regret it," she told him. "Thank you."

Quinn's steps seemed too loud as she descended the short staircase and hurried to Maisie's room. The door creaked as she pushed inside and released a breath at the sight of her pelt spread out at the end of Maisie's bed. Digging her fingers into the thick fur, Quinn tried to steady her heartbeat.

It was misting softly outside, but Jamie and Maisie had decided to spend the afternoon patching up the rest of the stone fence. Quinn found them huddled together near the entrance where the path trailed in a lazy curve down to the beach, which was out of sight.

Maisie, of course, spotted Quinn the moment she was in sight. Her hat was pulled low over her eyes and she had on her oilskin coat to protect against the chill, damp air, but Quinn could still see how Maisie perked up at the sight of her.

The smile on her face quickly faded when Quinn got closer. Her eyes dropped to the pelt clutched in Quinn's hands.

"Jamie," Quinn called, and Jamie's hands paused laying a stone as he looked up. "MacArthur needs you."

"He asked for me?"

"No," Quinn told him.

Jamie let his gaze travel over Quinn's face and the pelt in

her hands, then shot a quick look at Maisie, who hadn't looked away from Quinn.

"All right," he muttered. He set the stone down at the base of the fence and stood with a grunt. Quinn didn't watch as he headed toward the lighthouse, but she got the feeling he was glancing back at them as he left.

Quinn had left the lighthouse with no shoes on. The grass was sharp and cold, and she tried to focus on that feeling as she watched the torrent of emotions passing over Maisie's face.

"You're leaving," Maisie said.

"It's time," Quinn agreed. She checked over her shoulder to make sure Jamie had gone inside. "I need you to listen to me, Maisie."

Her keeper's brow furrowed, "What is it?"

"I haven't told you everything about me. I didn't think it was worth it for you to know, at first, but now I need you to trust me when I say I have never wanted to hurt you. You've been so kind to me," Quinn said quickly. "And I could never bear it if you came to suffer because of me, or because of what comes after me."

"If you mean Owen," Maisie started, shaking her head.

"Not only him," Quinn continued, stepping forward to take Maisie's hand. "The other men. The ones searching for their murderer." Maisie's fingers stiffened in hers, and she tried to rub some warmth back into them. "I couldn't live with myself if I left and they came and found you instead. I can't leave you here."

Quinn took in a shaky breath. She felt like a candle guttered by the wind, clinging to hope. "I have to leave, but I can take you with me."

Maisie's face was slack with shock. She mouthed wordlessly,

finally managing, "How? You're a selkie, a seal. I'm not made for the sea, you saw when you rescued me."

"Listen to me," Quinn begged her. "There's more to selkies than what you've heard. We can do more—I can do more than you know. My mother once told me a story of a selkie who wished to go back to the ocean, but didn't want to leave their love behind. So they brought their spouse to the sea and made a trade with the ocean. A piece of the selkie in exchange for a pelt for their love."

In between her hands, Maisie's fingers wilted. Quinn tightened her grip on them, heart racing as she watched a dozen thoughts flash behind Maisie's eyes.

Quinn pressed on. "Come with me. Maisie, come to the beach with me and let me take you away from here."

The wind sang across the island around them, and the crash of the waves beckoned from far below. Quinn was breathing hard and the blood was rushing in her ears. She could save Maisie and swim away from here so that Owen could never find her again. She could search for her family with Maisie by her side.

Maisie blinked, as if trying to awaken from a dream. "What if it's just a story?"

"There's truth to the stories," Quinn said. "I'd heard of selkies who could influence the weather, too, but I'd never thought it was real until it happened to me. You can ask MacArthur; his journals confirm that the storms came from me—"

"You went to MacArthur first?" Maisie asked, hurt plain on her face.

"I had to be honest with him before I left. The storms are my fault," Quinn explained. "Any of the storms that aren't in

MacArthur's predictions are because of me, because I can't control my emotions. The one that nearly killed you," Quinn said, but Maisie was shaking her head.

"It's just been a rough winter," Maisie said.

"Because of me," Quinn stressed. She tried to draw Maisie closer to her, but the keeper resisted. "When I'm angry, or afraid, or feeling anything so strongly that I can barely contain it in my body, a part of me calls out, and the storms answer."

"Weather is always temperamental by the coast," Maisie bit out.

Quinn took a steadying breath, feeling overly fond of and exasperated by Maisie's bullheadedness at the same time.

"But it's more than that," Quinn said. "I'm telling you now because I wanted to return all the honesty you've given me with the one thing I didn't want to tell you, because I knew it would change how you saw me. It may be cowardly to wait until I had to leave, but I needed him to know."

"You told him this?" Maisie asked.

"I had to," Quinn said. "Maisie, it's my fault he lost his arm. I caused the storm seven years ago. The same night his ship came by this island was the night my pelt was stolen."

Maisie's hand slipped from between Quinn's fingers. She was shaking her head as she took staggering steps back until her legs hit the fence. Quinn stayed where she was even as her heart began to sink.

Pulling the knit hat from her head, Maisie asked, "How long have you known this?"

Quinn met her searching eyes with as calm a face as she could muster. "Since he told me how he lost his arm."

It was too long, Quinn knew. Too much had happened

since that moment, and yet Quinn had said nothing. She had promised Maisie the truth and then withheld it.

"Maisie," Quinn pleaded, "I'm sorry I didn't tell you until now, but please, come with me. I can explain more once we're safe, but I can't stay here any longer and I don't want to leave you. Please come with me."

"She won't be going anywhere with you," Jamie said suddenly, and Quinn flinched around to see him standing at the edge of the lighthouse, a hard expression on his face. "Especially not to the sea. I was right to doubt you all this time, wasn't I?"

"Not for the reasons you thought," Quinn argued warily, cautious of Jamie's size.

"Oh, sure," Jamie said. "You didn't kill your husband, but you'll seduce a human and use them until they'll follow you to the depths. You'll let your emotions, your storms, destroy their lives and then won't apologize."

Maisie let out a strangled sound, and Quinn shook her head. "I don't want to hurt her. I want to save her!"

Jamie's face was hard. He took a few steps and stopped so he was closer to Maisie than Quinn. The keepers were both studying her, as if they could pry the true story out of her through looks alone. Maisie's eyes were welling with tears. The look of pity Jamie had for Quinn was wiped clean, though the one that had replaced it was complicated. Quinn shifted on her feet, picking up the heel of her injured foot and rotating her ankle to observe the way the newly pink, newly healed skin pulled taut and flexed with the movement. She thought about the young male seal in her herd that had died because his wounds made him slow, and the herd had not been able to protect him. The only reason Quinn had healed so cleanly was because of Jamie. She was standing freely because Jamie and Maisie had helped her do so.

Even though Jamie was barely containing his anger, Quinn turned away from him to face Maisie again.

"I never wanted to use you," she said quietly. "You remember what you told me about my freedom? How it is finally in my own hands?"

The thick mist was clearing, only for a fiercely cold rain to replace it. Like a frozen cloud lifting up off the island to release a bitter deluge. Wet tracks ran in tiny rivulets down Maisie's face, including two dripping from the outer corners of her eyes. Her face was crumpled, but she nodded, just once.

"You were my choice," Quinn told her. "But I can't stay here and risk losing you to my past mistakes. If there was any chance I could save you by making you a selkie, I would take it. I would trade anything."

Maisie was shivering. Her oilskin coat couldn't protect her from the rain sluicing down her hair and neck. It took everything in Quinn not to crush the distance between them and beg for Maisie to forgive her, to wrap the pelt around the two of them and hold Maisie where she would be safe and warm.

Maisie pressed her clenched hands to her chest, her chin dipping down as she muttered, "I...I can't..."

She couldn't even look at Quinn. When she parted her lips but no more words came out, Jamie moved between them.

"The agreement we had is over. You're healed. You need to leave us alone, before your mess ruins us all," he told Quinn. His gaze was colder than the wind. "She's made her choice."

Maisie's silence hurt, like Quinn knew she was hurting Maisie. This was the dagger that Quinn had been so afraid of from the moment Maisie had found her on that beach, the one she'd been watching come closer and closer to her heart, until the sharp point was flush to her skin, angled just so it could slide between her ribs like a whisper.

Quinn took a step back, and the thread between them snapped.

With her pelt clutched in her hands, and the startling sense of déjà vu from when Flora had handed it back to her for the first time in seven years and Quinn tasted bittersweet freedom on her tongue, Quinn turned and ran. The path was cold, muddy, and jarring under her feet. The wind and the rain were rushing in her ears, or else that was just her imagination as her heart beat maddeningly in her chest.

When Quinn made it to the beach, she risked looking back. Maisie hadn't followed her. Jamie watched her go before turning away, shepherding Maisie inside. Far above her at the top of the island, the lighthouse stood dark, the beacon unlit even as the clouds shadowed the sky.

The beach's rocks were slippery, and she staggered toward the cliff where she had lain those first few nights, alone until Maisie had made sure she was never alone again. There was nothing to indicate that Quinn had spent time there. Anything she'd had, Maisie had given her.

Quinn put a hand to her chest, resting over the thick knit of Maisie's sweater. Laying her pelt gently at her feet, Quinn quickly stripped herself of Maisie's clothes and, after a moment's hesitation, carefully folded them and tucked them beneath a large rock closest to the spot Maisie had found her in. Perhaps Maisie wouldn't want them back, but Quinn had no use for them anymore.

She picked up her pelt again. The waves slapped meaning-fully against the shore, as if beckoning her to hurry up. The sea beyond the waves looked dark and endless.

Quinn stepped into the path of the tide, and the freezing water rushed up to meet her. She shivered, her thin human skin prickling against the cold, and the pain of it was enough to pull her focus away from Maisie. She couldn't risk her pelt not working again.

Quinn sucked in a deep breath and drew her pelt tight around her shoulders. Leveling her eyes on the dim horizon, she charged into the water and dove headfirst into the waves.

It was like being swallowed by a snowstorm. The seawater churned around her, the shock of the cold threatening to squeeze the air from her lungs. Quinn pulled the two ends of her pelt tight across her chest and forced herself to think of nothing but being a seal again.

And slowly, as she kicked ineffectively with her flat human feet, she felt the pelt meld to her back, felt her knees knock together and the seam between her legs seal up tightly until she had a thickly muscled, powerful tail to propel her through the water. Her goose-bump-covered arms shortened into flip-pers. The skin slipped over her head, and Quinn blinked her eyes open to the expanse of ocean in front of her. Her nose twitched, whiskers caught in the push and pull of the tide.

A seal once more, Quinn twisted in the water to cast one last look at the empty beach and the dark outline of the light-house on the crest of the island. Then she turned away and swam into the deep.

Chapter Twenty

QUINN SWAM INTO DEEPER water. This time of year, the sea was warmer a few meters down than it was on the surface.

Her body was moving fluidly, as if no time at all had passed since she'd been forced to go ashore. There was a small starburst scar on her right tail fin where the spear had hit her. It would serve to remind her what humans were capable of, and perhaps in time the scar on her heart would heal as well.

Which made her wonder why she was heading toward the town. She should have set her nose north, where in her distant memory she could recall a shaky outline of the coast and the distance she would need to cover before she could round the top of the mainland and begin to make her way east. But instead, Quinn was pushing toward the beach where she had been captured all those years ago.

Perhaps it was her instinct, kicking free of her dulled human senses, and compelling her to go back to where it all started so she could leave this part of her story behind. Perhaps it was curiosity. Then again, she thought as she startled a small shoal of fish risking the surface to feed, the feeling that was tugging her forward had nothing to do with the seal instincts she'd grown up with.

No boats passed above her as she swam. When the seafloor began to rise up to meet her, Quinn rose with it and poked her head above the surface.

The town was gray and dreary in this weather, and Quinn's heart skipped a beat at the sight of it. She snorted and ducked below water before rising back up to try and shake off the nervous feeling. The dock was still a dozen or so meters away and crowded with boats. No fisherman would bother going out in this weather.

Quinn aligned her body so she could glide through the water a little easier, her nose and eyes skimming right above the surface. She gave the docks a wide berth and instead approached the stretch of beach she and the other young seals from her herd had explored that one fateful night.

What was she expecting to see? Seven years had passed since then. The herd was long gone, and she was no longer the carefree seal who had wanted to experience everything for herself. Still, she pushed herself closer.

Movement on the beach made her freeze. Who was out there in this weather? Not a fisherman; they never had any luck catching fish from the shore. Quinn sank as low as she could go in the water while keeping her eyes above the surface. It was hard for her to see at this distance.

She flicked her tail and came in a little closer until she could hear the waves crashing against the rocky shore. Three figures were huddled together in the rain. The tallest one raised her head, and Quinn's heart stopped.

It was Flora. Her hair, braided back in two messy tails, dripped with rain, but she gazed steadily into the water. Did she know Quinn was there?

On either side of her oldest daughter, Evie and Oliver were wrapped in their warmest coats. Evie was saying something to Flora, but Oliver was looking right at Quinn. The sight of them made the tugging feeling in Quinn's chest pull tight.

Her children had called her here.

Quinn looked up and down the beach, searching for Owen. Was he trying to lure her in the way she'd been when she was distracted by Flora?

There was no sign of Owen. Quinn moved a little closer, every muscle tensed in case she needed to make a quick escape. She saw Flora say something quietly to Evie, and her youngest daughter finally looked out to where Quinn was floating in the water.

Oliver, his gray eyes flashing like the inside of oyster shells, took a step away from his sisters, toward the shoreline. As if she were being pulled in by a net, Quinn came closer too.

When Oliver's small boots hit the water, he stopped. Quinn was only a couple meters away now. She drank in the sight of her children. Other than being drenched by the rain, they looked healthy and clean. Their clothes were warm and proper. Oliver had mittens on that Quinn didn't recognize. Owen had been taking care of them, and they had been taking care of one another.

Oliver was staring down at her with a funny pinch to his

mouth. Quinn remembered that this was the first time Evie and Oliver were seeing her like this. Flora had only had a glimpse of her before. She sucked in a deep breath, nose twitching, and rose up a little higher out of the water.

Evie gasped. Flora was looking at her without blinking, as if she could hardly take in everything about Quinn's appearance.

Oliver took another step forward, his foot sloshing in the waves. Quinn made a rumbling noise in her throat. She didn't want him to come too close. But was that for his safety, or hers?

Oliver stilled at the sound.

"Mama?" he asked.

Quinn snorted and dipped her nose down. His voice soothed the tight sensation in her chest. She had heard it so little in all the time she'd known him.

"Mama," Oliver said again. He wasn't crying. None of them were crying. They were simply together, here on this beach.

Then, Flora said, "Show her."

Oliver turned to glance back at his sister. She nodded encouragement, her eyes still on her mother. Quinn watched as Oliver turned back around and began to work off one of his mittens. He was slow and clumsy with it until finally he was able to pinch the end and slip it off. Oliver held out his bare hand to Quinn, fingers spread. Even from here, Quinn could see the thin webbing between each small finger, ending before the first knuckle. Her own fin flexed, the long bones and thick webbed skin a far cry from her son's hand, but indisputably similar.

Oliver had begun to grow fins. He opened and closed his fingers to show Quinn how much mobility he still had. When had this happened? She wondered what could have instigated this change in Oliver.

Did this mean he could transform fully?

Quinn looked at her daughters. Did they have this too? But Flora caught her look and shook her head.

"It's just him," she told Quinn. Her long, dark hair, her even darker eyes, her sharp cheekbones, all inherited from Quinn, and yet only this Quinn had not passed on to her daughters.

How long had she waited for something like this to happen? How many times had she run her fingertips over Flora's tiny hands, her chubby legs, searching for any sign that her daughter had kept a piece of Quinn's ancestry? She'd repeated that search many times on Flora, Evie, and Oliver, to no success. Their skin remained smooth and flawless. Their feet were flat and sturdy. Their eyes, though strange, had white rings around the pupil and iris that flashed like the lighthouse's beacon.

Quinn wanted to know why Oliver had developed these webbed hands now, but she couldn't ask. She made another low, rumbling sound in her throat, and Oliver cocked his head at her.

Tentatively, he took another step into the water.

Should she take him with her? If his webbed hands had taken this long to develop, there was a possibility he could transform all the way, but how long would that take? She didn't have the time to wait for Oliver to discover how far he could change his human form.

She had been ready to trade a piece of herself for a pelt for Maisie. If it worked, if Maisie had agreed to come with her, Quinn would have already been far up the coast. Maybe she would have never seen her children again.

But Maisie had not come. Quinn was alone, and again she faced a choice.

Quinn took her eyes off Oliver and looked to her daughters.

Evie was staring wide-eyed at Quinn, her body half turned into Flora's side, while her sister was giving Quinn a difficult look. It was similar to the look she'd given Quinn when she'd finally understood that it was Quinn's fault the townspeople treated them as strange, fearsome creatures, but there was a tinge of guilt mixed in.

Flora had given Quinn her pelt back. She had freed her mother, and in doing so, freed herself and her siblings from Quinn's tainted shadow. And yet, it couldn't have been easy for them to lose a mother, even one as unsuitable as Quinn.

If Quinn knew her children at all, Oliver had come to Flora the moment his hands began to change. It was possible they hadn't shown Owen yet. Had Flora brought him here to the beach hoping that Quinn would appear? Hoping that she would—what?

Oliver shifted and held his hand out to Quinn, palm up. His small face was set, his depthless silver eyes steady on her. But Quinn could see his fingers trembling. His mitten-covered hand was clenched at his side, the empty glove squashed in his grip. He was scared.

Quinn couldn't take him with her. She couldn't take her son from his sisters. She had already deprived them of their mother.

Mind resolved, Quinn pushed herself onto the rocky shore. Water streamed off her thick fur, and the tide frothed around her fins. Oliver watched as she hauled her way up the beach toward him. His shivering hand was still held out as an offering, and she rested her cold nose in it for a moment when she was close enough. He inhaled sharply.

Quinn pushed his hand aside and stretched up to lay her snout against Oliver's chest. She could feel his heart beat excitedly beneath his ribs.

Oliver laid his webbed hand against her fur. They stood like that for a moment, connected at two points, with the waves rushing around their feet, endlessly tugging them toward and away from the shore. But the sea would not decide this for them.

Huffing a breath against Oliver's thick coat, Quinn pushed her nose into his chest until he was forced to take a step back, out of the waves.

Oliver frowned. His hand tightened in her fur. Quinn whuffed again and pushed him back, shuffling herself up the rocky shore until he was all the way out of the water. When he was out of reach of the tide Quinn leaned back to look at him.

Flora had stepped forward when Quinn had begun pushing Oliver out of the water, and Evie came with her, until they stood right behind Oliver's shoulders.

Quinn rumbled softly in her throat. There was no guarantee that Oliver could make the full transformation. And even so, he already had a family that loved and needed him. She wouldn't take him away from that. If he could make that choice one day in the future, she swore to herself that she would be here for him, but until then, the sea did not call to him.

Quinn looked at each of her children in turn. There was a chance she would never see them again, and she tried to drink in everything about them.

"Mama," Flora said quietly. "We'll take care of him."

Her oldest knew the burden of what Quinn had given to

Oliver better than any of them. But so long as he had his sisters, Quinn knew he would be safe. Once they showed Owen, he, too, would protect his son. He had wanted Oliver so badly, after all.

Unlatching herself from Flora's side, Evie took a step toward Quinn and laid a small, plump-fingered hand against the other side of Quinn's head.

Quinn closed her eyes and sighed. She knew there would always be a part of her anchored to this shore, but it would live on in her children. Her children, who had been the ones to finally free her and give her the chance to make her own choices again. She wanted to return the favor in kind.

Blinking her inky eyes open, Quinn twitched her nose and let out a short bark. Oliver and Evie took their hands away from her fur, startled, but then Evie laughed as Quinn shook her head and sprayed them with salt water and rain. Flora circled her arms around Evie's and Oliver's shoulders and held them as Quinn backed away.

The waves rose up to meet her and helped her off the rocky shore. Quinn worked backward as long as she could, watching the distance between herself and her children grow. When the seafloor gave way, she swam with her head above water, floating on her back. The rain was coming down harder now, dimpling the sea where it landed and dripping heavily down Quinn's fur.

Finally, when she could no longer make out the details of their faces, Quinn tossed her head and flipped into a dive. She made sure to make a large splash with her tail as she descended and hoped that it was the sound of Evie laughing again that sent her off.

QUINN FINALLY LET HER instincts take over and began to swim north. She stayed low in the water and only came up to take a fresh breath of air when she really needed to.

The rain at the surface did not cease. When she paused to take a break and float along the top of the water, eyes scanning the thin strips of beach and cliffs in the far distance, it poured as if an endless urn had tipped over. The sound of the rain hitting the water coupled with the ceaseless movement of the ocean made Quinn feel uneasy, but she pushed forward anyway.

How long had the journey north taken the herd when she was younger? After so long of using the humans' measurement of time, her memories were muddled, and the days blurred together. Even so, she was not the same selkie she'd once been. She was traveling slowly and alone.

Night fell quickly after she left her children on the beach. Quinn had only managed perhaps an hour's swim north before she had to stop and find a place to spend the night. Cautiously, she angled herself toward the shore again.

She found an outcropping of bare rock to rest on out of reach of humans. Still, she slept very little that night. Without the journey to keep her occupied, the image of Maisie's crumpled face, of MacArthur's fractured control, and Jamie's anger flooded her mind. She wondered what they were doing now that she was gone. Would they be talking about her, and how she had betrayed them? Or had they already begun to forget about her?

She had not been able to resist checking over her shoulder as she swam away to see if the lighthouse beacon had been lit, but the sky had stayed dark.

Quinn had known her leaving would hurt Maisie, but she had selfishly hoped that Maisie would be able to rely on MacArthur and Jamie to hold her together once Quinn was gone. With Jamie and MacArthur likely cursing Quinn for bringing such destruction into their lives, she wondered how long it would take for Maisie to be poisoned against her.

Quinn shut her eyes firmly, back facing the direction of the lighthouse, and tried desperately to sleep.

THE NEXT MORNING DAWNED rainy and cold. Quinn had managed only a few hours of restless sleep, and the moment she woke, every choice she'd made over the previous day rushed to the front of her mind and filled her with doubt.

Rolling over on the rock, Quinn stretched her tail and looked around. The sea and sky were still swollen with rain. Shaking off the chill from the early morning, Quinn hooked her flippers over the edge of the rock and pulled herself into the water.

Quinn put some distance between herself and the cliffs before diving into the deep water and continuing her journey north. As she dove, swam, rose, breathed, and dove again, Quinn eventually felt her stomach complain. She'd been getting steady, reliable meals three times a day at the lighthouse, but now it was up to her to provide her own food again. She dove deeper in search of a fish shoal.

An hour later, Quinn felt something move in the water. She was deep, the water bitterly cold and influenced by the far stretching currents that wrapped around the land. But this wasn't the frenzied, scattered movement of a fish shoal. Something large was moving around her.

An orca? She didn't remember seeing them along this coast so late in the winter season. A whale? No, it was moving too quickly, and it was alone, like her. She listened hard for any clicking or moaning calls, anything that would indicate who was in the water with her.

She had a few more minutes at this depth before she would need to return to the surface for air. Should she try to swim for shore? If she wasn't faster than whatever was out there, darting away would invite a chase. Maybe if she kept moving forward at the same pace she'd been keeping, it would lose interest in her.

If Quinn had been with her herd, she would have felt safe in their numbers, and known that someone older and more experienced than she was would make the decision about what to do. But she was alone now. The choices were hers.

Quinn wouldn't race for the shore. She knew the dangers that lurked on land, and more important, she'd only just been able to return to the sea. She wouldn't let herself be chased off by another sea creature.

She was a selkie. This ocean was her home.

Quinn made up her mind. Twisting in the water, she faced the direction she'd last sensed movement and let out a loud, bubbling bark. Then she shot toward the surface.

The creature gave chase. She could feel the prickle along the back of her neck that meant she was being followed, and she pushed herself faster. Quinn was moving so quickly that once she hit the surface, she went airborne for a few moments before splashing back down.

Sucking in a huge breath, Quinn ducked back into the sea and swam in wide circles around the point where she'd made a splashing reentrance. In the dim light, she could only see shadows, until one broke away from the others. It swam incredibly quickly, slicing through the water like a beam of light through the darkness.

Quinn braced herself as it came closer.

Then, finally, she could make out the details. A long, equine head and neck, a broad, muscled chest, and razor-sharp front hooves attached to misleadingly delicate ankles and legs. Thick, seaweed-like hair led down its neck and far down its back to the point where smooth black skin gave way to closely overlapping scales covering a wide, lethal tail like a whale fluke. The scales seemed black at first glance but shone an iridescent dark green as it moved. There were clusters of the seaweed-like hair at the base of its front hooves, which fluttered madly as it galloped around Quinn. The tail was extremely flexible and moved fluidly through the water.

A kelpie. Quinn clamped down on the breath she'd taken moments before as she circled to watch the kelpie swim around her.

Her mother had told her about kelpies, of course, but no one had seen one since the generation before hers. Quinn had thought they'd all moved on, or died.

Her mother had told her stories about how the humans had coveted the kelpie, like the selkies, for their beautiful human forms and ability to grant them luck. Knowing that the humans' stories about selkies bringing luck were drastically exaggerated, she mourned the loss of the kelpie to the humans' greed.

But here was a kelpie, fiercely alive, and circling her like a predator closing in on its prey.

Quinn twisted in the water to keep the kelpie in sight. It moved nearly too fast for her to keep up, its front hooves slicing through the water as it flicked its tail, moving as effortlessly as a bird gliding through the air. Thin streams of bubbles trailed from its wide nostrils.

She could never outswim a kelpie. Quinn's heart beat manically in her chest as she hovered, her gaze catching on the kelpie's mouth as it pulled back its lips to bare large, flat, white teeth. Those weren't the teeth of a predator, but its eyes certainly were. They flashed red even in the dim light beneath the surface.

What should she do? Quinn thought frantically, trying to remember any stories her mother may have told her about escaping kelpies. But her mother had never met a kelpie and she'd probably thought Quinn would never see one in person either. She braced for the right moment when she could break out of the kelpie's circle.

I have not seen your kind in many moons, selkie.

Quinn jerked, a startled grunt making her lose half her air. The kelpie's pace slowed, hooves set to a slow trot rather than a gallop. She was looking at Quinn with one red eye, neck extended and head tilted.

She spoke again. *I mistook you for a common seal. Had I not noticed, you would have been my meal.*

The kelpie's voice seemed to pass right into Quinn's head. Her mouth didn't move at any point, lips still pulled back and teeth pressed together to flash menacingly through the blue haze of the water. The voice was overwhelming, soaked in brine and ageless wisdom, but it also seemed hoarse from disuse.

Where did you come from, selkie?

The kelpie suddenly reared up and pivoted with a massive thrust of her tail. Now she stared at Quinn through the other eye, still circling. Quinn could see a row of jagged teeth marks indented into the kelpie's right flank stretching between the smooth skin and scaled tail, long healed, but it had obviously been a deep wound.

Quinn thought, *Can you understand me like this?*

Yes.

Quinn shuddered, a mix of relief and unease as she felt the kelpie's presence brush against her own so they could speak.

I was on land, Quinn told the kelpie, *trapped for seven years. I finally escaped.*

Humans? the kelpie asked.

Quinn made an affirming grunt, and the kelpie tossed her head in anger. She stalled in the water again and slowed to a meandering clip. She no longer circled Quinn, but paced back and forth in the water.

Horrible creatures, the kelpie spat. *They take and take, giving nothing but death in return. They tear apart the cycles of this world for their greed.*

The kelpie threw her head again, and a large burst of bubbles billowed from her mouth, as if she was neighing. Quinn stayed silent. She had no love for humans like Owen, or the people in the town, and she knew that the kelpie spoke truly about humanity's greed since she had seen it with her own eyes. But still, Maisie lurked in the back of her mind, along with MacArthur and Jamie. They'd been generous with her. How could they be of the same population as the ones who had treated Quinn so badly?

I am the last kelpie in these waters, she told Quinn. *I fled to the ocean after my only remaining companion was caught and slain by the river we grew up in. I did not know these waters, but I learned quickly in order to survive. Humans can't reach me here, but that does not mean I am safe. As you can see, the ocean's inhabitants tried to eat me.* She twisted in the water to show Quinn her injured flank again. *But I escaped. Now I hide in the depths, as the salt water slowly wears me away like a stone in the path of a river.*

The kelpie ducked her head and gestured to her body. Quinn looked more carefully, and realized that the kelpie's horse-like front legs did not only appear weak, but they were also too thin for an animal of such size. Patches of skin around its ankles and shoulders had faded from black to gray. A full-grown kelpie like this one should have been able to live for many decades, but they were made for the gentle fresh water of the river, not the abrasive, unforgiving sea.

Why stay in the ocean? Quinn asked her. *Why not seek another river, where you may find another of your kind?*

The kelpie shook her seaweed mane and rolled a red eye to pierce Quinn with a hard glare.

I am too old for such journeys now. Too weak.

Quinn let out a bark of disbelief. *You are faster than any creature I've ever met!*

Not weak in that sense, the kelpie told her. *Too many years have passed since I lost my companion. I am not strong enough to have such hope that I would find another.*

This far beneath the surface and away from the shore, especially now that the kelpie was keeping a slow pace that hardly rippled the water, Quinn was distinctly aware of the stillness around her. She had decided to venture out to look for her herd on nothing more than a rumor and a hope. How could she accomplish such a thing, if a creature like the kelpie saw no worth in it? How could she accomplish what a kelpie could not?

The squeezing feeling in her chest was not only anger. With a frustrated grunt, Quinn darted for the surface and took a fresh breath. She dove again right away, worried that the kelpie would lose interest in her and leave her behind.

But the kelpie was right where she'd left her. This time, she closed the distance between them until there were only a few meters of water separating them.

I am searching for my herd, she told the kelpie. *I have nothing but the word of a human to go off of, but I am looking for them anyway.*

There have not been selkies in these waters for many years, the kelpie told her. *You are searching for ghosts.*

Better looking for ghosts than sitting around waiting to become one!

Quinn let out an angry bark with this thought, and the kelpie nickered like she was laughing. She swung her huge head around and stared at Quinn with a fierce red eye.

A ghost I may soon be, but I will live out my life as I choose. I can have no more offspring. My companion is long gone to the froth, and any kin I could seek out would not recognize me. My years in the salt water have changed me. I am no longer the kelpie that finds solace in others of my kind. The kelpie pawed at the water. *Tell me, selkie. You say you spent years on land with the humans. Have you not changed from who you used to be?*

Quinn knew she was changed. Her years with Owen, though she had done all she could to resist it, had changed the way she saw the world. But in that time, she had learned of her ability to influence the storms and send her rage into the world. She had met the washerwoman, who had not been able to fulfill her wish, but instead made Quinn recognize her power of choice. Her children had set her free. Maisie had given her everything and asked for nearly nothing in return, except for what Quinn would be willing to give.

When Quinn had left the herd that fateful night, she had wished to see what the rest of the world had to offer. She had found it, the good and the bad. If she returned to the herd now, if she was even able to find them, how could she ever settle into a life like that again? Her mother had raised her on stories, but Quinn had learned to write the story herself. She was no longer a fish in the shoal. She was the whole ocean.

I am changed, she told the kelpie. *But can I not choose the life I want?*

The kelpie arched her neck. *Of course you can. But are you choosing the life you want, or the life you think you should have?*

This made Quinn twist in the water as if she could shake off the feeling settling into her fur. She had left the lighthouse because she thought she should find her herd again and rejoin her kind, and because she was too dangerous to be around

Maisie and the others. How could she choose to stay with them when she had caused them so much pain? How could she choose to stay with a human, when so many years of her life had been stolen by a human?

How could she be a selkie and choose a life with Maisie?

Easily, was the answer. She wanted to stay with Maisie. She wanted a life with Maisie in it, whatever form that took. She could face the storms she'd wrought, and weather the storms ahead with the people who had brought her back to life.

Quinn rolled toward the kelpie again.

You hate humans, she said, not really a question.

I despise their greed, the kelpie replied.

Quinn pushed. *The life I want, it is with humans. But if I am like you, perhaps the last of my kind in these waters, shouldn't I try to find the selkies?*

The kelpie considered her. Even when her head was still, the deep ocean current tucked its fingers into her mane of seaweed and set it fluttering around her neck. Her broad chest and shoulders, still heavily muscled despite the years fighting against the erosion of the sea, gave Quinn the impression of a great boulder balanced at the edge of a mountaintop. She could hold steady and strong for ages, or one motion could send her charging forward like an unstoppable force.

The kelpie's sleek ears twitched forward.

I have only known humans at their worst. They have shown me nothing else. There is nothing they could offer me now that would make up for all I have lost. Her age-old anger bled through her movements, and she tossed her head as if to free herself from a rope. *But we are not quite the same, child. I am only made for the ocean now. You and your kind, you can walk on land as well as you swim the sea. You are made for both worlds.*

But my herd, Quinn said, because they would always be in her heart. Her mother and her stories, the elders who had warned the pups even when they weren't listening, the community of seals who had raised her, would always be a part of her. She had to believe they were somewhere out in the vast ocean. But they had moved on. And so could she.

Her herd had shown her what it was to be a selkie of the sea. Quinn had not seen what a gift that was when she and the other young seals had gone looking for their legs that night seven years ago, but she knew it now. She also knew that in finding her legs, she had suffered and grown, and eventually found herself amongst kind humans and a love she could not forget.

Her herd could be somewhere ahead, but they were already a part of Quinn's past. Behind her was Maisie, and a new herd that Quinn needed to protect.

The kelpie pawed the water again with a sharp hoof. *Don't be foolish with your freedom.*

This struck Quinn deeper than the kelpie probably intended, and it cleared her mind like a warm wind buffeting away the clouds to open the way for a bright, sun-soaked sky. She and Maisie had agreed to use their freedoms for themselves. Quinn had to go back. What use was her freedom if she could not share it with Maisie?

Perhaps the kelpie could see the thoughts settle in Quinn's mind, and it tossed its head.

I am glad to have not eaten you, child.

And I'm glad to have met you, Quinn said. *Could I ask, what is your name?*

With a snort, the kelpie stretched out her tail and kicked herself into motion, once again slicing through the water in a circle around Quinn.

It is lost, gone to the froth like my companion, the kelpie said. *As I will be one day. So long, my saltwater kin. I hope your humans are worth a selkie such as you.*

Quinn had much more she wanted to ask the kelpie, but she knew there was no point trying to stop her. The kelpie widened her circle, scales flashing as the powerful muscles beneath her skin flexed and stretched to their full extent. She moved as if she were a part of the currents themselves. Or perhaps the currents were a part of her.

Caught in her tide, Quinn leaned toward the kelpie as she suddenly broke her circling and galloped away into the deep, indigo-stained waters. Within a moment, she was nothing more than another shadow in the gloom.

Chapter Twenty-One

NOW

A STORM WAS BUILDING. It was not of Quinn's making, but she certainly felt its presence looming just as she felt the weight and importance of what lay ahead of her.

She had turned back toward the lighthouse and swam nonstop for hours after the kelpie had left her behind. In that time, she considered the disastrous way she had left the island. How could she convince Maisie to trust her again after leaving her in such a state? How would she be able to even set foot on the island that MacArthur called home without drowning in her guilt?

She had owned up to her truth, but she had not been gentle about it with the keepers. Jamie had believed that she was trying to steal Maisie away like the vicious selkie he thought her to be, and his loyalty to his fellow keepers had only strengthened his suspicions about Quinn. He would be the most difficult to convince.

But she had to try. The conviction she'd felt to go looking

for her herd had settled firmly and desperately into a desire to return to Maisie's side. Her herd would live on without her. She could not go on without Maisie.

So she swam straight through the night. Her muscles ached from overuse and exhaustion, but she worried she had already been gone too long. She passed a shoal of fish and only paused long enough to snatch a singular bite from the shimmering mass. Glittering scales drifted up from around her mouth when she sank her teeth into the squirming fish, and the satisfaction of the hunt propelled her onward.

This time, she kept close to the surface. As she was moving more quickly, she had to breach for air more often. Rain splattered down from the dark gray clouds above, and the waves grew choppy.

Had MacArthur predicted this storm? Quinn could picture the keepers settling in for a long night of minding the beacon to provide a guiding light for every vessel unlucky enough to be out on the water.

When morning came, it was hard to tell if night had relinquished the sky, and Quinn's only indication was the faint outline amongst the clouds that suggested the sun was behind them. Her instinct, which had obeyed her in her journey north, now worked to home in on the lighthouse. It was as though her internal compass was centered upon the island.

But if her feelings were right, Quinn should have been able to see the lighthouse's beacon by now. The light could slice through the darkness for kilometers.

She kept swimming and began to scan the horizon every time she surfaced.

Above, the clouds woke and shifted, as if pinched by an invisible hand.

Quinn saw the island from below the water first. The looming mountain beneath guided her toward its dry peak, and at its summit, a dark spire. The lighthouse wasn't lit. The sight of it sent a tremor through Quinn's bones, and she stayed at the surface for the final stretch to keep her eyes on it and because she didn't have the strength to dive.

A shape on the shadowy horizon flickered in the corner of her eye. She turned her head without breaking course and felt her heart sink into the depths.

There was a boat on the water heading straight for the island. It was rising and falling alarmingly in the waves, but Quinn could tell it was moving toward the island with a purpose. There were few people who would risk crossing the open water in such conditions just to reach the lighthouse.

The figures scrambling around the boat's deck were too small to make out, but Quinn had a dreadful feeling she knew who was aboard. She hesitated in the water for a moment before making a beeline toward the boat. She wanted to confirm her suspicions before heading to the lighthouse, staying low in the water so she wouldn't attract attention.

The men aboard were too busy fighting the waves to notice her small head surface alongside the hull. They were shouting to one another to be heard over the din.

As Quinn feared, Owen's voice called out commands from the helm. There had been no doubt in her mind that he would return to find her. But what Quinn needed to know was whether the two men who had been looking for Maisie were aboard as well.

The waves made every attempt to dash her against the side of the boat, and Quinn struggled to keep her head above water. Another male voice said something she couldn't make out, and then someone else spoke, so close he must have been right above Quinn.

"We couldn't wait another day! If our questions from the first visit didn't scare him off, we need to get to him before he disappears again."

Owen yelled from farther back, "Which one did you say was your man?"

"James Donovan," the man shouted. "Though that ain't his real name."

Quinn let the next wave drag her below the surface. She felt dazed, as if she had been knocked into the hull, but there was no confusing what she'd heard.

The men had never been after Maisie. They had been searching for Jamie and were returning to the island to arrest him now. Quinn remembered the way Jamie had gone stiff every time the investigators were mentioned, and how he had gone quiet when Maisie claimed they had been looking for her even when the details didn't entirely match up. Quinn had thought that he had simply been worried about losing his fellow keeper.

But Jamie had always been the target. He had let Maisie believe the men were after her and pushed the attention away from himself and onto Quinn, blaming her and Owen for the arrival of the men on the island.

This was the kind of selfishness she had learned early on in her time with humans. Quinn wondered how Jamie could be so light-hearted and loyal to the other keepers while lying to them. Had he tried to separate Quinn from the others because he wanted to protect them, or because he saw her presence as a threat to the fragile illusion he'd built?

Despite her turmoil of feelings toward Jamie, Quinn still had to return to the lighthouse before the boat. She didn't want Maisie to be caught in the cross fire of whatever confrontation was coming.

Even with the choppy waves and dark horizon, the boat was moving quickly, too quickly for Quinn to beat them to the island. She had to get there first and warn the keepers.

Quinn dove farther below the surface so that the water muffled the noise of the storm and closed her eyes. She reached for the emotions she'd trapped in her chest, holding on to them so tightly for fear of the destruction they could wreak, and they bubbled up eagerly at the slightest evocation.

Please, she begged. She had never felt in control of the storms her emotions summoned. They had simply come when called and run amok on her rage and fear. But this time, she needed them to listen. She needed the storms to give her time.

Quinn pulled the emotions from her heart and thrust them outward.

She waited, hung in the false stillness a meter below the surface. Then she felt a tug, as if a hooked line were testing its strength where it was connected to her chest. She tugged back and the storm broke loose.

Quinn swam up to see the chaos she had summoned. An otherworldly wind was tangled in the boat's sails and was pushing it away from the island while surging waves reached up and washed over the deck. For any sailor worth their salt, it wasn't enough for the boat to capsize, but it had certainly stalled their pace.

Quinn didn't have time to marvel at the control she'd finally managed to exert over the storms. She gathered up her remaining strength and sped toward the island.

The loose rocks of the beach clattered against one another as the waves tumbled and broke on the shore. Quinn swam right up to the edge of the water, rolling with the force of the waves, until it pushed her up onto the beach. She dragged herself up a few more paces before allowing herself to lie down flat for one moment. Her ribs creaked as she tried to catch her breath.

Quinn rolled herself onto her back and began to work her hands out of her fur. Her pelt peeled off willingly, but she kept it close to her skin, like a child who believed a blanket could protect them from harm. She draped it around her shoulders like a thick cloak and got to her feet.

Her exhaustion remained even in this body. Quinn pushed her wet hair out of her eyes and made her way up the beach to the path, legs aching with every step. But she'd made it back.

The climb up to the lighthouse was filled with Quinn's terrible thoughts—that the beacon was dark because the keepers had all left, that they were hurt and unable to move, or worse. She kept glancing behind her to see if the boat had wrestled its way to the dock, but the storm was doing as she asked. But it could not delay them forever.

When the building came into view, Quinn scanned every window for a light, for a lamp left on, but all the windows were as dark as the lighthouse, which loomed high above her as she approached its base. The wind buffeted her as she crested the top of the island, nothing stopping the gale from pushing at Quinn with its full strength. Quinn put her head down and shouldered her way toward the front door. As she came closer to the building, she could hear the wood creaking and groaning in protest at the force of the storm, the windows rattling in their sills.

Pelt clutched in one hand at her chest, Quinn put her hand on the door handle and pushed, but it didn't move. She blinked, water dripping down her chin and hand where it rested on the door. She pushed again and felt the same resistance. The door was locked. The keepers had never locked the door in all the time she'd spent with them. Why lock a door on an island where no one else lived?

Frowning, Quinn thought about circling around the lighthouse to check if the kitchen window had been left unlatched, or if she could see anyone inside. She stepped back and craned her neck to look up at the dark beacon room of the lighthouse. If they weren't minding the beacon, what could they be doing?

Quinn knocked on the door. The hollow sound was lost in the cacophony of the storm around her, but she knew it would echo through the long hallway inside. A few moments passed, and then a few more, and Quinn's heart picked up speed the longer the silence on the other side of the door went on.

She knocked again and called out, "Maisie?"

There—was that a scuffle inside? She left her knuckles pressed against the wood.

"Maisie, are you there?"

The door cracked open, and Quinn swayed forward to keep her hand in contact with it. A sliver of MacArthur's face appeared in the doorway.

The first thing Quinn felt was a warm rush of relief. Even if his lighthouse was not lit, MacArthur was all right. Then she remembered how she had left him the last time they'd spoken, and she pinched her mouth shut.

MacArthur regarded her with shock plain on his features, but she had also seen how his shoulder had dropped when he'd seen it was her on the other side of the door.

"You came back," he said.

Quinn nodded slowly, rain dripping down her cheeks and off her chin as she moved. She was waiting for him to shut the door in her face, to tell her to leave the island, to shout at her like she had been expecting him to react when she told him it was her storm that had caused his shipwreck. He did none of those things. The crease between his brows was prominent, but she was startled to see there was no anger in his eyes.

"Why?" he asked her.

Clutching her pelt tightly, Quinn flattened her other hand against the door to feel the wet grain against her palm.

"Because when I left, I was scared of your contempt," she said. "But then I realized I was even more scared of losing you all."

"All?" he repeated. The knowing look on his face added, *Not just Maisie?*

Quinn pressed her fingertips into the door. The wind was pulling at her wet hair, but she let it toss the strands as it pleased, keeping her focus on MacArthur.

"You let me stay," she explained. "Jamie—Jamie helped me

heal. Maisie is not the only reason I came back." She tilted her head. "She is also not the only one who could tell me to leave."

It was a question in disguise. If MacArthur didn't want her at his lighthouse, she couldn't refuse him. She had taken so much from him with her selfishness already.

MacArthur let the door open a bit more until she could see his entire face.

"You left because you were afraid of my...contempt, you said? Because of this?" He shifted his left shoulder forward and held up his forearm, pinned up behind his sleeve and sweater. When she nodded, something cleared in his eyes. "Quinn, when I told you to go, I did not mean away from the island. I just meant away from me, for a moment. I've mourned this arm already. But understanding that you can impact the weather and that my years of research, planning, and records can be reduced to a useless pile of paper based on aspects I can't predict was a bit much to process all at once. And," he added, "I thought you wanted to leave."

Quinn's mouth opened, then snapped shut like a clamshell.

"You don't blame me?" she asked, incredulous.

MacArthur looked down at the space where his left hand had once been, then rolled his shoulder back and straightened.

"You cannot blame a shark for biting, when it is in its nature," he told her. "Nor do I believe you can blame the tide for going out."

Barefoot, with only her pelt around her shoulders, Quinn felt as though MacArthur had unveiled a piece of her soul. The piece that was made from the ocean.

She asked, daringly hopeful, "And Maisie?"

MacArthur's head turned slightly when there was another

scuffling sound behind him. The hall was dark, so Quinn couldn't see anything in his shadows, but then a rare smile crossed MacArthur's mouth.

"I think she agrees with me," he told her, and stepped back to open the door the rest of the way.

Quinn barely had a moment to take in the two people who had been crowded behind MacArthur in the doorway, their broad shoulders taking up too much room to allow them to eavesdrop successfully, before Maisie was flinging herself from the house with her arms outstretched.

Maisie collided with Quinn with a force that could have rivaled the storm. Her arms went tight around Quinn's back, her face in Quinn's damp neck, and Quinn staggered back a step. The hand holding the two ends of her pelt at her chest was crushed between her and Maisie.

Then Maisie wailed into her ear, "I'm so angry with you!"

But Maisie was clinging so tightly to Quinn it felt like her ribs were being crushed. Maisie was crying, and despite her exclamation, her voice wasn't angry. It was honest, as Maisie usually was, but in that honesty, Quinn could hear a reflection of the same relief that was coursing through her veins. Even as Maisie compressed her ribs, Quinn's heart felt as though it would beat right out of the bones.

Quinn put her arm around Maisie's shoulders and hugged her back. Maisie was wearing a familiar sweater and no coat, and so Quinn put her nose right at the corner between Maisie's shoulder and neck and breathed in the warm scent.

"You left!" Maisie accused her, voice muffled as Maisie's mouth was still pressed against Quinn's collarbone.

"I left," Quinn agreed, softer, "and I'm sorry."

"You told me about the storms, and MacArthur, and turning me into a seal," Maisie went on, "and then you left!"

"Yes," Quinn said, lifting her chin to lean her cheek against Maisie's hair. Over Maisie's shoulder, she could see MacArthur and now Jamie standing in the doorway. Jamie was standing with his arms crossed behind MacArthur, like a bodyguard, his jaw beneath his beard tense as he watched the two of them.

"I know you had to leave because of Owen," Maisie cried. "But it still hurt."

At this, Quinn had to lean back, sliding her hand up to cup the back of Maisie's neck and draw her face up so she would look Quinn in the eye. Maisie's face was blotchy on the cheeks and her eyes were watering so much the tears stood out even in the downpour, but the sight of her face soothed the anxiousness in the pit of Quinn's stomach like nothing else could.

"I never wanted to leave," she said steadily. "I thought I had to. I thought I didn't deserve to stay here with you because of what I am."

Maisie's green eyes flashed, and she sniffed loudly, tightening her grip around Quinn.

"You can stay!"

"Before I left," Quinn said, hating to bring it up, but needing to be sure, "Jamie said you'd made your choice when you didn't say anything."

Maisie's eyes widened, and she shook her head, sending rain and teardrops flying. "I didn't mean that I wanted you to leave! I just couldn't bring myself to tell you"—her voice softened as she went on, descending from her panicked pitch to something more familiar—"that I knew what you were saying about wanting to choose your freedom. I didn't think I could go with you, but I couldn't ask you to stay when I knew that it would get in the way of chasing the life you wanted. I didn't want to be selfish with you."

At this, Quinn finally smiled.

"You, selfish?" She laughed. "The life I thought I wanted was just a memory," she said. "The one I really want is here, with you."

When Maisie smiled back at her, Quinn wished she could close the distance between them and crush everything unsaid into Maisie's mouth, but MacArthur and Jamie were still watching. Quinn glanced at them and met MacArthur's considering gaze, feeling like a weather pattern he had just pieced together. Jamie's eyes were shadowed by the hall, but some of the stiffness in his shoulders and crossed arms had loosened. He leaned down to MacArthur and whispered something to which MacArthur responded only with a pointed look.

The circle of Maisie's arms loosened a little, but then Maisie froze.

"What happened to your clothes?"

Only then did Quinn remember her borrowed sweater and pants, which Maisie had obviously not had enough time to discover hidden under that rock on the beach, which Quinn had forgotten about in her haste to get to the lighthouse.

Maisie saw what must have been a sheepish look come over Quinn's face, and she quickly twisted around while still holding on to Quinn's waist to hiss at the other keepers, "Look the other way!"

MacArthur raised a brow but turned obediently, reaching out to tug Jamie around as well and push him farther down the hall.

"Invite her in, won't you, Maisie," MacArthur called. "There's obviously much we need to discuss."

"Actually, it will have to wait," Quinn said, leaning around Maisie to make sure MacArthur was listening. "We're about to have company."

Maisie gasped, "Your husband?"

"And those investigators," Quinn confirmed, gaze locked on Jamie's back. "They've found their man."

"They're coming for Maisie?" MacArthur asked incredulously.

"No," Quinn said, tightening her grip on Maisie when she went rigid in Quinn's arms. "They're not here for her."

Jamie slowly turned around in the hall. Quinn worried that he was going to react like a cornered animal, lashing out at whatever was too close, but Jamie met her eyes soundly.

"They're here for me," he told the keepers.

Amidst the sound of the lighthouse complaining against the force of the wind and rain, a stunned silence settled over the keepers. MacArthur was staring up at Jamie with an open mouth. It was the most unguarded Quinn had ever seen the lead keeper, all of his control melting away in his surprise. Not even Maisie's confession had loosened his soldier-like posture. Jamie turned toward him seemingly without thought, but couldn't find anything else to say.

"What?" It was Maisie who finally broke the silence.

MacArthur's mouth clicked shut. He blinked toward where Quinn and Maisie stood on the doorstep, and then back at Jamie. A dawning realization settled over his face, and he pivoted around Jamie in a few sharp movements and disappeared down the hall.

Jamie closed his eyes. For all his bulk, it was as if he had shrunk two sizes when MacArthur turned his back on him.

"Come inside," Jamie told them, his voice low. "And I'll explain."

Quinn hesitated, aware of the men closing in on the island every moment they delayed, but Jamie looked to her in particular.

"I won't take long. And I'd rather you heard this from me."

He retreated to the kitchen, and Quinn wondered if they should have given the men a few moments to themselves before joining them. Maisie had no such reservations and pulled Quinn into the house. She did pause when they passed her room so she could grab Quinn a towel and a set of clothes to pull on over her chilled skin.

The pelt dripped seawater and rain on the floor as they made it to the end of the hall. The door to the kitchen was open, and MacArthur and Jamie were standing by the fire with their heads close together, though Jamie was the only one speaking. Jamie had to bend his neck quite a bit to get down to MacArthur's ear, and their bodies curved toward each other like they felt the pull of an invisible tide. When Maisie and Quinn entered the kitchen, Jamie quickly stood up straight, and MacArthur looked around. The corners of his mouth were still turned down.

"Why are those men after you?" Maisie asked, straight to the point.

Jamie glanced at MacArthur, who now stood with his arm behind his back and his gaze trained on the floor.

"Because I skipped my parole," Jamie answered her.

"But they said they were looking for a murderer," Maisie pressed, confusion and disbelief clear in her voice.

"Aye," Jamie said. "And I am one, I suppose. Though the way they've put it, it's like I broke out of jail or something. I served my time for it. But getting a job with my record is mighty difficult, even in the city."

"I think you'd better start from the beginning," MacArthur told him quietly. Jamie nodded, and looked to Quinn when she shifted nervously on her feet. He spoke as quickly as he could while being clear.

"I had a brother when I was younger. Duncan," Jamie began. "He was sweet as a mouse and strong as an ox, and too smart to be working in mindless construction with our dad and me. He was also too good to leave our father alone, even though that man didn't give two shits about us. Duncan got hurt on the job, the wall they'd been building collapsed and nearly buried him. His leg was shattered. He died from an infection a month later."

Quinn's foot twitched impulsively, and she recalled Jamie's careful assessment of her wound, the wide injury that so easily could have festered without his care.

"He wasn't even supposed to be working that day. It was supposed to be our dad and me. It was supposed to be our father there," he said, barely suppressed anger making his voice shake. "After Duncan was gone, my father and I went back to work. Everyone told us how sorry they were. They told my father how terrible it was to lose a son. He hadn't even come to watch them put Duncan in the ground.

"His drinking got worse after that. He was draining all our money. He knew I blamed him for Duncan's death. I didn't try to hide it." Jamie sucked at his teeth. "I should have just left then. But I was trying to put away any money I could so I could afford to get out of that city, and my resentment irritated him. He started taunting me, talking like it was my fault Duncan had died."

Maisie made a soft sound. Quinn gripped her fingers tightly.

"I should have just left," Jamie repeated. He took a breath. "We were at a new site, the same kind of work I'd been doing with Duncan when he'd been injured. Someone must have said something about Duncan to my father, and maybe it was my fault, but he was tired of hearing about Duncan all the time. He said, 'The most useful that boy's ever been is feeding the worms in the church yard.' "

A chill came over Quinn as if a sudden gale had swept through the closed window. Maisie's face was stiff with anger.

"I don't remember much of the next few minutes, but I remember the sight of his bruised face under my split knuckles, the smell of liquor on his breath, the way his blood sank into the dirt that had swallowed Duncan. There were four or five other men there that eventually pulled me off of him. He was pronounced dead before the doctor even arrived."

"How old were you?" MacArthur asked. As Jamie laid out his tale, MacArthur had raised his eyes until they were trained unerringly on Jamie's face.

"Nineteen. I could have swung, but a few of the men testified that it was an accident, and I was sentenced to ten years in Barlinnie. I served five years' hard labor and got parole, but no one was hiring men with records like mine when I got out." Jamie laughed, a hard, cough-like sound. "I was turned away at the door before I even said a word. With no money, no family to take me in, no friends to bear such a burden as I was, and a monthly parole I had to report for, there was nothing for me in Glasgow but a slow, cold end.

"Then I saw an advertisement, searching for workers to do hard labor on a remote island, and I thought it must have been the work of someone's god that put me in front of it. No background required. Only a commitment to the job and no strings. I wasn't going to risk such a good opportunity putting my paperwork first, so I skipped my next parole meeting and left town as soon as I could."

Jamie paused and gave MacArthur an unfathomable look.

"Don't get me wrong, I very much appreciate your dogged commitment to finding people to do the job regardless of where they come from. But you may want to rethink your policy on background checks in the future."

Quinn was shocked to see that this brought a twitching grin to MacArthur's face.

"You knew those men were after you," Quinn accused Jamie, drawing their attention to her. "When? At the docks?"

Jamie gave her an odd look. "How'd you . . . no, not then. It wasn't until they came here that I knew for sure."

"But you let Maisie believe they were after her," Quinn said, trying to temper her anger even as she heard the storm howl in response outside. "You blamed their arrival on me, when Owen might not have made it here had they not needed the passage and provided the chance for him to come here."

Maisie seemed to be wrestling with a few feelings at once: sympathy, for Jamie's past struggles, chagrin that she had been allowed to think she was being hunted for her own crime, and relief, that the men had never been after her at all.

"I have done you both wrong," Jamie acquiesced. He tilted his head toward MacArthur. "All of you. I'm sorry."

"But why lie?" Maisie asked him. "Why did you not tell us you were in trouble?"

As if he couldn't help himself, Jamie snuck a glimpse at the head lighthouse keeper. When he found MacArthur watching him with expectant eyes, he seemed stuck even as he answered Maisie's question. "I have lost everything before. I didn't want to see it all taken from me again. You've only known me for who I am now, instead of what I did before I got here. I didn't want you to think less of me, or fear me." His voice trembled as he admitted this, and whatever resolve MacArthur had been holding on to since Jamie's first confession crumbled. He took a step toward Jamie and then halted, glancing at Maisie and Quinn. But Jamie seemed to take strength from this and continued. "Ever since Quinn arrived, everything we've built seemed to be falling to pieces, and I wanted to believe that if she left, all our problems would disappear with her."

He laughed weakly. "Obviously, that was a foolish wish. The men tried to come to the island before," he told Quinn. "Right after you left."

Quinn's chest lurched, and every terrible thought that had plagued her journey came rushing back, every awful outcome of her time away could have been realized, and she would have never known. She shivered.

"Tried to?" she repeated. Maisie curled a hand around Quinn's elbow and applied a slight pressure. When Quinn looked at her, Maisie was nodding at Jamie to go on, but kept pressing until Quinn started to move. She led Quinn to the fireplace, where the smoldering coals let off just enough heat to be noticeable. Maisie installed her right in front of the mantel so Quinn's pelt could dry.

"I spotted them," Jamie said. "They couldn't make it past the wave break, and the swells by the dock were too aggressive for them to hope to tie up a boat if they could even make it to shore. But they were on their way here."

"They didn't make it," Quinn reiterated.

"No," MacArthur said. "But they tried."

"And they're trying again now," Jamie said darkly. MacArthur's mouth became a thin line.

"So," Quinn asked, "is that why the beacon isn't lit?"

MacArthur shifted uneasily on his feet. Quinn thought about what he had told her about the lighthouse, about how he had sworn to keep the beacon lit so that he could warn passing ships of the dangers ahead and provide a light to those lost in the dark.

"It is harder to find the island when the beacon isn't lit," MacArthur said carefully.

Quinn stared. She looked at Jamie, whose gaze was fixed so tightly on MacArthur it seemed it would take monumental effort to pry him away.

"When the boat finally gave up and turned back," Maisie said, instead, "we figured it wouldn't be too long before they tried again. But the storm continued, and the sky stayed dark, and if we lit the beacon, it would be like we were inviting them right to our doorstep the moment the waves calmed down enough for a boat to reach the dock."

"But when the storm does die, then what will you do?" Quinn demanded.

"You must go," MacArthur said softly, his head turned so that he was looking out the dark window, where four smudged, shadowed figures of themselves backlit by the fire were reflected in the glass. "You need not wait here for them to come and find you, if it means they would take you away bound like criminals."

"I am a criminal," Jamie reminded him.

"But you needn't live like one!" MacArthur shot back, spinning on his heel to pace the length of the kitchen. When he passed the fireplace, Quinn could see how his stubbornly set shoulders quivered slightly. "You told me that's why you came here. To live a life free of your past, which you have paid for in full. If staying here means you would be doomed to pay for it with the rest of your days, then—"

He cut himself off, facing away from the rest of them. Quinn didn't think he would be able to tell Jamie to leave. He could offer it, he could make it the only viable option, but he wouldn't *tell* Jamie to go. Even the revelation of Jamie's past and the repercussions that were quickly approaching his door, MacArthur could not abandon him.

Quinn shot a quick look at Maisie. She, too, would never be ordered to leave, but she risked just as much staying here as Jamie did. With their suspicions already high, the possibility that Maisie could be discovered as a woman in disguise seemed too great a risk. Could Quinn ask Maisie to come with her and leave behind the life she'd built again?

"I won't leave if it means leaving you here alone," Jamie said decidedly, eyes locked on MacArthur's back.

"I cannot leave the lighthouse," MacArthur said.

"You can," Jamie said, taking a step toward MacArthur. "You can. This stack of bricks won't crumble the moment you step foot off the island."

"I swore to keep the lighthouse running," MacArthur said, twisting around and circling the table as if to avoid Jamie getting too close.

"It's not running now," Quinn observed.

MacArthur jerked to a halt.

"Quinn," Maisie muttered, a concerned look drawing her face tight. Whether the concern was for her or MacArthur, Quinn didn't know. But, if she considered what she knew about Maisie, it was probably for both of them, for different reasons.

"Don't think I haven't considered the consequences of my actions," MacArthur said quietly. He turned toward her. "I have. I know the dangers better than most."

Quinn kept her gaze steady on him.

MacArthur said, "This storm was in my predictions. Any decent weatherman would have been able to see this storm coming and warn those who would be on the water when it hit. It has certainly lasted longer than I thought..." He gave Quinn a significant look, which she returned with a nod. "But they would know to be careful. They would know to sail cautiously. They would know, even without a beacon, to be wary."

"But it would make a difference to light it," Jamie argued. "Right?"

MacArthur opened his mouth, and then shut it again.

"Of course it would," Maisie said. "That is why you're here, right, Mr. MacArthur? To make a difference to those out on the water."

"What does it matter if I can help those out there," Mac-Arthur snapped, voice cracking as he shifted the intensity of his gaze to Jamie, "if I can't protect the ones who rely on me in here?"

A log on the fire, blackened and shriveled, cracked and clattered into the coals beneath the grate. The silence in the kitchen was thicker than the kilometers of ocean Quinn had crossed to be here.

"You don't need to protect me," Jamie said, but even as he said it, he was taking another step toward MacArthur. When MacArthur didn't move to spin away from Jamie again, he took another step until he had closed the distance between them.

"Finn," he murmured. Quinn was startled to hear MacArthur's first name out of Jamie's mouth, especially the way he said it, as if putting his breath to the word would scare it away like a bird startled from a branch. "You don't need to protect me."

"That doesn't mean I won't," MacArthur responded, pointedly not looking Jamie in the eye again. Jamie curled his shoulders in, and he could have engulfed MacArthur's slighter figure in his tall frame.

Quinn felt a slight touch at her wrist and looked down to see Maisie's fingers against her skin, sliding down until their palms pressed together and fingers interlocked. Quinn met Maisie's wide gaze. Maisie raised her eyebrows emphatically and nudged her chin in Jamie and MacArthur's direction.

Quinn wasn't surprised that Maisie had caught on to the same suspicions she'd been having about the two keepers. With the threat of discovery weighing heavily over their lighthouse, their carefully concealed secrets were being pushed to the surface. But if Maisie's unsurprised look told her anything, Quinn figured Maisie had been putting the pieces together long before she'd even arrived on the island with a bloody hole in her tail. The lighthouse wasn't so big, after all.

"Even if I did leave," Jamie was asking MacArthur, "where

would I go? No one else is blinded by their ideals enough to look past my records. If the choices are leaving and being on the run, always looking over my shoulder, never finding any work because to everyone else these are the hands of a murderer"— Jamie held up his wide, worn palms, the fingers calloused and sturdy—"or staying here to help you for as long as I can, I would rather stay."

MacArthur gave him an incredulous look, but Quinn saw the flicker of longing before it was quickly dashed away. "Only to be taken from me anyway!"

Quinn had a feeling the keepers would go around this carousel of bad choices and worse choices for a while if left unmeasured. She had returned to this island to find Maisie because she had finally realized the life she wanted was right in front of her, waiting for her to take it. Right now, with one hand in Maisie's and the other still holding on to her slowly drying pelt, Quinn remembered her children and Oliver's webbed hands.

She had considered taking him with her. Had thought about what it would take to make him fully a selkie, what he would need to make the ocean his home. But Oliver had sisters and a father who loved him. He had something tying him to the land.

The keepers, though they hadn't said it out loud, only had each other. And now, they had Quinn.

She turned to Maisie.

"I need you to answer a question honestly," she said quickly. Maisie blinked away from Jamie and MacArthur to look at her and turned fully when she saw the focus on Quinn's face.

"Okay," Maisie said. "Of course."

"I love you," Quinn said, and Maisie's fingers spasmed in her hand. Her green eyes widened and her mouth parted, but Quinn kept going. "That is why I came back. That is a truth I owed you. And if I asked you to come with me now, to trust me, would you?"

Maisie's hand, which wasn't as broad as Jamie's but was now nearly as labor-worn and calloused from her work on the light-house, twisted so that she could cup Quinn's hand between both of hers. She let Quinn's question hang in the air for only a moment before she said, "Of course I would."

Quinn smiled and lifted their joined hands so that she could kiss the tips of Maisie's fingers.

Maisie gasped, and whispered loudly, "Oh, and I love you, too!"

Now Quinn laughed as one burden lifted from her back. She kept Maisie's hands tucked around hers as she turned back to the other keepers, who were unsurprisingly still caught up in their own argument.

"If the problem is having nowhere to go when you leave," she said loudly, and the men looked around as if remembering they were not the only ones in the room. MacArthur's eye went unerringly to her and Maisie's joined hands. She met his resulting look with a raised eyebrow at the small distance that remained between him and Jamie. "I may have a solution. I can turn you into selkies, like me. You helped me," she directed this at Jamie, needing him to believe her. "Now let me help you."

Jamie was staring at her slack-jawed, likely reconsidering the conversation he'd overheard between Quinn and Maisie before she'd fled the island, but MacArthur's mouth was set.

He turned to Jamie and had to tilt his head back slightly to look him in the face since they were standing so close.

"You should go with her," MacArthur said.

"And leave you here alone?" Jamie scoffed. "You're capable of many things, but you don't need to bear this burden by yourself. Come with us."

MacArthur was already shaking his head and took a step back.

"I can't leave. I can't abandon my post. The lighthouse—"

"Will get new keepers!" Jamie exclaimed, holding out his hands as if asking MacArthur to lay down his concern in them. "It's only a building!"

"You said just a moment ago it would be best if I lit the beacon," MacArthur muttered, "and now you want me to abandon it. You don't want to be caught by the manhunt, but you won't leave while I'm here. You have to choose, Jamie. You can't have it all."

"You're wrong there," Jamie said. "I can have what I want. I just need you to choose to want it, too."

The kitchen was too small to pretend that she and Maisie weren't listening to every word. Maisie was breathing quickly through her nose, as if watching a race come to a galloping finish. Quinn spared a moment to look out the window, where the sky, like her heart, was slowly lightening. They were racing against borrowed time.

MacArthur's mouth was working silently as he stared up at Jamie.

"Finn," Jamie said again. MacArthur held up his hand, fingers trembling, and tried to wave Jamie away. "You're more than this lighthouse. You will still be you, outside these walls."

"I can't," MacArthur said. He took another step away, and the back of his knees hit the bench under the kitchen table. As if that one blow was enough to unbalance him, MacArthur sank into a seat.

"You can," Jamie said earnestly. He came forward and knelt down in front of MacArthur so that now he was the one looking up into MacArthur's face. Slowly, he reached out and picked up MacArthur's hand where it was braced on the bench by his thigh. Jamie brought their hands together over MacArthur's knee. "You won't tell me to go. But I will ask you to leave. Leave with me."

"With us," Maisie added softly, her eyes shining. Jamie flicked a glance at her and Quinn, and Maisie nodded encouragingly. Quinn didn't want to interject in what was very obviously a moment that had been building for months, perhaps years, but she knew that they needed a push.

"A washerwoman once told me that I live at no will other than my own," she told them, recalling that fog-ridden day in the hills and her desperation for a change. "She told me I do not owe humanity to humans because I can become one. You need not be a lighthouse keeper for the rest of your life, just because that is all you have known. She told me to make my choices. You can make yours."

"Aren't washerwomen omens of death?" Maisie whispered.

"Yes," Quinn said. "But she can also help prevent death, depending on what the person chooses to do when they see her."

Jamie hadn't taken his eyes off of MacArthur's face while Quinn spoke. He tightened his grip on MacArthur's hand and brought it to his broad chest, resting right over the point where his heart lay below layers of cloth and skin.

"Come with me," he pleaded with MacArthur.

In MacArthur's seat on the bench, Quinn couldn't see all of his face, but she could see the slumped form of his shoulders, the thin strip of skin between the top of his collar and the neat line of his hair as his head bowed forward.

"I cannot," he replied, the words short and weak, but they cut through Jamie like the sharpest blade. His face shuttered, cheeks paling as he let MacArthur's hand slip from his so that it fell limp at his side. MacArthur told him, "But you must live. You go."

Maisie was looking between them frantically, searching for the words to try to mend it, but there was nothing to fix. MacArthur had made his choice. Quinn felt a heaviness settle in her stomach, but she couldn't fault him for doing what she had told him. And they didn't have time to pick up the pieces and try again.

"If we're leaving, we have to go now," she told Maisie quietly. "The men could be here any moment, and I don't know how long it will take me to change you into selkies."

Maisie nodded reluctantly, wiping under her eyes with the back of her hand.

Quinn jerked her chin at Jamie, who was still kneeling, eyes unseeing, on the floor at MacArthur's feet.

"Get him up. I'll meet you at the door."

They untangled their fingers, and Maisie went straight to Jamie's side, crouching to get one of his arms around her shoulder, talking quietly the whole time. Only when she'd gotten him back on his feet did she look at MacArthur.

"Sir," she said steadily, "I owe you my life, and much more besides that. But if I may, Mr. MacArthur," she added, hefting

Jamie farther onto her shoulder, "I risked everything to be here, and got more than I could have ever dreamed of. I never thought, and still don't think, that you were any less brave than I am."

MacArthur raised his head, and whatever she saw on his face, Maisie accepted. She led Jamie out of the kitchen, his steps heavy. Quinn saw him look back just once before they were out the door.

Rounding the table, Quinn stood in front of MacArthur with her pelt between them. The fur was still a little damp.

"I wouldn't take them from you if there was any other choice," she told MacArthur.

Now that she had a good look at his face, Quinn could see that MacArthur was as pale as Jamie, his mouth red from how tightly he was keeping his lips pressed shut.

"They've always been free to leave," MacArthur rasped out.

"And yet, they never have," Quinn observed. "And never would have, if I hadn't forced the situation."

MacArthur looked up at her at that.

"It is my fault," she told him. "Everything changed when I arrived."

MacArthur's hand curled into a fist as he leaned forward on the bench.

"It is not," he declared. "Those men, the ones looking for Jamie, they would have come whether you were here or not. In fact, it is because of you that we've had this much time," he said, nodding to the window and the weakening storm beyond it.

"And it is because of them that I came back," Quinn said. "I thought I had to live for one purpose now that I had my freedom. But I was wrong. Because I had my freedom, I could choose to live the life I wanted."

She leaned down and pressed a kiss to MacArthur's brow. He stiffened beneath her touch and was staring at her with dark, wide eyes. His eyes, she realized, were a brown so dark they were nearly black, just like hers.

"Thank you for giving me shelter. I hope you can continue to find what you want here," she said.

Then she left him sitting alone in the kitchen, with only the smoldering fire for company.

Chapter Twenty-Two

NOW

In the hallway, Maisie had managed to lead Jamie all the way to the door but was peering over the edge of his considerable biceps to look for Quinn. She tossed her pelt around her shoulders and found Jamie's and Maisie's oilskin coats on the rack by the door and folded their bulk over her arms.

"Let's go," she said.

The trek down the island's path was quiet as they bulled through the fading storm. None of them spoke, except once when Jamie mumbled something to Maisie, and she let him take his arm off her shoulder to walk on his own. Quinn pretended not to notice how often he would glance back up to the dark lighthouse behind them. Maisie, following behind Quinn, would look back at Jamie to make sure he was still coming.

When they rounded the cliff that gave them a clear view of the beach, Quinn froze. There was a second boat tied to the dock. Owen and the men had made it to the island.

"Maisie," she warned, harsh and too loud so they could

hear her over the rain. She motioned to the beach until Maisie and Jamie realized the danger.

"This way." Jamie beckoned them off the path and into the slick grass and mud. Quinn looked behind them to see if they left footprints, but the rain was still heavy enough to wash away any indents they left behind as they climbed down the island.

Jamie suddenly stopped and crouched, waving at them to do the same. Whatever he was feeling about leaving Mac-Arthur behind, he seemed to have buried it to deal with the present threat. They huddled together, Quinn's heart pounding in her ears the only sound she could hear until something else rose above the wind. Men's voices. They must have been passing right over the path where Quinn and the keepers had just been standing.

"Let's go." Jamie moved slowly, as low to the ground as he could manage, his boots sliding in the mud as he led them away from the path.

The beach was empty save for the two boats rocking gently in the waves. Quinn took them right to the water.

She ran her fingers over the rough material of the coats in her arms, gathering up the drops of water that pooled in the wrinkles. She'd had the idea when she'd seen her children standing on the shore but hadn't gone through with it. Now, faced with putting it into practice, she wasn't sure if it would work.

Quinn turned to the keepers and held out Jamie's coat, which Maisie took. "Wait here."

"Do it quickly," Jamie told her. She gave him a look, but knew he was only speaking out of worry. His life was in her hands now, too.

Barefoot, Quinn walked into the surf with Maisie's coat in her hands. The ocean tugged at her ankles, then her calves and thighs, and Quinn stopped when the water swirled around her waist. Her borrowed pants and sweater were soaked through, but the pelt around her shoulders floated atop the water.

Quinn rubbed her thumbs over the coat and then submerged it completely. She closed her eyes, focusing on the coat in her hands and the ocean surrounding her.

When she was a pup, her mother had told her many stories, and nearly all of them were about the ocean. Even the ones about humans featured the ocean as something coveted by those on land, or as something they feared. Her mother had raised her with a great sense of respect toward the ocean. And in return, the sea listened to her when she needed it most.

For the first time, Quinn tried calling out to it on purpose. She thought about Maisie's freckles that darkened in the sun, she thought about Maisie smiling with tears in her eyes as she remembered her family, and everything she'd given up to be here with Quinn. She thought about Maisie, soaked from head to foot, sneaking away just to give Quinn a piece of bread when she could hardly move. She thought about Maisie's face when Quinn told her she loved her.

She asked the ocean, *Please.*

But the ocean was not magnanimous. When she called out with her emotions, the sea would take them and twist them into storms, using Quinn's fear or anger to charge the thundering clouds and uncontrollable rains. If she wanted to ask something of the ocean, she would have to give something in return.

Anything, she promised.

The water around Quinn frothed, the push and pull of the tide becoming a swirling tide pool as she gripped the coat tighter to ensure it wasn't torn from her hands. The coat was writhing between her fingers like a live thing. Eyes still squeezed shut, Quinn gasped aloud and held on as tight as she could.

Then, just as suddenly as it started, the whirlpool stopped. Quinn waited a few moments before peeling her eyes open and lifting her hands.

Maisie's coat was gone. Instead, Quinn held a thick, lovely, patterned gray seal pelt.

Quinn twisted around in the water and slogged her way back up to the shore, where Maisie and Jamie were staring at her.

"Quickly," Quinn panted, still ankle-deep in the water, "give me the other."

She held out the pelt and traded Maisie for Jamie's coat. The moment Maisie touched the pelt, she let out a gasping cry.

"Maisie!" Jamie said, reaching for her. Quinn had frozen in the shallow tide.

"It's mine," Maisie said, holding the pelt with both hands as a look of wonder overtook her face. "It's mine."

Quinn knew exactly what she was feeling. It was what she had felt the first time she had removed her pelt and seen it lying amongst the others. She would know it anywhere, as she would know her own heart.

Knowing that it had worked, Quinn splashed back into the water with Jamie's coat and submerged it. She repeated her request, hoping her payment in return still applied.

The whirlpool surrounded her again, and Quinn smiled as she held on tightly to the coat as it kicked and jerked in her fingers. The material turned to soft, wet fur from one moment to the next.

Jamie's coat had been significantly larger than Maisie's, and his pelt was no different. Quinn felt its considerable weight as she turned back to the beach. Jamie was looking at her expectantly, his hands open to take the pelt, but Quinn stopped dead in the water looking over his shoulder.

Maisie and Jamie both spun around at the call behind them, but it wasn't Owen or the men in hot pursuit.

MacArthur was running down the path. He stumbled once, arm wheeling to keep his balance, and Jamie shouted, "Finn!"

But MacArthur kept his footing and dashed the rest of the way down the dirt path to the beach, the rocks crunching and rattling beneath his footsteps. He slowed to a halt right in front of Jamie, chest rising and falling rapidly.

MacArthur was too breathless to find the words, so Jamie said them for him. "You came."

"I chose," MacArthur agreed, sending quick looks to Maisie and Quinn before looking back at Jamie. "It dawned on me only once you all had gone and the lighthouse was silent. I could think clearly, for the first time in years. I want to be with you. If that's still what you want."

It was good that Jamie hadn't taken his pelt from Quinn yet, because he needed both hands to reach for MacArthur's face and tilt his chin up to meet him in a resounding embrace. MacArthur stood with his arm at his side for a moment before he leaned into the kiss and raised his hand to loop his arm around Jamie's neck, pulling him further down.

Maisie was looking at them with her mouth fully open,

and she turned to Quinn with an incredible light in her eyes. Quinn let them have a few moments, smirking when Maisie's mouth snapped shut and she raised her eyebrows expectantly. Quinn cleared her throat.

The men broke apart, but Jamie didn't let go.

"We were leaving, yes?" Quinn asked.

"We're leaving," MacArthur agreed, straightening his appearance as best he could with Jamie still clinging to him. His sweater and shirt were distinctly rumpled from his run and the prize he'd received at the finish line. "I managed to slip out the kitchen window when I saw them coming up the path."

Maisie frowned. "You don't have your coat."

"No," MacArthur said, brow creasing. He looked at the pelt in Maisie's hands, and then at the one in Quinn's as well as the one draped over her shoulders. "Ah."

"He can't go back to get it," Jamie said.

"Wait," Quinn said, bending to put the pelt she'd just transformed into the shallow water at her feet. "Let me try something."

Jamie hadn't touched the pelt yet, so it hadn't been claimed. Running her hands around the edges of the massive pelt, Quinn felt for a place where it gave. When she found it, Quinn pulled with all her strength until the pelt tore into two pieces.

Jamie took a staggering step forward.

"It's okay," Quinn panted. "It should be fine, as long as it's the two of you."

MacArthur and Finn shared a look. Quinn held out the halved pelt to both of them.

With one hand on MacArthur's shoulder, Jamie reached out to take a pelt while MacArthur took the other from Quinn.

They inhaled simultaneously, a full-body sound just like the one Maisie had made. Jamie's fingers on MacArthur's shoulder tightened. They looked at each other, and an ocean of words seemed to pass between them.

When the pelts left Quinn's hands, she felt something squeeze tight in her chest, and she choked, dropping to her knees in the water.

"Quinn!" she heard Maisie cry, and felt her hands on her shoulders, her face, but Quinn was gasping for breath. It was like there was suddenly a giant thorn piercing her heart, and it was being drawn out, achingly slow.

"What's wrong?" MacArthur asked, his voice watery in Quinn's ears.

"I don't know," was Maisie's anxious reply.

Though it hurt like pain she'd never felt before, Quinn knew it would end. The water rushing around her knees showed her where to go.

"We have to leave," she gasped out. "Now."

She felt for her own pelt with numb fingers, and Maisie helped put it in her hand. There wasn't time to remove her borrowed clothes, so Quinn pulled the pelt tight around her shoulders and grabbed Maisie's hand with the other, staggering to her feet and leading them deeper into the water.

"Wait," Jamie called, "how do we put them on?"

"Like a coat," Quinn managed to tell him. She and Maisie were hip-deep in the water. Quinn looked at Maisie, who was pale, but watching her unerringly. Trusting Quinn. Quinn leaned in and pressed a hard kiss to Maisie's mouth and told her, "Like this."

Quinn pulled the pelt taut and met the next wave head-on.

The thorn in her chest was nearly out, and she gasped at the space it left behind. But her pelt was rippling around her, the fur spreading over her arms and legs, her body twisting as it found a new shape.

She was a seal again. Finally, the pain in her chest faded. The sea had claimed the payment for turning the others into selkies. When Quinn touched the place in her chest where she had kept the emotions that had called the storms, there was nothing there. She ached at the loss of a power she had only just figured out how to control, but she had promised the ocean anything. It had taken something of equal value.

Quinn surfaced and found three humans staring at her. Maisie, seeing Quinn's rounded face and black eyes, steeled her nerves and copied Quinn exactly, diving into the next wave. Quinn circled around her in the water, waiting. She couldn't help Maisie through this part. This was something she needed to do on her own.

Then, a head surfaced. It was a seal's head, with a great smattering of spots on the fur around its snout and forehead. Maisie barked, and Quinn barked back, swimming forward to brush against Maisie. In unison, they turned to look at the remaining keepers.

"Right," Jamie said, shaking his head. "Well, that's us shown."

Maisie barked again. *Hurry up.*

"Yes, yes," MacArthur said, pulling his pelt around his shoulders like Quinn had shown him. Jamie did the same, and then they both met the waves.

A moment later, there were four seals twisting and swimming in the waves. Three were struggling a bit to find their balance; the spotted seal was too enthusiastic and she kept bumping into the others. The largest, with a scar on his snout, was trying to use his front flippers to steady himself but kept rolling in the water. And the last was a sleek, barely patterned seal with only one front flipper. Despite this, he leveled out quicker than the first two and began to swim in tight, smug loops around the others. The fourth circled around them until all three were darting naturally through the water and then led them away from the beach, turning on her back to make sure the others followed. They did, one close behind and the two others following in a pair.

Quinn looked up at the lighthouse one last time, still dark and reaching into the sky. Above it, the clouds suddenly parted, and a bright beam of sun shone down on the island.

The three seals were waiting for her. Quinn sucked in a great breath, chose a direction, and began the swim.

Epilogue

BY THE TIME THE lighthouse board had word that the lighthouse on the small island off the coast had been dark, many days had already passed. A small crew was sent to investigate, including two men recruited from an ongoing police investigation and a local fisherman who had volunteered.

When they arrived at the island after struggling against difficult winds and curtains of rain, they found a boat still tied to the dock and an empty beach. They hiked up the path in silence and considered the foreboding presence of the lighthouse with its dark beacon waiting for them at the top.

Inside the lighthouse, they found recent signs of life, including coals in the fireplace, water in a kettle, unmade beds, and a single oilskin coat hanging on the coatrack by the door.

"Where are the keepers?" a man from the board asked, while the two men from the investigation searched every room. In a crowded office they found detailed reports of the island's weather, including reports on the strange storms that had swept over this part of the coast like a nightmare. The notes were detailed, but gave away nothing as to the whereabouts of the three lighthouse keepers who were supposed to be tending to the beacon.

The fisherman did not search the house. He had stopped in one of the bedrooms, the smallest, and was staring out of the tiny window to the sea below.

"There's nothing here," someone said from the doorway to the lighthouse, his words echoing up the empty, spiraling space. "It's like they disappeared."

Silently, the fisherman ascended the lighthouse until he stepped into the gloomy beacon room. As he turned in place, scanning the water below, the storm began to lessen. The rain petered out to a mere drizzle, and the waves smoothed into a glassy expanse. It was the calmest the sea had been all winter.

The glass door swung open silently when he stepped outside. High up on the cliff, the wind spun through the air and tugged at him until he grabbed the railing with one hand. The fisherman frowned at the water far below.

A wave was broken by a small, round head. It moved leisurely through the water, heedless of its onlooker. Three more heads surfaced behind it. A joyful bark was carried up to the top of the lighthouse on a breeze, and then the four seals disappeared back beneath the waves.

ACKNOWLEDGMENTS

THE EXPERIENCE OF WRITING this book was wildly different from the first, and I feel so lucky to have been able to write it. Selkie mythology has enchanted me from a young age and I've loved crafting a story around such an incredible piece of Scottish folklore. This book, like the lighthouse, took many hands to keep it going.

I am so grateful for my editor, Kirsiah Depp, who leaned into the niche selkie and lighthouse idea I had for her and helped to draw out the myth and the magic of the story. I'm thankful for the amazing team at Grand Central, Lyssa Keusch, Nicole Luongo, Luria Rittenberg, and Kamrun Nesa, for all their help and support, and Albert Tang and his incredible art team for their amazing work on the cover!

Melanie Figueroa was my own lighthouse in the uncertain seas of the sophomore novel, and with her direction I was able to find my way home.

From the group chat to our few and far between meetups,

I'm eternally thankful to have my Council of Women, Ally, Kellene, and Hannah, who have been my biggest cheerleaders and favorite readers.

I want to thank my dad for waiting as I finished this so he could finally have another book to read after finishing my debut. Having you as a reader means the world to me.

And for my mom, I will always be so thankful that you encouraged me to keep reading, and now to keep writing. The stories you shared with me inspired me to create my own.

I also want to highlight the following sources that I used while researching the selkie myth: "The Seal's Skin" from *Icelandic Folktales and Legends* by Jacqueline Simpson; "Supernatural Beings in the Far North: Folklore, Folk Belief, and The Selkie" by Nancy Cassell McEntire from *Scottish Studies*, Volume 35; and *Tales of the Seal People: Scottish Folk Tales* by Duncan Williamson. And a shout-out to the Blue Turtle YouTube account: I think I listened to every instrumental ambience video they ever posted while writing this book, many times over.

ABOUT THE AUTHOR

NATALY GRUENDER WAS BORN and raised in Arizona and found an escape from the desert heat through her library card. She studied English, creative writing, and classics at the University of Arizona and is a graduate of the Columbia Publishing Course. Giving in to the siren call of New York, Nataly booked it across the country, and when she's not working or writing, she likes to pet other people's dogs and spend too much time in used bookstores. She currently lives in Brooklyn, New York.